Praise for *An Address in A*

"Because I lived in Amsterdam through ⟨ ..... Occupation myself, the author had asked me over the years to check the historical facts and the verisimilitude of her well-paced plot. When the latest version arrived at my desk, I found myself pushing everything else aside to read it cover to cover and follow the development of the rich palette of characters—despite the fact that I had read sections of the book multiple times over seven years.

"Fillmore's tale of powerlessness and defiance, of death and love during the years of Occupation is woven into the rich tapestry of sights and sounds of the inner city of Amsterdam. Her language is that of a poet: sensuous and rich in metaphors and similes that reach deep. That is why I could not put the book down!"

—**Laureen Nussbaum**, Professor emerita, Portland State University,
Department of Foreign Languages and Literatures

"*An Address in Amsterdam* is a compelling story of the Jewish experience during the Nazi occupation of the Netherlands. Filled with richly detailed descriptions, obviously based on extensive research, the book follows the activities of Rachel Klein as she navigates the personal challenges of her emerging adulthood and the complex social dangers of working in the Dutch resistance movement."

—**Amy Belding Brown**, author of
Mr. Emerson's Wife, Flight of the Sparrow

"*An Address in Amsterdam* immerses the reader in both the light and beauty of the city and the dark, ugly atmosphere of the Nazi occupation. The protagonist, teenaged Rachel Klein, must find her way between the extremes, which makes her breathtaking story impossible to put down."

—**Katherine Bradley Johnson**, NextReads Bibliographer,
NoveList, a division of EBSCO

"In spite of the fact that *An Address in Amsterdam* is a novel, and frankly that word and the Holocaust in one breath bothers me, Ms. Fillmore has done a great job. Her research is impeccable. Moreover, it's an excellent read!"

—**Johanna Reiss**, author of *The Upstairs Room, The Journey Back*
and *A Hidden Life*

"This powerful novel seldom left my hands. Based on years of research, Fillmore's story gets at a universal truth about the dangers of prejudice."
—**A.J. Mayhew,** author of *The Dry Grass of August*

"Mary Fillmore was ahead of her time when she realized that this story is hers and everyone's story. She has given thirteen years to writing *An Address in Amsterdam*, and she has also given her life. This act of witnessing and great courage offers us sanctuary as we search for all the possible ways to survive the rising blood tide of brutality, violence and death. These times demand ethical scrutiny; and the question that Fillmore asked herself, that her characters asked, that the Dutch asked, is the question we must each ask ourselves: collude, collaborate or resist? Fillmore challenges us and sustains us simultaneously."
—**Deena Metzger**, author of *Entering the Ghost River: Meditations on the Theory and Practice of Healing* and *Writing For Your Life: A Guide and a Companion into the Inner World*

"This compelling and emotionally touching tale brings the Nazi occupation of the Netherlands to light, told through the eyes of a courageous young woman determined to put aside her fears and risk all for the noble cause of resistance."
—**Laurel Corona**, author of *The Mapmaker's Daughter* and *Until Our Last Breath: A Holocaust Story of Love and Partisan Resistance*

AN ADDRESS
IN AMSTERDAM

AN ADDRESS
IN AMSTERDAM

A NOVEL

MARY DINGEE FILLMORE

SHE WRITES PRESS

Published 2016
Printed in the United States of America
ISBN: 978-1-63152-133-1 paperback
ISBN: 978-1-63152-134-8 ebook
Library of Congress Control Number: 2016939976

For information, address:
She Writes Press
1563 Solano Ave #546
Berkeley, CA 94707

She Writes Press is a division of SparkPoint Studio, LLC.

Cover photo © Collection Jewish Historical Museum, Amsterdam

In memory of the Dutch Jewish citizens and others
who were murdered in the Holocaust, and in honor of
all who tried to help them.

With unceasing gratitude to my love, Joanna Rankin,
and to my great friend, Eliane Vogel Polsky
1926–2015

An address! There was magic in the word for people whose very lives depended on their finding one.

—Dr. J. Presser, *Ashes in The Wind: The Destruction of the Dutch Jews*

CONTENTS

PREFACE: JULY 1942

Rachel didn't linger, in case she was being watched. The canal sloshed uneasily below her. Looking both ways, she slipped close to another house. Was this the address where she was supposed to deliver the envelope? Yes. The white number on the dark blue metal plate corresponded to the one she'd memorized. She knocked three times. The door opened the merest crack, with no light behind it. One eye and a slice of a finely lined face. Rachel shrank back like the teenager she'd been before the Nazi occupation: a polite Jewish doctor's daughter taught to be cautious of strangers. Then she squared her shoulders and steadied her voice, forcing out the prescribed words. "Is Uncle Harry here?"

"Yes," came a whisper. "Come in." Rachel took a quick breath and entered. Her hands still trembled a little. Deliveries were riskier today than a year ago. She made out the outline of the thin man who'd answered the door. He stepped past her to the threshold and listened, taut and alert. His house must have been raided before.

The man stuck his head partway out the door and looked up the slick street. He took one swift step back, then closed the door quickly and quietly.

"Downstairs," he hissed, grabbing Rachel's hand, yanking her along behind him. Her feet responded before her mind registered his urgency.

She sensed rather than saw the looming furniture in the dark hallway. If this address was a trap, what would he do to her?

"Wait," Rachel said. She stopped short, jerking the man backward for a moment. He might be a collaborator. She'd heard so many stories, and she'd never delivered anything to this address before.

He pulled her arm hard enough that she was again forced to stumble along behind him.

"Shut up!" he spat between clenched teeth. She felt tears burning under her eyelids. She lurched along, fearing that he might dislocate her shoulder. He halted abruptly near the back of the house. A latch clinked as he shoved a door open. "Downstairs," he commanded, pushing her ahead of him. The steps squeaked under her uncertain feet. In the darkness at the bottom, the ceiling was shorter than she was, so she hunched over, breathing in dank air. The door closed above her. She heard the man's steps shuffle softly, then felt his hands on her shoulders, steering her. He switched on a flashlight.

"Go left, about two meters." He moved in front of her, and they crept along. When he stopped in front of a large storage wardrobe, he pressed his lips against the crack between the door and the frame to speak. She could hear the sound of his voice, but not the words.

A weak answer came from inside, as the door creaked open. How could someone breathe in there? So many people were crammed into attics and basements all over the city. At first, almost no one had taken the Nazis seriously. Like them, Rachel had believed the Netherlands would protect all of its citizens, Jews as well as Gentiles. It had been a sanctuary for the three centuries since her mother's family had fled the Spanish in the 1600s. But everything had changed incalculably since the German Nazis swarmed over the Dutch border in 1940. Although only two and a half years had passed, the era before the invasion felt as distant as her early childhood.

"Get in," the man ordered. She began to step inside, but drew back when she heard a soft cry.

"Be careful," someone whispered. "There are six of us in here already." The thin man nudged Rachel forward, her face toward the wardrobe's back wall.

"What's going on?" It was another irritated voice, a man's.

When the door shut, Rachel's ribs compressed so it was hard to breathe. The thin man must have stepped in backward to close the door, because his back was jammed against her spine. Since the wardrobe was a little shorter than Rachel, she had to slouch lower. Quick breaths pumped her ribs against his back. She felt her golden brown curls stick to the back of her neck. In front of her was the rounded form of another woman, pressing against Rachel's bony frame.

"What's happening?" A man's whisper, from a back corner.

The thin man said, "Five German Green Police. I saw them turn this way. They might have seen me. Or this girl might've led them to us."

A sudden stillness fell. No one could step away from her, but everyone who was touching her stiffened.

"You're crazy!" Rachel said. "Anyway, how do I know who *you* are?"

"Sure. We're pretending we have to hide. That's why we've been locked up here for days." She heard a sneer in the man's voice, then low mutterings from others. They might strangle her here, in these stifling quarters, if they thought she was on the other side. She'd have to risk telling them the truth.

"I work for the underground. I've brought your papers." She must not lose control of her voice. The silence this time had changed, as the unseen group recalculated.

"Sorry," a man whispered from the corner.

"Shhh," from the thin man. From the front of the house came one crack, then three others. The wooden door finally splintered. Some instinct made Rachel reach for the other woman's hand and clutch it. Heavy, booted footsteps stomped overhead. The air inside the wardrobe soured. Shouting, then clomping feet up to the second floor. A collective exhale in the closet as they realized the boots were not yet headed downstairs. Sweat stuck skin to skin.

After all the risks Rachel had taken in the months she'd worked for the underground, wouldn't it be ironic to be captured here, in a normal house-to-house raid? She'd carried coded messages, distributed illegal mimeographed newspapers, and—since she'd moved into even more dangerous work—delivered false identity papers. It had been hard to follow the orders never to tell her parents what she was doing, but now Rachel felt the rightness of that choice. If the Nazis came to the door to say she'd been arrested, her mother and father would say, "Not Rachel. Not *our* daughter. You must have the wrong address." And they would know nothing, no matter what the police did to them.

PART I:
RACHEL'S HIDDEN LIFE

MAY–JUNE 1940

A roaring noise jolted Rachel awake. Her attic bedroom shook, its ancient timbers and tiles jangled by the planes overhead. None had ever come this close before. Her carved walnut wardrobe and the mirror on her dressing table shone for a moment in the ghastly light. Rachel pressed her hands over her ears, thrust her feet into warm slippers and headed down to her parents' room. The noise abated for an instant, which meant she could think again. Those must be Nazi planes. Her radical mother had been right, not her father and most Dutch people, who thought the Netherlands could stay neutral the way they had in World War I. The noise wracked her again. At least she heard no explosions, just planes overhead.

No sign of her parents in their room, but a crack of light leaked under the kitchen door on the floor below, so she went down. The noise lessened again for a moment just as Rachel opened the kitchen door. Her mother was yelling at her father, her face blotchy and red, her silvered brown hair in rare disarray.

"Why? Why aren't we in London with my aunt instead of here? Can you tell me that?"

Rachel stood still in the doorway. In her eighteen years, she never remembered a scene like this. Her parents, Jacob and Rose, noticed her and froze, just as another barrage assaulted them. Her father sat at the table, his long face haggard rather than serene and competent.

Her mother stood stiff and straight by the stove, her round face defiant in its beauty. Water was coming to a boil for the coffee whose fragrance was already in the air.

Moving toward the table, Rachel broke the spell. While her mother turned back to the stove, her father looked up. Rachel put her arm around him and kissed his cheek. She felt his bristly goatee, not as well trimmed as it would have been during the day.

"What's happening?" she asked, right into his ear.

"Your mother thinks the Germans are invading."

"Who else would it be, the Chinese?" his wife snapped as the racket increased again. Rachel's parents rarely disagreed, despite their contrasting backgrounds. Jacob's bourgeois Jewish family had arrived from Germany in the early 1900s, while Rose's diamond-cutting Sephardic people had lived in Amsterdam for three hundred years. The usual harmony in the house had been strained as Hitler's hold on Germany strengthened.

When the coffee was ready, Rose put it and three porcelain cups on a tray, and pointed to the living room where they could sit more comfortably. Once her parents settled in their chairs, Rachel sat on the couch facing the huge windows overlooking the Lauriergracht canal. Its procession of linked, centuries-old row houses was invisible. Was the noise from guns as well as planes? It was too frequent to allow for more than scraps of conversation. Only once, Rachel heard a moment of a melody from the nearby Westerkerk carillon, its intricate bells rippling through her body as they had every quarter hour since she was born.

As the noise intensified, she lay on her side, one ear to a velvet couch cushion, the other covered by her hand. Her mother's baby grand piano and the potted palm beside it were mere shadows against the tall windows. Rachel closed her eyes and tried to focus her thoughts elsewhere. Where was Michiel? Her new friend was a university student in Leiden, a few years older than she. He might be there, or here in Amsterdam where his mother lived. Just the morning before, Rachel had opened his invitation to take a long bike ride the next Sunday. The orchards might be in bloom, and perhaps some lilacs. Their date was just a dream now. The Germans were flying over Amsterdam without stopping, but where were they going to drop those bombs? Surely not Leiden. Rachel remembered Michiel's soft brown eyes, a color like the soil in the forest after years of leaves falling and changing. He'd looked at her intently when they were last together.

The noise hammered its way into her head again. She hated to feel the house shake. She'd lived there all her life, with well-laden bookshelves, her father's leather armchair and medical clinic downstairs, her mother's piano and rose-garlanded china, her own ample closet with clothes carefully tailored in the Kerkstraat.

What would Hitler do if he took over the Netherlands? Her father's brother wrote letters from Germany that were full of hidden messages and obscure literary references that he knew they would understand. Rose had done everything she could to persuade him and his family to move to the Netherlands after Kristallnacht in 1938, the night of broken glass and killings and beatings of Jewish people. His wife's elderly parents wouldn't budge, so they all stayed in Germany. What would happen to them now?

✗   ✗   ✗

The next few days brought worse news almost every hour. German paratroopers landed, sometimes in Dutch uniforms to deceive the population. The longtime family housekeeper couldn't reach her cousins by phone, and she was frantic. Rotterdam was bombed to smithereens, with hundreds of civilian lives lost, and the Nazis threatened the same for other Dutch cities. Jacob tried to rationalize his native country's actions, saying that the Germans had to invade

Holland to prevent a possible attack from Britain, but as usual Rose wasn't buying it. She stored away as much canned food as she could get her hands on, and dove into Trollope's *The Vicar of Bullhampton*. Books were her favorite escape, and she loved England, where her aunt had immigrated after marrying a well-off shopkeeper. She often reminisced about their London home on an oval park with huge trees at its heart. It had been a welcome contrast to the smelly tenement where Rose had grown up until her father and others organized the Diamond Workers' Union.

On the evening of May 14, the family sat by the radio. The top Dutch general Henri Winkelman announced that the Netherlands had surrendered. Rose drew in a quick breath and covered her mouth. After a spasm of shock contracted his face, Jacob tried to compose his features. *What will this mean?* Rachel asked herself. She walked to the windows and looked out. The canal waters danced below her, on their way to the nearby Prinsengracht. In the evening light, a soft gold hovered over the greenish brown water. She could hear the percussive wings of a heron as it flew by.

The doorbell sounded, grating and insistent. Glad to leave the radio behind, she climbed the stairs down to the ground level, where her father's clinic was located. It wasn't a patient, however, but their next-door neighbor Gezin, an esteemed school athlete in her class.

"Rachel, I have to talk with your father."

"Of course. Come on up."

To her surprise, his breath was heaving behind her on the stairs. As soon as they entered the living room, he told her parents, "Something awful has happened."

"What?" Rose asked. "The Germans overrunning our so-called neutral country? The Dutch army forgetting to flood the dyked land so they couldn't just walk in? The so-called Queen fleeing to London?"

"Enough," Jacob said. "Let the boy speak." Gezin's family were longtime patients as well as neighbors. They turned to the doctor in any time of trouble.

"One of my father's cousins—his whole family—they're all dead."

"Oh, no! Were they killed in Rotterdam?" Rachel's thoughts veered to Michiel.

"No," Gezin said, his eyes wide. "Right in their own home. The father killed his wife and two children, then himself."

Rachel stepped back. "What? Who did you say this was?" It seemed too incredible. But who would make such a story up?

"My father's cousin, Mozes Moffie, in Den Haag."

Jacob put his hand on Gezin's shoulder. "He must have been out of his mind. I'm so sorry. What a terrible thing! Please give my condolences to your parents. Do they want me to come over tonight?"

"No, tomorrow would be better. They just wanted you to know what happened." Gezin hesitated. "Cousin Mozes left a note saying all the Jews were going to end up dead under Hitler anyway." Gezin sank to the sofa, and everyone else sat back down. Rachel couldn't believe what she had heard. Her father was right; the man had been mad.

"I told you, Jacob," Rose said, her voice low and tense. "I've been trying to tell you ever since Kristallnacht. Is there any chance we can still get on a ship?"

Gezin shook his head. "My aunt just got back from the port at Ijmuiden. She's in an awful state. My uncle tried to drive there, but the Germans were strafing a huge traffic jam of Jewish people trying to get out. Finally, he pulled the car off the road and they walked to the dock. The guards kept everybody away, even people with tickets. An old woman offered her pearls, but they wouldn't take them."

"So it's too late." The bleakness in her mother's eyes shocked Rachel. Would it really be that bad to stay in Amsterdam and wait out the war? Especially with her new friend Michiel nearby in Leiden. Her mother was exaggerating. All the fighting was over now, so it was just a question of enduring the occupation. If the Allies won, they'd know the Dutch had been invaded and wouldn't take revenge.

Her father said, "The Germans aren't at the door yet, my dear. Don't let them undermine your morale. We can't let them get us down. Come on, you two, let me see which of you I can beat at cards." At first reluctant, Gezin allowed himself to be distracted, just as her father had hoped. Rachel's mind wandered instead to the most peaceful place she knew: the enclosed courtyard of the Begijnhof, where she and her parents always sought out the first snowdrops, delicate white flowers that muscled their way into the light. In a few days, she could look forward to another treat: her friend Sonja's eighteenth-birthday celebration with her two other best friends, Paula and Anna.

✕ ✕ ✕

The gathering was held at Paula's on a chilly spring evening ten days later, after Hitler had appointed a stiff-looking Austrian the governor of the Netherlands. At least he left the Dutch civil servants in place to do their jobs—good news to everyone, but especially to Sonja whose father worked for the city. Rachel cycled around the Prinsengracht canal's half-moon shape, its waters flowing ultimately to the wild North Sea where she used to ride with her friends, about twelve miles away. After she parked her bicycle in front of the huge glass storefront of Paula's family's art and antique gallery, she gazed into the front windows. Tonight, *art nouveau* chairs in ivory upholstery streaked with gold sat around an ornate marble coffee table. She must bring Michiel to admire it when they met on the weekend. Heading upstairs to the family apartment, Rachel could hear Paula's mother, Mrs. Posner, call down to her.

"Rachel, at last!" She filled the stairs with her rich voice. "The others are waiting to cut the cake." Her ample figure and pretty features seemed unchanged, including the dimples she'd passed on to Paula. She didn't look as if there was a war on at all. "I know you have plenty to talk about, so I'll leave you to it."

As Rachel went through to the parlor, she couldn't help noticing the art. Wasn't that a Rembrandt etching of the goldsmith with the Madonna and Child he'd just gilded? No matter how many times Rachel saw the room ahead, she always had to stifle a gasp. The chandelier suspended hundreds of crystals, each sparkling from dozens of facets. The intricate shadow they cast on the ceiling was a work of art in itself. Rachel's own family was comfortable financially, but this was a whole other level of wealth.

"Come on in!" Paula said, effusive as usual, her brown eyes vivid and her face animated. She jumped up to give Rachel the ritual three kisses, her fine full figure shown off by a well-cut brown dress. "Anna and I have been waiting for you. Doesn't Sonja look elegant?" Although Sonja was wearing a becoming slatey blue, she still looked gawky, even at eighteen. She was taller than the others, almost ungainly, her features too big for her face. Her expressions were usually so animated that no one noticed she wasn't pretty in the ordinary sense. That night, however, Sonja's face looked tight whenever she wasn't talking. Anna, a blond pastor's daughter, also looked tired, but smiled as Rachel sat down beside her.

The four friends tucked their chairs close around a small round table so their knees touched. Paula poured the coffee, and soon cake crumbs were finding their way to the rich coral and burgundy Armenian carpet. Talk naturally veered to the invasion and what it would mean. Even Paula toned down her enthusiasm. Rachel sighed inwardly, and spoke up.

"Please, can we keep the Nazis out of the room, just for tonight? I'm tired of hearing my parents fight about whether we should have gone to England, and what will happen to my uncle in Germany. I want a night off."

"Me too," said Sonja, her face pinched now. "At least your parents are arguing about England. Mine are talking about going to Paraguay. Almost nobody can leave anyway. But I'm not supposed to say anything about it."

"Then let's talk about celebrating instead." Paula managed to laugh again. "Should we order a case of French champagne for your birthday?" Her smoothly coiffed auburn hair glowed in the light from candles on high, polished brass sticks. No wonder the boys' eyes lingered on her.

"I don't know about a whole case," Anna joked. Everyone called her "The Librarian" because she loved books and wore huge, unbecoming tortoiseshell glasses which obscured her large blue eyes. Her shapely figure was lost in the lackluster clothes that her pastor father could afford. She continued, "The last I heard, Sonja's boyfriend is still in town. I bet they'll find a way to celebrate!" Maybe Anna wasn't as straitlaced as Rachel often thought. They all giggled as Sonja's fair skin turned pinker, while she shifted her long body and tapped her foot impatiently.

"Are you and Daan thinking of making any . . . announcements? Any diamonds in your future?" Rachel teased. If things were getting serious, Sonja would be the first of her friends to marry. Rachel couldn't imagine it. She was more than ready for a boyfriend to have good times with, but not a husband. Not for years.

Sonja pursed her lips and her face fell. "We'd like to, but my father says we can't right now, because the times are too uncertain. What kind of reason is that?" She tossed her head back, took a quick sip from her cup, and set it down hard, making a cracking sound. "I'm old enough to get married. Then I could just stay here with Daan, no matter where my parents go. My mother already had a baby when she was my age."

Paula said, "Our parents are so conservative about us, but it was a different story when they were young." Paula dropped her voice even though the apartment was huge. "I found a gorgeous taffeta skirt in the back of my mother's closet with a wild pattern in fuchsia and black stripes. I asked her when she wore it, and she said, 'While I was engaged to Alistair.' I'd never even heard of him. 'Was he Jewish?' I asked her. You can't always tell by the name. But she shut up and wouldn't say another word." Paula's dimples deepened at the recollection. She had a boyfriend for every day of the week and liked it that way. Rachel didn't want that many, but she was hoping Michiel was someone she could enjoy being with.

Anna looked away. She was always busy after school with some church project. No boy had yet seen past what she wore, probably donated from the parish, and her glasses. Rachel sighed in sympathy. Even if she herself hadn't ever had a real boyfriend, at least there had been some flirting.

As the others chatted, she sipped her coffee, its complex flavors waking up her whole mouth. Rachel wondered about her own parents' lives before they met, and tried to remember the few stories she'd heard. Her working-class mother had a lot of spirit or she wouldn't have married into a much richer, more conservative and religious family. But engaged to a Gentile? She would never have done that. As the girls said goodnight later that evening, Sonja smiled only briefly when she said she was going off to meet Daan. Rachel felt sorry for her, but even more for Anna, who was more caught up in her father's church work than a teenager should be.

✕ ✕ ✕

A few days later, Rachel put on her coat to go and meet Michiel for the third time. Rose raised her eyes from her book and tried to smile, which happened less often these days. "Have some fun if you can, dear. And boys are good company, too, not just your girlfriends, delightful as they are." She was curled up with yet another Trollope novel, looking up only when necessary. From the age of five, when her baby brother died and her parents withdrew into their grief, books had become her best friends.

The world outside felt warm and effervescent after a spate of rain. The clouds overhead moved as fast as water, the thin ones streaking below the billowing cumulus. The breeze stroked Rachel's bare legs. As she headed around the curved Prinsengracht canal toward the Three Herons Café, she stopped for a moment to look at the houses her parents had taught her to love. Every one looked as individual as a human being, with its own address. The linked facades were written on Rachel's inner eye like the shape of her mother's body. They had seen wars come and go, and still stood. Rachel started walking again, toward the place where she and Michiel had first met only weeks before.

✕　✕　✕

She would never normally have been there. Her mother had told her not to go into a café unescorted, as she quaintly put it. However, Rachel hadn't had a choice. She had been riding home from Centraal Station when she realized that her sanitary towel had slipped. The nearest toilet was at The Three Herons, an old-fashioned café she had often passed. When Rachel opened the door, a gust of smoke and coffee and beer hit her, along with loud voices crooning a sentimental song she didn't recognize. She calculated that the toilet must be in the back.

Bracing herself, Rachel had made her way first through a loose crowd, then a denser pack of men at the back. She dreaded unwanted contact with those who might take advantage of the tight situation. Clasping her satchel, she had moved ahead. One man in the smoky back room caught her eye. He was tall, with fair hair and coloring. However, his eyes were brown, not blue, and soft rather than bright like hers and her mother's. He used his forearm to ease a companion aside so she could pass easily. "Please," he said somewhat formally, with a little bow and a slight smile.

Rachel met his eyes and entered the tiny ladies' room. Her face in the mirror looked pliable and open. She told herself that he was just a guy like anyone else. By the time she finished washing her hands, she knew she had to find him again.

He was waiting by the archway to the next room. "My name is Michiel Drogt," he said, extending his hand. "And yours?"

As she told him, she felt the warm breadth of his palm, his long fingers. She wondered if he would recoil at her Jewish name—a question that had only ever come into her mind recently—but he didn't. His face was long and well formed but not especially interesting except for his eyes. They were deep and alive.

Moving closer so he could hear her over the din, she said, "I'm surprised that so many people are having a good time in here. Sometimes people just aren't in the mood anymore."

"You're right. I'm a student at the University of Leiden, and there are days when it's hard even to study." A quick tightness passed over his face. A roar of laughter from the front room almost drowned out his words.

She looked at the clean, bare floorboards. "Is this one of your favorite cafés?" Rachel asked, suddenly aware that a few others were watching them. Perhaps his friends?

"It wasn't, but it is now." He only looked into her eyes for an instant.

"I'm usually in the neighborhood about this time," Rachel improvised. "Perhaps I'll see you again." It would be wonderful to have a male friend of her own.

"This time tomorrow? I'll meet you in front." Michiel gave another slight bow and a quick smile in response to her nod, and returned to his own comrades. Their next meeting had interested her even more. The invasion had kept them apart, but at last they were about to meet again.

X   X   X

As Rachel turned the bend in the Prinsengracht on her way to the café, the Westerkerk carillon played a sweet musical phrase as if to greet her. Michiel slipped into her mind at least as often as the dozens of tuned bells did, every quarter hour. Despite the frightening developments around her, thinking of him always brightened Rachel's mood. She gazed up at the Westerkerk's elaborately carved tower, almost as tall as Big Ben. Its dark gray stone seemed etched against the soft blue sky with a few puffy white clouds racing across it. Would Michiel be as eager to see her as she was to see him? He seemed to like listening to her, and he always asked interesting questions. She was intrigued by their political conversations.

When they settled at a favorite table in the corner over coffee and apple tart, the café was noisy enough that they had to sit close to hear each other. Rachel thought her skirt was touching his pants leg, but she wasn't sure. She liked seeing him up so close and smelling the soap he must have shaved with, clean and unscented. When Rose talked with her about boys, she'd always said it was good to have fun, that kisses were OK, but that was where it stopped "until you're going to get married. Then we'll have another talk." Feeling Michiel so close made Rachel wonder what it would be like to let him kiss her, but he was on another track right now—and no wonder, with the Nazis all over the city.

He spoke passionately as he predicted dire consequences of the Nazi occupation. "Mark my words, they'll be shipping Dutch farm goods to Germany, and drafting us to fight on the Nazi side or work in their factories. The next thing we know, they'll be diverting Dutch companies to produce guns and who knows what else." Could he be right? It was too frightening for Rachel to contemplate. Her father had reassured her that the changes wouldn't be that drastic.

Before she could reply, the noise level increased. "Let's go outside," Rachel suggested. She loved the sound of his voice, even when what he was saying upset her.

The afternoon was cooler but fair. They found a bench by the glittering side canal, in the shade of the soft new leaves. When they sat side by side, Rachel could see the watery reflections on Michiel's face, brightening and changing it as the waves flickered.

He was still preoccupied. "The Germans are acting like savages."

She couldn't let that pass. He was talking about her father's native place, after all. And about her.

"Have you forgotten that I'm half-German? Am I a savage?"

"Of course not! But look at how they threatened to blow up all our cities if we didn't surrender." The wind picked up a lock of her hair and tickled her cheek. Was he even noticing?

"True, but most invaders would have bombed them the first day. At least they gave us a choice." She'd heard her father say this.

"A choice? Give in or we'll destroy you? What about what they're doing to the Jews in Germany? Look at the attacks on some of the Jewish shops right here. The Dutch Nazis are gearing up. And a lot of Jews agree with me, or they wouldn't have rushed off to Ijmuiden to escape." Rachel could see he expected a response, and she wanted to provide one. She liked the give-and-take.

"But, Michiel, the Dutch Nazis are just a tiny minority. All the Dutch civil servants are still in place, and they aren't going to let the Nazis get away with anything big." He listened to her, even when he didn't agree, his head cocked a little to the right and those deep brown eyes focused right on hers.

× × ×

As the summer progressed, Rachel began to agree with Michiel's pessimism, which unsettled her. Although she loved and respected her father and wanted to believe him, she was alarmed when the Allies were forced to evacuate all their troops from France. Rachel wondered aloud whether any place was safe from Hitler. Michiel nodded grimly, but he was still sure the Allies would prevail in the end. Rachel let him convince her, which meant it was just a matter of time until the war was over. They just had to get through it somehow. When the two of them rode their bikes or sat and talked about anything and everything, she felt that she would be able to face whatever came. A serious relationship with a Jewish boy could develop later, when she had finished her education and was ready to think about marriage. For now, she and Michiel could be good friends, even flirt sometimes.

The more time they spent together, the more they confided in each other. Rachel admitted that she didn't want to be a doctor like her father for reasons she couldn't quite articulate, and felt guilty about it. They talked about their futures—her hopes for a home and family and becoming a teacher, Michiel's to be both a scientist and a poet. Another time, he recounted his father's rages and how he had beaten his son for breaking a pencil box. Rachel saw the hurt stiffness on Michiel's face when he talked about it, and reached out to touch his arm as he sat beside her in the café. How had he become such a gentle person?

"He hit my mother, too," Michiel added softly, "especially at night." He turned directly to her and put his hand on hers, warm and thrilling. "That's why I never, never want to make a woman do anything. Not unless she wants to. Not even a kiss." Rachel took in a deep breath, relieved that he would never ask more than she wanted to give, so things could never go too far. Even if sometimes she might want them to.

X   X   X

When her friends asked how she and Michiel were getting along, she was pleased to be asked, but answered evasively. He was, after all, a friend, and couldn't be much more than that in the long run. Michiel probably felt much the same way, although they hadn't discussed it. He came from a solid Protestant background, and his parents wouldn't accept her as a serious girlfriend—any more than Rachel's would accept him. Still, in these times, it was wonderful to have someone and something to look forward to. Rachel didn't want to explain all that to the others.

Paula kept up a campaign of relentless teasing. Sonja, in love herself, was subtler but equally insidious, looking down at Rachel from her considerable height to cross-examine her. "You're spending a lot of time with him. Has he kissed you yet?"

"We're friends," Rachel snapped. If only he would kiss her, just once. Then she'd know what it was like. "Just friends, nothing more."

Only Anna, who'd never had a boyfriend, looked as if she believed her.

JULY–AUGUST 1940

One warm, late evening with the orange sun slowly slipping down, Rachel and Michiel strolled toward the billowing trees of the Westerpark. Her hand was tucked into the crook of his elbow, and every now and then he squeezed it to his side. Through his thin shirt and undershirt, she could feel his warm flesh. It made her want to be even closer. If she felt this strongly about someone who wasn't really her boyfriend, what would it be like when she found her husband? Crossing a broad drawbridge to the Houtmankade, they gazed up the canal to the gleaming open waters of the harbor.

Four German police clustered at the edge of the park, like a group of boys hanging around a ball field. "Let's cross," Michiel said, but she could feel his arm tighten. As they approached, the men heard them and straightened up. One tipped his hat and said *"Guten abend."* Before she could stop herself, Rachel replied in German, her father's mother tongue. It was a reflex to be polite, even to them.

The men's faces broke into smiles, and they all spoke at once. "You speak German!" "Where did you learn?" "Your accent is good." Michiel's elbow tensed beneath her hand, pulling her away, but she couldn't be rude to them. *They're our age,* she noticed. *If they were tourists, we'd chat with them. Instead, they're the enemy.* Given Michiel's reaction, however, she decided to play dumb and repeat the German greeting rather than start a conversation. Their smiles turned to polite disappointment and nods of farewell.

If I'd been alone, Rachel thought, *would I have talked to them for a while, even if they're on the other side?* She loved the German language. She and her father spoke it together sometimes to keep in practice, and he had read aloud to her from his favorite authors when she was growing up.

"Don't ever say too much to them. You need to protect yourself," Michiel said as they walked under the huge trees on the edge of the park. Rachel pulled away a little.

"From what? They're boys, like the ones I go to school with. Unless I flung a bomb at them, they'd never hurt me, especially not if I spoke German to them. They're probably homesick."

"Come on, Rachel!" His tone was impatient, even dismissive, his lips pursed into a tight line. Rachel didn't want to spoil the mood between them, but she didn't like his comment, either.

"Think about it. They're far from home, some of them are probably believers in Hitler but some probably aren't, and they just want to speak their own language. Is it wrong to give them that for a moment?"

"Maybe not. I didn't mean to snap at you. It's been a rough day." She waited for him to say more, but he didn't. His apology made her like him even more, and there was a place she wanted to show him.

They walked on in silence. She steered him toward the view of a small island with a copse of high trees, set in the middle of a pond. The scent of fresh water filled the air.

"Look," she said, "the herons nest here, and they usually start coming home about this time, from the whole city." They chose a bench and sat near each other. One huge heron flew toward the trees, tilting its broad wings and extending its spindly legs.

Rachel edged closer before she spoke, not quite touching but wanting to. "Michiel, remember how terrified people were before the invasion? Our neighbors knew a family where the father killed everyone, then committed suicide. But you have to admit that the Germans have behaved well so far. The Dutch Nazis have attacked some Jewish businesses, but the Germans themselves have hardly done anything to us."

"I agree, but that's because they still think we Dutch are their Aryan brothers, and that sooner or later we'll see the light. One day, guys like the ones on the corner will figure out how many of us hate them." He moved away, and she immediately felt the deprivation.

"Those boys were standing around, minding their own business. I'm totally against what they believe," she said as he opened his mouth to protest, "but the Germans haven't done a lot of things people predicted. What's the big deal if we aren't allowed to watch English or American films? You can't blame them for not wanting us to see propaganda." Listening to herself, Rachel realized that she sounded more like her father than her fatalistic mother, but she couldn't help herself. Maybe things would work out after all, no matter what Hitler said. When she felt Michiel's arm around her, even for a moment as they passed through a door together, she felt hope.

The sun's bronze light tinged his face. How could she have thought it was plain, with the strong jaw and well-drawn nose? He said, "They're under strict orders to behave themselves. They believe they can win us over. What makes you think the Germans will keep on acting like gentlemen? All our good, conscientious Dutch civil servants are working for them. When the Germans jerk the puppet strings, those bureaucrats will do whatever they want." His dark brown eyes flashed.

"That's not true, Michiel. My friend Sonja's father works for the city. He would never do anything that goes against his principles. And he's Jewish." To see how Michiel would respond, she added, "My father thinks the Germans only invaded us to get a buffer between them and England. They need more labor for their weapons factories, and they know we're good workers."

She heard Michiel draw his breath in sharply, and his hands clenched.

For a moment, she thought he would blow up, but he stopped himself. So maybe his father's temper was in there somewhere. "I hope he's right. I should walk you home. It's getting late," he said in a tight voice.

They made peace with a few observations about the herons, and Rachel slipped her hand through his arm on their journey home, glad that things had warmed up again between them despite their wrangling. He was a good friend.

✕ ✕ ✕

Although their political and personal conversations continued, Rachel and Michiel also talked endlessly about books. Neither had ever met someone else their age who loved literature so much. At school, most other students seemed diligent rather than passionate about their studies. Passing volumes back and forth, Rachel and Michiel discussed every nuance chapter by chapter. His French was excellent, so he brought her Molière's plays. They split their sides laughing over *The Hypochondriac*, which gave Rachel a chance to tell him about accompanying her father on house calls.

Because her English was better, she introduced him to the challenges of Shakespeare, blushing as they discussed Juliet's passion for Romeo.

"She's too young!" Michiel protested. "A girl that age wouldn't fling herself at a boy that way."

"Of course she would. I don't know why everyone talks about boys in love. Girls feel at least as deeply." She felt her cheeks redden as she said so.

"But would she defy her parents that way?"

"Well . . ." Rachel thought of Sonja's loving Daan despite her parents. "Yes, she would have. Even in Shakespeare's time."

"Just a little before your mother's ancestors were settling here."

She couldn't believe how Michiel remembered every detail she had told him about herself. *Maybe he cares about me,* she thought, and her chest swelled as if with oxygen. A little romance wouldn't be bad as long as they both knew which lines couldn't be crossed. Michiel certainly knew how to respect a girl—maybe a little too much at times. Rachel wouldn't mind if their greeting and farewell kisses were less perfunctory.

✕   ✕   ✕

Like Rachel, Michiel exulted in the outdoors. They cycled along the canals into the countryside whenever possible, often side by side in conversation, or looking around to drink in the fragrant fields, the melodious birdsong, and the fleeting sun. One balmy afternoon, things changed fast. "Look, Rachel, the clouds over that steeple are starting to thicken. We'd better find shelter." He pulled his bicycle up beside hers.

"I know a spot about a mile up the river. Let's try to get there."

She pedaled fast, happy that she could keep up with him although his legs were longer. They didn't quite make it before the rain began drenching her light cotton dress. The top stuck to her slip, revealing the shape of her breasts. Would he notice? Her stomach fluttered, but she did her best to ignore it. Michiel glanced at her and took a quick breath, then looked away. It must go back to that father of his. Every now and then, his eyes took in all of her, even before today. When Michiel put his jacket around her shoulders, she shivered toward him, and he almost held her. She didn't think about where it all might lead.

× × ×

The next time they were together was a bright afternoon, when they parked their bikes on the bridge facing the vast Rijksmuseum. Every inch of its surface was colorfully decorated, so unlike the canal houses with their elegant stone or brick facades.

Michiel said, "It's more like a palace than a museum." They paused on the bridge.

"Like the Louvre. Wouldn't you love to see it?" Rachel moved closer and touched his arm for a moment. His starched shirt crackled under her fingers.

"Paris is fabulous. And it's not that far away," he said. "I'm surprised you haven't gone already." They lingered a moment on the bridge, leaning against the railing to watch the weeping willow branches strumming the water as they swayed in the warm breeze. Overhead, immense mounds of cumulus clouds blew around and over each other.

"We normally go every year to see our relatives in London," Rachel said, "but not since the war started. My great-aunt Sophie said it was too dangerous to travel, but sometimes I wish we'd visited and just stayed there." She moved her arm closer to his. Was he moving toward her? She didn't know why this scrap of closeness mattered so much to her.

"If you had, we wouldn't have met each other." A happy shiver touched her, like a breeze. So she did matter to him. He continued, "I could have gotten out, too. I have an aunt in New York. She tried to persuade me to move there for university. My mother is still pestering me to consider it, since the Americans are having an easier time than we are."

Rachel looked into his eyes. Could he really leave, just like that? "New York? Why would you go?"

"You know the Nazis want all the unemployed Dutch men to register for war work, or else they'll lose their benefits?"

Rachel nodded. "Yes, but that doesn't apply to you."

"My father's afraid there might be a labor draft soon, even for students."

"Oh." What would that mean? Could they write to each other? What if he were in Germany and everything was censored, and the Allies were bombing the labor camps? All this went through her mind in seconds.

Michiel seemed to read her thoughts. "I don't like it either, Rachel. Let's hope it doesn't come to that. We came here to enjoy the paintings, not to worry. Let's go." He put his arm all the way around her. It felt like the branch of a strong tree, and she eased into it as they approached the heavy wooden door to the left of the dark, arched passageway. Was that gesture mere politeness? Surely not. The slight pressure of his arm sizzled through her coat. Rachel knew her face must be more vividly pink than usual, and she'd chosen the brown raincoat specially. The sunshine fell on the two of them.

"What would you like to see if you got to New York?" he asked.

"Everything. Especially the skyscrapers. But I'd go to Paris first. I want to see the Eiffel Tower, the museums, the fabulous clothes. And the shows, too, with the famous cancan girls."

Michiel's eyebrows shot up. "Why?"

"Why *not*?" Rachel asked. "Didn't you ever see Toulouse Lautrec's paintings of the dancers at the Moulin Rouge?"

Michiel pushed the heavy arched wooden door open. "Peace, peace," he murmured, putting his hand up. "I didn't mean to offend you. But you have to admit that most girls like you aren't interested in the Folies Bergère."

"What do you mean, girls like me?" she asked, her face turned away. She didn't want him to see her reaction to whatever he would say. They began winding their way up the spiral staircase with its illumined stained glass windows.

"Smart, beautiful, well brought up." At least he gave her that, and he listened. She liked wrangling things out with him, and the feeling of his arm around her. She nodded, and he smiled back at her. He reached over and adjusted her soft golden scarf, touching her cheek lightly as he did so.

"It was slipping off," he said.

✕   ✕   ✕

Did Michiel wonder why Rachel never asked him to pick her up at home? She couldn't have explained exactly why she told her parents she was meeting one of her school friends, Sonja or Paula or Anna, instead of him. She didn't usually lie. Her mother and father were happy to see anyone she brought home. They wouldn't make any assumptions about a romantic attachment, but an instinct made her want Michiel to herself. It was a shame he wasn't Jewish, and she was sure he understood what that meant in the long run. But they could enjoy the pleasure of each other's company right now.

Their debates about the consequences of the occupation took a more serious turn in early July. Jews were banned from the Civil Air Guard, although the Mayor of Amsterdam pleaded that they wouldn't have enough guards to cover the city center. The Nazis wouldn't take unemployed Jewish men for labor in Germany when they drafted the others. Yet life went on.

✕   ✕   ✕

One resplendent afternoon, Rachel and her friends strolled along the intimate Egelantiersgracht, as the houses' reflections shimmied in the water. Anna said she'd heard rumors that Jewish people were being threatened. Sonja leaned down to her shorter companions and lowered her voice.

"My parents are worried about my brother—and the rest of us, especially if the Nazis change their minds and start drafting Jews, too. My dad is still talking about Paraguay or somewhere."

"That's ridiculous!" Paula exploded, her dimples disappearing. "We can't let these stupid Nazis get us down. Besides, nobody can get out of the country now anyway."

Rachel agreed with Paula, but she didn't want her friends to argue. She'd had enough of that at home with her parents' debates about what lay ahead.

She asked, "Anna, has your father heard anything about where those unemployed men the Germans drafted are being sent?" Rachel was still haunted by Michiel's father's concerns for his son, and she knew Anna's father had his ear to the ground.

"No, but he worries about them all the time." Anna's glasses were slipping down her nose as usual. "Everyone wants his advice, but he doesn't know what to tell them. The Germans and their Dutch police are everywhere these days. Look, there's a clump of helmets going over the bridge." A duck galumphed up onto the edge of the street and wandered toward them, as though it too wanted to know what was happening. Although the girls turned to other topics, their hearts weren't in it anymore.

X   X   X

However concerned she might be about the Germans, Rachel relished her secret friendship with Michiel. She brushed her hair a hundred strokes before going off to meet him. He had such good ideas about what they could do together, and he was interesting to talk with. Their disagreements usually felt exciting rather than distressing, and he did pay attention to what she said, unlike some of the boys who had flirted with her before. That dress wouldn't do, too frumpy. Where was her good silk slip?

Perhaps they could go dancing one day. It would be such fun to feel his arms fully around her. He was nothing like the other boys. When she had let a few of them kiss her, their efforts were disgusting. He would never slobber the way they did, but it would be nice if he tried something. Lots of girls had male friends—even real boyfriends—before they found the man they'd marry. She checked her hairstyle. Would Michiel like it this way, puffy over each ear, like a cancan girl's? He'd said the red gold in her hair was shining in the sunset the other evening. Had she imagined that his last three kisses on her cheeks were a little closer to her mouth?

✕ ✕ ✕

"You look lovely." As Michiel said it, Rachel realized how much she'd longed to hear that from him. That evening, they were sitting on a bench beside a small canal ruffled by the breeze, outside the city center. The houses blushed in the opalescent light. The sky was busy with dashing clouds, painted every color from charcoal to a peachy dove gray. The warmth of Michiel's arm against hers made Rachel feel dreamy.

She was unprepared when he asked, "May I come and meet your parents, or would you rather visit my family first?" His face was open and almost afraid. Rachel closed her eyes. Was he more serious than she'd meant to be? Part of her rejoiced at the possibility, but surely his feelings couldn't have moved that fast. She needed to nip this in the bud. She'd loved their time together and hoped for more—but involving their families was a danger signal that he wanted something else.

"No! Our parents don't have to meet everybody we know." She didn't want to give up her one big secret from her parents.

Michiel's face sagged like a disappointed child's. She would have to find a kinder way to tell him that she wouldn't invite him home. She didn't want to hurt him.

He said, "Of course I don't introduce all my friends to my parents. But I've told them about you, and they'd like to meet you. No matter what the Nazis are saying about the Jews, my family isn't like that, I promise you."

"What did you tell them?" Her voice was soft and she sat very still.

He turned away a little, looked down at his large hands. He took a deep breath, and turned back. "My mother saw it first. She asked me directly if I was in love. What could I say but yes?" Rachel's eyes widened. Before she knew what she had done, she drew his face toward hers and kissed him, lingering. His mouth first felt feathery, then yielding and pliable.

Michiel pulled away for an instant, then wrapped his long arms around her and squeezed her to him. His eyes scanned to see if anyone was watching. Someone was: a frowning elderly woman in a flat opposite them, her face framed by the seventeenth-century window.

Although he let go, Michiel and Rachel held hands and looked at each other. Rachel listened to the roar in her body, like the ocean crashing against the dunes. Every time she thought the waves would subside, they came back. She longed to put her arms around him, over and over again, to lie down with him for hours and feel his breath and heart. She had not bargained for that, not at all, but she wasn't going to think about the future at that moment.

Without speaking, they walked along the canal. She luxuriated in their interlaced fingers, but she wanted more. Rachel pulled Michiel into a shadowy corner to hug him fully at last. She stood on tiptoe to reach his mouth, and felt the full height of his body. Pressing her breasts against his chest both relieved her and opened an aching emptiness inside her body that she had never felt before.

After a searching kiss, she heard his jagged breath, then a retreat.

"No," Michiel said. "Not this way." He stepped away from her.

Rachel reached for him, but he eluded her. Was he going to take this hunger away as soon as she'd tasted it? Her body had liquefied, and suddenly it tightened up. She knew they could only go so far, but it had felt wonderful.

"Someday we'll be together," he continued. "If you'll marry me . . ." His voice was so quiet she could hardly hear it.

"Marry?" She felt cold and sad. Things really had gotten out of hand. Hadn't he heard her when she talked about being Jewish? "But, Michiel, that's impossible. I'm not ready to think about being married. And my parents would never agree. I love being with you, especially today, but I couldn't hurt them that way. They'd never understand if I married a Gentile."

Michiel recoiled as though she had whipped him in the face. "But if your parents see how we feel about each other, wouldn't they change their minds?"

"Being Jewish matters more than ever now. I'm sorry, Michiel, I didn't understand. You hadn't even tried to kiss me, and I thought we were just getting to know each other."

"I've respected you, I've listened, I've done everything I could to show how interested I was in you. Didn't you notice?" His voice was louder. Was there any way to salvage the situation? She didn't want to lose him, but maybe it was the only way. Otherwise, she'd just hurt him more.

"I didn't understand it had gone so far for you. I thought we could have some good times together, and we have."

"The way you kissed me, I was sure . . ."

Rachel blushed harder than she ever had. "I'm sorry, Michiel. I should have known better. I'd better go home now." Pulling away felt horrible, but she had to.

X   X   X

Rachel threw herself into her schoolwork as never before. Her teachers praised her redoubled efforts, and Paula commented on how
far Rachel had moved toward the top of the class. She tried to stay
focused, doing her best to ignore the news and the Nazi proclama-
tions posted throughout the city. When Michiel wrote to ask her
to meet again, she sent back brief responses, then none at all. She
didn't dare see him and lose her self-control, and she didn't want to
face his pain. There was no point. He wanted marriage, which she
could never give, no matter how much she enjoyed and wanted him.
How could she have thought that he was just a friend? She missed
their conversations and even their arguments, the tilt of his head,
his legs and eyes. Her body betrayed her again and again, especially
at night. She couldn't rest unless she quenched her thirst for him,
vividly remembering the press of his long body against hers. She had
no idea that the longing would be like this. How could she ever have
thought that they could stop with a few kisses?

At school, students watched each other uneasily, not sure where
each one stood, although the teachers—Jewish and otherwise—
continued to set a high standard. Students who heard anti-Semitic
remarks at home felt free to mutter "No wonder, she's Jewish," if
someone made a mistake in class. Rachel worried when she heard
about even worse incidents from Sonja and Paula, but luckily didn't
experience them herself. She wondered what Michiel thought about
what was happening, then stopped herself.

According to the newspaper, swastika flags fluttered around the
Eiffel Tower. Would she ever see Paris with Michiel—if she ever saw
him again? When she caught herself talking to him in her mind, as
though the two of them were still involved, she whisked him away
with a mental broom.

✕ ✕ ✕

A few weeks after the surrender of Paris, Jacob came to breakfast with an uncharacteristically worried expression, reporting that the German bombers were attacking convoys of British ships in the English Channel. Rose poured coffee from the silver pot polished every week by their housekeeper.

"Is that a surprise to you?" Her steady voice was challenging.

"No, my dear. This is war. But it still saddens me to see my countrymen engage in it. I know my father would be ashamed of them." He buttered his toast and passed the jam.

Rachel asked, "Hitler can't win, can he?"

Rose spoke first. "We can't take victory for granted, not after this week. If the French can't defend their own country any better than we Dutch did, why couldn't Hitler win? Especially if England falls."

"What do you think, Paps?" He must have had German friends at school and camp who were Nazis now, but he loved his adopted country and must feel torn.

"I'll have to leave that to you. My schedule today is packed, especially since some doctors are leaving the city. Meanwhile, I'm waiting to hear about Mrs. Feldberg's pregnancy. She's a little overdue, but that's not unusual with the first one." He rose from the table and kissed them both, Rachel on the top of her head, Rose on the cheek. Then he headed for the stairs to his office to care for patients from all over the city, some well-off and many not. Unlike his daughter and his wife, he could set all his worries aside.

✕ ✕ ✕

As summer's long days shrank, the Westertoren's tall silhouette incised itself against the dark sky ever earlier, soaring over the houses.

Rachel watched the change from her desk overlooking the canal, beside her mother's piano. Schoolwork helped her stay sane, especially mathematics and the other sciences. You could learn it, and it was done, not like the less exact subjects in the arts. Sometimes she raised her eyes from her work to gaze past the tall burgundy drapes to watch the intricate patterns of light and water on the murky canal. When still, it reflected the houses opposite, with their subtly carved windowsills and doorways. The elms' leafy branches filtered the intermittent sunshine, layer upon layer. Rachel loved looking up from her books and knowing such beauty was still there, despite the ubiquitous German presence. They had put up ugly posters slathered with propaganda, detailing the latest restrictions on the Jews. More and more, she wondered if Michiel's predictions had been right. She hadn't stopped missing him.

Rachel spotted Sonja locking her bike to the iron railing by the blue stone stairs. A burst of affection filled her, despite having been furious recently when Sonja had said, "It's high time you forgot this man you say you aren't in love with. You need a new boyfriend." A rap sounded on the heavy carved door. The resulting noise inside was low and dull, but pleasanter than the doorbell. In a moment Rose opened the door and Rachel heard her say, "Sonja! It's been a long time. Come have some cake. You look wonderful. What vitamins have you been taking?"

Once they arrived in the living room, Rachel rushed across the room to hug Sonja, who looked better and better, her face open and full and her long spine straighter. Rose had diminished, like most people. Soon the three women were seated together with hot drinks served in Rachel's grandmother's coffee cups, and almond cake. Their housekeeper, ever the professional, kept baking, even when the ingredients were sparse and had to be adapted. "If there was ever a time to bake a cake, it's now," she often said.

"Where's the doctor?" Sonja asked. He had cared for her through every childhood illness. As a little girl, she doted on his old-fashioned way of talking to her like a real young lady.

Rose chuckled. "He's gone to see an Orthodox patient who's had stomach trouble ever since last week, when they banned ritual slaughter," she began, but Rachel interrupted her.

"Please, Mams! To some people," she looked meaningfully toward Sonja, "it's important."

"I don't mean to make light of it. Our butcher will be devastated. I don't know whether he'll be able to hang on long enough to keep the business alive for his son. What if he has to choose between handling unclean meat and feeding his family?"

Rachel said, "His son is my age, Mams. He doesn't need to be fed."

"Jaap has stopped eating?" Rose joked, then lost her smile.

Despite her apparent joy in life, Sonja's face fell when asked about her father, a civil servant who worked in the municipal housing authority. "He was finally up for promotion. We'd planned a big family vacation to celebrate, a whole weekend of cycling before the winter sets in."

Rachel looked up sharply. "What happened?" Her spine pressed against her chair.

"Yesterday the Germans decreed that no Jews can be promoted at all. He's been in that office since I was born, and he works such long hours. Those Germans just hate us for no reason." Sonja's spoon clanged on her saucer.

Rachel reacted instantly, her voice rising. "They're inciting the Dutch Nazis, too. Somebody burned up the synagogue in Zandvoort the other night. And my Uncle Rab's letters are weirder than ever." She picked one of the envelopes off the table beside her, the German stamps cancelled out and the long black inked letters perfectly formed. "Listen: 'The seasons are like Titania's and everything is topsy-turvy but some birds may never make it to their homes this winter.' He's clearly trying to warn us about something."

"You sound like your grandmother," Rose said, with more than a hint of pride in her voice. "She ranted when she read her communist newspaper in the morning. Opa was the sunny one, who used to say that Jewish people were freer here in Holland than anywhere else in the world. But not now. I'm glad my parents didn't live to see this Occupation. It would have broken their hearts."

"Yes, Mams, but what about what's happening today? What about the synagogue they bombed, and Uncle Rab, and Sonja's father? He deserves—"

"Yes"—Rose raised her hand like a traffic policeman—"we all agree with you, but there's nothing we can do about it. Especially not as long as your father keeps his head in the sand. Let it go for now. Sonja, who's the young man?"

Sonja fidgeted with her spoon, opening and closing her mouth slightly. Her expression indicated that she might lie. After all, Rose was of her parents' generation, but the families didn't know each other. She finally said, "It's Daan da Costa, but my parents don't want us to get married. They're very orthodox, and they think it's the wrong time."

Rose gave Sonja an appraising look. "But things are different in wartime, aren't they?"

"They certainly are," Sonja flashed back. "My crazy parents want to leave the country! They're talking about going somewhere in South America—even though everybody says it's impossible to get out now. My parents might make me move there if they can arrange it somehow. Even if they don't, Daan and I may not get another chance to be together if the Nazis go on winning."

As Rose poured more coffee substitute and sympathized, Rachel listened without speaking. Was Sonja right that this could be her only chance at love? *What about me?* Rachel thought. *What if the war gets worse and I never see Michiel again?* She missed everything about him: their arguments about politics, their bike rides, that amazing kiss, even his wanting to marry her.

"Rachel . . ." Sonja interrupted her thoughts. "I actually came by to take you with me to a party near here. Get ready so we can go."

"But I don't want to."

"You'll enjoy yourself," Rose said. "You need to get out. Go dance with somebody and forget all this for a while."

"At least put on lipstick," Sonja ordered.

Rachel went upstairs. *Well, why not?* It might distract her. She changed into her newest dress that would do for a party, a tawny brown that complemented her eyes and hair. When she came down, Sonja said, "That's more like it. Come hop on my bicycle," and they were off.

The strong breeze made it a playful challenge to keep her equilibrium. The houses scrolled past across the canal, the details of their facades blurred by the wet air, like a pastel. Sonja stopped for a moment. "Rachel, I need to tell you something that nobody else knows. I know you can keep a secret even if you don't approve, and I have to tell somebody. Daan and I have decided that we're really married, even if we haven't had the ceremony. If they'd let us, we would."

Rachel was stunned. Did this mean what she thought it did? "But what if you get—you know?"

"Then my parents might let us get married, do you see? And Rachel, I'm so much happier. In fact, being with Daan is the only thing that's making me happy right now. So I'll stay at the party for a few minutes, but then I'm meeting him."

"Be careful, Sonja. I understand, but a lot of people wouldn't."

"I know. Let's get going."

They heard the flat before they saw it. "Stardust" blasted at full volume over a roar of laughter and voices. When the two young women entered the stuffy ground floor room, someone handed

Rachel a beer. She sat on the first rickety chair she could find and began looking at all the young men, wondering if—when?—the Gentiles among them would be forced to work in Germany. Wasn't that a classmate of hers chatting up a petite girl with carefully curled hair? Rachel tried to remember if they were both Jewish, but gave it up as a silly exercise. Religion didn't matter much except at the holidays, or when a relationship began to get serious, as she realized too late it had with Michiel. If only he were here to dance with her. None of these boys had his sexy eyes, his charm. Her mind jerked her heart back. Someone reached around her to knock ashes into a nearby receptacle, filling her nose with smoke.

A thin, dark-haired man touched Rachel's shoulder. He was handsome in a clichéd way, with slicked-back hair and a thin mustache, about her height. He didn't try to shout over the noise, simply offered his hand, which she took. In a moment, they swayed together. "Georgia—Georgia on my mind," the singer crooned. Rachel let go a little, her feet moving in perfect time to the music. The man tried to draw her closer. Rachel stepped back a bit, but smiled. Their bodies moved well together. At last she stopped thinking of Michiel. Her nipples tightened, and she wondered if the man could tell.

When the music changed back to "Stardust," the lights went out. Shrill cries burst out briefly, replaced by shuffling feet, the occasional inarticulate murmur or breath quickly drawn in. Rachel's partner moved closer. This time she did not pull away. Their cheeks were joined, his clean-shaven and scented, hers silky. Her breasts tingled, light against his chest. Before she knew it, he was kissing her, nibbles followed by a searching tongue.

Wait! Rachel thought. *I don't know even your name.* She pulled her head back and closed her mouth, but he pressed forward insistently. *Why are my panties wet?* she thought. His tongue felt huge and she didn't like it. She inserted her hand between their chests, pushing lightly. She shook her head.

"Why not?" he whispered in her ear, kissing her earlobe.

Rachel wondered, too, but he was the wrong man. Even though her body was zinging with an energy she had not felt in weeks, Michiel was the man she wanted to be with. She wanted to be kissed, squeezed, thrilled—and she had never suspected how much until she'd kissed Michiel. Although she had tried to work him out of her system, she longed for his lanky sturdiness, and the look in his eyes when he'd said he loved her. Could she find him now, if she let herself look? But that was ridiculous. Their relationship had no future. She broke away, slipped through the crowd, and walked back home in the dark. She hoped her parents would already be upstairs, and call down to be sure she was safe rather than coming to greet her. But she was a little disappointed when she didn't get to tell her mother that yes, she'd had some fun. Kind of.

SEPTEMBER–NOVEMBER 1940

"That can't be right. It's just another rumor." Rachel stood in line in the Jonas Daniel Meijerplein marketplace, waiting to buy the scrawny vegetables which were all that the family's longtime green-grocer Mr. de Jong could get.

"I'm sorry, but it's true," her friend Anna insisted, shifting her market basket from one arm to the other. Her coat sleeves were too long. "My father told me."

"They can't ban Jews from all the markets except this one." Rachel shook her head sharply. The truth was hard enough without amplifying it with rumors.

"But—" Anna said.

"It can't be right. The Jews sell too much of the food all through the city, and we're a lot of the customers. You should know better." Her friend's puzzlement had turned to hurt. Rachel was ashamed, then embarrassed when she felt tears coming to her eyes. "I'm sorry, it's just . . ." How could Anna ever understand how Jewish people felt, with her flaxen hair, blue eyes, and impeccable credentials as a pastor's daughter? "We'll ask Mr. de Jong, then, when it's our turn. Come on." Rachel pulled her forward.

Mr. de Jong had known Rachel forever, and her mother and grandmother. Visits to him were always a treat to her as a child. Sometimes he leaned over her little basket to pop a fresh Frisian strawberry into her mouth, sharp and sweet. Whenever Rose finished her purchases, he used to ask, "Rachel, how much does your mother owe me today? Let's figure it out." He inclined his kind face with its oversized nose and eyes, and held out his compact hands for her to count on his fingers. Thanks to Mr. de Jong's lessons, Rachel headed every math class she ever took.

He stood beside the vast Portuguese Synagogue as usual, in an advantageous position to observe the whole square. Suddenly, he looked old, with his grizzled beard, and his broad face more wrinkled than she remembered. He was waiting on a careworn woman as they approached, but soon looked up and caught Rachel's eye, his taut face breaking into a smile and a wink. As he counted out change, Rachel nodded back and relished the earthy smell of the root vegetables. She fingered the delicate skin of the onions. At least a few things remained the same.

Mr. de Jong greeted the two young women. "Everyone's been too serious today. Rachel, you're just the sunbeam I need, though even you look a little cloudy. Who's your friend?"

She introduced them, and Anna blurted, "Tell her it's true about the ban on Jews in all the markets except this one. She wouldn't believe me."

Mr. de Jong stood still for a moment. "I've been here forever and I can stay. Most of my customers will stick with me. But the merchants who are banned from the other markets can't survive here. Only a few of their Jewish customers will follow them across the city."

Rachel unwittingly squeezed the onion in her hands. *Was it possible?*

He continued, "So Anna's right. What do you want, carrots again? Take this last green lettuce. It's wilted, but I don't know how long I'll be able to get it. The Germans don't let us have anything much these days, you know. The good stuff goes to them and their cronies, or into the black market." He weighed the carrots and other items on his pan scale, with clanging weights on one side and vegetables on the other.

"I don't suppose you can add those up for me," Mr. de Jong said. Rachel tried to smile, and handed over her folded money.

"I wasn't following," she admitted. What would the Nazis do next? If they broke the British forces, then Hitler really could win.

Mr. de Jong pressed coins, cold and dead, into her soft palm. As they said goodbye, he reminded her, "At least we're in Holland. People like your friend here won't let the Germans go too far." She kissed Anna before she walked away, sad to see that her friend's eyes were still clouded from their spat earlier.

Rachel had hoped to get her mind off Michiel and the war, but now she felt even worse despite the sunny day, especially after passing a poster announcing that no more Jews would be hired in the civil service. She looked back at the square. On either side of the Jonas Daniel Meijerplein, the brooding synagogues—Portuguese and Ashkenazi—looked as secure as the high elms between them. The sun tinged the dark brick of the Portuguese Synagogue with thin gold. It was at least four stories tall, with its monumental arched windows reaching almost to the roof. *My people built this,* Rachel thought, *my mother's people, over three hundred years ago.* Amsterdam had been the safest place for them to flee the Inquisition, and the diamond merchants had brought a few cutters like her ancestors with them.

To lift her spirits and distract herself, Rachel decided to detour through the nearby Jewish Waterlooplein Market to see the thousand things the merchants offered. Soon she was squashed in a crowd from all over the city, which swirled away her thoughts. Here they were, everyday citizens doing everyday things—like people in London or even Berlin. The September air blew warm and sparkly, an effervescent tonic. At least the Nazis couldn't take that away. An elbow poked her sharply. It was time to move on.

On her bicycle once more, Rachel pedaled hard. The golden September air tangled her hair and reached deep into her lungs, consoling her with its fragrance. Her body ached from hours of study and desire. When she let herself want Michiel, a hand reached inside her and opened slowly, the way a flower's petals slip against each other and unfurl. But that was a fantasy. Nothing would come of it.

She finally pulled up to her house, and looked for a moment at the carved stone above the door, a sculpture of a woman from the days of sailing ships, holding an anchor in one hand, and gazing at a bird held aloft in the other. The word Hope was written below. Rachel liked living in a house old enough that her address was more than a number. She let herself in, hauling the small bag from Mr. de Jong. "I'm home," she called, but there was no response. When she peeked into the living room, Rose had pulled her piano bench to the window and was staring out at the newly yellowing leaves on the elm.

When Rachel walked around the big potted palm to kiss her mother, she saw the stoniness in her face. It felt cool to the touch. "What's wrong?" she asked.

Rose looked at her vacantly and whispered, "They've bombed London."

"What?"

"Hitler has bombed London. He says he'll burn the rest of Britain."

"London! Where's Great-Aunt Sophie?"

"Still at her cottage in the country. But not everybody has that luxury."

"I know." Rachel couldn't stop herself. "So, Mams, it's good that we didn't go there. Hitler would have followed us."

Her mother sighed deeply but did not argue, just took her daughter's hand and pulled her down to the piano bench. They held hands and watched the pale gold elm leaves flicker, reflected as yellow dots on the surface of the greenish ripples in the canal. A few mallards landed noisily, leaving a V-shaped ripple in the water. A heron sailed overhead, its majestic crossbow form silent and exact. *They're still here,* Rachel noticed in surprise. How could birds occupy the same sky as Hitler's bombers? How could Amsterdam be safe while London was burning? And where was Michiel?

X   X   X

The city felt less safe a few weeks after the new restrictions on the market were imposed, when Rachel and Sonja came upon a rare sight in their generally well-ordered schoolyard: two boys slugging it out. Rudi's father had been fired from the Civil Air Guard because he was Jewish; Han's was a well-known Dutch Nazi Party member. A circle formed around them, with shouting on both sides.

"What's going on?" Sonja asked a girl on the periphery.

"Rudi was bragging about how the Royal Air Force was beating the Nazis. Han hit him and said that Hitler was just biding his time." At that moment, Rudi's arm angled back, and he squashed the other boy's nose. Rachel shuddered when she saw the spurt of red as Han howled and went for Rudi's throat.

"Boys!" The hefty physical education teacher's baritone voice bellowed. Han let go. The teacher stepped between the contestants.

"Rudi, for your sake I hope you didn't hurt Han too badly. If his nose is broken, you can get expelled for that. You Jew boys have to learn to control your tempers."

"Wait a minute. That isn't fair—" Rachel began, but the teacher stopped her.

"Quiet, young lady, or I'll send you to the principal's office." They would call her parents. Sonja gave Rachel a meaningful look that told her to shut up. Nobody, however, could stop her from giving Rudi a sympathetic smile, and feeling more worried than ever.

✕ ✕ ✕

In the low light of a late October afternoon, Rachel stopped on the bank of the pale blue Amstel River, and watched an elderly couple standing arm in arm on the nearby Skinny Bridge. As they moved closer together in the high wind, she wondered if they had once longed for each other the way she longed for Michiel. Perhaps. The man looked frail as he inclined his head toward the woman's broad and smiling face, but such tenderness flowed between them.

The more she had tried to banish Michiel from her thoughts and heart, the more strongly her body remembered and demanded him. Rachel asked herself: *I hardly know him. Could I honestly miss him that much?* From her depths came an answer. How could she have thought she didn't want to marry him?

But Mams and Paps . . . her thoughts whirled in the river, where the sunset sheen now tinged the water a sizzly bronze. Why had she left him? Things were getting worse all around her. The Luftwaffe seemed invincible. Earlier that month, civil servants, including teachers, were forced to sign an "Aryan attestation" about their forebears. Professors drew up petitions against it, a number of students protested, but it didn't make any difference. Sonja's father was one of thousands of dismissed officials. Jewish businesses had to register—why?

Walking or biking along the canals, Rachel had to watch for German uniforms, Dutch Nazi thugs, and the Dutch police who were often collaborators. She'd heard lots of reports about what could happen, even in broad daylight. Perhaps Sonja's parents' wild idea about fleeing to South America wasn't as crazy as Rachel had first thought. No wonder Sonja and Daan felt they couldn't wait until their parents approved of their marriage.

Across the Channel, the bombing in London was endless. The

BBC said that 250,000 people were homeless. St. Paul's Cathedral was hit directly, after everyone had said that Hitler wouldn't dare bomb Sir Christopher Wren's dome. Was Great-Aunt Sophie really OK? Letters weren't allowed between England and occupied Europe anymore. Uncle Rab's occasional missives from Germany became harder to decipher, but it was clear that life was worse for the civilian population there, too.

The war was spreading, and the Netherlands was a logical potential battleground, positioned between Britain and Germany. Anyone could be killed in a war. Michiel could be forced into the German factories or work camps, which the Allies would surely bomb. Or, if he acted on his beliefs, he might be arrested, or have to hide to avoid it. If he planned to disappear, would she even know? How could she be sure? She might never see him again. Her body ached for him, day and night. How could loving him be wrong? The rules for ordinary times didn't apply to an era when neither she nor Michiel knew what might happen to them.

She had to find him.

✕   ✕   ✕

After the months that had passed, Rachel had to look hard. She took the hour-long train ride to Leiden three days in a row. Being in the quiet university city soothed her after the bustle of Amsterdam. She realized how much she wanted to find Michiel as the days wore on. Because they'd spent almost all their time together in Amsterdam, Rachel wasn't sure exactly which were his favorite cafés, or where he lived. When she overcame her reluctance to ask at his Physics department, they told her to look at the library. Her first attempt to scan all the students sitting at long tables failed, and she went home discouraged.

The next afternoon, Rachel finally spotted Michiel outside the library with an unusually short man. When their conversation seemed to be breaking up, she walked over, her heart loud in her ears.

"Excuse me—Michiel?" She waited. His face, thinner and sharper, went slack with surprise. He said nothing.

His friend didn't move, so Rachel said, "How do you do? I'm Rachel. It's nice to meet you." His eyes fell on hers in a way that said he knew something was up. Had Michiel told him about her?

"Same here. I have to go to chemistry class. See you around, Michiel." Funny that he hadn't said his own name.

Michiel turned his back on Rachel and walked away into the raw drizzle.

"Wait!" she called, and ran to keep up. "We need to talk."

The face he turned to her had altered more markedly than she could have imagined. Colder and more lined. The deep brown eyes recessed into the sockets. All the bones accentuated.

"Please," she begged, her eyes smarting with tears. Maybe he didn't want her anymore.

"All right," he agreed gruffly, and led her into an ancient building. She followed him up to the top floor to an empty classroom, with long rows of desks and high windows. Noticing how his shoulders curved forward and down, a posture she didn't remember, she hardly knew what she wanted to say to him. She just wanted to feel his arms around her again.

He waited for her to sit at a table, then sat opposite her, stiffly. He spoke first, formally. "Rachel, I don't know why you're here, unless your father has finally changed his mind about us, or about the Nazis."

"No, Michiel, it's not that. He thinks still we're safe here. I've stopped agreeing with him, though."

"Hasn't he heard that even the Jewish university faculty are being dismissed? He's living in a dream world." Michiel was stiff with restraint. "But tell him that a very few people are somehow buying their way around the travel ban. I still think the Allies will win, but the Nazis can do a lot to Jewish people in the meantime." His body softened a little as he looked at her more closely.

"Mams agrees with you, but Paps keeps on working and saying everything will be all right." Somehow, Rachel believed Michiel and Rose rather than her father. Things could get much worse, very fast. In fact, they already had. Worse than she could possibly have imagined. Why not be with the man who loved her, whom she loved, before something awful happened to her and her parents, or even to him?

"What are you going to do?" Rachel whispered, melting under his kinder gaze.

"Don't ask," he added, pulling away again. It was like watching a ship leave a wharf, irretrievable.

"Michiel." Her voice was low, hardly recognizable. It startled him into facing her. She slid her foot across the floor to meet his, but he retreated, and turned to leave his chair.

She said, "Maybe there's a way we could marry. If you want me enough."

He looked at all of her body that he could see above the table where they sat on opposite sides. He met her eyes, then looked quickly aside. "Want you? I was the one who wanted to marry you, remember? You were the one who said no. Of course I want you."

"Michiel, so much has happened. It was never that I didn't *want* you."

Rachel slipped over to Michiel's side of the table, and stood beside his chair. When she pressed her breasts against his face, he first jerked his head back, then met her eyes and let it fall forward. Rachel drank in what she had been longing for—but knew he'd stop any second. He did.

"We can't, Rachel. I can't take advantage of you." His voice was squeaky. "What if you get pregnant? Who knows if I'll be in Holland, or even alive? I have to do something about the Nazis. I can't just sit here. One day I might have to go underground, and you'd be stuck with a baby and no husband. It's wartime. Who knows what will happen to us?"

She replied simply, "I love you. If I do get pregnant, I think my parents would let us marry. Why can't we be together now? It may be all we have."

Michiel stood up and took her hands, but held her away from him, his arms stiff. "I have to think." He kissed her hands in the courtly way she used to love. "We can't rush back into this," he said. "Let's meet tomorrow at the Vondel Park, by the gates. I'll be there at five, and we can talk more."

Rachel didn't know exactly what would happen, but if Michiel came to his senses, surely they could figure it out. Sonja and Daan had, and they weren't married, either.

✕ ✕ ✕

She had tucked the woolen blanket into her book satchel, ready to spread on the ground. For once it wasn't raining. She explored the Vondel Park until she found a private place in the more forested part under an immense plane tree, then returned to the elaborate cast-iron gates. Michiel's large frame eventually emerged from the crowd, bent into the wind. His face showed resolve, a bad sign. When she kissed his cheeks, she smelled his soap. Would she ever watch him take the wet shaving brush and whisk it around to make lather in the morning?

"Let's sit and talk," she said. "I found a nice place by a tree."

"Good," he replied, sounding relieved, following as she led the way. "Here, you can sit on my jacket." Something told her not to pull out the blanket. The ground was strewn with golden leaves.

"Thanks, I'll use mine." Side by side, their backs against the tree, neither spoke for a few minutes.

"I've been thinking," he began. Rachel put her hand lightly on his thigh and began stroking it. He jolted in surprise but did not move away. Their eyes locked.

"Let me," she said. "Please just let me."

He leaned over and kissed her near cheek, holding the other in his hand, turning her face toward his. He began nibbling her mouth. By the time their tongues met, Rachel was in a rage of hunger. Her vagina was clenching and then opening, each time feeling slipperier. Rachel slipped her hand toward his crotch.

Michiel's hand suddenly covered hers and pushed it hard against something bulky, over and over. She recognized the rhythm from her own explorations, and pushed in time with his thrusts. Giving a thin cry, he stopped all of a sudden, then kissed her more deeply than ever before. Rachel was fascinated, and even more aroused. If he could use her hand, she could use his. She grabbed it, but he stopped her. "Wait," he whispered, reached under her skirt, and touched her bare thigh. The whispers of his fingers made her skin quiver. It was so intense that it almost hurt. Her body became a creature with its own will and hungers.

When Michiel's broad hand awkwardly reached the slippery places between her legs, he seemed to be touching her everywhere. She arched toward him over and over, until the huge horse she was riding took an unimaginable leap.

X   X   X

After that, they met whenever he could come to Amsterdam. Rachel counted the hours until their next time together. Her body simmered, no matter what she was doing. Walking down the street, energy streamed into her limbs. Someone occasionally lent Michiel a room where they could make love, learning not to hurry when they had time. They approached the ultimate act gradually. When he did slip into her, the pain was easily overridden by her desire. The blood terrified Michiel because of his violent father, but Rachel reassured him. It was like her period. The next time, he brought a condom and used it. "I want to leave you with good memories, not a squealing baby. These days, anything could happen," he said.

She didn't argue. The news was almost unbearable. Hitler said he would beat the English, then shattered Coventry Cathedral along with four thousand homes around it. Eggs and cake were suddenly rationed, which meant that treats were scarcer. The school hours which used to captivate Rachel now bored her. Each felt like a huge concrete block between her and Michiel. What lay beyond them she didn't dare to think.

When the two of them could only meet in public, they sometimes went to the movies. When the newsreels began to show the usual Nazi propaganda, they joined much of the crowd and booed the officials with their straight-armed salutes. During the features, hands could stray without attracting much notice. More often, they sat in the Three Herons Café and talked endlessly. Rachel's other friends faded away except for school hours together. Sonja was busy with Daan, Paula had plenty of boyfriends, and Anna's father kept her busy with good works in the parish.

The conversation between Michiel and Rachel was often about what would happen next, but he merely hinted at his own political activities. Rachel knew he wrote for a student newspaper, but surely he wasn't silly enough to do anything that would put him in real danger. Once, when Michiel was in the men's room, she reached into his satchel to find something to read, and stumbled on a broadsheet denouncing the Nazis: "Stop the pogrom!"

"What's this?" she asked when he got back. His eyes evaded hers. "Just something from the university."

"Do you honestly believe there could be a pogrom?"

"Yes. That's why I can't talk with you about what I'm doing, Rachel. Please understand. I wish to God"—she had never heard the word from his lips—"that you had gone to England when you could have, and stayed there with your family."

"Even if we could have, my father wouldn't be happy there. He had too many bad times there as a boy after the first war. Now he's saying that even if the Germans have gone crazy in their own country, our Dutch countrymen won't let them harm us. I'm not so sure anymore."

Just the day before, Rachel had seen a policeman she recognized as Dutch going into the corner tailor shop and shouting at the owner, an elderly Jewish man who had fled Germany five years ago. "Where is your registration? What makes you think you can get away with this? I could arrest you right now. In fact, I'm going to. Get your things."

Even from outside, Rachel could hear the whimpering, conciliatory tone the old man used to try to calm the invader.

The policeman said, "Well, all right, I'll let you get away with it for now. But I'll be back, and you'd better be ready for me next time." It wasn't hard to guess that he meant that he could be bought. How long would it be before the police came after a doctor like her father, too, just because he was Jewish? She hardly dared let the thought enter her head.

When they talked about the larger Nazi threat, Michiel seemed sure that he knew more about what was going on than she did. Every now and then, he implied that he was working against the Nazis, but he'd never say how. She would have liked to help, but she was a girl, after all, and her parents wouldn't let her get involved. If she were at university with Michiel, she could have made sure he didn't do anything foolish.

✕ ✕ ✕

The night before while she was cleaning up the kitchen, Rachel had heard her parents arguing in the dining room. It had become the norm rather than the exception. "Excuse me, Jacob, *my* people have been here since the 1600s. Yours arrived when you were just a boy." Rose rarely rubbed it in. "We faced anti-Semitism here from the beginning. They wouldn't let us in the guilds, remember?"

"But no one has ever hurt us. The Nazis tried to get the café owners to put up those signs about Jews, but most of them won't keep us out. This is Holland, my dear. You seem to be forgetting where you are."

"The Dutch aren't in control anymore, can't you see that? They're knuckling under." She was as agitated as he was calm. "The latest German refugees say the raids and beatings there are worse than ever. Your own brother Rab is trying to tell you that in his letters. It's too late to go to England, but what about Switzerland? I know it's an outside chance, but we just might have enough money to make it happen." They kept arguing until the dishes were done, and Rachel didn't doubt that it would continue long after she was in bed.

DECEMBER 1940–JANUARY 1941

What were those Nazi thugs doing near the entrance to the Three Herons? Rachel heard the shouting, and she and Paula darted across the nearest bridge to put some distance between them and the café. At least five men were shouting and running down the Prinsengracht, carrying signs. *What if they catch sight of us?* Rachel just wanted to get away.

"Faster, Paula. Come on!" Once they were around the next corner, she pulled her friend into a doorway. They were both breathing hard enough that they couldn't speak for a few minutes. Paula's brown wool coat heaved up and down. She clutched the rabbit fur collar around her neck.

"Who were they?" Paula asked.

"It must be some of those pro-Nazi street fighters. But why would they be at The Three Herons?" She walked cautiously to the corner and peeked. "They're leaving now." Her body stiffened, ready to bolt, but the men went the other way and soon were out of sight.

"Let's go over. I have to know what happened," Paula said.

An ugly sign awaited them outside the café: "Jews not wanted." But Paula led the way, and a tense Rachel followed.

Paula flirted with the perky young man behind the counter and asked, "What were those guys doing here?" Rachel would never have taken the risk.

"They left that stupid sign. We'll leave it there, in case they stop by again. Who's going to come here if we get rid of all the Jews? We'll still let our friends in, like you. What'll you have?" Rachel's heart eased, but it still raced.

✕ ✕ ✕

"Could you get away for a whole night?" Michiel asked Rachel with rare urgency as they walked in the cold rain. It sounded so heavenly, the idea of going to sleep with him, and then waking in his arms. She hated lying to her parents, but she would. Sonja was the logical one to help with a cover story.

Rachel and Sonja met after school near the Rembrandt House, and walked across the street toward an ancient café perched over the narrow locks between the Amstel River and the Oudeschans. The wooden supports which anchored it in the muck under the city had sunk unevenly, leaving the walls canted at a funny angle.

The two young women sat on a bench which faced the café, and soon Rachel's story was out. "I'm so glad you told me," Sonja said. "I thought I was the only one who'd ever—you know—without being married." There were tears in her eyes. "I'm still hoping my parents will let me marry Daan if I get pregnant."

If Michiel would cooperate, could that strategy work for Rachel? She wasn't really sure. She imagined Rose patting her pregnant belly, shaking her head, and making the best of a hasty wedding. But would the wounded look ever disappear from her father's eyes? Besides, she couldn't imagine having a baby now. That was for later.

✕ ✕ ✕

Rachel didn't let herself think, but packed a small bag and sped through the wet streets on her bicycle. Using her city map, she found the obscure address Michiel had given her, where a friend had made a flat available. Michiel greeted her with uncharacteristic intensity, and led her upstairs. They entered the studio, which served all functions except the toilet. The bed was covered with bright red cushions which could easily be tossed out of the way. Rachel let her eyes fall on the candles on the table, illumining real chocolate cut into ten perfectly equal square-centimeter pieces presented royally on a china plate.

"Chocolate!" Rachel exclaimed. "Wherever did you get it?" But Michiel wasn't listening. He stripped off her coat, then clasped her tightly so she could hardly breathe.

Then she knew. He was about to leave her. She wanted to cry out, but instead returned his swift embrace. Her mouth covered his and searched as if for the depths of his soul, but it was his body she wanted, all of it. The buttons on his shirt wouldn't yield easily, so she pulled the whole garment up and squirmed her head under it, panting.

He tried to hold her still, but she fought him off, undid his pants and found herself licking his penis for the first time. It felt sturdy under her tongue. He was moaning by then, saying her name, over and over. But kissing wasn't enough. She slipped off her panties and pulled him over to the bed, where he half fell on top of her. At last, she felt him stretch and fill her to the depths. Her pelvis plunged toward his, faster and faster.

Michiel grasped her breasts roughly, as he never had before. Could that be her voice crying out?

Over the next hours, they dozed and made love, each time more slowly. She couldn't bear to think this wouldn't happen again and again. Her body vibrated like a bell.

"Do you have to . . . ?" she asked.

"Yes. The police are looking for me. I don't want to say exactly why, but you can imagine. It started after they fired the Jewish professors."

"Where will you go?" she whispered.

His breath whistled as he sucked in air. "Somewhere north. They don't tell us. But I have to go. They may not let me contact you, for your safety as much as mine. But I promise, after the war, I'll find you somehow."

Promise? After? She knew better, but she said nothing. Real sleep was out of the question for her, but his body claimed him, and soon he was snoring lightly. She felt his ribs under her sticky fingers, and her drowsy mind began to drift to the ribs of ships that had brought her mother's people to this country. To safety. His warm breath scented the air with a remnant of the chocolate they had fed each other sometime during that long night. Rachel listened to the carillon's music for the hour, the quarter, the half, the three-quarters, each time with its own melody, over and over.

At first light, Michiel woke and wept. She saved her tears until his were done, heating water on the little stove and washing him, from his cold toes to his sweaty head. Then he did the same for her, wordlessly. They helped each other dress. "You go first," he whispered. He wrapped the chocolate they hadn't finished in crushed paper, and passed it to her.

"No. You might need it," she replied, and handed it back. He stood by the door.

She knew better than to kiss him one last time. She just left.

✕   ✕   ✕

After the New Year, Rachel huddled with a group of friends for coffee after school. It was part of her plan to keep busy. Her mother was delighted that she'd brought some fellow students home on an otherwise dismal day, and pulled out some cookies saved in a tin from before the Occupation, made with real butter. The group sat around the Kleins' dining table by candlelight, while frigid rain spattered against the already dark windowpanes.

Everyone was complaining about the Germans pressuring young Gentile men to work in Germany alongside the unemployed who had already been shipped off. Some students had already been threatened with arrest for political reasons, like Michiel, and a few of them had disappeared. Rachel could hardly bear to think of him, yet she did—constantly.

"At least they don't want *us* to work for them," Rudi joked. "And we don't have to worry anymore about passing the exams for university next fall." Rachel recoiled at being reminded that her dream of going to the university was over, at least for now. Jewish students weren't allowed to enroll without special permission by the Secretary General, which was highly unlikely. School, which had always held Rachel's attention and often delighted her, felt pointless now.

On top of that, every bit of Rachel ached for Michiel. Sonja told her she'd changed in a month's time, and not for the better. Rachel was ever leaner, and she noticed a biting undertone in her own voice. Alone, she often cried for no reason. As she passed the plate of goodies around, Rachel noticed that even the inveterately cheerful Paula was losing her dimples. The family art and antiques business must be suffering these days.

"It's getting worse in the streets," Paula said. "The other day I saw two Nazis push an old Jewish man up against the wall. They smashed his glasses! I couldn't believe it. He was lucky he didn't lose an eye."

"He might as well have, with the outrageous price of spectacles," Rudi said. The others laughed, but it wasn't funny. Were they really helpless against attacks like this? Rachel burst out, "Can't we do anything about it?" More and more, she found herself getting angry. Everyone fell silent except Rudi, who tossed back "Get a pair of padded gloves and practice!" Many Jewish men were doing exactly that; the boxing clubs attracted more members than ever.

"Women can't box," Rachel said tersely, "but there must be

something we *can* do." Her fists clenched and her buttocks tightened, as though she were getting ready to jump up and fight.

Someone quickly turned the conversation to the latest cabaret act at the Schouwburg Theatre, where the songsters Johnny and Jones were making fun of the Nazis again. Although anyone could come to hear them, the audience and performers were largely Jewish, and the Nazis had renamed it "The Jewish Theatre." It was one of the few places where people could laugh about what was happening.

"Let us know when you set up that club for women boxers," one of the boys goaded as the group broke up. All evening, Rachel sputtered clever things she should have said at the time.

✕   ✕   ✕

Her spirits weren't improved the next day by going with her parents to register as Jews, after a fight about whether to comply. Rose had argued against it, but Jacob prevailed by reminding her that the efficient Dutch Population Register already had a list of everyone in Amsterdam, complete with their addresses and religions. As they stood in line in the saturated chill, Jacob fretted about his office hours as they stamped their feet to keep warm. When they reached the head of the line, he paid a fee to the Nazis to register each of them.

✕   ✕   ✕

Rachel dreamed of floating in the loose circle of Michiel's arms, moving closer to his body which then slipped away like an eel in the canals. A sound interrupted this dream, a kind of ringing that kept coming back. In an instant, she was out of bed, pulling on her bathrobe. The doorbell. But it was pitch dark, and the clock showed 2:30 a.m. Who could it be? *The Nazis can't be looking for me,* she thought, *all I did was say a few words against them in my own house.* She rushed downstairs while her parents were still rustling around. If it were the Nazis, she'd try to divert them rather than let her father aggravate the situation. Rachel braced herself to face a phalanx of aggressive men and unlocked the door. Instead, a tall, sobbing girl poised her finger on the doorbell for one more desperate ring. Her coat and scarf were soaked. She looked up, and it took Rachel a moment to recognize her.

"Sonja?" Her friend's eyes were swollen, her face a vivid red. Rachel took her freezing hands and pulled her inside, dripping and trembling. Rachel didn't understand. Adrenalin swept through her. Had Sonja been attacked?

By then, Jacob had arrived in the vestibule, his hair combed and his bathrobe neatly tied. "It's Sonja," Rachel said, in case he too had trouble recognizing her. Rose joined them, her face white. Jacob spoke to her quietly. "You see, my dear, it's not the Nazis." He turned to Sonja, his longtime patient.

"Doctor!" Sonja fell toward Jacob's arms.

"Not a word until you're warm and dry," he replied, taking her freezing hands and looking her up and down after a quick hug. "Rachel, run a hot bath."

A few minutes later, Sonja sat on the bathroom stool while Rachel and Rose peeled off her wet clothes.

Her soaked underwear stuck to her breasts and belly, more rounded than Rachel remembered. Much more. Could she be?

Sonja caught her looking and said suddenly, quietly, "They called me a whore."

Rachel's hand moved over her mouth. "Who?" she asked, her voice muffled. Rose shook her head at her daughter over Sonja's raw face, but it was too late.

"Paps and Mams," Sonja whispered.

Rose half-lifted Sonja into the hot water, saying, "They're just angry. Maybe they got carried away before they were married, too."

Rachel asked herself, *Why does Sonja get to be pregnant and not me?* Envy surged through her like a flame. She thought of Michiel, and left the bathroom. She couldn't bear to stay there and wonder why he hadn't left her a baby with his deep brown eyes. Then again, what would she do with one now, no matter how much she loved the child?

To distract herself, she made tea. Her father came into the kitchen, having dressed well if not as impeccably as he would have under Rose's supervision.

"Let's sit down," he said, and they did. He patted Rachel's arm, and it comforted her.

"You're such a good friend to Sonja. No wonder she came here. But her parents must be frantic. I'll call and let them know she's safely here with us."

"Don't bother," Rachel said. "They threw her out." Was there any chance he would do that to her, if he knew?

His body jolted backward. "But why?"

"She's pregnant. She needs help."

He sagged into a chair. "I thought I saw a change. The poor child. They'll have to talk to the father first and see about marriage. That is, assuming she wants the baby."

"What do you mean?" Rachel had heard whispers that doctors could do something when a woman became pregnant at the wrong time.

"She might prefer to give it away. This isn't exactly a good time to start married life." Her father spoke firmly.

"But, Paps, of course Sonja wants her baby. If her parents had let her marry Daan, this wouldn't have happened." And then, to her great shame, Rachel burst into tears and found her father's arm around her, smelling of his heathery sweater. "There, there," he said as he patted her back, the way he used to. "Most girls want a baby one day. But if the boy won't marry Sonja, she can't raise a child without a father, especially if her parents won't help her."

Rose bustled in and reported, "I put Sonja to bed. She was exhausted." Flopping into a chair, Rose looked up. "What's the matter now?" she snapped, a reaction that often followed her tenderness. "Why are you all dressed, Jacob?"

Rachel spoke for him. "He was going to tell Sonja's parents not to worry." She let out a sarcastic laugh, embarrassed that her mother had caught her crying like a child.

"Where's the boy?" Jacob demanded. "He ought to marry her."

"He wanted to," Rachel replied, "but her parents wouldn't let him. The Germans caught him sneaking into the movies after the ban started. His family sent him north. The last time they tried to contact him, there was no reply. Maybe he's found a new address."

Rose rolled her eyes. "Pour me something hot. Her parents are absolutely furious—I knew they would be—"

"You knew?" Jacob asked, reaching for the teapot.

"I guessed, from the way she was talking, that it could happen. But no matter how angry they were, they shouldn't have called her ugly names and thrown her out of the house. Especially with the Nazis roaming around." The three of them sat at the table, the shiny silver teapot at the center, its lid reflecting the chandelier overhead. Rose took the cup of tea and went on. "She told me the whole family was trying to leave the country next week—"

Jacob opened his mouth to speak.

"I know it's supposed to be impossible now, but with enough money it's still worth a try. The go-between, a good Christian no doubt, is charging a fortune. At least Sonja's family can afford it. They were supposed to report to an underground address this week, and travel from there. Where, I don't know." She paused, sipped.

Jacob shook his head. Rachel listened closely. The tea felt hot on her tongue.

"Anyway," Rose said, "the man who was helping them said specifically, just adults, no children. He quizzed them to be sure Sonja's mother wasn't pregnant—at her age!—because he'd been in charge of a woman whose morning sickness created a lot of problems."

"You mean," Rachel asked, "her parents are angry because she might spoil their plans to get out?" She put down her cup, her eyes on the teapot. Her heart felt frozen.

"I can understand it. They thought they'd finally found a way to leave. Just the way we would have, if we'd gone to England when we could. At least I know that Aunt Sophie's out of London and safe. But are *we*?"

Rachel's mind awoke. Mams was asking the same questions that she was. Her eyes met her mother's in an instant of understanding.

"Rose, that's ridiculous," Jacob said. His wife reached out and held his hand midair as if to stop him from waving the idea away. Rachel sighed. No matter how dire his brother's letters were, her father still couldn't see.

"Not now," Rose said, "let's rest, and we'll see what we can do in the morning."

They tiptoed upstairs to look in on Sonja. Now Rachel was more sorry for her than envious of her pregnancy. Sonja lay asleep in the guest room, her large body angled on the bed. How would she manage?

In the morning, Rachel heard Sonja's broken sobs even before she knocked to bring tea. She rapped loudly and went in to find her friend trying to muffle her noise with a pillow.

"I can't. I can't have my baby." Each word seemed to tear something away from Sonja. Rachel sat on the bed beside her and held her hand, feeling the agony in it as she gripped hard. If she herself were pregnant, Rachel couldn't imagine giving up her one tie to Michiel.

"Don't you want it?" Rachel asked. What if Sonja never saw Daan again?

"Of course, but what does that have to do with it?" Sonja broke down again, her face worn and puffy as it had been the night before.

"I don't know where Daan is. All I have is my family. I was so sure my parents would want a grandchild, and that would make it all right."

Rachel put her arm around her and waited for the shaking to subside. Finally, Sonja blew her nose and shook her head. "Their contact said he won't help anyone who's pregnant. Your parents might know someone who can help me. I'll come down once I wash my face."

When Rachel reported this conversation, Rose said, "You have to take care of her yourself, Jacob. Don't you have to do this sometimes?"

"Yes, but for medical reasons. This—"

"—is to save her life. Isn't that medical enough? And if you do it, she'll be able to have other babies. Someone inexperienced might botch it, and anything can happen. Besides, she trusts you."

Jacob was clearly troubled for the next day and night, barely present as Rose and Rachel continued with daily routines and tried to keep Sonja calm and distracted. Ultimately, he agreed to do the procedure, but he hardly spoke, and his face looked pained. "If there's any hint of trouble, I'm taking her straight to the hospital," he told Rachel, "and I don't care who knows what at that point."

Taking Sonja downstairs to her father's clinic unsettled Rachel. She held her friend's hand in the waiting room, with its immaculate floor and antiseptic smell. Everyone was gone, even the nurse.

"Nothing can go wrong, can it?" Sonja asked. "Oh, Rachel!" She let her face fall for a moment, and her anguish peeked through. "I wish I didn't have to do this." Her hand held Rachel's so tightly that it hurt.

"At least you had those times with Daan. It's wonderful when you're together, even if it's so hard now that you're apart." She didn't say more, but perhaps Sonja knew she understood.

Sonja nodded, and took a long breath. Then Jacob came to the door and said, "Please come in. Leave her with me, Rachel. You can wait upstairs."

× × ×

After a few days of crying jags alternating with naps, Sonja gained strength, even sympathizing about Michiel's absence. In about a week, Rachel took her back to her parents' home, a princely canal house with carved gables giving a calligraphic flourish to the rooftop. When Sonja tried to let herself in, the locks had been changed, and the house looked deserted. A neighbor saw the two women standing by the grand entrance, and pressed a note into Sonja's hand. "Your mother gave it to me," the elderly woman said. "It's their address. She said to tell you she'd handle your father." Sonja thanked her.

A block later, Rachel said, "Give me the note," looked at it and memorized the address on Egelantiersgracht, then tore up the paper and put the small pieces in her coat pocket. Through the fragrant smoke from the chimneys, the music of the carillon bells soared over the tiny restless canal, echoing off the rosy brown brick houses. As they counted off the house numbers, Rachel tried to focus on the decorative stonework rather than their imminent parting.

"Look!" Sonja stopped by the base of an elm, where someone had removed five or six bricks out of the sidewalk to make a tiny garden. A few snowdrops were on the way, their slender spears piercing the earth once more. No flowers yet, but the leaves had made it to the surface. Just like in the Begijnhof.

Rachel didn't want to face the fact that she might not see Sonja for months. Who knew where she'd be, or whether they could write to each other again? They would have to wait and see. When they arrived at number 452, Rachel held Sonja tight, then withdrew to stand on the nearby bridge, gently curved over the narrow canal. She watched a door below sidewalk level open to Sonja's knock, and her friend vanished behind it. Rachel took the torn bits of paper out of her pocket. If only she could tell Michiel how cautious she'd been, so he'd be proud of her. She wished that he could send a coded message sometimes, the way Uncle Rab did, but he'd warned her that long silences were ahead. She let the scraps of paper fall into the glowing canal, where they refused to sink.

✕   ✕   ✕

Rachel and her former classmate Joost walked toward the popular ice cream parlor. Taking his beefy arm, Rachel enjoyed Joost's confident stride. He seemed like a bull compared to Michiel's graceful, colt-like slenderness, but she was happy to have his company.

Perhaps because he'd sought her attention before with little success, the lines in Joost's angular face had lifted when she'd said yes to his invitation. "Good. Meet me at the corner of van Woustraat and the Albert Cuyp Market, and we'll go from there. I want to get to Koco's early. It's not as safe as it used to be in the streets." This was strange news, coming from a member of a leading boxing club. Joost was her height but solidly built.

Rachel was glad to accept. She'd gone to Koco's Ice Cream Parlor with her grandfather for special treats, and some of her friends might be there to cheer her up. A few knew about Michiel and realized he had disappeared, even if they were too tactful or afraid to speak of it. Besides, Koco's was fun, a happily crowded small place on a busy street. Two jovial German Jewish immigrants ran it, and everybody went there, Jew and Gentile alike.

The winter evening had already fallen, but at least it wasn't raining and the days were lengthening.

"I heard that some windows were broken near Koco's," Rachel said.

"Me too. We're trying to put a stop to it. Tonight, I'm on guard duty, but believe me, there isn't much to do. We can sit and have a chat."

People bustled through the streets to get all their errands done. Food was harder and harder to come by. Even their housekeeper had shrunk like many older people, her back hunched over. Rachel asked, "The Dutch Nazi thugs wouldn't come to Koco's, though, would they? Everybody goes there, not only Jewish people."

"They seem to be getting bolder. The Germans love the way the Dutch Nazi Party does their dirty work for them. Did you hear about the Jewish boys who fought back the other day? They showed those cowards up for what they are. A whole pile of them went crying home with bruises, and one had a busted lip that messed up his fancy coat, I can tell you that for sure."

Rachel peered at him. "I don't suppose you were there to watch, were you?" Even through his thick wool coat, she could feel his strength. She remembered Michiel's torso straining against hers, and put it out of her mind.

"Not me, my dear, oh no! I wouldn't hurt a tabby cat. You look stunning in that shade of brown, by the way. Here we are." As usual, Koco's was jammed with full tables of friends talking, although no one she knew well. The conversation had an uneasy undertone, like the brooding section of an orchestral work. The smoke smelled more like alfalfa than real tobacco. Joost led the way to a strong-featured, buxom girl they had known slightly at school. He bent over to speak close to her ear, but Rachel heard him. "Something wrong?"

"Later," she replied softly. Aloud, she said, "Oh, this stomach thing that's going around! I hope Koco's ice cream will cure it." So even here she didn't feel safe talking. They chatted amiably enough while Joost stood in line and bought the tiny dishes of ice cream. Rachel's favorite was still chocolate.

Each time the door opened, everyone glanced up. The moment of quiet quickly passed once the person was recognized. Rachel noticed that one man sitting near the door was keeping watch, and Joost sat so he could face the street. The group next to them talked about their school days nostalgically, as if they were already middle-aged. Rachel didn't feel much like conversation. She already missed Sonja as well as Michiel, and she wondered where Paula and Anna were that evening.

As Rachel raised her spoon to her lips to take her last bite of the rich chocolate coldness, a noise exploded behind her, and something light hit her head. Glass splintered onto the table, into her ice cream. The door burst open. Rachel cringed and put her hands over her face. Joost shouted, "You dirty bastards!" and jumped between her and the attackers, who were spitting out abuse.

"Filthy Jews!" She heard more glass shattering and cowered.

"Take this, Nazi scum!" Joost's voice made her look up. He and the other boxers were landing blows, but the attackers were using truncheons to smash heads and arms. One boxer fell to the floor, bleeding from his scalp, and rolled under a table to get out of range. While the thugs' attention was diverted, Rachel stood up to flee.

She felt a hand grip her from behind. Someone spoke right into her ear. "Get out! Through the kitchen." The man turned her around and pushed her toward the door, like a doll, guarding her retreating body with his. She could do nothing except save herself. She had never struck another human being in her life. The kitchen door opened, and one of the owners rushed over to her.

"You"—pointing to Rachel—"get out, fast." He grabbed her hand and pulled, and she let him take her out the back door. At the end of the block, the man shoved her in one direction, then ran off in the other. Without knowing how she got there, in a few minutes Rachel found herself on Diamond Street, where her mother's parents had lived by the Asscher Diamond Factory. She heard her heart galloping, as if she had been running. The owner had spoken to her in German, their common tongue.

Beside the small houses with their dainty lace curtains, Rachel traced her way to the nearby tram. Avoiding the eyes of other passengers, she eased herself into a seat, listening to the comforting ring of the bell. Her breath was still strained. She fingered the back of her head to see if she'd been cut in that first crash, but nothing was wet. She could still see the blood gushing from the boxer's scalp, and hear the sound of the truncheons against the soft bodies. Joost could take care of himself, but she'd have to get word to him that she was all right, or thought she was.

Would she have to face thugs like this again? Then what? She had escaped only because others had helped her. Jew haters hurt people, on purpose. For the first time, Rachel saw that it could happen to her. She kept quiet about it when she went home, and stayed in the next day, pleading a headache. If she had told her parents about the incident, they wouldn't let her go out at all. When the doorbell rang, she did her best to be the first to go. At last, Joost appeared, and they had a moment alone.

"Joost! You're safe!" She almost hugged him.

"Yes, and so are you. I asked the owners if they'd seen you, and they told me they'd escorted you out like gentlemen." For a flashing instant Rachel yearned to yield and cloak herself in his bearlike warmth. She longed to feel close again, and she'd heard nothing from Michiel in so long.

When Rose left the living room to the two of them, probably hoping that a romance was in the offing, Rachel whispered, "What happened?"

"We took care of them in the end. Just some neighborhood boys looking for trouble. Next time, we're really going to be ready. One of the guys is setting up a gas canister we can set off. That'll be a nasty surprise for them. I'm sorry things got rough." She studied him for a moment. His nose was awfully prominent, she thought, then castigated herself for accepting the Nazi standard of Aryan beauty.

"It scared me, I have to admit. I don't think anybody's ever broken a window anywhere near me before, or . . ." She couldn't continue.

"Now maybe you understand why the Jewish Action Groups are so important. I've always liked boxing, but now it really comes in handy. I've got to go. We're training again tonight."

After she saw him out, deep piano notes filled Rachel's ears and body, and she moved quietly back into the living room. The music and the warmth from the fire drew her like gravity. Under the piano's angled lid, her mother's face focused on the score, her arms and shoulders in constant motion. She'd told Rachel that, when she and Jacob became engaged, she had said, "I don't need a diamond. My father works with those every day. But I've wanted to learn the piano all my life, and my parents couldn't afford one." Jacob gave her the baby grand piano as an engagement gift, along with lessons. She had practiced almost every day ever since.

As she listened to the music, Rachel wondered what she should be doing. The raid at Koco's had been terrifying. When Rose paused, Rachel stood up and asked, "Mams, could we at least talk with Paps about going somewhere safer, maybe renting a cottage?" She put her hand on her mother's shoulder and sensed it tightening.

"I've tried and tried. If he thought you were in danger of any kind, he might change his mind. If you hear about any place specific, let me know. But he loves this house, and his patients. It would take a miracle to get him out of here—or a catastrophe. As long as he's here, so am I. Let me get back to this waltz."

FEBRUARY 1941

A tall German was walking toward Rachel on her bike. The rare sun was reflecting off his black helmet, so it was hard to see the face underneath. She stiffened and slowed down, trying to keep her eyes straight ahead. Even though they generally behaved well, you never knew. He might demand some paperwork from her, or anything else. He had the right to do whatever he wanted. She caught herself quivering in the cold, her hands trembling on the handles. He was only a few feet away now.

But his gait was relaxed, unofficial. Take away the uniform, and you'd have a student heading for an evening out. He was going to speak. She straightened her spine.

"Beautiful day, isn't it?" he said as he passed, with a smile.

To Rachel, it wasn't. For the first time, she'd seen a barbed wire fence as tall as she was, and signs saying "Juden Viertel, Joodsche Wijk." Jewish Quarter, in German and Dutch. Amsterdam had never had a ghetto; would it now? She thought of their butcher and his son Jaap, just her age, living inside that barbed wire. How would he feel? How safe was he? The Jewish boxers had actually beaten the Nazis in the Rembrandtplein, and everybody was afraid they would retaliate.

× × ×

Despite that fear, the days lengthened. On her way home from school, Rachel wondered whether snowdrops already bloomed at the Begijnhof despite the cold winter. Last year, she had gone alone to find the very first one. The gatekeeper had invited her to mass, but closed the door in her face when she said she was Jewish. Rather than encounter her again, Rachel crossed Dam Square past the Royal Palace, empty of the Queen, and made a beeline for the happy memories of Prinsestraat, where she and Rose used to shop for clothes and trinkets.

Pedaling along quickly, Rachel almost missed seeing two men running suddenly out of a side street well ahead of her. They dashed toward an elderly couple, the man with the distinctive broad-brimmed black hat of a Sephardic Jew, walking carefully with a cane. An old woman, perhaps his wife, steadied his arm. In an instant, the men were upon them, pushing them to the ground, then spitting on them. Rachel couldn't hear what they were saying. She felt like fleeing, but she wanted to stop them. She wished Joost were with her, and thought, *They could beat me up, too.* Her helplessness swept through her body like nausea.

The two men disappeared as suddenly as they had come. Racing across the bridge, Rachel knelt to help the old man up, but he moaned in pain. His face contorted. The woman wailed, "No, don't make him get up, he's hurt!"

"Stay here." Rachel stood up and ran into the nearby café, causing a stir among the few patrons. "Somebody's hurt. Who can go for help?" A gawky male teenager stood up and nodded. "Get my father. He's a doctor, at 3 Lauriergracht." It was Jacob's lunchtime, but he'd come. The boy headed for the door.

The old woman was sitting on the sidewalk by the injured man, whose eyes looked unfocused. Rachel tried to reassure them until Jacob's bike clattered nearby. In a moment, he knelt beside them with his black bag, examining the still-trembling man. After he confirmed that nothing was broken, Jacob told him to take it easy for a couple of days. Once they'd seen the couple home, father and daughter rode home silently. The sun had crept up a few degrees since the depths of winter, so in early afternoon it coated the houses in pale warmed silver.

"What happened?" Rose asked as they sat down to a late lunch of bread, a little cheese, and apples saved in the cold cellar. The more drastic her view of the larger situation, the more she retreated into books. She quaked at Rachel's report, and twisted the silver bracelet she always wore around her wrist.

Jacob said, "A patient told me about attacks like this. He said they virtually destroyed the Alcazar nightclub in the Rembrandtplein. I hate to say it, but the Jewish boys really hurt a man there."

"I heard about that," said Rachel. "He just died. His name was Koot, or something like that. But our boxers won! The others ran off with their tails between their legs." She studied her father's puzzled expression. Wouldn't he be happy to hear this?

"It's a terrible thing when we behave as savagely as the Nazis," Jacob said quietly, shaking his head and cutting an apple into ever-smaller slices.

"Paps, how can you take their side, especially after what you saw this morning?" Rachel felt the bite of the sharp old Gouda cheese at the back of her throat, along with her exasperation and fear.

"Because otherwise we're no better than they are."

Looking across the table, Rose spoke up. "Jewish people have to take care of ourselves, Jacob. Our own fellow countrymen are attacking us. It looks as if the Dutch anti-Semites have been waiting for the chance to beat Jews up and break our windows."

Rachel chimed in. "The Germans may not be attacking us on the streets the way the Dutch are, but they're attacking us, too. I don't just mean making us register and all that. Now they're talking about a Jewish Council, supposedly to coordinate between them and us—as if we were different from other Dutch people. Can you imagine anybody founding a Protestant Council? It's ridiculous." Her hands twisted her napkin. How she missed talking about things like this with Michiel.

✕ ✕ ✕

A few days later, Rachel fumed while holding the newspaper *Het Nationale Dagblad* under her mother's nose. It pictured three Jewish youths posed with pipes and axes beside an article about the uprising of Jews. "Look at this! They're blaming us for that man Koot's 'senseless murder.' They call us terrorists—but they attacked us first! Mr. Asscher has called a meeting at the Diamond Exchange to tell us what's happening, and I'm going. There's no point in bothering with school today." She moved toward the door defying her parents to stop her—or to insist on accompanying her. They didn't.

"Mr. Asscher is a good man, at least," Rose said grudgingly. He owned the factory where her parents had both worked. "He built my parents' house on Diamond Street, after all. Tell us what they say, and be careful."

Holding her tongue with difficulty, Rachel kissed her parents goodbye and heard her father's affectionate farewell as she ran downstairs. In the lightly spitting cold, she pedaled her bicycle quickly, curious to hear the latest. Mr. Asscher might be influential enough to stop the Nazis—maybe. Would he?

The bridge over the pale gray Amstel River was crawling with people and bicycles. Rachel had to get off her bike and turn into a canal where moorhens were making ugly sounds and fighting. At last the Exchange came into view, right across from the ultramodern Jewish Invalid Hospital, a globally respected facility. The Exchange's huge windows allowed the maximum daylight in, as if it housed workshops where diamonds were cut by men like her grandfather. *Built by the Jews they wouldn't let into the guilds,* Rachel thought.

She spotted Joost struggling up the entrance steps among the throng. His familiar broad shoulders turned when Rachel shouted his name, and she pressed her way toward him. At least he'd be with her when they heard the news.

"Quite a scene," he remarked. "Let's see what the boss has to say." Rachel smiled back. They squeezed through the noisy crowd to the auditorium, its chandeliers sparkling. Mr. Asscher took the podium, a stocky, compact, well-dressed man, totally at ease. His vibrant energy was apparent even at a distance. After announcing that a second session would be held for those still waiting outside, he got down to business. "The Jewish terrorist attacks have to stop. We have to surrender our weapons."

Because she and Joost were seated in a back row, Rachel had trouble hearing. But she caught the gist, and asked herself, *Can he be saying this? Who are the terrorists here?* Mr. Asscher went on to decree that the German invaders would disarm the Jews if they didn't do it themselves. The audience threw out questions like grenades, but Mr. Asscher had no real answers.

"He sounded like a mouthpiece for the Nazis," Rachel said as they rose and began their slow progress to the stairs amid a flood of expostulations and questions. When they reached her bicycle, Joost spoke in an undertone. "Control yourself in public, Rachel. You never know who's listening." They kissed ritually on both cheeks, Joost's lips coming closer to her mouth than she would have wished.

Rachel took a long way home so she could calm down before reporting to her parents. Her mother would be even grimmer and more withdrawn; her father would find excuses for the Germans. As long as he could stay in his beloved home and tend to his patients in relative peace, that's exactly what he would do. She and her mother would stay there with him, no matter what. Wouldn't they?

Rachel rode in front of the pale golden brick diamond factory where her grandparents had worked for years, emblazoned with Mr. Asscher's name. Gripping her bicycle handles hard, Rachel remembered her grandfather and their trips to Koco's. It seemed like centuries ago, although she was only nineteen now. Once she was on Prinsengracht, the half-moon shape of the canal meant that the ancient houses were illumined for one part of her journey, then darkened as though the sun had gone down. As though she had traveled through time as well as space.

Whatever calm Rachel had achieved by riding her bike evaporated quickly when her father justified the German demand for weapons because Jewish boys were turning into thugs.

"Thugs!" She couldn't stop herself. "Who do you think started this? The Nazis have been crashing into the cafés and shouting terrible insults and dragging people out to the street. If our boys are starting to fight back, I don't blame them. If I were a man, I'd do the same thing!" Her mouth was trembling, and she could feel her cheeks turning pink.

"Rachel! Don't say that." Her father looked genuinely shocked. "Becoming a criminal is never the answer." Her mother met her eyes and shook her head.

Rachel went to the window and stared out. Through the high windows with dark red velvet drapes pulled back, the light was lingering later each evening. A thin skin of rain accentuated every line of the elm outside. A heron flew straight past, its huge wings flapping so it could go anywhere it wished.

X   X   X

As Rachel left the house after dark one evening that week, a man slipped out of the shadows as she unlocked her bicycle. She froze, wondering if he meant to attack her. Instead, for an instant, he stepped under the streetlight. A heavy muffler covered most of his face, and he pulled it down so she could see him. His jaw was heavily bandaged, and he could hardly speak.

"Joost?"

He nodded rather than the usual leaning forward to peck her cheeks. "Can't talk." He tried to smile, but tears formed.

"Come inside!"

He shook his head. They moved back into the darkness between two streetlights. "Koco's, tonight." He made a gesture like an explosion.

"Do you mean that somebody set off that gas canister they put in after the last attack?" He nodded.

"Big attack, not WA. Germans. Mad."

"Oh, no! You mean Germans got hurt?"

He nodded. She continued, "Your jaw looks awful. Come in and let my father have a look at it." She touched his good cheek.

Joost pushed her hand aside, shook his head again, and disappeared into the night. Rachel realized Joost didn't trust her father to treat him secretly. To her horror she wondered if he was right.

✕   ✕   ✕

A few days later, the Nazis said they weren't satisfied with the number of weapons which had been turned in. What would Michiel say about it? What would he do, if he were here? She kept having conversations with him in her head, but at least the aching in her body had subsided during the day. Nights were harder.

The family still needed to eat, no matter what insanity the Nazis were up to. The deadline for turning in weapons was extended, to everyone's surprise and relief. Before the war, mother and daughter had often argued about politics, since in Rachel's view Rose colored everything red or at least pink thanks to her own parents' radical views. She had to admit, however, that Rose had warned against Hitler the moment he was elected, when everyone else thought he'd be out of office soon. Great-Aunt Sophie used to make funny drawings of Hitler in the margins of her letters. Rose must miss those witty epistles even more than Rachel did, now that no mail was allowed between the occupied countries and Britain.

She set off with her market basket attached to her bike, wearing her warmest coat and muffler but shivering in the February cold. A little snow curdled on the ground, not melting as it usually did, and the wind slashed through her buttonholes. Riding along the Jodenbreestraat was still enjoyable because of the bustle from the nearby Waterlooplein Market. She wiggled through the crowds of other bicycles and peddlers with handcarts. When Rachel passed the Rembrandt House, she wondered whether her favorite painter would have allied himself with his Jewish neighbors as he had in his actual lifetime—or would he have moved out of the Quarter and painted Nazi generals?

On a side street to her left, Rachel noticed a group of Germans and Dutch police near the huge brick Boas Diamond Factory, their helmets shining like the hard shells of beetles. She couldn't understand why they were out in such numbers. They'd been furious about what happened at Koco's, but hadn't they simmered down by now? Especially after the three-ring circus funeral complete with marching bands for Koot, the man allegedly killed by Jewish terrorists. Weapons were still being turned in, albeit slowly, and the searches of houses in the Jewish Quarter hadn't revealed much. What more did the Germans want?

Rachel crossed the street, continuing toward the market, and putting distance between herself and the mysterious group. They must be doing a military exercise. Nothing at the market would draw them—just some beaten-up vegetables. Although the wind bit her cheeks and fingers, Rachel was relieved to be out of the house.

Jacob was more on edge since he and other doctors had to sign a declaration about whether or not they were Jewish. Maybe he was beginning to let the truth in. Rose knew approximately what was going on, but she often retreated into the nineteenth century with Chopin and Trollope and Zola.

When Rachel found Mr. de Jong, he looked thinner, and the lines around his eyes had deepened. He had almost nothing to sell, and joked, "Look, Rachel, I could retire today if I could just sell this huge stock of valuable merchandise!" She managed an uneasy chuckle and sympathized. After making her few purchases, Rachel heard a loud mechanical creak.

Someone murmured, "They're pulling up the bridges." What could that mean? Who would do that and why? She turned around, and saw the uniformed men who had assembled by the factory surrounding the square. As the drawbridges swiftly tilted upward, Rachel realized that the market could easily be cut off from every direction. Now that the bridges were all up, how would she get home? Another instant passed, while the Nazi Green Police massed in the square.

Rachel shivered; she wanted to shrink. Where could she hide? Other women screamed. Guns were pointed at them and they stopped. Rachel slipped behind Mr. de Jong's cart. She had never seen anything like this before. When Uncle Rab wrote that the hornets were swarming, was this what he meant? Mr. de Jong's small arm went around her, a welcome pressure against her back. His face was cramped in fear. In a few minutes, the Nazis had herded several hundred men in the middle of the square.

"What are they doing?" Rachel asked Mr. de Jong, as she scanned the tense faces of the captives. All men, their hands overhead.

He said, "They're coming after us."

"*Us?*" she asked in panic. Would the Nazis force her and him into the square, too?

"Us Jews."

The fury she'd felt when she saw the old couple shoved to the ground surged back through Rachel. Almost instantly, it turned into the nausea of danger, and tautened her every muscle. The Green Police were shoving the men down a gauntlet of blows and jeers, and ordered them to squat. Rachel could feel the guns as if they were stabbing her. This was so much worse than the single moments of violence she'd seen before, against only a few people. The Nazis here were in deadly earnest, not scattered thugs. She couldn't believe her eyes. Surely they wouldn't fire their guns? Would she have time to duck?

The crowd fell silent. All that could be heard was the bark and bite of orders. One German sneered and grinned, poking the back of a man who was desperately trying to keep his balance, his legs bent like a frog's. Rachel and almost everyone else stood stock-still. What else could they do? The Nazis had the look of men engaged in blood sport, volatile if the prey dared to turn on them. The one nearest Rachel, thankfully yards away, looked to be about her age, a fresh-faced country boy whose fidgeting showed he was ill at ease. If she walked up and put a restraining hand on him, would he stop, or would he shoot her? Had it been like this in Germany?

"How long will they keep this up?" she whispered to Mr. de Jong. Surely the Nazis would have their fill of this deadly game and move on soon, lower the bridges again, and let these people return to their selling or shopping.

"Who knows?" he responded. "As long as they want to."

Several hundred men teetered low on the snowy pavement, their hands still held up in the air. How that must hurt after a few minutes. Rachel repositioned herself to see their faces more clearly. She spotted the rabbi who had officiated at her cousin's wedding, a formal man but kind—hands overhead. A pimply youth a few classes behind her who had won a history prize—hands overhead.

Wasn't that the butcher's son Jaap? They'd known each other since they were children. He was a terrific athlete and scholar, the pride of his parents. Over there, a thickset boy her age from Diamond Street whom her grandparents had loved. No sign of Joost, thank goodness. But what was going to happen to these men? She shook uncontrollably. Mr. de Jong held her tight, but it didn't help. She was awakening from the dream of her life as she had lived it.

The police forced new clusters of young men into the square between the synagogues, and added them to the mass in the middle. Rachel craned her neck to see whether she recognized anyone in each new group. Into the scuffling silence punctuated by insults, a four-year-old girl set up a howl. A nearby Nazi turned his gun on her, pointing straight down her screaming throat. Rachel wanted to rush forward between the gun and the child, but she didn't, couldn't. A woman—the child's mother?—covered the open mouth with both hands, holding it tight. The child's eyes bulged as she tried to close her mouth. The adult flinched as her hands were bitten inside the child's mouth, but she held on. Would Rachel have had the presence of mind to do that? Luckily, an order turned the man's head and weapon away, and in that instant the crowd silently sucked the two offenders out of his view. When he turned back, they had disappeared. Rachel was weak with relief, and leaned against Mr. de Jong.

Across from her, one Nazi's cheeks kept puffing out, as though he might be sick to his stomach. Was Rachel imagining that? He might simply be cold. He held his rifle aloft, his eyes fixed on its lethal tip, and stayed on the edge of the crowd. Rachel thought she saw him flinch when another Nazi kicked a man in the kidneys. Couldn't he have said or done something to stop his comrade? But she was doing nothing herself. She spotted one of the Jewish boxers squatting on the ground, helpless. Why didn't he fight back? Maybe he didn't want to die on the spot. Rachel tried to see Jaap again, hoping to catch his eye and at least wave, but he'd disappeared in the crowd.

The afternoon grew colder and colder. The weak sun set. How she wanted to go home! More orders snapped out, chilling her further. She'd never seen the Nazis in action like this. *They are really after us,* she realized. It wasn't a game, and it wouldn't stop with a few attacks on the street. Her feet had passed from numbness to pain and back again. How could the men bear that cramped position for so long? Those who lost their balance and toppled over were ridiculed and forced back into place. Rachel felt frigid through her good coat. She tried to move her toes and, after excruciating effort, they responded.

Finally, trucks rolled in on huge tires. Three hours had dragged like days. The men were compelled to stand if they could, and tumble on board. The rest were flung in. Rachel recognized two policemen who used to patrol their neighborhood, now helping the Germans. *How could they?* she wondered. *They were so nice to me when I was little.*

"Where are you taking them?" was the question on everyone's lips, but there was no answer. The crowd broke silence to call out to the captives, called their names, waved as the trucks roared off over the newly lowered bridges, spewing exhaust. Rachel spotted Jaap and shouted to him, but of course he didn't hear her. The crowd choked on the fumes. Rachel lost her remaining doubts about whether the Nazis would harm Jewish people as well as harass them. If she fell into the hands of men like these, anything could happen to her.

"Take care of yourself, Rachel. Get home as fast as you can," Mr. de Jong said. His face looked as gray as his beard. She replied, "You too." Dashing across the bridge, she wondered if she would ever cross it again without fearing that it would clang and trap her.

With her fingers barely able to grasp the handlebars and her feet still numb, Rachel could hardly control her bicycle as she rode home. When she reached the doorstep, she struggled inside and upstairs. Rose looked as if she'd been ready to scold, but restrained herself when Rachel staggered into the living room. Her teeth were chattering so that she could hardly speak.

"You're half-frozen! Jacob, come here. What happened? Did they stop you?"

Rachel couldn't even cry. After her father rushed in to see what was wrong, he put her first-ever glass of brandy into her hands. It stopped one kind of shivering, but not the other, especially after she told the story. Rachel saw in her mother's eyes that she had expected it all, and even her father looked more anxious than ever. The day before, he'd told them that Jews were no longer allowed to give blood for transfusions—which had hit him harder than the raids on libraries, or the ban on Jews attending the cinema. Would the events at the marketplace sink in?

When she finally retired that night, Rachel kept seeing all that had happened—the men squatting, the Nazis making fun of them, the other bystanders' frozen faces. The trucks at last coming, her shame at her relief to see them so she could come home and get warm. And Rachel had stood there. She had let them take the men away. *Why didn't I stop them?* Rachel asked herself. *And what if the rest of us hadn't been watching? What would they have done then? What would they do to me if they trapped me?* As she thought of the Nazis, her Uncle Rab's first coded letter came back to her. He had written about the rage of two boys, stomping on every ant they could find.

After what I saw today, I have to do something to stop the Nazis, she thought. And wondered exactly what that might be. That day, even the boxers from the Jewish Action Groups had been rounded up. Physical force alone wasn't going to stop the Germans. What could?

X   X   X

Just a few days later, when Rachel went by Diamond Street to drop some food off for an elderly friend who had known her grandparents, the old man showed her a mimeographed notice announcing a general strike for the next day, February 25:

STRIKE!! STRIKE!! STRIKE!!

Protest against the awful persecution of Jews!

Organize a protest strike in all enterprises!

Fight unanimously against this terror!

Require immediate freedom for the arrested Jews!

Show your solidarity with the severely hurt Jewish part of
the working people!

Protect Jewish children from the Nazi violence by taking
them into your families!

She knew she had to go, even if the Nazis went after the strikers the same way they'd gone after the men in the Jonas Daniel Meijerplein.

×　×　×

"Come with me, Mams." Rachel, already bundled up, stood by the armchair where her mother had been reading.

"I can't upset your father any more than he is already. He doesn't show it, but he's ashamed of how the Germans are behaving, especially now. He's worried sick about Uncle Rab and his family. The last thing he needs is his own wife marching against the Germans in the streets. And I don't want to go behind his back. You go. Just be careful and get out at the first sign of real trouble. If anyone's at school today, I'll write you a note."

Rachel left the house and walked through the snowy air past the Westerkerk, wishing she had company and uneasy about what might happen. The carillon was playing as usual, but the familiar squeak of the trams was absent, so the strike really had begun. A few yards away, Rachel spotted a red-haired woman her age waving the Dutch flag and laughing as she marched in a crowd toward the

Noordermarkt, the church square in the heart of the neighborhood where their handyman lived. Rachel couldn't remember the woman's name, but they'd met long ago at her grandfather's Diamond Workers' Union functions. She pushed her way through the crowd and was out of breath by the time she caught up with the woman, who shouted a greeting immediately.

"Hi! Isn't this amazing?" the woman said. Rachel could hardly hear her over the loud voices bellowing out old favorites. Everyone felt like singing that day.

Rachel nodded and smiled. In a pause between songs, she said, "If only it was more than one big day. I wish I could do something." She didn't like the helpless feeling she'd had when she saw the old couple hurt or in the Jonas Daniel Meijerplein, and it kept returning.

The singing started again, and the crowd halted as more people tried to get into the square in front of the small church. The woman handed Rachel the flag, and pulled a scrap of paper and a pencil out of her pocket. As she wrote, she yelled, "Here's my address. Come find me."

Rachel looked back in confusion. They hardly knew each other. Leaning over so her mouth was right by Rachel's ear, the woman said, "If you do want to help. Remember, I'm Amalia. We communists got this strike going, you know."

Rachel thought she wanted to take some action, but she wasn't sure. She thought back to some of the espionage novels she'd read, with heroic deeds that saved the nation, or at least the day. In her fantasies, she imagined being applauded at a state dinner after the war for rescuing prisoners or code breaking or helping children escape to freedom. But what would happen if she was caught?

X   X   X

First the elation of the strike fizzled away. Then it was pounded out of people. The leaders were in custody, and their fate was uncertain.

As the crackdown pervaded the city, Rachel wanted more than ever to work against the Nazis despite her fears, although her doubts about what she could actually do persisted. She was a young woman, not a boxer like Joost, and she wasn't brave like Michiel. She was sure he'd helped organize student protests, even if he kept it to himself. No matter what, it couldn't hurt to visit Amalia and find out what she was up to. After all, she'd given Rachel her address. It wasn't far from where she and Sonja had parted, which gave Rachel a pang. She hoped the family was somewhere safe.

As Rachel rode toward Amalia's along the narrow Egelantiersgracht canal, the Westertoren's intricate clock and carillon tower floated above the ancient houses. *And they're still standing,* she reminded herself. This isn't Rotterdam. The Dutch surrender had saved the physical structure of Amsterdam. Leaning her bicycle on the easy curve of a nearby bridge, Rachel paused to take in the chilly beauty for a moment. The canal shimmered before the cold rain which was brewing overhead. She hoped Amalia would be home.

A few minutes later, the two women were standing together in a doorway on a back street.

Amalia said, "I'd invite you in, but I don't want my parents over-hearing us. They don't even know I've joined the communists. At least the party is standing up to the Nazis. Let me get my coat so we can talk." Her long face looked defiant as she dove back into the house. While Amalia was gone, Rachel remembered why they hadn't become friends when they were younger and their grandfathers were both in the union. Amalia had been a hard-core flirt who paid little attention to other girls, only to her bevy of suitors. The times must have sobered her.

"What do you think about what's happening?" Amalia asked once they crossed the bridge and were away from her house.

"It's awful! I was in the Jonas Daniel Meijerplein myself. When everybody came out for the strike, I was thrilled, weren't you? But since the Nazis have squelched it, things look worse than ever."

"In a way, yes. But a few people are trying to do something about it, and that's good." They aligned their paces, bending into the wind and blinking rain out of their eyes. "Did you mean what you said at the strike, about wanting to do something?"

They ducked into an arched doorway out of the wind. The rain, suddenly finer, beaded their coats. Amalia searched Rachel's face and waited for her answer.

Rachel laughed nervously. "I think so."

"A few people hope to form an underground against the Nazis. Of course, it could be dangerous. They'd arrest anybody they catch."

"I guess so," Rachel replied, even though she had not given it much concrete thought. A few days behind bars would be uncomfortable, but surely she could manage until her parents bailed her out. She didn't like to think of it, but if worse came to worst, she could always make friends with the guards. They'd quickly catch on that she was a nobody, not an activist like Michiel. A more grown-up voice suddenly spoke inside her head: maybe they'd be just as hard on her as they had been on the men in the square.

Rachel realized that her red-haired companion was standing in the rain, getting damper, waiting for her to say more. "Even if it's dangerous," Rachel said, "it's worse to let the Nazis do whatever they want. If we let them get away with all this, what will they do next?"

Her answer surprised her, but felt right. Michiel was gone. She'd had one postcard telling her not to expect any more, and to destroy it. She kept it for two days, then burned it. Anything she could do to shorten the war would bring him back sooner. If he wasn't all right, what difference did it make what she did? And somebody had to stop the Nazis.

Amalia spoke. "The men do most of the dirty work, like the boxers defending the ice cream parlor and the Jewish businesses, but women can help too. I asked a few people about you without revealing anything, and they said you were reliable."

"What can I do?" Rachel leaned closer to hear of some heroic deed.

"If you're willing to help, I have some papers that need to be delivered tomorrow."

"Papers?" This was not at all what Rachel had imagined, but she supposed it had to be done. "Where?"

"29 Nicolaas Witsenkade. Forget the address as soon as you deliver it. Really forget, not just pretend to. I scramble numbers in my mind and imagine myself erasing them. It works. Don't tell your friends what you're doing, Rachel, even if you think you can trust them. And of course not your parents." She turned toward a door, shuffled papers in her satchel, and handed over a regular-sized brown manila envelope. Rachel tried to tuck it into her purse. It didn't fit at first, but she found the right angle to conceal it.

"When will I hear from you again?"

"Someone will be in touch with you, but not me. We try to keep things separate so it's harder to connect people. Bye now."

They parted, heading opposite ways along the canal, now agitated by the breeze that brought the rain. Rachel wondered what was in the envelope: instructions to help someone like Michiel escape? Information about what the Dutch Nazis would do next? She stopped herself from opening it to see. There was no reason why the police would stop her before she got rid of it, was there?

MARCH—APRIL 1941

The envelope was burning in Rachel's purse until the next morning, when she told Rose that she would meet a friend after school. It was the same excuse she'd used about Michiel. If she started working against the Nazis, she'd have a life of her own again. School just didn't mean that much now that university was out of the question. Would Michiel be proud of her if he knew what she was up to? Would she be able to tell him one day?

It was absurdly easy to walk past her favorite pancake place, an old carousel converted into a café, then under the huge London plane trees that lined Nicolaas Witsenkade. Their light mottled bark made it look as if the sun was shining. She found the house number readily and dropped the envelope through the mail slot like an ordinary postman. The hard part was forgetting the address. It kept coming back to her, even after she was asleep, inserting itself into her dreams, insisting on existence.

✕ ✕ ✕

When she and Joost next met in a café, his wounds had healed enough that he could be out in public. He leaned toward Rachel whenever she spoke, and moved his chair closer. When she started to talk about the Nazis, he put his hand on her arm and shook his head. "Let's take a walk." Surely it would be safe to let him know she was hoping to help, even if Amalia had warned her not to tell anybody. Joost was a boxer fighting the Nazis, and an old friend. As he pushed aside the red velvet curtain that protected the outside door, she planned to ask how long it would be before someone contacted her. Rachel hoped he'd be impressed that she'd volunteered.

Before she could speak, Joost said, "Rembrandt here is coming, too." A hulking man in his thirties with deep-set hazel eyes and short-cropped dark blond hair followed them out.

Once in the street, Joost introduced them. "This is Rembrandt, and he has something for you. I'll walk behind while he explains." Seeming to read Rachel's thoughts, Joost said, "Someone told him to be in touch with you." He stopped to fiddle with his bike, and Rachel strolled ahead with the other man.

"Rembrandt? Did your parents name you that?"

"Well, no. But I am an artist," Rembrandt said as they strolled along in the raw but promising air. He had a long stride, which Rachel easily matched. "Joost and I are comrades from the boxing club. Amalia's brother goes there, too."

"Oh! Did she send you?"

He didn't answer. "Tomorrow right after school, take this envelope to the Golden Guilder café on the Rozengracht. Order a coffee and mention Scheveningen. Someone else will say it too."

"But why Scheveningen?" And going into a café? By herself?

"The Germans can't pronounce it. When the other person says it, hand over this envelope without being obvious. We're just starting to organize some real resistance, which depends on people doing boring little tasks like this. Don't talk to Joost or anyone else about this. The less any one of us knows, the better. If we're captured, we have less to tell. They can make it worse for the women, so don't do this lightly." Rachel recoiled.

At Rembrandt's signal, Joost rejoined them. He put his arm

around her until she moved away from him. They circled back to the café for their bikes, and said goodnight normally, in case anyone was watching. His kisses on her cheeks were light. It had been so long since Michiel disappeared, but her body felt nothing for Joost.

Cycling home, all kinds of thoughts wove through Rachel's mind. *Worse? For the women?* She could not bear to think what that meant. She had hoped to help with jobs that would help stop the Nazis in their tracks. Instead, the underground wanted her to deliver envelopes. How would that thwart Hitler? It didn't sound interesting, and was definitely not worth the risk of being victimized, or sent to prison.

She wouldn't do it. It had been an impulse when she was carried away by the mood of the strike. She should be paying attention to her schoolwork, even if university was impossible now, not involving herself in silly efforts that could be better done by the post office. It would have been different if they'd offered her an assignment she was enthusiastic about.

Still, she left Rembrandt's envelope in her bag, and again told Rose she was having tea with a friend after school. Her bicycle strayed into the bustling Rosengracht near the appointed time. A tram zipped past her, its bell ringing loudly and interfering with the music of the carillon. Despite the promise of spring, the cold rain had glazed the sidewalks and street, reflecting the watery bright gray sky. Mist clung to the pavement. Rachel found herself on the corner of the tiny cross street where The Golden Guilder was located. *Why not go in for a moment?* Her heart thumped. She'd almost never gone to a café on her own. The last time might well be when she'd met Michiel.

As she opened the heavy door, Rachel smelled stale beer and leftover smoke, amplified by two pipes and a cigarette from the rear. Rachel swallowed and approached the bar, where a couple of scruffy men were already well into their cups.

A worn young woman served Rachel and a dozen others efficiently, while the local patrons grumbled about the weather. After her "coffee" was served, Rachel winced at the taste of the brown powder substitute in hot water. She screwed up her courage and said, "Amsterdam is too much these days. How I'd love to see the sea—an afternoon at Scheveningen would do me good." The men muttered agreement.

A woman sitting alone at a table near the window looked up from the *Jewish Weekly*, the paper that informed Jews about community events and the latest Nazi decrees. She might have been in her seventies, colorless, with gray hair and dark clothing, no makeup. "Scheveningen," she offered quietly. "I had an aunt there once." Then she went back to her paper. Rachel was astonished. She'd expected a man.

After a decent interval, Rachel carried her drink and book toward a table beside the nondescript woman's. "May I?" she asked, her back to the crowd, slipping the envelope out of the book and onto the table.

"Of course," the woman said, covering the envelope with her newspaper. More customers had come in, and the general noise increased. "In a few minutes, I'll leave and go to the corner of Bloemgracht. Give me five minutes, then come meet me."

Rachel hesitated, but nodded. She was curious. A rendezvous with a complete stranger in a seedy café (which she wouldn't normally be caught dead in) fit Rachel's fantasy of the underground better than delivering an envelope. No one she knew would see them in Bloemgracht, a narrow canal lined with ancient warehouses as well as homes.

A few minutes later, the woman was waiting as promised, and she strode over to Rachel's bicycle with delight and energy. "They call me Eva." Surely a pseudonym. "I'm glad to meet you."

"Me, too. I didn't expect you'd be . . ."

"An old woman?" Eva laughed at her discomfiture. "My best

friend started some underground work a few weeks ago and got sick one day. He asked me to fill in, and I've been at it ever since. I like it." The woman had a lively, thin face, attuned and receptive. Her eyes were deep blue, like a lapis brooch Rose wore sometimes.

Despite the chill, they strolled along the canal, as the weather brightened over surprisingly still water. Eva asked Rachel all about herself. Somewhat to her own surprise, Rachel talked about her parents—not just about the Nazis or the war or the increasingly miserable food shortages and rationing. Soon Eva knew about the debate at home about how seriously to take the Nazis.

"Rachel, do you tell your parents everything?" Rachel shook her head as Eva continued, "Have you ever kept a secret from them—I mean a real secret, not a little thing?"

"Yes," Rachel whispered. She could feel Michiel's arms around her, but they weren't.

"Did you tell anyone at all?"

"One person. Otherwise, no one." Rachel shook her head again, and to her surprise, began to cry.

"Who was he?" Eva's arm felt warm on her shoulders.

"A student at Leiden. He wouldn't tell me exactly what he was doing, but he had to go underground. After the war," Rachel began, feeling the air fill her body like a balloon as she imagined that time, "if we can find each other again, maybe we could get married."

"Why not?"

As Rachel explained, the two kept moving. It was too cold to stand still on the slick sidewalk. Even the ducks on the water had pulled their heads down. A shiver started at Rachel's tailbone and moved through her body. A new breeze blew under her skirt and warm woolen coat, reaching her bare thighs. She should have worn heavier stockings.

After sympathizing, Eva said, "Let's get back to our work. I know you can keep a secret, but you do realize you'd be running risks?"

"Yes. I was at the Jonas Daniel Meijerplein." She remembered the men squatting in the cold. Maybe someone else should do whatever Eva wanted—someone who wasn't an only child whose parents would be devastated if something happened to her.

"We're just getting started, and we need girls like you," Eva declared. "Intelligent, dedicated, and pretty. Young women often make the best messengers. You could get away with a lot, especially since your face doesn't fit their stupid ideas of what Jews look like. I'll show you something I shouldn't." The Westertoren played the half-hour melody.

Eva took the envelope Rachel had given her out of her purse. She ripped it open, then removed the enclosed page. When she unfolded it, the page was blank, and only a few ashes folded inside it floated to the ground.

"But why a blank page?" Rachel asked.

"Frankly, it was a test, like the first papers you delivered. Some new workers get too curious. If you had steamed open the envelope and resealed it, the ashes would be gone. Here's a real assignment. Take this envelope to 1127 Prinsengracht as close to three today as possible. Walk like Queen Wilhelmina, and they probably won't bother you. If they do, say honestly that someone gave it to you and you don't know what it is. Act like a silly girl and flutter your eyelids. Let them think they can buy you for a few chocolates or a pair of silk stockings."

What could Rachel say? Eva had confidence in her, and Rachel had had practice acting in the drama club. With Michiel gone and school less relevant than ever, it was exciting to think about doing something useful against the Nazis. If Eva thought the envelopes were important, they probably were. Wouldn't it be glorious, when the war was over, for Rachel to astonish her friends by telling them what she'd done? Even Paula, with her fancy clothes and palatial apartment, would be at least a little jealous. How could Rachel ever have considered not meeting Eva and getting to work?

✕ ✕ ✕

Hiding the envelope inside her coat, Rachel walked the half circle of Prinsengracht. The afternoon had turned cool and sunny, and the water sparkled as she passed the warehouse where trucks used to unload the pectin that housewives needed to make jam. She looked up the canal toward the accidental bomb site of the bakery that made cookies shaped like a dog with small ears. Her parents had loved them.

Two chunky men in German uniforms marched toward her on the narrow sidewalk, and Rachel started to shrink into a doorway. Then she remembered Eva's advice, stiffened her spine, and walked past them, her head high, her fine shoes clicking sharply on the dry sidewalk.

One man smirked appreciatively and elbowed the other, whose gaze lingered on Rachel's breasts. She ignored them, and let out a breath when they passed. *They didn't stop me!* she realized.

Using the same haughty strategy, her next three jobs went smoothly. Rachel found a smelly back street in the Jordaan she'd never known before, using a big city map which she studied every night now. She picked up and dropped off the envelopes exactly as instructed. When she saw the Nazis coming, her stomach tightened but no longer turned flip-flops. She loved knowing that she was fooling them, and that she was part of an effort to defeat them.

✕ ✕ ✕

When Rachel met Eva for a Saturday walk and talk in the Westerpark near the heron nests, she felt a deep pang as she remembered being there with Michiel. But she couldn't help boasting to Eva about not getting stopped. "Those Nazis make lewd comments sometimes, but they never ever think that a girl like me"—she blushed a little— "could be carrying something important. What's in those envelopes, anyway?" She wondered if Eva would answer.

They walked on for a few paces. The day was bitter, but Rachel was glad to be outside and at the Westerpark. The small pond which surrounded the herons' island showed ice along the edges.

Instead of answering Rachel's question, Eva said, "So you think you can handle the Nazis?"

"Yes. I did what you told me, and it works." Rachel waited for Eva's nod of approval and a juicy new assignment—like delivering one of those underground newspapers she'd heard about.

Instead, the older woman frowned. Rachel had thought she'd be proud of her.

Eva kept her arm in Rachel's, but stopped walking. "That's how I lost someone last week. He thought he was smarter than they are. A neighbor saw him dragged off, and we don't know where he is. We may never find out."

"What had he done?"

"Exactly what you're doing—delivering envelopes."

"But he must have told someone, or gone to the wrong place, or—"

"He might have, but I don't think so. I knew him well, and he had been careful. Sometimes that isn't enough." She looked directly at Rachel, who balked and frowned. Could she actually be caught and imprisoned?

"I really should tell my parents what I'm doing so they won't be totally shocked if something happens. My mother probably suspects, but my father—"

"Don't!" Eva raised her voice, then lowered it. "Don't even consider it."

"Of course they'd be upset at first."

"Upset! 'Upset' is the least of it. What about the danger to them, and to you?" Eva's sea-blue eyes flashed. Rachel remembered Michiel refusing to tell her anything, but surely he had just been overprotective. Eva tightened her grip. "If someone arrests you, what happens? Of course the Nazis would go to your house. If your parents know anything, they'll tell, sooner or later."

Jerking her arm away, Rachel strode to the end of the pond, breathing hard, tears close. Her parents had brought her here when she was little to see the huge heron nests and baby birds opening their mouths to be fed. Until she got too big, she used to swing between her mother's and father's hands. If she were caught, she'd break their hearts by disappearing, or cost them their freedom or their lives.

Rachel came back and took Eva's hands. "All right. I won't tell them anything. And I'll be more careful," she said.

"Or sometimes bold, or in your case brazen. That wouldn't work for me anymore." Eva's smile was thin but genuine. "You're risking a lot, Rachel. But if you do nothing, you're helping the enemy. Those are the only choices left."

"What do you mean? A lot of people just mind their own business. They aren't helping the Nazis."

"Aren't they? Could the Nazis operate without them ignoring what's going on? At least you're aware and you're doing something about it. Even if it's just delivering a message. Remember, that envelope could make all the difference to someone."

As it often did, Rachel's mind went to Michiel, not her parents, and she looked back at the big trees. The pond's surface glittered a little, like diamonds. "I know you can't tell me exactly what's in the envelopes, Eva, but can't you give me an idea?"

"Usually, they're messages that would sound like nonsense to anyone else. That's what we try for, anyway."

"Can't I deliver more important papers?"

"Perhaps one day. For now, take these."

Rachel nodded, and Eva told her the addresses she must first remember, then forget. The pale, mid-afternoon sunlight was fading rapidly behind a thin cloud layer, lending a misty, apricot-tinged backdrop to the intricacies of the gray tree branches. More ice would form on the pond before morning.

$$\times \quad \times \quad \times$$

When they next met, Rachel pressed Eva again for other work. No one had stopped her yet, so why not? If she was taking such big risks—and Eva seemed to think so—she might as well do something more important. "I want to do more than deliver messages. I don't mind working part of every day, except that my parents worry," Rachel told Eva. "My mother probably knows I'm doing something—no, I didn't tell her anything, she just knows what she'd do herself if she didn't have my father to consider. And he just wants me to be safe, no matter what." The two women walked arm in arm along a small canal near the Diamond Exchange. Even that limited contact warmed Rachel. The low sun skimmed the canal's quiet surface. A few people passed them.

"I don't blame him," Eva said, "especially after seeing how the Nazis reacted to the strike. They didn't think we Dutch had it in us, did they?" She chuckled and squeezed Rachel's arm. "They certainly didn't expect the Gentiles to strike over what's happening to Jewish people. I've never seen as many people in the streets for anything. It really brought the whole city to a halt. That's when my friend decided to get involved and brought me in. Now that the Germans know what we're capable of, they're more dangerous than ever."

"Exactly. That's why I want to do more, Eva. Especially since I heard they executed Ernst Kahn. He led me out of his ice cream parlor that night I was caught in the raid. He was always so friendly. It's awful."

"It is, but did you know he didn't tell them anything, even when they tortured him? Not everybody can be so brave. I doubt if I would be. That's why I carry pills. If the Allies finally invade, things will get better, but until then we have to do everything we can." Eva spoke quietly.

"Let me do more, then. I can find my way almost anywhere now without a map." Like the early cartographers, Rachel envisioned the city center as a half wheel bounded by the Prinsengracht. She'd studied every spoke of the smaller canals and streets which led from the straight edge to the outer rim. "I walk by Germans and police all the time, Eva. They've never stopped me."

"One day, they will, and you need to be ready. Are you afraid of them?"

Rachel knew Eva was watching her closely. Her heart beat faster, and her breath rushed into her throat. Her mouth tasted metallic. She could bluff the Germans, but Eva? "Yes, I'm afraid," she admitted. "I've just learned not to show it."

"I'm relieved to hear that. The people who aren't afraid don't last long. Or they do stupid things that other people pay for."

Apart from talking business, Eva asked Rachel about the rest of her life at least briefly, every time they met. Once, when she asked why, Eva said, "Partly because I like you, and partly because I need to know. A few workers can't stand the stress. I try to catch things before they get to that point. You're handling it well, but you have to take a break, in case someone's watching you."

"I'd rather not, but if you insist, I will. Can't I do something more when I come back?"

"Soon. Meanwhile, catch up with your friends and your studies. Just two weeks, to be sure."

Rachel sighed and agreed. When she caught sight of Paula shopping in the market, Rachel asked about her parents' art and antique business. Her friend shrugged.

"Nobody's buying anything, so it's tough. Have you seen Sonja?" Her basket was barely filled. Surely the wealthy Posners weren't having to cut back. It must be the poor supplies in the market.

"No, I think she's gone." They left it at that. Rachel was relieved when she could get back to work a few weeks later. It kept her mind off things.

✕ ✕ ✕

The city of Amsterdam itself was eerily the same to her—its austere interlinked houses, the ever-shifting canals, the pale northern light, the seasons and their effect on the flowers and trees. But everything else had changed. People hastened past each other in the streets. Suspicion was like a stench in the air. Nasty posters were plastered everywhere, barring Jewish people from this or that, or telling everyone else how wicked they were. You couldn't walk more than a few blocks without running into some kind of police or soldiers. Violence could break out any time. People could be snatched off the streets like rabbits plucked by birds of prey.

School, once Rachel's main occupation, had changed. People who had been friendly before were distant. The other day, a French girl she used to enjoy bicycling with had deliberately turned her back when Rachel walked up to her. Even the teachers seemed preoccupied or worse. One man had assigned his class to write a report on a Nazi propaganda film. When Rachel told the truth, that it was a half-baked effort to justify an unconscionable philosophy of hate, she received a low mark and was reprimanded. She didn't tell her parents.

On her way to find Eva one sleety afternoon, she noticed more and more café signs proclaiming "Jews not welcome," even near the Waterlooplein, traditionally a Jewish stronghold. Many café owners were complying now rather than ignoring the prohibition. Her breathing shallowed as she scurried past, especially when she saw the sign in the window of her grandfather's favorite ancient café—the one tilted at a precarious angle, past the locks. When Rachel was six, he had given her hot milk there with a spot of coffee in it. She'd felt very grown-up.

Sleet peppered her until Eva appeared, her shoulders hunched against the wind. "Let's walk. It's too cold to stand here. I know a place where they'll let us sit in peace." She nipped around the corner into an alleyway and knocked on a door that looked as though it must lead to a storage cellar. Instead, a stout grand-motherly woman smiled broadly when she opened the door and beckoned them in.

"Come in! To what do I owe this honor? Do you need a free space for a little rendezvous?" She let them in and winked at Rachel. "Not interested today? Use the living room. It's seen stranger couples than the two of you."

"Rachel, this is Bet, and she has terrible manners. Cut it out, you'll scare the girl."

"She doesn't look as if she scares easily. If she's with you, how could she? Sit down and I'll bring you some coffee, unless you want to be alone." She threw a mock leer at Eva, and motioned toward the overstuffed chairs, then disappeared.

The room was cozy, with a deep red rug underfoot and a stained glass lamp casting a warm circle. Rachel settled in, on guard. She'd vaguely heard of such women, but she had never met one. Surely Eva wasn't like that?

"Don't take her too seriously, Rachel. Bet's not that different from you and me, except that she'd rather share her bed with women than men. And believe me, we couldn't do our jobs without her. The Nazis are after people like her, not just the Jews. Enough of that. Tell me, how are things at home?"

"I just don't see why my father isn't facing the truth. Every now and then he seems to let a little in, but then he puts the blinders back on."

"I imagine he has a lot at stake. He was brought up German, even though he's been here a long time. He probably can't imagine that the Nazis are out to harm good, solid citizens like him just because he's Jewish. And what about his medical practice? I'm sure he doesn't want to abandon his patients."

"I just wish I could sober him up by telling him what I'm doing."

"He'd try to dissuade you—and be a danger to all of us, as we've discussed before. You'll have to let him see the light in his own time, Rachel. One day you may need to do something for yourself—whether he's ready or not."

"For myself?" Her mother would never leave her father. If Rachel did something for herself, it would have to be without either parent. How could she?

"Yes, but for now we have work to do. I've been thinking about your offer to do more dangerous work. You've proved yourself in these last weeks, and if you still want something more, I'm prepared to trust you with some underground newspapers, too. You'd have to be able to talk your way out of a bad situation, or face the consequences. I think you could now."

"I hope so." Rachel wanted Eva to believe in her, and she wanted to believe in herself. She smiled.

Just then, Bet came in with two cups and a pot. "Here you are, girls. It's pretty disgusting, but such as it is, here it is. The last time I bought black market coffee, I couldn't pay the rent. So you'll have to make do." She left the tray on a low table and departed quietly.

"I have something else to talk with you about," Eva said. "Some news. I tried to trace your Michiel."

Rachel gasped, and leaned in as if her life depended on the next words.

"It was stupid of me, but I know how much you think about him, and what a distraction it is for you, which could put you at risk. The trail led to Drenthe, but it stopped. That's a good sign that people are keeping secrets the way they should. It's a fine place to hide because of all those spread-out farms, but there are some Nazi nuts out there too, so people have to be careful. I don't have any real information for you. He's probably on one of those remote farms, much safer than here."

Rachel let out her breath. "Thank you, Eva. I know you're not supposed to do that." She tried to imagine Michiel helping out on the land by day and doing something brave by night. When she imagined him caught, she resolutely put it out of her mind, and brought back the farm.

As she and Eva left, Bet looked Rachel straight in the eye, serious for the first time. "Don't let the bastards get you down, dear. It can't last forever."

✕ ✕ ✕

The next time Eva was to meet her, Rachel found the sheltered doorway they'd identified on a side canal. When the Zuiderkerk carillon marked the full hour, the notes wove Rachel into their melody, deep and clear. When they sounded again after fifteen minutes, Rachel decided she couldn't wait longer without being conspicuous. She returned to Jodenbreestraat and browsed in the window of a bookshop. Many things could have detained Eva, so Rachel wasn't unduly worried when she made another pass by the meeting place, and heard the melody for the half hour. As she waited longer, she began to wonder not just about Eva but about Bet, and whether she was still safe. What a strange life she led, with no man in it, but she seemed happy.

When the three-quarter-hour melody rang out, Rachel's stomach tightened with anxiety. She walked another few blocks to the

Hortus Botanical Garden and peered through its fence at a carpet of sky-blue scilla alongside the first daffodils. After one last look at the meeting place, she waited until the next hour struck, and then had to go home.

After an anxious night, Rachel scooped up a note from the mailbox, telling her to go to a particular vegetable stall in the Waterlooplein right along the canal. The graying man there was tall, his face tight, especially around the mouth. He looked winded and weary. His eyebrows met in a frown as he made change. Rachel waited until everyone else cleared away for a moment.

The man greeted her. "Good afternoon. Do you have your ration coupons?"

She nodded yes. "I've been to visit Uncle Harry." She saw his face relax slightly at the use of the password Eva had given her. "What about you?" She wanted to be sure.

"I was in Scheveningen just the other afternoon."

"Where is she?" Rachel asked.

He leaned toward her and lowered his voice. "We have a new contact for you. He'll find you wherever you are at four o'clock tomorrow—anywhere out of doors. Leave school as usual. In a few blocks, he'll stop you and ask you to help him find an address."

"But Eva?" She searched his lined face.

"Gone."

"Captured?" Rachel hated herself for it, but her first thought was not whether Eva was safe, but whether Eva would betray her name. Seeming to understand, the man said, "Don't worry. She had the pills with her, and she used them." Rachel felt as if she'd been slugged. Eva—gone? Gone forever because she knew too much? She pretended to blow her nose to hide the tears. Her face felt cold and wet. She stood aside to let another customer approach, then walked away as the man sold a limp carrot to another thin customer.

On her way home, Rachel found a quiet alley, and sobbed for a long, long time. No one could console her; she could tell no one. Not even Paula, or Anna, who knew how to keep her mouth shut in ordinary circumstances. *I could quit right now,* Rachel thought. *But that would be the worst betrayal of all.* Eva had trained her, and would be furious if she thought Rachel was shirking now. Her work must continue, but how she would miss the conversations. Without Eva's guidance, she wouldn't have stayed safe for half an hour on the streets. Another thought lurked: if the Nazis could catch Eva, careful as she was, wasn't it only a matter of time before they caught everybody, including Rachel? She felt more alone than she ever had in her life.

✕   ✕   ✕

"Rachel!" Rose banged the front door shut. Her alarmed voice carried all the way to the rafters. Rachel clattered down the stairs as fast as she could. She had lived in dread ever since Eva's capture and suicide.

"What's wrong?" Rachel grasped her mother's hands and looked her straight in the eye.

Rose shook her head, loosing raindrops and huffing, barely able to summon words. Her dark blue coat felt wet. "Get me 500 guilders. From the hiding place."

"But why?"

"Books. From the Diamond Workers' Union Library. The Nazis stole them and my bookseller has some. I gave him money but it's not enough."

"*Books?*" After losing Eva, Rose's urgency about saving mere books seemed preposterous. At night, Rachel imagined Eva's jail cell, the moment of choice, how hard it was to swallow pills without water, how awful it must have been for the other women imprisoned with Eva when she died. Day after day, Eva wasn't there anymore, to walk arm in arm along the canals. To no one else could Rachel open her heart and say anything at all. She'd even thought of going to see Bet, but that would probably only add risks for both of them.

Fortunately, after Rachel had followed Rose back to her favorite bookstall by the Oudemanhuispoort, the volumes she wanted were still for sale. The bookseller who had fawned on Rose in former days would barely deign to take her money. As they loaded the books onto their bicycles, Rachel remembered that her grandfather had taken her mother to the Diamond Workers' Union Library every week until she married.

Rounding people up was horrifying enough, Rachel thought. But books, too—and from the union building her grandfather used to call "our other house"? She didn't know what to say to console her mother. All she could do was slip off to pick up a sheaf of envelopes to distribute around the city, one address after another, until it was fully dark.

MAY–JULY 1941

As she rounded a corner a few days later, Rachel was jolted by an unexpected jab of fear. The envelopes in her satchel sizzled against her side, and caution clamped her jaw. Eva had taught her never to pause while she was making deliveries. Her task was to get the items out of her hands as soon as possible. However, she recognized a familiar figure coming toward her—a woman who had been her best friend as a child, in the last years a more distant acquaintance. She couldn't avoid Mia, although they'd drifted apart. Could the short but svelte figure approaching Rachel be the same person she'd met in the sandbox years ago?

Mia waved and grinned. "I haven't seen you in forever! Let's go and have a coffee, such as it is."

"I can't go into most of the cafés around here."

"Why not? Oh, right. My brother works on the next corner. He'll let us in." Mia's stylishly cut blond hair had a heavy wave swept back from her forehead, showing off her deep blue eyes. Her clothing was carefully chosen and everything looked new.

After they settled in and exchanged pleasantries, the conversation turned to the situation in Amsterdam. When Rachel expressed concern, Mia said, "Even you have to admit that the Jewish boys went too far, killing that man Koot. And they started that riot at

Koco's. Paps says the local lads don't mean any harm. They're just enthusiastic."

"Wait!" Rachel burst out. "They attacked us first. Our boys were defending themselves. I've been to Koco's many times, and so have you. Did you hear that the Germans executed one of the owners? It's just an ice cream shop, for heaven's sake!"

They were sitting beside the cast-iron stove to stay warm in the spring chill. Outside, the rain was pounding nails into the canal and streaking the windows, but the tips of the tree twigs showed new buds. Mia dropped her voice so much that Rachel had to cup her hand around her ear. A few people had been listening to the conversation. "Be careful. Don't talk so loudly. You never know who might overhear. Paps says the Dutch Nazi Party's orders are to keep their ears open all the time, because terrorists are everywhere." Her eyes slipped around the room.

Rachel looked down at her satchel, full of envelopes, and fingered the worn handle. "Your father . . ." she whispered, as if they were children again.

"Don't look so grim," Mia said, with a stiff face. "It's only politics, after all. But you do need to be careful about what you say." Rachel's back slumped in her chair and tried to meet her friend's eyes. Mia avoided her gaze and said, "Paps has a Dutch Nazi Party meeting tonight and he wants supper early, so I have to be going."

X   X   X

As she undressed one cool spring evening, Rachel was startled by a piece of soft paper at the very bottom of her skirt pocket. Could someone have slipped her a note without her noticing? Or it could be an old bill or card she hadn't noticed. But when she pulled the paper out, unfolding the many creases, she stood frozen when she recognized Michiel's handwriting. His schoolboy's script with its careful vowels and ornamented consonants squeezed her chest. Had he put it there? She had worn this skirt when they were last together, and had hardly touched it since because of all the memories it brought back. Rachel sank to her bed and curled up. He didn't use his name, or hers.

Dearest,

I write to let you know that you are as much in my heart as always, and my hopes that we will be united forever are unchanged. One day, I hope we will persuade your parents that we belong together.

For now, though, I know we are both better off with me out of the city. I'll just be working somewhere else. It wouldn't help us, or the cause, if I were imprisoned or worse. Sometimes you've been angry at me for saying too little to you. I wonder if I am asking too much: that you have faith in my love when you will almost never hear from me, and don't know where I will be.

Every word we exchange will imperil us, so I ask you not to write back or try to find me through people who could betray us. Hold me in your heart, stay alive, and be ready when I come back. Yours, with all my love.

A strange consolation swept through Rachel, like the shadow of a cloud moving across a stormy sea. Yes, times were terrible. Their radios had been confiscated, and all the Jewish musicians had been fired from the Concertgebouw orchestra. For once, though, all that left her mind. She felt Michiel's arms around her again, her body easing as his words sank into her. Would they really find each other again? Everything argued against it. Yet how could she not believe it? Their love was the deepest truth she had ever felt, singing in her very bones.

X   X   X

As the family sat at breakfast one burgeoning spring morning, the windows let in a soft breeze that carried the fresh smell of water, both from the canal and the gentle rain that pattered lightly on the new leaves. The houses opposite looked like nuanced watercolors. As she poured her parents' coffee, Rachel looked from her mother to her father. Rose's pallor was accentuated by her black high-collared blouse. Jacob's face showed deep lines, new since the last semi-hysterical letter from his brother.

Rose suddenly choked on her toast as she read the *Jewish Weekly.* "What is it, Mams?"

"The death notices. For those young men they took from the Jonas Daniel Meijerplein. Oh, no, not Jaap! Heart failure? A strong young man like that—how stupid do they think we are?"

Jaap . . . they'd known each other as long as Rachel could remember, meeting whenever she'd accompanied her mother shopping at the butcher's. How could he be dead? And the others? One by one, Rachel held their faces in her memory, their hands raised high overhead as they squatted.

"Mams, we have to go and see his parents. This will be horrible for them."

"Unimaginable. We should all go." Jacob's offer was surprising, since he nearly always left social matters to Rose and Rachel. "I never thought they'd hurt those boys, just work them too hard."

X   X   X

At last, Rachel had the more hazardous assignment she'd hoped for. Her new contact, Freddie, had asked her how she would feel about carrying something new. Rachel nodded. She'd do it for

Jaap. "I've been hoping for that. Can I know what it is?" Could it be what Eva had promised?

"Mimeographed newspapers. You must have seen them—they're being printed all across the city, and this is one of the best, for the workers. But if the Germans catch you with a bundle of them, it's bad. They can haul you off to prison, beat you up, or even torture you. It's not like having an envelope someone might have slipped into your bag."

She nodded curtly. She'd never be ready for ugliness, but she couldn't let that stop her.

"Do the papers go to separate places?"

"No, I'll give you one bundle. Someone else takes it from there."

"Tell me the address." She'd do what Eva had taught her. Every day, she missed Eva's company and heard her voice as if she were still alive. And where was Michiel? Their time together seemed like ashes now. She could hardly ever feel his love as the living thing it had been, even when she let her mind drift back over their time together. Every week, it was harder to remember his voice, his hands, even when she wanted to. Rachel shook herself back into the present moment, and packed the bundle into her satchel. As she walked along the canal in the spring breeze, two swans floated beside each other, their white bodies propelled by barely visible black feet, their mustardy-white necks high and stiff. Free.

X X X

Whenever she dropped off the newspapers, Rachel felt exhilarated by knowing she was doing something to counteract the lies and craziness around her. Virtually every day in May and June had brought new restrictions. Certain streets were named as Jewish streets. The Nazis required everyone to carry identity cards, so street photographers made a fortune. Rachel resented the prohibition on swimming in any public places. So much for the beach. When she learned that parks were off limits, too, she felt that part of her body had been amputated. Parks had been ideal meeting places for her and Eva—earlier for her and Michiel—and her solitary walks among the trees had provided escape and solace. She'd miss watching the heron babies up close as she had every spring for years.

Back at home, Rachel tried to stretch a small amount of meat and a few turnips and potatoes into a meal for herself and her parents. Rose was an unusual doctor's wife in preparing many meals herself, but today she was deep in Chopin, and Rachel didn't want to disturb her. Their daily life had been different for months because their housekeeper, who had helped with cooking, was long gone. When she left abruptly in January after the Nazis prohibited Gentile servants working in Jewish homes, Rachel felt as if all the lamps in the house had been dimmed, and the extra hours she and her mother spent working around the house now really added up. As long as Rose could read and play the piano, however, she could cope with her fatalistic streak. How she would manage without those outlets Rachel could not imagine.

Rachel was often glad to be in the kitchen, since she could give in when her thoughts irresistibly returned to Michiel. She saw now that she had added to his distress by pressing him for information that he rightly didn't want to give her, but they'd made up easily. Once, he'd brought a little cake, obtained who knows how, and teased her by feeding it to her a morsel at a time, like a baby bird. She remembered their next to last time together, when they had wrapped their sweaty arms around each other as their bellies stuck together, hair tangling in their mouths. "Don't forget me," he had whispered, after he thought she was asleep.

She had held him, wide awake, and ricocheted between fantasizing about the two of them wandering in Paris or New York hand in hand, and dreading the void that she would feel if he actually left her. Each time Rachel tried to speak to him, her throat closed, so she said nothing. She didn't want his last memory of her to be red-faced and sobbing. They'd met once more before he disappeared. A few weeks later, Rachel had received that vaguely phrased postcard about a friend visiting relatives in the north, telling her in so many words to destroy the card. At least she'd known that he was safe—or had been when the card was mailed. The letter she'd found in her pocket consoled her, but said nothing about his safety now.

As she diced potatoes ever smaller, Rachel wondered if she should try to convince her parents to get out of Amsterdam. Last night, they continued to wrangle over dinner, but her father had sounded more exhausted than exasperated. Rachel's work for the underground was important, but someone else could do it—and, the way things were going, a Gentile could carry papers more safely than she could. Rumors slipped through the city like fog about what might happen to the Netherlands' Jewish citizens. Now that more people were beginning to look for places to hide from the Nazis, maybe her father would take it more seriously.

As a Chopin waltz Rose loved radiated through the house, Rachel stole into the living room to listen for a moment. She sank into a carved chair facing the piano and the tall windows. The pedals squeaked softly as Rose pressed them, an undercurrent to the melody. Seeing her mother's rapt face as her head dipped and rose to the rapid tempo, Rachel envied her absolute absorption—something she only experienced herself when looking for a new address.

Outside, as a gray drizzle clothed the trees in a thin smoke, Chopin scattered bright notes like butterflies. The days were longer, and the new leaves were soft, each one languidly hanging around its central spine. A heron shot past as if from a crossbow, its imperturbable elegance gliding through the air. When the music ended, Rose looked up and smiled at Rachel. Her mother's lifelong dream had been exactly this: a loving husband and child, a comfortable home with books to the rafters, and a piano she knew how to play. No wonder she could find happiness sometimes.

"What are you musing about, Rachel?" she asked.

"Mams, do you think we could ever convince Paps to leave this house and go somewhere safer?" She was beginning to wonder if any Jewish person could be safe in Amsterdam anymore, even the most innocent.

"Not even to live in a palace," her mother replied, "but he may have to go anyway."

✕ ✕ ✕

Fortunately, Rachel had always studied hard, so the final exams which obsessed almost everyone else were a sideline to her. She was too busy with deliveries and anxiety about the overall situation to fret about her grades, as long as she passed so she could go to university after the war. If she made it. Four days before the exams, she took time off to review and focus. To Rachel's surprise, her mind was sharper than ever. When the exam results came in, she wasn't right at the top of her class as usual, but she'd done well.

✕ ✕ ✕

The next week, Rachel carried her empty satchel to Paula's luxurious apartment one wet evening when the sharp air was full of spring scents. It was always a relief to get the deliveries done, and she was eager to meet up with Paula. Between Rachel's newspaper deliveries and Paula's active social life, they hadn't seen each other lately. Rachel missed the quick grins her friend sported suddenly, like the sun coming out from behind the clouds driven east from the North Sea. More than she ever would have imagined, Rachel still missed Eva. And Joost hadn't been in touch lately because he was involved with a new girlfriend.

Pale green elm leaves shimmered in the lengthening evening light. Maybe gazing at them made Rachel stumble and fall over an uneven brick. On all fours on the hard sidewalk, her body felt jostled but not hurt. From behind, Rachel heard footsteps running toward her, and started blushing. As she lurched to her feet, she felt a light touch on her arm.

"Are you all right, *fräulein?*"

"Yes, thanks." Only then did she realize that he had asked, and she had replied, in German.

The soldier's blue eyes pleaded with Rachel's when she finally let herself look at him. *Maybe I could learn something from him*, she thought. He was leaning slightly toward her.

"*Bitte*—uh—*astubleeft*—*guten morgen*," he stammered out, his soft voice mingling and mangling his language and hers. He drew back and looked sweaty and embarrassed. *He's my age*, Rachel thought as she looked at him more closely. *How can he be carrying a gun and invading my country?*

"It's evening now—*avond*," she corrected. "We say '*goedenavond*' here."

"*Abbend?*" he tried, and Rachel sharpened her criticism until he said it properly.

"*Avond.*" He was making an effort. Because her satchel was empty of anything incriminating, she could keep up her end of the conversation.

"Coffee?" He made an inquisitive gesture, but Rachel shook her head decisively. He could not, absolutely could not, buy her anything, particularly not in public. His face fell, but regained its dignity as he nodded and left her.

Rachel couldn't help feeling sorry for the lonely figure as he retreated, then caught herself. *He's our enemy. He could have been there at Kristallnacht smashing up Jews. Well, no, he'd have been a boy then, a little younger than herself.*

The warm, liquid air soothed her skin like a gentle bath. Up and down the canal, elm branches swayed in a tender breeze, their greens still strong in the fading light. Although the sun would not be setting for another few hours, the water shimmered. What a spring! Nature had never been more beautiful, or more indifferent. Yet she would not want it to be otherwise.

Rachel was getting her bike out when she heard someone approach with quick footsteps. The German was following her, holding something in his hand. Rachel stepped back half a pace.

"For you," he gestured, his hand outstretched. "Thank you for 'avond.'"

"*Avond?*" she echoed. Could learning a word mean so much? He put something rectangular into her hand that felt like a chocolate bar.

"Your name, *fräulein?*" he asked softly.

Did anyone see us? Rachel put whatever it was—*could it be chocolate?*—into her pocket quickly, hardly knowing what she had done.

He saw that, and smiled.

Rachel shuddered. What had she been thinking? She nearly reached into her pocket to return it. Instead, she whispered, "Diena," and was gone.

$$\times \quad \times \quad \times$$

A week later, Rachel accepted another invitation from Paula, making an exception to her usual practice of going to work. Anna was coming too, also taking a rare afternoon off. Even she looked tenser and more tired now, and Rachel wondered how the Nazis might affect her father's church. She admired the way Anna visited sick people and the elderly, but that wasn't going to stop what was going on right under their noses.

Rachel knew their conversation would inevitably turn to the situation on the street, and sighed. What had they talked about before the Nazis, when they were together? Their families, boys, and weddings sometimes. Would Rachel ever know what married life was— when you could keep a clean house where everyone felt safe, have babies, celebrate holidays, make dinner, and sleep together night after night?

As the three young women strolled along the narrow sidewalk, often in single file, the air felt like a caress. Summer was everywhere, and the bustling clouds often parted to show the sun. Trees towered overhead, and clouds of blossoming clematis covered the brick walls. The elegant, austere house facades were all right up against the sidewalk, but behind them grew full-size trees and ornamental gardens like Paula's.

As they approached her house, they heard the disturbance before they saw it: raised voices and the throb of a loud engine. A big police truck was blocking the intersection off to the right of the main canal, but they could see the news and tobacco shop on the corner. Two tall Nazi Green Police pressed into the shop.

Anna pulled on Rachel's sleeve. "Let's get out of here." Rachel's first instinct was to agree. She couldn't afford to be arrested or captured at random, since the Nazis might realize that she was better bait than she seemed to be.

Paula said, "Wait, that's our newsagent. I can't just leave her." She led them to a high stoop which they could partially hide behind. Rachel was about to argue, when three figures burst from the shop— the newsagent pushed by two policemen. Rachel moved closer to her friends and felt Paula shaking, Anna shrinking into the corner.

"Get your hands off me!" The large woman was spitting like a cat. Rachel remembered her, always outspoken and never hesitant to point out the foolishness in the world.

The police did not bother to reply. They grabbed her arms, hard enough for her to cry out. One of them let go of one arm and struck her across the mouth. She squealed in pain and squirmed to get away, but could not. The other man yelled for the driver, who opened the back of the truck, and they shoved her in.

Will they drive toward us? Rachel wondered in panic, but they didn't. In a roar, they were gone. An elderly woman who had seen it all hobbled toward the three friends.

"Paula! Did you see that?" she asked, her cane trembling.

"Yes, but why? Did she do something?" Paula steadied her by grasping her elbow.

"She was bragging to the tailor next door about how the Brits sank the *Bismarck*. Then she said she didn't want to sell any more Nazi drivel. The tailor saw the Green Police coming and tried to shush her, but they must have heard."

"We'll have to do something," Paula said. "Come on, we'll talk to my father. We can't let them just take her away." As a wealthy art and antiques dealer, Mr. Posner had lots of connections. If that didn't work, Rachel once would have talked to Eva, but she wasn't sure the new contact would listen. Maybe Bet could help, but Rachel hated to draw attention to the basement which no doubt hosted many underground activities. Meanwhile, she felt as cold as she had in the winter.

A week later, after Mr. Posner had pulled the needed strings through Gentile friends, a subdued newsagent was back in place, and the three friends rescheduled their tea together. It was too nice a day not to walk, however. The music of the carillon bells cascaded down, first a few solitary notes, then the overlapping deep voices. The air had cooled, the sky clearing but for a few puffy clouds hastening in from the North Sea. *What will the clouds see,* Rachel wondered, *as they pass from our country to Germany? Will they see the difference from up there? And what is the difference now?*

"Look ahead." Paula spoke quietly. Anna took in a quick, audible breath.

Two Germans approached them, walking casually on the narrow

brick sidewalk and laughing. Would they move into the street or block the way, forcing Rachel and her friends to step into the street? She first felt afraid, then reminded herself, *It's our sidewalk, and there's no reason to think they're coming after us.* Anna was quivering visibly, and melted behind the two others. Rachel exchanged a glance with Paula to know they formed a solid front.

The gap between the three friends and the two Green Police began to close. Without slacking their pace, Rachel and Paula made bright conversation. They were looking at each other rather than at the approaching men, willing them to move out of the way. The harsh German words grew nearer, and the hard boots clicked on the bricks.

The Germans laughed more loudly as they approached more closely. Rachel braced herself for whatever would come—and then recognized the soldier who gave her the chocolate.

"*Goedenavond,*" he said in Dutch with a significant smile. Seeing her stiffen, his face changed and he added, "Did you enjoy the chocolate?" He and his companion stepped into the street, and erupted into guffaws as the friends passed.

Rachel flushed and couldn't think. She could lie, of course, but not to Paula and Anna. It was bad enough that she couldn't tell them about her work. She'd taken the chocolate in a moment of weakness, when she felt sorry for the man—and it had been forever since she'd had any sweets.

Rachel turned to Paula, who was crying softly, and felt the accusation implicit in those tears. She asked herself, *How could I have forgotten that he was a German? Am I any different from the women who sell themselves for stockings and real tobacco?* Rachel was about to stammer out an apology, an explanation, something—when Paula spoke.

"I didn't *mean* to take the chocolate," she said tearfully, "but he was nice to me."

"To *you?*" Rachel asked incredulously.

"He noticed me in the street . . ." When they compared notes, all three began laughing, harder than they had in months, great whoops of laughter that unclenched their jaws and bellies. Part of it was mirth, part shame, and part relief. Anna, who had not been offered chocolate, didn't laugh as heartily as the others.

X   X   X

When she heard about a German officers' club being blown up in the Schubertstraat, Rachel was cheered that someone had upset the Nazis, which happened more often these days. She wasn't sure if she had the guts to set off a bomb or to steal blank identity cards the way other people did, but she did her own work faithfully. A few weeks after, she heard on the illicit radio that the whole Luftwaffe telephone exchange at Schipol Airport had been destroyed. Her first reaction was glee—but then she wondered how the Nazis might take revenge.

X   X   X

A week later, Rachel found out. She and Paula were walking along the border of high trees surrounding the Westerpark, which was forbidden to them. Soft summer afternoon rain beaded Paula's auburn hair and the intensely green grass. They could smell the June roses blossoming inside the park. Dozens of herons on the island in the middle of the nearby pond were making a cacophonous racket. The trees all shone green, taller than those along the canals whose roots had to exist in one mere square meter of soil. The girls' pace was slower than usual.

"What do you mean, they took Kees away? Why?" Rachel didn't understand.

"Remember how they sent all the Ag College students to board in Amsterdam a few months ago?"

"Of course, but he's in classics."

"Yes, but now that they've decided they want the Ag students back, they raided any house boarding someone from the college. While they were there, they took away any young Jewish man they found. Then they pulled more men out of the cafés and the sports clubs. I'm worried about Joost, unless he was out of town visiting his new girlfriend." Paula took Rachel's arm and spoke softly.

Rachel filed quickly through her mental list of friends, wondering if anyone else she knew might have been seized. Out loud, she asked, "Where did they get the addresses where the students were staying?"

Paula turned toward Rachel, moving closer. "The Jewish Council must have told them. They have card files on everybody. I don't think the Nazis are actually sending anybody back to the college. They wanted three hundred Jews for labor to retaliate for the airport bombing—terrorism, they called it. They may take them to Mauthausen, where some of the Jonas Daniel Meijerplein market men died."

Rachel said, "Like our butcher's son Jaap. Kees won't be much good for hard labor, but he can recite Greek poetry by the hour." Rachel looked closely at Paula's more pinched face. Everyone was getting thinner on the diminishing rations. They talked more often about food, and Rachel found herself getting short tempered near mealtime.

"All this makes me wonder if Sonja's family was right. I wonder if they're in Switzerland, or farther away. It must have cost a fortune to get the papers and find someone to smuggle them out." Paula shook her head.

"At the time I thought it was extreme, didn't you? I was afraid to talk about it, even to you."

"Now I wish that my parents had sold the gallery before the invasion, so we could have started over somewhere else. I have to go, Rachel. My mother's expecting me, and these days I don't like to keep her waiting. See you soon." Rachel enjoyed meeting Paula more often, as her popular friend's non-Jewish companions dropped her, but she felt sorry for her. It couldn't have been easy to see friends turn away.

✕   ✕   ✕

A few weeks later, Rachel walked slowly along the edge of the Westerpark before going home after her deliveries. The smoothly laid brick sidewalk barely registered under her feet, her eyes scanning for danger as always. A few unwitting words could be passed to someone who would watch her, discover what she was up to, and take the next steps. *Who would tell my parents if I were arrested?* she asked herself, as she had many times before. *Would it be the police, or would a friend take the chance? Or would a letter be slid under the door?* A letter . . . she could leave one for them, an envelope to open in the event of her death, letting them know that she'd made her choice without revealing anything that could harm them.

The underground took up most of her free waking hours. Her parents accepted her excuses, but they were both uneasy overall. Having no mail from her mother's family in England was as bad as the occasional coded, incoherent letters from her German uncle. Rose suspected that Rachel was up to something, and subtly encouraged her. It was harder for Rachel to be patient with her father's evasions. If his attitude was changing slightly, it was taking a long time. What would have to happen for him to take the situation more seriously? By then, would it be too late—if it wasn't already?

Rachel began composing the letter in her mind, and imagined her parents opening the envelope, bending over it together. Rose would be proud no matter how sad she was, and she would understand why Rachel had chosen her dangerous tasks. Of her father's reaction

Rachel could not bear to think. He would never comprehend why she had risked the life he and Rose had made for her.

Continuing her walk along the edge of the park, Rachel noted how high the sun was above the trees, although it was already after five o'clock. The year was advancing. It seemed like an eternity since she and Michiel once strolled here together. How much news would he get? He was probably still in the Netherlands. Would he be able to find her again if they both survived the war? Would he still want to?

Only a few people walked inside the park. No Jews allowed, and others were staying home more. A heron flew, graceful and steady, toward the island. At the moment of landing, when its feet had to reach for the branch and its wings rose and folded, it lurched and became awkward. Whenever it wanted to, it could lift off again, and reach any part of the city in a few score strikes of its strong wings.

✕ ✕ ✕

When Rachel returned home, Jacob was reading in his favorite brown leather easy chair and smoking his pipe. She sat down on the footstool at his feet, even though she hardly fit on it anymore. He smiled, his face shining despite its sallow cast.

"How was your walk?"

"Lovely, thanks. I stood on the edge of the park and watched the herons. They take such good care of the babies. I saw a parent bring in a little fish, and the young one snapped it right up." She illustrated with her fingers, and they both laughed.

"You loved that park when you were little. Nothing has changed there, has it? The herons seem to be raising their young or hatching them, the same as always."

Rachel looked up at him. "That's right. I'm the one who's had to change." And she left it at that.

X   X   X

When the *Jewish Weekly* announced even more restrictions on admissions for Jewish university students that fall, Rachel excused herself from the breakfast table, went upstairs, and fumed. How dare they make it virtually impossible for her to do what she'd always intended to? At least they couldn't stop her from learning. Wrestling with a difficult equation strengthened her mind the way her long bicycle rides around the city strengthened her muscles. Rachel had so looked forward to university life, where she could study alongside others as keen to learn as she was. She'd once imagined that she would meet her future husband there. Now, all she dreamed of was doing her work without being caught.

AUGUST–NOVEMBER 1941

Rachel never looked at an address before she needed it. She closed the door softly behind her on a drizzly summer morning, smelling the soft fragrance of the white rose next door. Its canes somehow clung to the brick facade, the clumps of small leaves surrounding each blowsy, emerging bud and blossom. Around the corner, when she saw no one, she pulled a sealed envelope out of her skirt pocket, read where to pick up the underground newspapers, and shredded and discarded the notepaper as soon as she safely could. It helped her forget.

Over time, Rachel had learned that the newspapers were mimeographed secretly, then fanned out to various points. The stencils themselves were sometimes transported to different machines around the city, or the bigger distributors picked up lots and delivered them to others, who broke them into still-smaller lots for couriers like herself. Anyone could read the news, if they were willing to be arrested for it.

All over the city, she confronted pillars plastered with Nazi propaganda posters. The worst pictured Jewish people as monsters or rats. To counteract the constant flow of false news, the family gathered every evening around the radio concealed in the back wall of Rose and Jacob's bedroom. The BBC's "This is London" transported them, at least for a few minutes, to a place where they could have walked freely now that the Blitz was finally over. They also listened to Radio Oranje, the voice of the Dutch government and royals exiled in London. The hourly BBC broadcasts began with Big Ben striking loudly against the deep tones of the Westertoren carillon outside. Rose sighed deeply when she heard the six notes. When the broadcast was over, sometimes she muttered, "We could have been there right now." Rachel and her father didn't respond.

✕ ✕ ✕

Crossing the Singelgracht canal, Rachel stole a glance at the ornate black wrought iron gates leading to the Vondelpark, knowing that the long lines of flowerbeds would be at their peak now. Was it another lifetime when she had met Michiel across the city with her concealed scratchy blanket? Her vagina squeezed tighter, the way it had every single time he kissed her, even lightly, an involuntary response. *I'm still alive,* Rachel thought. *I wonder if Michiel reads newspapers like mine.* The radio was no substitute for the information she was carrying. The imperfectly printed letters on cheap paper railed against the Nazis as Queen Wilhelmina could not do—and the BBC had little idea what it was like on the ground in the Netherlands.

"Halt!" Two police marched toward her, both Dutch.

How had she not seen them coming? Carelessness could cost her life, or her freedom. The taller man had spoken, his features fair enough that they looked blurry. The other, thinner than his companion, had acute blue eyes in a well-worn face.

"Good afternoon," Rachel said, as pleasantly as she would to a friend's elderly aunt.

"What's in there?" The older one jerked his head at her satchel. He smelled of a cheap tobacco substitute.

"My books. Shall I open it?" She flipped open the flap, and

revealed two of her father's old university textbooks, and the edge of rags beside them.

"You read German?" The taller man's eyes narrowed.

"Yes, I studied it at school." Would this be in her favor, or the reverse? Rachel's gut tightened.

"What's this?" The second man pointed to the rags.

"Oh, well, they're, they're rags. Women use them." She hoped she was turning pink. "I'll take them out if you'd like."

"No, no." They looked away, embarrassed. "Get along now."

Rachel closed the satchel, walking for a block before she dared to glance back, or unfreeze her mind. *Free!* she thought. *Free!* Her ploy had worked; she had been ready with these props in her satchel, wrapping the newspapers in the rags. She'd escaped. Her step lightened and she began to hum as she passed the swanky American Hotel. Then Eva's face hovered before hers, the sharp features and intense eyes focused on Rachel's. "As soon as you think you're clever, you're halfway into the enemy's hands."

When she found the trash can she was seeking, Rachel checked three times before she left off the parcel of newspapers, and picked up an envelope taped to the lid's bottom side. She'd never opened one that wasn't meant for her, but it could contain a list of where the newspapers were to be distributed. Slipping away in the wrong direction, she checked to be sure no one was following, then searched out a semi-basement a mile away. Rapping three times on the door, she waited. A young man, unkempt and hunched over, opened up and looked at her appreciatively. "Any trouble?" he asked.

"Not this time," she replied.

✕ ✕ ✕

"What are you doing, Mams?" Rachel asked on a muggy August afternoon. She peered over her mother's shoulder at lengthy forms in fine print, filled out in Rose's careful calligraphic script. After a long series of deliveries, Rachel had just been stopped again. That time the rags didn't work. Luckily, nothing incriminating remained in her satchel, but she was jarred and sweaty after the encounter. Every time she was stopped made it harder to keep going. Sometime, her number would be up.

"Your father asked me to do this, or I wouldn't. The Germans have told all Jewish people to make a list of our assets, and transfer everything liquid into the Lippmann Rosenthal Bank. At least it's a Jewish institution so the money won't just disappear."

Rachel felt her head shake, but she couldn't speak. Plucking at her pale green summer dress, Rose added, "I have to go in person, to be sure it's all in order. And"—she looked at the door and spoke softly—"between you and me, to set some cash aside." By the next evening, the two women had collected family funds from several sources, and had put a credible amount into Lippmann Rosenthal— but only after waiting three hours in the sticky humidity with other Jewish people. Once home, they dispersed the remaining funds in hidden spots around the house.

"But, Mams," Rachel protested, "money won't help us if they take us to jail."

"Money helps no matter where you are. You wouldn't know. You didn't grow up the way I did," Rose said tersely. "Here, sew some into this skirt pocket, and don't forget where it is. And, while we're at it—" She took out the bottom drawer of her dressing table, turned it over, and slid a small panel off the bottom at the back. Inside was an apricot silk bag the size of two of Rachel's fingers, suspended on a matching twisted silk cord. "Put this around your neck and tuck it into your bra. Don't ever let it leave your body, not even at night. Open it carefully now." She handed it to Rachel, who fingered the diagonal pattern of the cord, the smoothness of the fabric, and small, bumpy things inside.

When she opened the bag and inverted it onto her parents' bed, five matched diamonds caught the light in the room, split it up, and subdivided it into rainbow colors. Rachel picked up each one and felt the complex facets. She couldn't take it in.

"Where did you get these?" she asked.

Rose talked over the distant melody of the carillon. "Your Opa cut them for you. They were meant for your wedding. He saved and saved, and Mr. Asscher let him pay them off a little at a time. He was so proud of turning a rough rock made from ashes into a sparkling star."

Rachel didn't know what to say, or how to feel. Opa had meant these for another time, not now. After the war, if Michiel . . . but not now. This new measure of how alarmed her mother was terrified her.

"A wedding doesn't seem likely right now." Rachel knew her voice crackled with regret and anger.

Putting down the needle, Rose looked at her steadily. "I know. But Paps won't think about leaving Amsterdam, and we might end up arrested just for being Jewish. If that happens, those diamonds might buy your way out."

"Mams, if you think it's that bad, shouldn't we try again to persuade Paps to hide?"

"I've done my best. You try. Just choose your moment carefully."

X   X   X

As Rachel delivered papers, she heard about more people vanishing since, like her mother, they feared arrest. Because Jacob had an independent medical practice, the family was unaffected when employers were allowed to fire Jewish employees without cause, but it was a sign of the times. Her father was unwilling to leave the city, but couldn't Rachel at least persuade him to hide in Amsterdam? If they did, what would happen to her underground work? Hadn't she done her share? Snaking her way through a narrow alley to drop off a package, Rachel heard something behind her and whipped her head around. A rat; unpleasant, but nothing to be afraid of, unlike the news. Hitler advanced steadily on the Russian front. How long could the siege of Leningrad go on?

At night, Rachel often went to sleep from exhaustion, but she awoke to the slightest sound. During the days, Rachel's longing for Michiel was still a low ache, like a cello's part in the orchestra—faint but nearly ever-present, beautiful and painful. At least it was no longer at the forefront of her body and mind at all times, except when she went to bed. Reading and exhaustion distracted her, but Rachel often resorted to putting herself back into Michiel's arms as soon as her eyes closed. It was a place of longing, not repose, and, if she relieved it, the result was often tears and wakefulness. It's not worth it, she decided, but eventually her body demanded otherwise.

X　X　X

As restrictions tightened on where Jewish people could go, Rachel had to be more cautious with deliveries, especially those outside the Jewish Quarter. Finding public places where she could meet safely with her contacts would be harder in the winter, and lingering out-doors would be more conspicuous. Rachel was banned everywhere she wanted to go: the parks, a theatre, the library, and concert halls. And now Jewish students had to attend an all-Jewish school, with others from around the city who had absolutely nothing in common except the Nazi definition of being Jewish.

Everywhere she went, "Forbidden for Jews" signs blared out of café and shop windows—not the once gentler "Jews not welcome." One evening, she sat down beside her father on the sofa. He looked pensive, which was a good start. "Paps, have you noticed how much worse things are on the street? The cafés have really changed. This time, they're putting those awful signs up instead of refusing the way many of them did last fall."

Instead of his usual defensiveness, her father said, "Yes, I've noticed. And I have more cases than ever of stress-related illnesses." His expression was bleak. "And when I think of my brother . . . If only we had visited them more often. Maybe we should have tried harder to persuade them to come here."

"Maybe. But now we need to think of our own safety. I'm sure we could find a place to hide." She saw his mind close with his eyes, but he spoke without anger.

"You must have been talking to your mother. No matter what else the Nazis are up to, they wouldn't dare hurt the doctors; they need us. And even though I'm Dutch now, to them I would still be German. They won't harm one of their own countrymen. Regardless of that, as long as I have patients who need me, I am keeping my clinic open."

Rachel knew better than to stand between him and his duty as a doctor, no matter how strongly she felt. Maybe Eva had been right. Maybe she would have to hide without him, which meant without them both. Could she face that?

X   X   X

Anna looked frustrated one afternoon when she and Rachel went to Paula's for a break together. It was harder for the three of them to meet now than it had been when they all went to school together and ran into each other almost every day. They were sitting on a silk-covered carved loveseat with a matching chair, looking out over the garden where they had sat among the roses earlier that year.

"People were lined up for blocks to put their assets in the Lippmann Rosenthal Bank yesterday. I hate to see Jewish people cooperating with the Nazis," Anna said.

"Have you noticed what happens to people who don't?" Rachel asked.

"Of course, but—"

"Some people are even trying to hide. Almost nobody can get out the way Sonja's family did anymore," Paula said, then put her hand over her mouth.

"Is that what happened? You've always ducked the question whenever I asked about her." Anna's tone showed that she was hurt. "You don't know everything about me, either. You're not the only ones who have reason to be afraid. Please don't lie to me."

Rachel felt badly. Maybe she had underestimated Anna, and perhaps her church work wasn't as innocuous as it seemed. They drank homegrown mint tea, and managed to laugh before the afternoon was over.

On Rachel's way home, the sun's last light tinged the houses ahead of her, so the curved flourishes of the gables burned over the calm gray facades. As her steps followed the curve of the canal, she left the stretch where the houses were still lit, near her father's parents' mansion in Keizersgracht. When they died, she had overheard the conversations about selling the house, since neither Jacob nor his brother Rab was interested in its opulence. Hadn't Rose said something at that time about putting the proceeds into a Swiss bank? Had she? Could they get to that money if they needed it? The darkness eased down to the canal slowly, almost undetectably.

When Rachel arrived home, her mother stopped reading, and handed her an envelope with a confidential smile. "Look, dear, here's something from Joost. At last! He's practically disappeared. I don't know what's wrong with him. Rachel, when I was your age, I had so much fun! Mams told me to enjoy myself before I got married, but to be careful."

Rachel nodded, hoping Rose would say more.

"I wish all this wasn't happening in the best years of your life."

Her smile was gone now, her cheeks sagging. When she wasn't reading or playing the piano, the shadows often fell across her face, and her spine slumped.

Rachel restrained herself from telling her mother how exciting her life actually was. She even felt a crazy impulse to confide in her about Michiel. Instead, she said, "Me, too."

In her attic room, Rachel opened the unmarked envelope. Inside was an invitation from Joost to an "anniversary party" the next afternoon. It was a relief not to deal with his attraction for her now that he'd found a girlfriend, but Rachel missed his company. She'd dress in her silky deep wine-colored dress to maintain the pretense of a party, now that she was trusted enough to meet with a group sometimes. One never knew who could be depended upon. People changed. Rachel heard of a Jewish woman who took up with a German officer, and gave him a list of people she suspected of being in the underground. Rachel's leader had whispered to her about even worse rumors, that Jewish people in Germany had been deported *en masse* to Poland.

The next day, after a lunch of watery turnip soup, the doorbell rang. Joost came in eagerly when she answered. He asked, "Are your parents here? Oh, good." The exchange of ordinary pleasantries acted like a tonic on Jacob, who no doubt appreciated a visit from someone too vigorous to require his ministrations. Rose turned on the charm that had served her well as a young woman with many boyfriends. How would she really have responded if Rachel had dared to bring Michiel home? Had it been a mistake not to?

"Let's go, or we'll be late." As much as she loved seeing her parents brighten up momentarily, she could not wait to talk freely with Joost.

Rachel slipped her hands through her coat sleeves as Joost held it for her. It could be chilly outside later. He kept up the light chatter as they left the house.

"How's the new girlfriend?"

"She's lovely, and I'm sorry it's been a while since I've seen you. They've kept me busy, and we've had to deal with a few betrayals."

They stopped beside a large elm, its roots heaving up the bricks around it, its leaves having lost their summer vigor. The uneven ground set their feet at odd angles. Joost faced Rachel, and put his hand on her shoulder. "Watch out, Rachel. You're doing dangerous work. Maybe you should be thinking about hiding."

She flinched, nodded, and looked away. Across the canal a thin-faced woman was watching them under her white lace valence. *What does she see?* Rachel wondered. *A young couple having a misunderstanding?* Unexpectedly, she felt a queasy nostalgia for what her young womanhood might have been without the war: boyfriends, parties, a student's hours and frivolous diversions. *I could have loved Joost once, when we were younger.* Was that only a year or two ago? He looked like a boy to her, after Michiel. Had he ever made love as she had, slowly, with complete abandon?

"Do you have the address for the party?" he asked.

"I know it." She slipped her hand back into the crook of his elbow. The canal's ripples would turn from brown to silver as the sun set. As they walked on, the afternoon light was already melting under a thin, mobile cloud layer. Rachel released her breath.

The "party" was for women like herself who needed physical training to fight back if attacked, or to startle an enemy and run. The hardest part was learning to slug someone, by punching a bag stuffed with sand. Her first efforts were lackluster. "Come on, Rachel. They'll never expect it, and that's your biggest advantage."

She closed her eyes and aimed again for the target. This time, her fist smashed it hard.

Joost nodded. "Good. Do it fast if you have to, then run."

✕ ✕ ✕

Rose stepped aside again when Rachel went home to confront her father. She couldn't give up on persuading him. She wished she could shock him with what she'd had to learn about protecting herself, but she wouldn't go that far.

"Some people say they're sending Jewish people off to Poland," she said.

"Some people are always saying something like that. You and I know better than to believe rumors, don't we?" Her father had that patient look.

"Even if only ten percent of them are true, shouldn't we get out of the line of fire, at least until this blows over?"

Instead of answering, he said, "My parents taught me to be proud of being Jewish, and I still am, especially now." He reached over and took Rachel's hand. "We've survived as a people for thousands of years. I'm not blind, Rachel. I worry more every day. But I still believe we'll get through this, and we'll do it here, in our home, not in a rundown dictatorship in South America, or in some farmer's shed in Drenthe. Now I need to go back to the office."

With this admission that even her father was worried despite his determination to stay in their home, Rachel's undercurrent of anxiety became the jitters at times. She had to work hard to calm herself enough to pay attention on the streets, and she knew that was dangerous. When she came home at night, she felt worn out, and she couldn't get to sleep. She kept seeing the last time a soldier or policeman had stopped her, and how easily she might have ended up in prison.

X X X

One late fall morning, Rachel wearily drew her curtains open to discover a glorious Saturday. The elm leaves had turned gold, and the air for once was crisp rather than damp. She'd done deliveries in almost every spare daylight hour for weeks. She started to cry quietly, and once she started, she couldn't stop. She'd be crazy to go out on the streets with dangerous cargo. In the mirror, her face looked blotchy and haggard, her red-rimmed eyes set in puffy flesh.

She wanted one day, just one day, when she didn't have to deliver anything, or quiver every time she saw a Green Policeman, or remember what happened to Eva, or Jaap, or Kees. One day when the images of the roundup in the market didn't flash before her eyes sometime. And when she didn't struggle to remember exactly what Michiel's eyes looked like. The sea—that was what she needed. No, too far, and much too risky, as much as she loved it. But the Amstel River, not the canal, not something man had made, but something traced by the hand of the earth—the river would help.

When she went downstairs, her parents were already out. Rachel grabbed an old apple, left a note, and soon sped up the Amstel River. She cycled as fast as she could in the cold air.

As she escaped the city, a thin sunshine burnished the fields. Rachel gave herself to the ride, and thought of little but the fresh smells of the water, the occasional squawk of a heron, and the bounce of the pathway under her wheels. Her heart was pounding, and her blood zinged through her legs and arms. When she spotted the modest spires of Oudekerk ahead, she decided to visit the Sephardic Jewish cemetery. No one could keep her out there.

Even the graves from the 1600s were mounted carefully and well tended. The stones were dark gray slate, the Hebrew letters and numbers carved deeply. Rachel's body and soul calmed immediately. She spotted a tall elm, even larger than the one in the Begijnhof. *The bones of my people are in its roots,* she thought, *reaching over me and turning into branches.* Somehow that gave Rachel rest as she sat with her back against the tree and closed her eyes. When she woke up, the low sun barely touched the golden elm leaves which had fallen all over her body.

✕ ✕ ✕

On her way home the next Monday, Rachel rounded the arc of Prinsengracht in the early November gloom. Police were swarming around Paula's family's antique store and gallery. Fortunately, Rachel had nothing incriminating on her person. She checked herself every night to be sure no scrap had escaped. And she wasn't remembering any addresses, that she was sure of. Before she slept, she jumbled them in her mind, throwing in false ones until she couldn't tell where she had been. Rachel's hands tensed on the bicycle handlebars. The Posners' apartment upstairs could easily be a Nazi target, as well as their business. Every delicate Louis XV chair, every impressionist drawing, every Armenian carpet, was exquisite in itself. The Germans could have their eyes on those treasures, or on Paula's older brother Jan, a scholarly boy.

Should Rachel stay and try to help in some way? Just then, Paula appeared by the window in the family quarters, looking right at Rachel, shaking her auburn head and her index finger. Rachel rushed home on her bicycle to await news.

Rose had left a note that she was visiting a friend forced to move from a village to Amsterdam. "If I wait long enough," Rose had half-joked that morning, "Hitler will bring all my friends from other towns here to Amsterdam. They're getting us all out of the provinces so we can enjoy the delights of city life in the Jewish Quarter here."

Every time the doorbell rang—for a peddler, a neighbor, then a passerby wanting directions—Rachel dashed downstairs. She was particularly worried about Jan. He hadn't been working—how could he, in public, with his stereotypical Jewish features?— and he was subject to drafts for the new Jewish labor camps.

The fourth time the doorbell rang, Paula at last appeared. She was so furious that she didn't say hello. "Who the hell do they think they are? They broke in like a gang of thieves." She banged past Rachel, letting in a blast of sleet-laden air.

When Rachel caught up with her, she saw a bitter smirk that was a caricature of Paula's usual warm smile. Although they'd known each other since they were little, Rachel hadn't seen this side of her friend. She didn't know what to say.

Paula tossed her soggy coat toward Rachel. "My mother's gone crazy."

"What do you mean?" Rachel put Paula's coat near the fire to dry. The fur collar was soaked.

"When the Germans stormed up the stairs, she started yelling. A policeman slapped her and knocked her down. I got her upstairs before she could make it worse." Paula flung herself on the couch and pressed her mouth with her fist.

"I'll get you some tea." By the time Rachel came back with a steaming cup, Paula was railing again.

"Stop, Paula. Tell me what happened." Rachel had to know.

She took her first sip. "They came at one o'clock. Wouldn't you think they'd be taking a lunch break with all the good food they get? They're taking almost everything. They said no Jew is going to profit from the great Germanic heritage. Right. Then why not leave us the Fabergé eggs or the English highboy?" Her eyes focused at last. "They're going to make us move—"

"Move? Out of the gallery?"

"Yes, and the apartment. They're putting us in some awful place in Amsterdam South. A German officer is going to live in our house. We can only take a few boxes of household things. But everything valuable stays right there, or it goes straight onto the barge."

"What barge?"

"To Germany. Paps says they've already sent away hundreds of barges piled up with furniture, art, anything the Nazis want."

Rachel looked around her own living room—at the piano, at the rustling scarlet and gold fire, at the windows which were magnificent even when streaked with sleet. Her home was far humbler than Paula's, but still qualified as a comfortable canalside residence. Would the Germans want it, too? She spoke. "I wish I could have helped."

"Don't be silly. When I saw you outside, I was terrified they'd catch you. You've never said anything, but I know you're the type who—"

"Never mind that," Rachel interjected. "What about Jan?"

"He wasn't home, or those bastards would have taken him."

Paula crumpled and clung to Rachel, and cried at last. Rachel held her friend as she had only held little children and Michiel before. Was her family targeted specifically, or had the Germans made up some new rule that applied to them?

When her sobs slowed down, Paula began apologizing for crying. Rachel hushed her. "Your father needs us, especially since your mother is upset. Dry your eyes and wash your face, Paula. And think of something funny to say when we get to your house." She wrote her parents a quick note and began to bundle up against the falling November evening.

Darkness had descended fully when they left the house, and cold rain plummeted from the low clouds as they raced around the curved canal. By the time the two young women reached the Posners' splendid display windows, only one policeman stood guard. The door leading upstairs was open.

"I live here," Paula told the guard with a hint of her former fire. He checked their identity cards closely.

"For one more night," he said.

The apartment, a museum of treasures a few hours before, was a mess. Paintings still hung on the walls with the best furniture ranged underneath them, but otherwise chaos reigned. The back stairs linking the apartment to the gallery downstairs had been locked and sealed with red wax.

"Paula dear." Her father's voice trembled a little. He looked pale as he put his arms around her. "And Rachel. How kind of you to help us. My wife is—resting. If you could pack a few kitchen items . . ."

Paula swallowed and said, "We're going camping, is that it?" She managed a small smile, and so did the others. Then they packed.

×   ×   ×

At breakfast in the late-dawn half-light later that week, Rose handed Rachel an envelope. "Someone put this under the door. Love finds a way, dear," she said, but with a wink. This was as close as they came to discussing Rachel's mail and her absences these days. One recent afternoon, her mother had been blunter. "If I were your age and didn't have your father to take care of, Rachel, I'd be out on the streets doing something useful. You're my daughter and I want to be proud of you after all this is over. But watch yourself. Don't take stupid risks, just necessary ones." Even if they couldn't talk about the details, Rachel felt comforted to know her mother wasn't completely in the dark.

DECEMBER 1941–FEBRUARY 1942

"682, 48, 143, 79, 56," Rachel chanted on her way home, scrambling the numbers and then the canals or streets to help her forget the addresses. "Keizersgracht, Geldersekade, Lastageweg." At six o'clock it was already dark. She nearly ran into a slightly older neighbor from years ago who looked more vibrant than she remembered, unlike almost everyone else. In their brief conversation, Rachel learned the reason: the woman had gotten a good job with the Jewish Council, and she'd been promoted. Now that she was a supervisor, she asked Rachel to call if she'd like to work there with the Population Registry cards.

As Rachel walked home in the chilly fog, she couldn't help reflecting. *That's how I could be safe: do a nice clean job filing cards, keeping them up to date. No wonder the Council employs thousands of people. How many cards could I lose? Anyone whose card disappeared could simply vanish—or work for the underground. It would be much easier than what I'm doing now, and it might work better. Nobody would ever have to know a card was gone, and that way I'd know I was actually saving lives.* She shook herself like a horse shucking off an unwanted rider. No matter what good the Council was doing, in the end they were making it easier for the Nazis to find Jewish people and persecute them. How many cards would she have to "process" correctly for every one she could lose? It was unthinkable.

X   X   X

As the winter deepened, Rose often reminded Rachel to be careful, but never asked her where she was going, only when she would be home. Jacob kept up his optimism about the Dutch, especially after 4,300 doctors signed a petition against the Artsenkamer, the professional organization the Nazis ordered them to join. "You see, Rachel, the Dutchmen aren't all as bad as you think they are," he said.

"I don't think they're bad, but they're letting the Nazis—"

"Just a minute, my dear. My Gentile classmates from medical school are taking a stand."

"Yes, Paps, but they're the exception. The other professions are knuckling under. Aren't you afraid of what they might do to you if you refuse?"

"Not as long as the other doctors are standing with me. There are too many of us."

Maybe if he'd been in the Jonas Daniel Meijerplein that day, he would understand. And now she had another danger to face: if he didn't register, the Nazis might arrest her beloved father, who insisted on believing the best of them.

X   X   X

Rachel felt strange talking with her underground contact about events she couldn't discuss at home. Did she trust a relative stranger more than her parents? No, she cared less—a realization that made Rachel uneasy. How far could she herself be trusted by her colleagues? Could she keep her mouth shut to protect people with whom she didn't feel a deep bond—especially if the Germans threatened her parents? She'd heard about situations like that, and they made her gut constrict.

On the days when Rachel was delivering papers, she took care to look as drab as possible. No lipstick, hair pulled back severely. Though she couldn't conceal her relatively expensive clothes, she chose neutral colors. Looking in the mirror didn't give the satisfaction it used to. Her skin was sallower, her cheeks hollower, and her figure was bonier, especially around the ribs. No one ever complimented her on her appearance anymore.

The address she needed was never revealed until the day itself, and Rachel never knew how it would come—buried in the text of a letter (as in "we used to work in the diamond factory at 49 Ruysdaelstraat"), or revealed by a stranger who stopped her in the street with the password, or another way. There was no pattern. Rachel went out for a ride every single day, regardless of the weather, so that anyone suspicious of her would see only an invariable routine. Finding a new address had become child's play. Years before, her English cousins had told her of the stringent examinations imposed on London cab drivers, who had to locate street numbers from memory, in tiny alleys. Rachel patterned herself after them, and was proud of the results.

At one new address, Rachel left her bicycle outside and climbed five steps up. She rang the bell, two shorts and one long. A huge window reflected the shivering elm branches. After a short wait, the door opened, and a slim young man about Rachel's age greeted her.

"I'm looking for Uncle Harry," Rachel said, and stepped inside. The warm room smelled of boiling potatoes. After the war was over, she never wanted to eat one again.

"Wait a minute," the other replied, disappearing to the back of the house, and reappearing with four packets. "This is a lot, but we've lost someone." It was happening more often, and Rachel couldn't ignore that. Hitler had decreed that underground workers should be punished by disappearing into the "night and fog," so their families would not know where they were or whether they were still alive.

The man recited the addresses, easily memorized and located on her mental map. "Be particularly careful. We don't know how much the other courier may have told them. These are new addresses, but still . . . watch out. And cheer up. The Soviet Army is finally fighting back around Moscow." America had at last entered the war. Could it be over in a matter of weeks?

Outside, Rachel lashed the heavy satchel to her bicycle. She glanced both ways, and no one seemed to be noticing her. Still, in the densely populated heart of Amsterdam, windows were everywhere. Her Uncle Rab used to say it was amazing that the brick architectural frameworks could hold such expanses of glass. It had been weeks since they'd had any news from him. As she swung her bicycle into the street, Rachel rehearsed what she would say if she were stopped. What if they beat her enough to make her bleed? Would the addresses come spilling out with her blood? Even after all these months, Rachel felt her stomach tense up at the thought. How much longer could she deal with the fear?

The first two deliveries went easily. She moved swiftly and confidently after checking out the passersby. She spoke to no one, dropping a package where it would be found but could be denied—concealed at the top of a stairway, or inside an internal vestibule. Rachel started off on her bicycle again, feeling light sweat on her back despite the chill. Then she noticed him. Still in the next block, in uniform, headed straight for her. A Dutch policeman, but he might well be as dangerous as a German.

Rachel's diaphragm clenched as she glided forward on her bike. In her mind's eye, she saw the scene as though in a movie shot from overhead, showing herself and the policeman on a collision course. She still had two packages to deliver.

"Where are you going?" he barked. She rode closer so they would be at equal height, although when she dismounted he was much taller. Close shaven with fine-grained skin, perhaps in his thirties, the policeman's nose was bulbous and his mouth asymmetric and large.

Rachel's heart surged with relief. He was one of their neighborhood cops.

"Remember me? Rachel, Dr. Klein's daughter. You helped us when a patient punched my father, remember?" The eyes she remembered as pale now sharpened.

"Answer!" he shouted, taking a long step toward her.

Eva had taught her to swallow her pride and try deference. "I'm going home to dinner, sir." Rachel cast her eyes down.

"What are you carrying?" he pointed at her satchel. Another uniformed man, this time a German, was approaching. Often their presence made the Dutch police act tougher.

"A few potatoes for my mother for supper," which she in fact had packed as camouflage. "She'll be angry if I don't get home soon." Rachel tried for the flustered tears of a child who might be punished. She was terrified, so it wasn't hard to do.

"Get out of my sight!" the man bellowed, with a side-glance at his approaching colleague. "And don't let me catch you again, do you hear?" He gave Rachel the slightest possible wink. So he just wanted to look strict. He didn't even know what she had.

"No, sir," she replied meekly, and scurried off. In the wake of her fear, she was furious. Pedaling wildly down the canal past others who were also hurrying home, she was angrier than ever. If she had been alone in the world, Rachel could have leapt at him and hit him the way Joost had taught her. They would have locked her up as another crazy Jewish terrorist. *Yes, terrorist,* she thought, *the more they brutalize and go after us, the more they accuse us of being the aggressors.* A terrorist is someone every civilized person is authorized to hate.

When Rachel got home, she couldn't help telling her father all about the policemen and how they had treated her. "Yelling at me in the street!" she sputtered. "How much longer are we going to have to put up with this?" He didn't answer, but his misery showed in the sag of his face.

✗   ✗   ✗

When Rembrandt, whom she hadn't seen for months, invited Rachel to join him at an artists' party one evening, she agreed, although listlessly. He had hardly contacted her since their first encounter, but he was probably as busy as she was. His dark blond hair was longer now, and those distinctive deep-set hazel eyes shone out. They rode side by side along the frosty canal in the slow cold rain until he pulled over, a few blocks from Bet's basement haven. "Let's leave the bicycles here." He smiled at her and reached over to steady her machine as she got off.

Rembrandt was right there, right then. Michiel was somewhere far away. She missed Joost, too. He had disappeared after a theft of blank identity cards, and might be hiding in Drenthe. The country was safer than the city if you could get there, but the risks of traveling were enormous.

Rachel and Rembrandt walked close together on the narrow street, past windows which used to be full of jewel-toned scarves and fragrant cheeses from the countryside. No one else was on the street, but they didn't speak. As they turned another corner, the force of the wind hit them full blast, with fine icy needles propelled by a stronger gale. When it punched Rachel in the chest, she moved behind Rembrandt's stolid figure. They turned another corner, and the wind abated. Their roundabout route had led them to a back door on a deserted alley.

"You won't have to worry about anybody here," Rembrandt said in a low voice. "I've known them all since art school. The boys who beat people up or blow up the train tracks or bridges slow the Nazis down for a day or two. But we artists give people papers that mean they can stay alive."

The party of forgers was in a basement, dark except for a few precious candles. Rachel could make out quiet figures who drank a smelly homemade brew. A subdued conversation was in progress about the Americans' arrival in Britain. Rachel looked around the smoky room, speculating about whether she might work with these forgers. Her anger at the neighborhood cop had fueled her determination to do even more to counter the Nazis. The underground newspapers had been a good although dangerous step up from simply delivering messages, but she'd love to put false papers into someone's hands. To create a new identity, a hunted resistance worker or Jewish person needed a new name or address, or a photograph with bleached hair and eyebrows, or even a different gender. If Rachel were caught, delivering false papers was worse than the illegal newspapers. Was she ready to take the additional risk?

"Come along," Rembrandt said, helping her up out of the deep couch. "It's time for the next shift." A false door opened behind them to reveal a brightly lit artists' workshop. Four or five weary women and men slipped past Rachel. A woman said, "The finished ones are in the pile."

"Fine," Rembrandt said. "And you left the ones still to be done on the table?"

"Yes, all five thousand of them," a retreating back grumbled.

As Rembrandt showed Rachel around, she marveled at the fine-pointed engraving tools, the rubber stamps, the small letter presses and type to be set. On the desks were neatly arranged authentic models of documents to work from, and an assortment of ink colors and pen nibs. Bright light from gooseneck lamps helped the artists trace from one document to another.

"It wasn't easy to assemble all this equipment, believe me," Rembrandt said. "The fees we charge barely feed us. Here's a card

I did." He handed it to her, and Rachel touched his warm fleshy fingers. His hands were so broad, so unlike Michiel's slender ones. Could she imagine Rembrandt touching her? She let the thought flit through her mind for the first time.

"See how the seal sits right on the edge of the photo?" he pointed out. "And getting the background right on the ration coupons isn't easy, either. See those wavy lines where it says 'Distributie Nederland'?"

"Yes. I had no idea it was so complicated."

"Almost nobody does. Sometime I'd like to show you the real art I used to do. I have a series of color studies you might enjoy. In fact, I could lend you one if you'd like something cheerful for your room." His face was open like a child's, hoping she would accept. She said yes. It encouraged her to see how hard others were working, too. At least she could do her part in the open air. If the artists were raided, they were stuck.

X   X   X

The winter was so cold that year that Rachel's warmest coat barely protected her as she navigated her way from one address to another. Now that she was usually delivering false papers, she was more on edge. No cover story would account for a batch of identity cards without a J, or ration coupons. As she passed the Diamond Exchange building on her way to pick up a delivery, Rachel saw a crowd gathered outside, and recognized Mr. de Jong. What could he be doing here? She parked her bicycle and braved the police to speak to him. Slipping through the crowd, she felt a gust of fear.

"Hello, Mr. de Jong. Are you here to sell diamonds today?" She'd hoped to make him smile.

The man she remembered as hearty and humorous looked timid

and ashen. "They came into the Quarter and picked us up, any street vendor who happened to be there. What about my vegetables?"

"In this cold? Not a chance they'll spoil." Still no smile. "Why did they bring you here?" She looked around the crowd. All men.

"The doctors will check us out and say if we have to go to those labor camps. If anybody says no, they'll come after our families. How will my wife manage? Will you help her, you and Mrs. Klein?" He was close to tears, desperate.

Rachel felt unsettled under the nose of the guards. "Of course we will. Don't worry. Tell me your address." Even though the Jewish Council had already helped the Nazis call up hundreds of Jews— some said it was several thousand—the Germans demanded more men to work in labor camps in Drenthe, or somewhere. It was so cold up there that a few crews had been sent back, but that didn't stop the recruiting process. The demand for false papers was escalating. No wonder Rachel was so busy delivering them.

"You!" A policeman grabbed her arm. "Get out! This has nothing to do with you." He thrust her roughly out of the crowd toward her bicycle. She knew she had to leave, but when she looked over her shoulder, Mr. de Jong was still watching her. Could she do anything for him, anything at all? Even if she could somehow give him papers, where could he go?

By the time she reached home, Rachel had thought of something else. "Paps, don't you have a patient who's an official in the Jewish Council?" When he nodded, she told him about Mr. de Jong. Perhaps the patient could help, the sooner the better. Her father said, "I couldn't misuse a patient that way, asking for favors. He'd never trust me again." Rachel argued, even brought her mother in, but Jacob didn't budge. The family was split, which made Rachel feel even shakier.

X X X

Despite all the underground's precautions, every week or so Rachel heard about someone who simply disappeared, either taken away or voluntarily diving below the surface of society. Even the streets seemed emptier somehow. One day, at the back alley door of an elegant canal house where she'd been directed, an envelope was pinned to the papers, with a sketch of a heron where the address would normally be. Rachel recognized Rembrandt's style. He knew they were her favorite birds. Ripping it open, she read only one line: "Sometimes it's time to fly away. May we meet again." Below it was a deft drawing of the Royal Palace bedecked with the Dutch flag as if the Allies had already won. Rachel stared at the paper in her hand. Why was she crying? Had he been that important to her? What would happen to his art now, and the cheerful work he'd offered to lend her? She slipped the note back into the envelope, and tucked it into her bra. With luck, she wouldn't be arrested before she destroyed it, but she couldn't bring herself to tear it up just yet.

Strangely, Rembrandt's departure reawakened Rachel's longing for Michiel. At the least, they'd have to wait months to see each other again, maybe years. Her body still longed for him, but she was usually so busy and in sufficient danger that she forgot. Rachel's former life seemed boring in retrospect, even if she occasionally felt nostalgic for its simplicity. One morning when spring looked as unlikely as the apocalypse, Rachel headed into the wealthy nineteenth-century canal neighborhood to deliver an envelope she had inserted into the hidden pouch in her coat lining. Rachel didn't let her growing skills deceive her into feeling safe. It was sobering to hear about a classmate—observant, agile, and strong—locked up at the grim prison on the Weteringschans.

The weather was still cold enough that no one would ask her to remove her outer garments. Placed carefully not to show a bulge, the envelope was almost undetectable. Rachel had inserted a hidden zipper for that purpose. Riding past the castle-like Diamond

Workers' Union building made her sad, because her grandfather had taken such pride in it. A few diamond people were still at work, but now all their products went to Germany. He would have been ashamed.

She counted off the house numbers—62, 86, 110—until she found the right one, unusual in that the house stood behind a front garden of rhododendron, blooming hellebores, and—yes!—a small clump of snowdrops. Virtually everywhere else in the city center the facades were right on the sidewalk, with the gardens hidden behind them, as Paula's used to be. Rachel let herself in the plain wrought iron gate. On either side of the entryway, shiny tiles showed herons fishing in the marshes. When she knocked, a grizzled old man answered, smelling of licorice. Where did he get it? At first she thought she'd made a mistake, when she only had identity cards for his son and daughter-in-law, but he told her he was staying put. "I'm too old to leave. This way, they have a chance. Thank you." In such moments, Rachel knew that what she was doing mattered— and they balanced out the unfortunate times when a recipient was snappy or rude, or didn't seem to care.

The next address was for a pickup. Back on the main road through the Plantage neighborhood, Rachel heard children's high voices as they played in the courtyard of a child care center. The icy wind sharpened. The rain pierced her face with stiletto-like precision, so unpleasant that she almost didn't hear a voice from overhead.

"Rachel!" The voice, insistent but secretive, came from a window high overhead in the child care center. It was Klara, a homely girl she used to go to school with, now sporting a starched nurse's uniform. She put a finger to her full lips as she used to in class, pointed downstairs, and mouthed, "Meet me." What could she want? They'd never been close, but Rachel had enjoyed her. Her family were patients of her father's.

Inside, the center entrance was decorated with bright drawings on the walls. Klara appeared in a moment. "They gave me five minutes off. I told them it was urgent. Come into the staff room with me so we can talk."

"What's going on?" They were settled on an upholstered sofa. Klara's kind face looked shriveled, as if she hadn't relaxed in months.

"I'm going to take a chance, Rachel, because your father has always been so good to my family. My brother's in trouble. He's strong, he's the age they're after, and they just took his best friend. Do you think your father could get involved? He must know people who could help."

"I'm not sure." Was Klara setting her up? It wasn't impossible. Someone wandered in, then withdrew.

"Please, at least ask your father? I'd planned to go and see him myself, but we're working such long hours now. Then I saw you in the street. Take these photos of my brother. I had them done last week." Klara's thick brows contracted. She reached for Rachel's hand.

"All right." She'd have to think about this. Rachel stood up, breaking contact, but she took the photos. "I'll let you know."

✕　✕　✕

Rachel did not like to help people she knew, because the links between them would be easier to trace. Still, she couldn't ignore Klara's situation, and tried connecting with Rembrandt's friends. Because they were overextended, they suggested a group far from the city center to create the new identity card. Rachel didn't want to deliver the photos and wait for the card herself. In a rural community, she'd be vulnerable to questioning. She needed someone unimpeachable for the job, but who?

MARCH–JUNE 1942

Rachel's heart stiffened as people turned away, especially the class-mates who would have been her fellow students at the university. Now, they barely spoke when they saw her. While she'd never been the most popular girl at school, Gentiles as well as Jews had included her in parties or games, and she had her close circle of friends. A few prejudiced kids had occasionally harassed the others, but was the separation deeper than that? Had she not seen it?

A notable exception among her Gentile friends was Anna. Her blond hair kept showing up among the predominant brown in the Jewish market, and at Rachel's and Paula's homes. Although Rachel had always seen her as a do-gooder for her father's church, she was proving a loyal friend who seemed to feel for the predicament of Jewish people, and sometimes hinted that she might be helping in some way. Rose, who had looked smart all her adult life, told her daughter, "I should take that girl's wardrobe in hand," as she con-templated Anna's poorly cut skirts and boring blouses. "She has a fine figure, but who will ever notice it?"

Rachel briefed Anna before they went for a first call at Paula's cramped new address in Amsterdam South. "It's not just the Posners," she said. "They've taken over all the Jewish galleries in the city."

After they climbed up the dirty steps to the third-floor apart-ment, Paula hugged them both hard. Even she was beginning to look thinner and scrappier. Her older brother Jan was bending his unruly chestnut curls over a book in the corner of the living room. He wanted to be a veterinarian, not run the family business as his parents wished. His long, well-shaped fingers caressed a kitten he had rescued, carefully avoiding the paw he had bandaged. Rachel saw that Anna, a lover of animals of all shapes and sizes, noticed every stroke.

"What are you reading?" Anna asked, in a voice that sounded different than usual.

Startled, Jan looked up, his brown eyes deep, as though the book had entered them. "About squirrels. Did you know they bury their food in up to a thousand places every fall?" She did, and the two sailed off in a realm of their own, pointing out illustrations to each other and disputing small points amicably. Watching them, Rachel couldn't help but remember that Jan was the right age to be taken away, and he looked like the Nazi caricatures of Jews—deep brown wavy hair and an olive complexion, a broad mouth and a distinguished hooked nose. His parents must have despaired. Anyone could already spot their son, and now Jewish men were being sent to labor camps like all the others.

✕   ✕   ✕

A few days later after a harrowing delivery, Rachel returned to the Posners, and to her surprise found Anna and Jan sitting side by side on the sofa, murmuring over a fine old leather-bound *Atlas of the Americas* from Mr. Posner's remaining collection. Somewhere Anna had found a deep blue blouse that matched her eyes.

"At last you're here!" Paula exclaimed, her dimples suddenly alight. "I'm bored to tears. All these two ever do is read and look at pictures."

When Anna glanced up, blushing, Rachel saw that they were

conducting a courtship under the eyes of his family. She felt almost matronly. "Why don't you two go and have a look at the heron nesting area in the Westerpark? You can see pretty well from the edge," she suggested. It was a good distance away and would give them time to talk. Then she thought of Jan's Semitic features, and Anna's blondness. "Actually, there's a closer place," Rachel added hastily, since herons were almost ubiquitous.

Paula laughed. "Birds of a feather." The couple bundled up and left.

Mrs. Posner asked the girls to help her darn a moth-eaten woolen blanket. She had shrunk so that her clothes no longer fit properly, but her middle-aged face was dignified if stiff, her long, graying hair in a carefully tended bun.

"I never thought we'd need this blanket, but it's been freezing in here." The apartment was drafty and small, graced with only two of the splendid paintings which had hung in their old home. They must have bribed someone to be able to keep them.

"Rachel, I've been meaning to ask you." Mrs. Posner threaded a new needle awkwardly. "What do you know about Anna's family? Do you think her parents know she's coming here?"

"I've met Anna's parents," Rachel replied, "and I'm sure they know. They belong to the Reformed Church—the one that speaks out against the Nazis sometimes. Her father is a pastor and her mother's a housewife." Rumor had it that Anna's father was quietly asking his parishioners to help the Jews, but she was afraid to say so.

When evening fell, they heard footsteps below. Mr. Posner appeared, quivering from the chill but smiling as he peeled off his soft leather gloves.

"Where are the lovebirds?" he joked, sipping the hot brown liquid his wife handed him.

"Out looking at other birds." Paula rolled her eyes.

"It's late," Rachel remarked uneasily, reflecting on the

disappearances she knew about. A few minutes later, her fears were proved groundless. Two radiant beings rushed up the stairs.

Jan held Anna's hand. "Mams, Paps—Anna and I wish to be married. As soon as possible."

The parents froze. Rachel watched as Paula ran across the room to embrace her brother and her friend.

"That's wonderful," she exclaimed. "It will give us something to celebrate."

"But—" Mr. Posner began softly, his voice full of concern.

"Abraham!" was Mrs. Posner's quiet remonstrance. The couple and Paula were too involved in congratulating each other to hear her, but Rachel did. "Be practical. This could save his life. The sooner they marry the better, before the Nazis can ban it."

The couple looked at Mr. Posner, awaiting his verdict.

"My only concern is for the young lady's family. It isn't exactly a good time to marry a Jew, particularly when he's been stripped of his inheritance. But your mother accepted me when I was poor, and I see that Anna has said yes."

Paula disappeared for a moment, and brought out a tray with tiny crystal glasses. They toasted the couple with a long-stored liqueur that sang of herbs on a summer meadow.

Jan put his arm around Anna and drew her closer. That gesture made Rachel ache for Michiel. If she could only hear from him, just one more postcard . . . But they had never imagined a real future together. She had been so sure her parents wouldn't let her marry him that she had never allowed that.

Mr. Posner had slipped away for a moment. He whispered to his son as he gave him something.

Jan turned back to Anna. "For you," he smiled. "Hold out your hand." When she did, the diamond ring sparkled in her palm, a star coming out from behind a moving cloud. Jan put it onto her finger.

Mr. Posner smiled, too. "I've been keeping it hidden. Are you really sure your family won't object to your marrying a Jewish man, Anna?"

"My father is a pastor. We hold prayer meetings every Friday night, while you have your Sabbath." Rachel saw Mrs. Posner flinch a little. Anything short of a High Holiday usually went unnoticed in their household. "Every Friday, as long as I can remember, we've prayed for God's chosen people to have their own home. A place where you could finally live in peace and safety."

Both the prayer and the idea seemed far-fetched, but for that moment the Posners were reassured, agreeing that the wedding should take place as soon as possible. Anna and Rachel left together, arm in arm. Anna's face glowed the way sunrise transforms the sky long before dawn breaks.

Rachel squeezed her friend's arm and said, "My mother would love to help you with your dress, I'm sure. Come over tomorrow afternoon. Unless you think your own mother—"

"No," Anna laughed, still giddy. "I'm sure she'd rather not struggle with it."

They breathed in the evening air as they stopped on top of a curved bridge. The canal reflected the bridges ahead and behind them, the echoing forms shadowy and wavering in the silvered water. "Look up, Rachel, a star! It's a good omen."

It certainly was for Jan, since marriage to a Gentile would put him into a less vulnerable category. Rachel thought of Klara's brother's problem. The answer was right beside her.

"Anna, do you remember Klara from school?"

"Of course." Her face was puzzled.

"Could you pick up a package for her brother and deliver it? It's something he really needs."

"Of course. What is it?"

"I'd rather not say. It could get you into big trouble. It's a matter of delivering something, waiting, and then taking it to Klara. It's probably better if you can honestly deny that you know what it is. Let's go to my house for a moment to pick it up." Could she ask this of a woman right before her wedding? But a man's life could be at stake.

"Of course, as long as we can make it quick. I'll take care of it before I come to visit you tomorrow. Just give me the addresses with the package. I'll be at your house after lunch, once it's done."

✕   ✕   ✕

Rachel was sure her mother would object to the interfaith match, but Rose saw eye to eye with Mrs. Posner, and took over the important matter of the wedding gown with pleasure. "I have a dress we can alter. I've hardly worn it."

By 2:30 the next day, Rachel was beginning to fret about Anna. Had she been stopped? *What will Jan think if he finds out that I put her in danger?* For an hour, Rachel sat by the window and watched the rain make concentric circles on the brownish canal. Apart from those plops, the tree reflections were like mirrors, but they gave her no comfort. The carillon's music barely reached her.

"What's wrong with you? She's only a little bit late," Rose said.

Rachel kept worrying. Every outdoor sound made her jump. At 4:00, she at last heard a knock.

"I'll go!" Rachel shouted, flung open the door, and threw her arms around Anna. "Are you all right?" she hissed.

"Of course. When I got to Klara's, her brother started telling me all about how worried he is about his sister. He asked me to keep an eye on her once he's gone, that sort of thing. I couldn't cut him off. But here I am!" Rachel's relief was as intense as Anna's enthusiasm while they bustled upstairs to Rose's dressing room, its walls covered equally by English chintz and bookcases.

Rose kissed Anna, ordered her to shed her plain cotton dress, and handed her a cream silk party frock from Rose's youth.

Anna, normally so serious, giggled as she slipped it on. Rachel held the pins as her mother took in a tuck or two here and there. For the first time in weeks, Rachel was fully absorbed in something other than her work. She basted in the alterations while Rose piled Anna's hair on top of her head. A few gold locks cascaded down her neck.

When Anna stepped into the dress, her fine figure transformed it from merely pretty to beautiful. The gently form-fitting top ended below the waist, where the skirt flared out, falling to mid-calf. Gold undertones in the cream set off Anna's finespun pale blond hair. She looked with wonder at the shimmery skirt.

Rachel couldn't believe her eyes. "Mams, how did you do it?"

"It's not just the dress and the hair," she replied. "Anna's in love." Rachel turned away. *If Michiel came back, he would hardly recognize me, I look so different,* she thought, and felt tearful. *Stop it,* she told herself. *Be happy for Anna.*

✕   ✕   ✕

Within the week, the Posners and their guests gathered at City Hall on a cloudy but bright spring day, wearing their best clothes for the first time in months. Jan's unruly hair had been temporarily tamed, and he looked less ungainly in a suit. Paula was dazzling again, wearing the diamond earrings her father had given her for her eighteenth birthday. "Someone's coming to meet us," she said, and pointed at a tall figure a block away.

The woman walked confidently toward them in a long, gray coat that fit her as nothing ever had before, her golden hair visible from afar, her white teeth showing as she laughed. The thin man whose arm she'd taken laughed, too. "Is that Anna?" Jan whispered to Rachel. She squeezed his hand and nodded. Michiel had loved her as deeply as Jan loved Anna, but what good did that do her now?

After the brief ceremony, they all signed the register, and dined at one of the few remaining Jewish restaurants, which produced real, tender lamb and a proper cake from somewhere. Rachel suspected that Mr. Posner had sold hidden diamonds or art to pay for the occasion. She tried not to think about a corrupt Nazi officer buying them at a high price to dress up a Dutch traitor.

Anna's parents sat next to Rachel for the wedding supper. Rose and Jacob shook hands with them, praising the bride's beauty. Commenting on the flowers adorning the table, Jacob recounted how he and his father went cycling in a daffodil field shortly after they arrived in the Netherlands. "The gold reached all the way to the horizon, and they smelled so sweet and sharp. My father picked one to show me. 'See the Star of David?' he said. 'This must be Holland. The flowers don't even mind looking Jewish.'"

After more stories, the pastor turned to Rachel and said, "We've all been busy lately—Anna and I, and perhaps you too?" Rachel's antennae quivered. The rumors could be true.

The pastor raised his glass.

"To Anna and Jan—to their future together!"

X   X   X

Rachel often thought of Mr. de Jong the vegetable man and wondered where the Nazis had sent him, but she knew better than to ask anyone. When Rose and Rachel had called on his wife, it had been awkward. The best way to help her was to buy as much of her produce as they could. Nobody had anything fresh for sale, and the market looked like an old garment, worn-out and lackluster. Mrs. de Jong kept up appearances at the vegetable stand in front of the Portuguese Synagogue. She looked skimpier despite being in the food business, but her striking head of gray hair still looked elegant.

"It's the latest fashion," she said sarcastically. "Everybody's wearing those yellow stars."

"Can you believe they make us *buy* them?" Rachel asked, forcing a smile. Everyone was complaining about it.

Mrs. de Jong sorted through the withered turnips. "Here, these have sprouted. It will give you a little green. Of course we have to buy the stars. Otherwise they wouldn't make any money from them. Don't forget the penalties for carelessly pinning them on rather than sewing them." Mrs. de Jong snorted.

Trying to enter the spirit of the occasion, Rachel added, "Yes, and of course we have to launder them to keep them clean and bright." They shook their heads. It was easier to joke a bit now that a chilly spring had lured the daffodils and early tulips out of hiding.

But the star wasn't funny. That morning, she and Rose had sat down to the aggravating task of sewing them onto most of their clothes. A meter of mustard yellow cotton was printed with stars stamped with JOOD written in a pseudo-Hebrew script. Before, Rachel had been able to slip around the city anonymously. With the star, she was exposed. When she was making deliveries, was she safer with her new false papers without the J and no star? If she carried her real papers and wore the star, she was legally correct and could recognize other Jewish people with a nod and a smile, but she would be subject to heightened scrutiny. *I can't win,* she thought. You were supposed to wear the star everywhere you went, over your heart.

✕ ✕ ✕

Rachel's underground contact at that time was Janneke, an unemployed librarian. Tall and lanky, she could pass unnoticed in a crowd, with her typical graying blond hair and nondescript wardrobe. She had resigned from her job when she was ordered to remove any book considered hostile to the Germans. She drew the line at John Dos Passos. "I told them I was sick," she'd told Rachel. "I persuaded my doctor to give me a notice about female trouble that required me to quit." A wry smile illumined her face.

"Why didn't you resign in protest?" Rachel asked. They were standing by the doorway of an empty house, looking out on the drippy gray scene outside. At least the trees showed the hazy pale green that presaged real leaves.

"Because I want to do underground work until they catch me. There would have been no point in being imprisoned or shot first."

"But don't you have a good chance to survive the war if you're careful?"

Janneke's face hardened for a moment. "Think of how many leaders you've worked with in these last few months, Rachel. We do rotate, of course, but . . ." She paused. "Enough of this. Here's something for you." Rachel took the papers and left.

The rain was warm, but pressed by a mighty wind from the North Sea. She quaked as she tried to keep the umbrella from inverting. Rachel was on foot, through no choice of her own. The Nazis had banned Jews from riding bicycles and using public transportation. She couldn't flee as easily, and her overall pace was slower. She reminded herself how important the packages were to those who received them, as she thought for the millionth time about the dangers. Her insides tensed and her feet stopped feeling the ground.

She thought, as she had many times, about the men the Nazis rounded up in Jonas Daniel Meijerplein in February last year—especially Jaap. When Rachel closed her eyes, she could still see the Nazis forcing the men to hold their hands over their heads while squatting on the ground. How were the butcher and his wife managing after the death of their only child? Was Bet still safe in her basement? If so, she would have lasted longer than any of Rachel's contacts. Remembering all that made her feel more vulnerable than ever. Now that Hitler had successfully attacked the Soviet Union, he looked invincible.

In case anyone still had valuables, the Nazis had ordered all Jewish people to turn in all their precious stones and silver, artworks, and anything else worth more than 250 guilders to the same Jewish bank that held their other assets. The deadline was the end of June. Rose was already assembling a credible amount to turn in, and planned to hide the rest. "They'll let me keep my wedding ring, and a fork, a knife, and two spoons for each of us. Aren't they generous? I'm keeping this silver bracelet on no matter what they say. It was my mother's, and that's that."

X   X   X

A few days later, Jacob arrived to lunch in a rush, flapping his napkin as he sat down. "Did Mrs. Schelvis say anything to you about leaving?"

"No." Rachel had known her father's plump, expert nurse as long as she could remember, and she almost never took a day off.

Holding out a note, her father sputtered so much he could hardly speak. "She says here that she'll be gone for at least a year."

"Paps, her son is a communist, remember? A union man. She probably decided to go underground with him."

"I always thought Mrs. Schelvis was so sensible! She's not just the nurse, she keeps the records and does everything else."

Rose was bringing the soup tureen to the table, an elegant container for meager contents. "I'll help you," she said. "It would take my mind off things. Even I can only read so many books."

X   X   X

When Rachel arrived home late one day after a long delivery, her mother was furious. "Do you know what time it is, Rachel? Your father is half-starved and so am I. It's bad enough to have to cook these scraps, but to overcook them . . ." And she went on, until they had the food on the table. The full hour's carillon melody flowed into the room as she lit the candles.

"What happened, Rachel?" Her father at least was interested in the explanation.

"I'm sorry to be late," she began, tasting the mushy vegetables. They stuck in her throat. She invented a quick but credible reason, then asked her mother what was upsetting her so much. Surely she knew Rachel wasn't at fault for being late.

"They're going to cut off the phone next week. How can a doctor run an office these days without one?" Rose's voice was high and harsh. "Just four Jewish doctors in all of Amsterdam will have one. What if someone has a heart attack?"

"Calm down, Rose. Hitler will never win in the end. We have to stick it out, just the way my brother is." Jacob had actually raised his voice, which was rare.

"Paps, maybe you're right. But what if you aren't? Other Jewish people already escaped to Switzerland or England or Palestine before the Nazis came, or they've started to hide until the war is over. Won't you at least think about it?" She couldn't stop now.

Jacob started to interrupt Rachel. "But—"

"How can you not see it? They've herded all the Jewish people from the provinces into Amsterdam. They've made us wear the yellow star. We can't even go fishing in the river anymore. We have a curfew. Kids have to go to all-Jewish schools. They're sending Jewish people away. What are you waiting for before you'll believe we're in danger?"

Silence fell. Rachel had never talked back to her father. She usually disagreed with him politely, after cooling off. He looked astonished and angry. Rose's quick breaths sounded loud in the quiet room, but she didn't speak. To her embarrassment, Rachel knew tears were on the way, and swallowed hard. She said, "I didn't mean . . ." but she did. They all knew it.

"I'm waiting for sanity to return to my own family. Excuse me." Jacob put his napkin beside his barely touched plate, and left.

Rose turned to her daughter. "Of course we should consider hiding, but you know I'll never leave your father." Despair settled on Rachel like fog. She was going to be forced to make a choice. Her mother was still talking. "If you want to go underground, I understand, and I'll help you if you don't have the contacts already." Rachel jumped back, surprised. "I still know people, my dear. If you set something up, there's a chance your father would agree to keep us together—especially if he loses enough patients. We can't count on it, though. His heart would break if anything happened to you, Rachel, not to mention mine. Of course you can't tell me what you're doing, but be as careful as you can on the streets with those Nazis roaming everywhere. I know I've said it before."

Rachel looked into her mother's eyes and saw the pain and knowledge there.

"I'll try to be careful, Mams." In her own mind, she added, *But they might not get me out on the streets. They might come for me here.*

JULY–AUGUST 1942

Deliveries continued, but with even more caution than before. Even so, the Green Police were spotted on the corner while she was making a delivery, and Rachel was dragged down into a basement and crammed into a wardrobe to hide. At first, the five men in it didn't trust her, but she convinced them to. As they waited for the police to break into the house, Rachel registered that her thin belly was pressed against another woman's surprisingly full one. *What are they feeding them down here?* she wondered. *Black market steak?* She hated the way her formerly well-cut clothes hung on her body. Then the shock of pounding boots overhead. The woman struggled to put her arms around Rachel, who squeezed her back, their embrace more intimate than any hug since Michiel's. Her skin yearned for him, even in that moment.

One hand slipped from behind Rachel's back and tugged on her fingers so she could feel the woman's rounded stomach. Oh. She must be pregnant, not eating luxuries. No one wanted to hide a pregnant woman, with the prospect of labor and a baby with its unpredictable noise. She must have to conceal her situation from the men, but she wanted someone else to know. Rachel first put the woman's hand to her own cheek as she nodded, then guided the mother-to-be's short finger to trace her smile. The finger felt soft, light, encircled by a ring with a cut stone, maybe a diamond.

Above their heads, the boots ran up another flight of stairs. Before long, they would descend—how far? The two women touched foreheads and noses. They breathed each other's breath. A baby, Rachel thought. Wouldn't it have been wonderful to have had something of Michiel left inside her when he disappeared?

She sighed. What a disaster it would have been if she'd gotten pregnant. Apart from her parents' reactions, working against the Nazis would have been impossible after the first few months. If she could finally convince her parents to go underground—since the raids were ever closer to home—nobody would agree to hide them with a noisy baby. Still, Rachel wanted a tiny being floating in a sea within her, the promise of its whole life ahead. Nothing but a little skin and muscle separated her empty womb from the full one in front of her. Their foreheads touched as they listened to the steps pounding high overhead. Wildly, Rachel longed to know the woman's real name, the one her mother called her, not a false name scrawled on a forged identity card.

The police boots crashed down from the second story to the first. Something smashed, possibly china. The thin man's spine flinched with each step. The invaders were swearing. They tramped to the rear of the house, above the wardrobe.

"Hey!" Someone bashed the basement door open. "What's down here?"

Breathing became panting. An acrid smell filled the wardrobe. Someone must have peed.

One policeman started down the stairs. They creaked as he descended. Rachel tried not to breathe when she saw thin wisps of light on the wardrobe's back wall, where his flashlight leaked through the fissures in the door. Had he seen it, or was he focusing only on the steps? *At least the baby hasn't been born,* Rachel thought. *It could get us killed.* She shivered, remembering that infants had sometimes been smothered to avoid giving adults away. The other woman tightened her embrace.

"Damn!" the policeman yelped. The woman and the thin man jerked.

"Anything down there?" A shout rang down.

"You can't stand up. Damned roof nearly knocked me out!"

"Don't be such a sissy. Have a look around."

The injured policeman said he would, but in fact they heard no movement at all. Maybe he'd decided it wasn't worth risking another bump on the head.

"Not a thing," he reported.

"All right, get back up here. Let's try next door."

The police stomped out the way they'd come. No one moved inside the wardrobe. The woman whispered, "Sometimes they come back."

We'll suffocate, Rachel thought. Instead, they waited. She thought of Michiel, of carillon bells getting ready to ring the curfew out over the darkening canals. Of her parents. What if she disappeared? They would never recover, even if they lived through the war.

At last, the thin man spoke. "I'll open up, but everybody stays by the wardrobe. No lights till the girl's out of the house." As he unlatched the door and stepped out, the others stumbled into the basement.

"You can't let her go out there, with police all over the place," the pregnant woman protested.

"They'll be gone soon. She shouldn't risk being out after curfew."

Rachel breathed in the musty basement air. After the stultifying wardrobe, it smelled delicious, the breath of life. She said, "I'll leave the envelope with you and get out of here. But I want another address along this street. If they're after me, I need a place to go if I can't make it home." She spoke with more bravado than she felt.

"How far do you have to go?"

"Six blocks." Her parents would be waiting for her, wondering why she was out this close to curfew. If only she could persuade her father to hide, too.

"I'll give you an address before you leave." Of course, why say it in front of all these people who could be arrested any time?

"I'm going now," Rachel announced brusquely. Her legs trembled as she searched her bag for the envelope. "This is for you. Good luck." She held it out in the direction of the man's voice. The light weight left her hand.

"Wait." The pregnant woman found her in the dark and hugged her again.

"Thanks—" Rachel paused.

"I'm Rebekka. Rebekka Feinstein."

"Take care of yourself." Rebekka—her grandmother's name. Rachel wanted to reciprocate with her own, but she was still alive, free, and she wanted to stay that way. What if these people were captured?

The man preceded her upstairs, and they picked their way through the broken objects in the hall with the help of dim light from outdoors. What a relief to be out of that basement! How could people live without light and fresh air? But they were—Jewish people, underground workers, and Gentile men drafted for labor in Germany—despite the fear of being discovered in systematic, street-by-street raids. Some neighbors would turn them in for money.

At the door, the man began to speak. "Listen, I'm sorry—"

"Forget it," Rachel said. He opened the door to the gentle sounds of the murky canal, the staccato of cool rain falling on water, and the wind in the leaves of the elm trees that lined the city's canals.

She could clearly see the man's gaunt face now, his alert eyes and tense expression. Giving her an address, he said, "Go quickly."

Like a diver, Rachel plunged into the cooling evening. Her pale blue dress was drenched with sweat. Despite her shivering, she took care to look brisk, watching for nooks where she could duck out of sight before she came to the safe address. She'd tell her parents that she'd been at a friend's house. That usually worked. Then Rachel took refuge in remembering Michiel, their long walks and bike rides, their entangled bodies.

He'd never believe that I'm working for the underground, she thought, rushing toward home past the clean doorsteps abutting the sidewalk. *He was the activist, not me. I liked talking about politics, not risking my life. Not then.* As it rained harder, she moved faster.

Suddenly, movement in the next block, by the fragrant bakery on the corner. She caught her breath. Two men, side by side, their cigarettes lit. One tapped ashes onto the street. She was too far from the next address to go there.

As she darted into a narrow alley with simple workers' housing blocks behind the canal houses, Rachel remembered her instructions for the thousandth time. Don't run. Take a deep breath. Notice everything. Months after Eva's death in prison, Rachel still heard her voice: when you're afraid, think of someplace calm. She imagined herself in the safely enclosed courtyard of the nearby Begijnhof, where she and her parents had sought the first signs of flowering snowdrops every year before the war. Overhead, she registered the beating wings of a broad-winged heron, the sound repeating like quickly exhaled breaths.

Five minutes later, the men had moved on. The rain stopped. Rachel patted her unruly hair back into place. The Westertoren carillon began to play the short but glorious melody reserved for the full hour. In the waning light, Prinsengracht's restless waves churned. Then she heard the tolling that ended the music. Eight o'clock.

After a few more quick paces, Rachel turned onto the lane bordering the much narrower waters of the Lauriergracht, as straight as a seventeenth-century surveyor's tools could make it. A few steps along was her own doorstep. She pulled out the key, let herself into the entryway, and locked up again. If the police broke down this door, where would she and her parents hide? How absurd to feel safe simply because she was at home. Her spine slumped, then straightened up. Her parents would need her good cheer.

Rose bustled down the stairs, wearing her favorite English tweed skirt. Her face looked haggard. "At last! We've been worried." She inspected her daughter's sweaty, mussed-up dress, wrinkled her nose, and recoiled instead of the usual warm embrace. "Where have you been?" Lowering her voice, she whispered, "Whatever you're doing, Rachel, be careful. And don't tell your father." Rachel nodded and rearranged her face. Her mother wasn't as blind as she'd hoped. Then, at normal volume, Rose said: "Go take a bath, then come down and drink something hot with us."

Rachel nodded again. She climbed the narrow stairs after her mother to get to the living room level. Because its door was cracked open, Rachel spied part of her father's slight, anxious face tilted upward as Rose said, "She's fine, Jacob, just tired. She'll be down in half an hour . . ." He came out anyway and bent down to kiss his daughter's wet forehead. He was still dressed for work, everything about him immaculate including his well-trimmed goatee, but his long, kind face and wide-set brown eyes were marred by worry.

"At last you're home," he said. "I keep hearing about girls being bothered on the streets. With the raids . . ."

"I'm sorry, Paps." Then she fled to take a bath. Was he finally taking the situation more seriously?

At last, when she sank up to her neck in soapy water, Rachel breathed deeply, closed her eyes, and relaxed. She wanted to dissolve away her own sweat and everyone else's—except Rebekka's. How different their bellies were. Rachel's pelvic bones formed thin ridges under the water, with a sagging hollow between. Michiel used to love her ample body, but it had shriveled.

Her hand floated below her navel, which rose and fell with her breath. As her pores drank in the warm water, her dreams resurfaced.

What might life be like after the war—if she survived? She sipped her fantasies like strong gin. Other people her age moved away from home in normal times, but she couldn't imagine a house she would love more than this one.

She let herself taste the fantasy that somehow Michiel might return to her. Her tongue barely touched the sweetness, but then she couldn't stop, and let her thoughts go further. She imagined that the Allies would win. By then, her parents wouldn't even care that Michiel wasn't Jewish. It wouldn't occur to them that he could have been her lover. Somehow, they would find each other. Rebekka Feinstein would come to their wedding, and propose a toast to Rachel because she'd risked her life for the underground. After a suitable time, a little girl would be born, another Rebekka. As the soap bubbles sank into the cooling water, she let herself believe.

✕ ✕ ✕

When Rachel met with Janneke again, they agreed things were getting worse. The Germans had demanded four thousand Jews, a record number, to send east for labor. They raised the age for the draft to fifty. Many new addresses were needed to help the men hide. News from outside the country was equally grim: Hitler had overrun Minsk. Stalin was calling for a scorched-earth policy, which meant inconceivable suffering. Even so, the Nazis had advanced into the Ukraine.

Frequent raids made Jewish people frantic. When too few men appeared at the appointed place and time for the labor draft, the police rounded up seven hundred more to fill the Nazi quota. All kinds of false papers—identity, exemptions, and ration coupons to keep people in hiding alive—were needed more desperately than ever. If she were caught with hidden documents, Rachel would be shipped off to Westerbork like others she'd heard about, or imprisoned and even tortured. The sweet talk or little tricks that had served her well before might well not work anymore. Her fate depended more on luck than ever.

X   X   X

"I can't let my parents go to that Westerbork Transit Camp by themselves," Paula said. Her eyes had lost their radiance, and her dress hung loosely in the wrong places. "They look so much older. The idea of them in a work camp! It's ridiculous, and it could be dangerous."

On that sticky hot Saturday, Paula had come to say goodbye. She and Rachel talked quietly, sitting side by side on the bed where they'd once giggled and whispered their dreams to each other.

"Paula." Rachel squeezed her hand. "Your parents love you. They want you to get through this. If you go with them—even though you still haven't been called up yourself—what can you really do to help them?"

"At least they'll have a few laughs. I can try to keep them out of trouble. And Jan is safe for now because of Anna." Her eyes darted around the room.

"We don't know what happens at Westerbork, and you might end up in Germany, or even Poland. Nobody knows."

"The Jewish Council is sending out lists of what to take to Westerbork, so they must think it's OK. I can't let my parents cope on their own while I'm somewhere safer. So this is goodbye for now." Paula pulled a little package from her small black leather purse. "I brought you something." Rachel opened it slowly.

Of all the gifts Paula could have chosen, this was the best: Mrs. Posner's multicolored Venetian glass necklace. The girls used to try it on sometimes, as a special treat. The light pooled and swirled in each bead. But Paula's leaving was unbearable. For Rachel, a star would be extinguished.

"Let me help you fasten it."

As Rachel touched the necklace, her fingers pinched the beads, and one of them was sharp. She pressed it hard, grateful for the distracting pain. She could not speak.

At the door, she asked one last time, "Are you sure?"

Paula nodded. Their farewell was muted. Only when she closed the door after her friend did Rachel notice the blood on her finger where the glass had cut it.

X   X   X

A rare meeting of underground workers to discuss the raids was running late. Rachel whispered, "I should go," to the host, Mr. de Vries, a short man with a slight hump on his back. It was 7:35 on a warm July night and her parents would be beside themselves if she wasn't home before the eight o'clock curfew. Without a bicycle, she had to allow more travel time. Since she gambled with her parents' ultimate peace of mind every day, at least she could avoid smaller infractions. The telephone had long since been cut off, so she couldn't call to let them know she was safe.

Across from Rachel, a man said, "The Westerbork Transit Camp is so close to the German border. Maybe they're going to send them to work in the nearby factories. All the German men are on the front."

"In the last raids, they took away women and children, too. What use would we be in the factories?" a young woman with a perpetual frown asked.

Rolling his eyes, Walther, an outspoken socialist, roared, "It's property they're after! What else?"

Rachel pointed out that all Jewish assets over 250 guilders had already been transferred to Lippmann Rosenthal Bank long since, as well as the land and personal effects of value. What more could the Nazis want?

"All that fine furniture the rich German Jews brought with them from Berlin," Walther answered.

"Just a minute," an icy male voice with a German accent interjected. "We've been warning you about the Nazis since 1938. Most of us had to abandon everything to come to Amsterdam. We thought other Jews would take care of us . . ."

"And we have," another man responded. "We've done nothing but collect money and food and everything else for you for the last four years. All you do is complain." His face tightened.

"Excuse me," Rachel said. "Aren't we all here for the same reason? To get as many Jewish people safely hidden as we can." She looked at her watch. Suddenly, it was too late to go home. Her breath fluttered, but what could she do? The meeting broke up, and those who lived nearby scattered quickly.

Mr. de Vries invited her and Walther to stay in his two humble but immaculate rooms, where the meeting had been held. He was once a tailor, and said his wife had died several years before. Rachel could sleep on the overstuffed living room couch, and Walther could use the bedroom floor. Rachel had to accept the fact that she could not get a message to her parents. Despite the warm evening, she helped the tailor close the dark curtains and windows tight for the blackout.

At one point, Walther puffed out his chest. "I'm sure they'll come after me," he said proudly. "The right-wing Dutch police never did like radicals, and they have a new excuse. Lots of comrades are already in prison."

"Prison"—a word Rachel tried not to think of. If she had only her own safety to consider, she would have scurried through the streets to get home, and taken her chances. She winced when she thought of her parents' worries. But if she were caught, she knew too much now. No matter how hard she worked to scramble the addresses in her mind, she couldn't get rid of them all anymore. Her nightmares regularly included an interrogation in which she spilled everything. At least she knew only fake names rather than real ones.

Rachel cleaned her teeth as well as she could in the basin, and sought out the toilet down the hall. It was quiet by then, 11:00 p.m. She was uneasy in the hall by herself, but comfortable curled up on the sofa. She was drifting off to sleep when she heard a vehicle screeching up the street. She jolted to a sitting position. The noise halted about half a block to the north. "What's that?" She got up and headed for the window.

The tailor appeared in his pajamas. "Don't open the curtains!" However, a bay window at a slight angle allowed them to peek out of the long slit between the blackout curtain and the glass.

A police vehicle halted, spilling German Green Police everywhere. Dozens of them. Rachel involuntarily grabbed the tailor's hand, and he held it tight. "The boy's asleep," he whispered. "If they come up here, we'll have to try to hide him. And you." But where, in this tiny space? After all the chances Rachel had taken already, would she be rounded up like this, more or less at random? Her breath beat percussively inside her chest, like a sob.

Nearby, the Nazis were pounding on doors and ringing bells. Two of them smashed through a lock. Moments later, a screaming woman carrying a toddler was thrust into the street. A tall policeman slapped her hard, and she staggered before he thrust her and the child into the back of the truck. A man, apparently her husband, rushed out to join her with a suitcase, probably prepacked per the Jewish Council's instructions.

Rachel realized she must be breaking the old man's hand. She tried to release her grip, but could not. The tears on her face were cold and strange, like someone else's. How she wanted to look away, as the street filled with people in their nightclothes, some grasping at the sleeves of their captors, apparently trying to bargain. At any time, the Nazis might knock on the door downstairs.

A girl about five years old held her mother's hand and obediently climbed into the truck: a child Rachel might have helped to save. Somewhere deep within, in a moment of brutal, intuitive clarity, she knew the girl would never return. The life force inside Rachel surged into another deep knowing. If she avoided being captured that night, she had to hide and take her parents with her, whether they wanted to go or not. She quaked when she remembered how she had been trapped in the wardrobe with six other people while the raid went on overhead. She couldn't take any more. She could not have lived with herself if she had let the Nazis run over her country unchecked. But she was not Janneke; she was not going to work to save others until she was killed. She had a life to live, and she was determined to live it, somehow.

The police were hauling a man by the shoulders of his trench coat. Her own shoulders shrank upward as the Germans tossed him in with the others. Hands reached out from the back of the truck to try to cushion the blow. The tailor wrenched away his hand, made a gagging sound, and sagged onto a nearby chair. Rachel rushed to give him water, as though it could wash away what they had seen.

"What's going on?" Their rumpled, half-dressed companion emerged from the bedroom. Neither Rachel nor the tailor could answer. Walther rushed to the window, tore open the curtain, and gasped when he glimpsed the scene below. Rachel ripped the cloth out of his hands and closed it instantly. "Are you crazy? They'll come after us if they know someone's here."

"But they're taking people away! We have to stop them!" He rushed back to the bedroom to dress. Rachel ran after him, hissing, "No, you can't! You'll get us killed!" The tailor followed her.

Walther's excitement glittered like a sparkler. He sat on the bed to get on his shoes. "Come on! At least we'll put up a good fight." He glanced up at them as one hand pulled out the tongue of his shoe, and he eased in his heel.

Rachel calculated quickly. He couldn't be reasoned with. That she knew. He would tear out of the door on a rampage. The Nazis would gun him down and storm the building. She and the tailor would be on that truck in less than half an hour.

Walther's eyes were downcast, his hands busy with the other shoe. She did the most difficult thing Joost had taught her. She hit Walther as hard as she could, full in the face. Blood spurted from his nose, and he shrieked. The tailor sprang from behind Rachel and muffled the terrible noise with his hands.

"Keep him still just for a minute," Rachel ordered. Walther was in so much pain that he couldn't react yet. She seized the advantage, pressing directly on his carotid artery. He slumped in an instant.

She recoiled, shaking as if she were in the truck going over cobbled brick.

The tailor went to the window. "You saved our lives."

Rachel looked at him across a vast distance. She could not speak. Walther—thankfully still breathing—had fallen back on the bed. His blood had stained her dress, his shirt, and the little rug by the bedside. It was sticky underfoot when Rachel stepped back. What had she done?

"Come and sit down. I'll get you some coffee." Mr. de Vries led her back into the living room and over to the couch, where she sat slumped with shock. In the far distance, she heard him wash his hands and make the coffee.

After the wave of adrenalin, Rachel felt very, very sleepy. Drinking too much alcohol must feel like this: her extremities and her thoughts were floating clouds touching a hilltop for an instant, then blowing off and touching another.

Someone was touching her hand—oh yes, a nice elderly man. She sort of remembered him. "Drink this," he told her, and guided her hand around a hot mug. But she'd rather sleep, she was so tired.

He cupped his hands around hers and raised the mug to her lips. Something sweet touched her tongue. Real sugar.

As she was about to drink, she thought of her father, and sputtered the hot liquid out. "I have to go home!" she announced desperately. "They'll be so worried."

"Drink this, and don't worry. You'll go home in the morning." The man kept raising the sweet hot drink to her lips, then eased her onto the pillow and talked to her quietly. The tale he told entranced her in spite of her worries, and soon she fell asleep.

When Rachel woke, Mr. de Vries was sitting beside her, holding her hand and dozing. "Where am I?" she asked in alarm, waking him. He reminded her of the night before, more fantastical than a legend, and drew the curtains to reveal the newly risen sun. Rachel, seeing the blood on her dress, remembered. Then she looked at the closed bedroom door.

The tailor said, "I'll see to him. He'll be happier if you're not here when he wakes up. People pay to have their Jewish noses redone; you did it for him without charging a guilder. Go home and reassure your parents."

Thank goodness her raincoat would hide the bloody stains on her dress. She had to get home as soon as possible, and it was a long walk. She tore herself away from the tailor after thanking him as best she could. The Germans were an orderly people with an excellent card index compiled and kept by the Jewish Council. They would catch him the next night unless he hid, but that was up to him, not her. It was her own family she had to save now.

The journey home through the warm, sunny morning was a blur. Running would attract attention, so she walked as fast as she could. When police were ahead, Rachel slowed to the pace of a busy woman doing an urgent domestic errand. None of them stopped her. Finally Rachel heard the Westertoren carillon's sweet middle notes carried by the underlying boom. Could she find a place for herself and her parents to hide where they could still hear the bells? Who might help them? Convincing her father would be the real challenge, although his arguments had shifted. The night before her meeting, they had argued again. "How would we live in hiding?" Jacob sounded incredulous. "Where would our food come from? It's completely impractical."

Hustling along the brick sidewalk, Rachel hoped that her story of the raid would persuade him. What would she say about the blood on her dress? Finally, her own gable stone appeared: the figure of the woman with the anchor and the bird poised over the word HOPE. Rachel ran the last few paces, unlocked the door, and shouted as loudly as she could, "I'm home!" Then she sat down on the bottom step and wept, but not as hard as her father did when he ran down the stairs and held her in his thin arms. Rose leaned over him to kiss Rachel's head. "I thought you'd be all right," she said, "but your father has been out of his mind."

Rachel pulled back from Jacob's embrace to look at him— unshaven as she'd almost never seen him, his eyes swollen, his cheeks strangely hollowed. He clutched her arms, trying to find words.

They stood together, and then Rachel held her father rather than the reverse, feeling his bones and the trembling in them. *This is what it will be like when he's an old man,* she thought. *If he lives to be one.*

"Paps, I'm so sorry. We have to talk." Her words were muffled against his shoulder.

"Yes, we must."

The three went upstairs into the morning light. The sunlight sparkled on the canal, glorious and indifferent. Rachel was grateful for it, now that she was home.

Before taking off her coat, she said, "I'm afraid my dress is ruined."

"You were attacked?" Jacob bolted out of his chair. "What happened?" His face was wrinkled with worry and lack of sleep.

"I was with friends," Rachel began. Her mother gave a thin smile. "One of them had a bloody nose, so I stayed to help him. Suddenly it was too late to come home. I knew you'd be upset, but they've started raiding Amsterdam South, and I was afraid to leave."

Jacob started to speak, but Rachel held up her hand. "No, Paps, it isn't a rumor. I was there overnight, at Mr. de Vries's, an old man who was kind to me. We saw it happen. We saw the Nazis break into buildings, drag people out, and put them on a truck—even children." She waited to hear her father's shocked protests.

Instead, he said, "I know. One of my patients from the Jewish Council told me something big was planned. That's why I was so afraid last night. I thought they had taken you." His voice shook again. "We can never go through another night like that, your mother and I. We have to go into hiding until this is over."

Rachel and Rose turned to him, openmouthed. "What did you say, Paps?"

"We have to hide."

At last! Rachel thought, and said aloud, "I'll start looking for a place. And I know people who might help us."

"No, no." Jacob shook his head dismissively. "We already have a place; we just have to make contact. Wim told me about it."

"Wim?" Rachel and Rose asked together. Their Gentile handyman seemed the unlikeliest person to help.

"He was already thinking that we might need to hide." Jacob regained his composure as he sipped the hot brown liquid. "He told me he had a cousin I might want to meet, Els Brinker, at 452 Elandsgracht. I asked if she was ill, and started to make a note. He shook his head and said, 'Don't write it down. Just remember the address. She has a nice big basement, and she likes guests. You can trust her completely.' I didn't understand at the time."

Suddenly, Rachel longed to be in her own room and go to bed. Her body felt thick. She could hardly move. Rose read her face and said, "Good, that's settled. You can rest in a minute, Rachel. Everyone's used to your going out every day, so you can call on Mrs. Brinker later today. Since we aren't allowed to visit Gentiles anymore, take your false papers—don't look at me that way! I know you have them—and of course don't wear the star. After you rest, we'll have lunch, and then you can go. And as for you, Doctor, I've never seen you look so peaked and disheveled in our married life. Shave before you lie down, please. I won't have whiskers like that in my bed."

Jacob and Rachel let themselves be led upstairs, he to his shaving mirror and she to the tub. By that time, Rachel's fumbling fingers couldn't undo the buttons on her dress. Her mother helped her undress and wash as if she were a child. "You were doing some underground work, weren't you?" Rachel nodded. That much she could safely say. "That's what I thought. Bloody nose? I wasn't born yesterday, even if your father was."

Rachel hardly spoke as she found her way to her clean bed with her mother's help. As she was dropping off to sleep, the Westertoren played the musical phrase of the half hour. *Elandsgracht,* Rachel thought. *I hope it's better than the basement where I was trapped in that wardrobe last week. Maybe it will be cozy like Bet's. Elandsgracht is just two blocks away, but if we're in a basement we won't be able to hear the carillon.* Outside, the canal would be shimmering in the sunlight, reflecting the delicate elm leaves overhead. *A basement.*

X   X   X

"Find out as much as you can," Rose told her daughter. "A basement could mean anything. And of course settle the costs. Remember we don't know how long we'll be there, so the less the better." How strange that her mother would leave this to her. She must be afraid of what she might find.

The two women sat with Jacob over a late post-nap lunch, eating dry bread with a few slices of Leiden cheese and preserves from the back pantry.

"I'll go this afternoon as soon as I do a few errands," Rachel answered. Minimally, she had to let Janneke know to make other provisions for her duties. People were vanishing so much more often that it might not matter, but she didn't want her contact to think she was yet another person who disappeared into the night and fog.

When Rachel left home, she turned around and looked at their house, at the sculpted gable stone which had seen some ships wrecked, others returned. After telling Janneke the news, Rachel was surprised to feel at least as much relief as regret. More people might volunteer for underground work now that the urgency was clearer. Many Gentiles were hiding from the draft that now applied to both working and unemployed people, which meant more were willing to offer addresses—but it was already too late for so many Jewish people.

As she had so often before, Rachel searched for an address, this time for her own family. How long would she be able to walk freely? At most a few days. Could that house be the one? It was neat but small, two stories tall with a glass shop front on the ground level, and a hardware sign. So often, the safe addresses belonged to people who didn't have much themselves. Two such houses could easily have fit into her home on Lauriergracht. What would the basement be like?

When she rang the bell, a tidy Dutch housewife answered the door. Els Brinker stood at Rachel's height, with graying gold hair and a serene face. Underneath her hazel eyes, her cheeks still looked pink. That boded well for the food supply. The curved white collar on Els's yellow dress had been starched and pressed. Rachel introduced herself with her own name, and Els invited Rachel through the storefront to the kitchen at the back of the house. It must have been scrubbed an hour before. They sat at a neatly set table.

Els came right to the point. "Don't come until Friday evening; our current guests are moving that morning if everything goes smoothly. Tell your parents that I'm stricter than a lot of people—I don't allow guests upstairs, not even at night. But we haven't lost anybody yet." They agreed on a price that was more than fair. Since Jews were prohibited from moving household goods or traveling, someone else would pick up three suitcases from Lauriergracht the night before the move.

Rachel walked home as the light became gentler, approaching the evening. The Westertoren's music sank into the silvery waves scattered by the winds, but she barely heard it.

✕   ✕   ✕

In the past, they had brought their suitcases down from the attic for holidays or weekends away. Choosing what to bring had meant delicious anticipation—a bathing suit, a party dress for a fancy dinner, presents for Great-Aunt Sophie and her daughter.

This time, the cases gaped open on the guest room bed. Rose was in organizing mode, to Rachel's relief. "It's a basement, remember, and we could be there all fall. So pack a sweater."

"That won't be enough for the winter," Rachel protested. "What about coats?"

"We won't be going outside," Jacob replied, "and the war may not last much longer. Let's use the space for blankets instead; we can wrap up in them." So one suitcase was assigned to blankets and sheets. Rose slipped four of Jacob's grandmother's rose-patterned china plates between the layers, explaining, "They may ask us to share with someone else. And no matter what the food's like, at least we can eat it on something beautiful."

After they had selected warm nightclothes and a few changes of day clothing, they had at least twice as much as would fit in the cases. Once they had decided on the clothing, each sorted again to see what else they would need to sustain life, beginning with paper, pens, and toothbrushes for them all. "Let's share a hairbrush," Rachel proposed. They added a razor for Jacob, and a single compact of powder and lip rouge for Rose and Rachel. Next, they had to choose among books. Rachel went first, and grabbed two comfort books from childhood (fairy tales and poems), a Dutch English dictionary, and *The Complete Shakespeare*. At least she could improve her mind while her body lay idle. Finally, Rachel clutched at a few essential objects: her bunny Paul, who had never left her, and the necklace Paula gave her.

"I know what will keep me busy," Jacob said. He disappeared downstairs, returning with an immense tome. "My anatomy text," he explained. "I always meant to review it."

Seeing its size, Rachel groaned. "That's all you get, Paps."

"I can read it for days if I have to. Otherwise, I'm ready. I already sent a note to Dr. Fink to let him know he may see some extra patients. They know to go to his clinic any time I'm out of town."

Meanwhile, Rose issued another order. "Rachel, go downstairs and get the Diamond Workers' Union Library copies of Tolstoy and Turgenev, and *Middlemarch*. I can't leave them."

At last three leather suitcases rested on the bed, bulging but closed: one for household goods and linen; another for books, toiletries, and light clothing; and a third for everyone's heavier garments. Then Rose and Rachel assembled the cash they had hidden from the Lippmann Rosenthal Bank, and the diamonds that might also be essential currency one day.

"Let's not put diamonds in the suitcases. We hope the carrier is honest, but who knows if he is?"

"Or she," Rachel added quietly. "Let's split the stones up. That way, if we're separated, each of us will have something." Rose spilled them onto a dark blue blanket, their sparkles making it like the midnight sky. Jacob counted the stones out among the three of them.

X   X   X

"I'm starving," Rachel said after the preparations were done, and Jacob nodded.

"Isn't there champagne somewhere in this house? Mr. Feldberg sent it when his baby daughter's fever finally came down."

Rachel and Rose prowled through the kitchen like thieves, and tossed items onto the table like spendthrifts. The pantry held nothing except a few potatoes—and luxuries like champagne and their favorite smoked eel, a gift from the fish merchant who had undoubtedly been shipped off to work for the Germans. The unusual indulgence in champagne went right to their heads. Rachel had never seen her parents tipsy before.

"So we get to drink the precious champagne!" Jacob raised his glass to it. "If I'd known that, I'd have suggested that we go underground earlier." He took a sip and refilled his wife's half-empty goblet. Rose's hearty laugh sounded a few registers higher and louder than usual.

Rachel giggled, then put her hand over her mouth. But she was still laughing and could not stop. A little spit bubbled and hissed between her fingers as she tried to quiet down.

At that moment, they heard a loud knock on the front door. All three went silent. Rose reached for Jacob. Rachel suddenly felt stiff and sober as she asked herself, *Is that the police? Were we one night too late? Or is it the carrier?* After an interminable few seconds, two more knocks rang out, the signal. Everyone exhaled.

X   X   X

After a restless night, the two women cleaned the house thoroughly. Once the floors were scrubbed, the furniture dusted and polished and the rugs beaten, Rachel helped lock up the armoires, having ensured that the linens were well stored and would not be attacked by insects in their absence. They'd agreed to leave as late in the day as possible without violating the curfew.

When Rachel came downstairs at the appointed hour, she found her parents already waiting for her in the foyer. They didn't look at each other, or at her. "We're going out," Jacob said quietly. "If we're stopped, I am on my way to visit a Jewish patient—let's say Mr. Da Costa. That's why I have my medical kit. You two know his wife, so you are accompanying me."

Rachel turned her head sharply toward her father. At least he was thinking ahead. She put a light jacket over his left shoulder, then grabbed a shawl and sweater for herself and her mother. Rose gave a quick nod. All three stayed a moment before the threshold, feeling behind them the weight of their beloved house, and its smell of beeswax and dried roses. Rose stepped outside first, then Rachel, then Jacob, who turned the key in the lock. After sticking for an instant, it clanged into place.

They walked the few paces along Lauriergracht in silence. The canal shone softly in the late light, rippling gently in a breeze more like spring than August. Although Rachel had sometimes noticed the houses opposite theirs, she'd never tried to memorize every detail before. One leaned so far left that the inhabitants must have grown up crooked. Next door, a square gable stone showed a draper's carefully folded cloth. The late afternoon light coated the rosy brick and gray stone facades with a pearly sheen.

As they turned into Elandsgracht from the Prinsengracht, Rachel showed the way to Mrs. Brinker's house, squeezed between taller homes on either side.

"This is it?" Jacob asked. Although his patients came from all kinds of circumstances, Rachel knew her father had never lived any-where as humble as this shopkeeper's dwelling. He swallowed as she nodded, and put his arm around Rose. At home, she had busily gone through the motions, with one brief outburst of tears. Now that her work was done, the house packed away, and their belongings win-nowed and organized, she looked lost. It hurt Rachel to see it.

She again remembered the basement where she'd been crammed into a wardrobe. What would their hiding place be like? How would her mother cope, much less her father? Rachel gulped in the fresh air as deeply as she could before ringing the bell. They waited. Was Els away? Had they been betrayed? Footsteps sounded from inside. The door opened enough to let them into the dark shop. They could hardly make out the figure who had opened the door.

"*Goedenavond*. Let me show you the way," Els said, "and then we can have light."

They shuffled behind her through the shop to the kitchen, whose blue-checked curtains were closed.

"I was expecting you," Els said unnecessarily, looking to Jacob and Rose. "Rachel, introduce me to your parents." They shook hands courteously, attempting to smile.

"Before you sit down, just in case, let me show you the way to the basement. Doctor, I'll put your satchel down there. If anyone comes—if you hear anything at all from the front of the house, go downstairs as fast as you can." Rachel had expected this, but saw Rose and Jacob draw back in revulsion.

Els rolled up a rug near the stove deftly, and took a flat-bladed, heavy spatula from the counter. "It's right here," she indicated. "Between these two boards, you can pry up the hatch. It's safe, no hinges at all. We haven't lost anyone from this house, and they've come twice already to look. It's cramped down there, but I think most people would rather be a little confined and worry less. I cer-tainly would." She headed through the opening and down a ladder, then must have put the satchel somewhere below. In an instant, Els's gray head popped up again. The basement couldn't be very tall. Rachel tried to dismiss her vision of a smelly, dark hovel where they would have to crouch for years.

"Let's have tea, then, not the real thing of course," Els said briskly. "I'm sorry there's no more coffee, and sugar's hardly to be thought of." Their hostess reheated the water on the stove, and set four cups on the table.

"I have a little sugar in my purse," Rose offered. They sat down, and she produced a small, sealed envelope.

Els protested, "If that's all you have, why not keep it for a rainy day?"

Rose's mouth twitched. "If this isn't a rainy day, what is?" Each stirred a few grains into the fragrant mint tea. It tasted fresh and alive.

"From my garden," Els said. "The mint likes the shade, and it keeps growing."

Jacob had hardly said a word.

Els turned to him. "Wim said you're an excellent doctor. I'd like to consult you sometimes about people who get sick in hiding. Of course we couldn't bring anyone to you, but you could tell us what to try."

Jacob nodded, but his "Of course" sounded hollow.

"Paps, you always said you could practice medicine on a desert island."

"Let's call it that," Rose put in. "Let's call this our desert island. Fortunately, the natives are friendly."

Els's laugh lit her austere face. *Good,* Rachel thought, *our lives depend on this woman's carefulness and goodwill. If we can make her laugh, we're safer.* Els said, "Let me tell you a little about life on the island. I can't provide cooked food for you myself. Someone will bring you groceries—such as they are—every week or so, with anything fresh she can find. She's a friend of mine from grammar school. I trust her completely, and sometimes let her come downstairs to bring the food if the coast is completely clear."

Rachel worried about how long their cash might last. "But we thought you'd include food in the price."

"I did. Don't worry," Els interjected. "People charge three times as much as I do, or more. I'll show you how to use the electric burner, and I'm sure I don't have to tell you to be careful. The ceiling is low, so watch your heads when we go down."

Rachel knew it was time to face the basement. "May I help you with the dishes first?" she offered.

"Yes, and let's dry them and put them away. Leave the table set for two. They look for discrepancies like that." Moving her hands in circles to dry the plates soothed Rachel, as well as the look of the pale blue dishes against the yellow kitchen tablecloth.

"Why don't you three go down first—here's a flashlight—and once you move aside at the foot of the ladder, I'll follow and show you the arrangements. Don't bump your heads. It's not fancy, but you'll have what you need. At least for now."

PART II:
THE FAMILY IN HIDING

AUGUST 1942

Jacob

Jacob heard the summons to descend, but hesitated to approach the hatchway. His daughter met his eyes. Her serious face looked paler than he ever remembered. If one of his patients looked like that, he'd suspect anemia. Had he missed it? Would there be a way to send a blood sample out? Rachel's hair shone under the light that hung over the kitchen table, and she started down the ladder first. The night when he wondered whether the Nazis had taken her had been the worst of his life. Here, with any luck, they would be together and safe. However unpleasant the basement might be, Rachel would be less vulnerable than she would be anywhere on the street. She'd been out so much lately. Rose was the one he worried about. She hadn't lived in dirty conditions since she was a small child, and she had that streak of depression sometimes.

"Don't bang your head," Els reminded him. "The ceiling is low, but you'll get used to it." A creak sounded from the ladder, and Rachel disappeared one step at a time. Rose was right behind her, fidgeting. She probably wanted to get the descent over with. When they married, he'd given her a home with everything she'd ever wanted: shelves and shelves of books, a piano, space, and ultimately their child. How would she cope?

Even when Els looked at him pointedly, Jacob could hardly leave his chair. Her hazel eyes were kind but insistent, her graying hair pulled back from her face. This little scene—the green-shaded light overhead, the perfectly starched and embroidered tablecloth, the four chairs drawn close together—made him want to linger. However, he was the father, and it was time to dive into the basement.

The top rung felt slightly wobbly, but the next one was firm, and the next. Now his eyes were level with Els's waist; to be polite, he turned them instead to the cooking stovetop. Another step, and only the oven door was visible. Then the stove legs. When the kitchen floor was over his head, a raw, moldering stench thrust up his nostrils like two big fingers, inescapable. He felt the strange softness of the floor under his other foot. What could it be made of? Dirt. He heard Rose warning her daughter, "Be careful! You can't stand all the way up."

"Move along, Doctor, I'm coming down."

"Ouch!" He had cracked his head. The pain made his eyes water. The only light came through the hatch from the kitchen, so he could see almost nothing. But the smell! When he'd thought about hiding, he'd never imagined that.

"Over here, Mams. I think there's a couch." He heard them rustling. How could he live in a place where he couldn't even stand up straight? Els brushed past him. Surely someone would help them find a better environment if they paid more. He didn't want to hurt Els's feelings, but this wouldn't do. If it were only a question of his own comfort, he could stand it, but it wasn't.

A click sounded as Els switched on a lamp between an overstuffed chair and the couch where Rachel and Rose had perched. A cursory look showed that the furniture had seen better days. Even Els's head was inclined to accommodate the low ceiling. "The light helps," she said, "and so far we still have electricity."

Rose sat forlornly on the worn couch, with her feet resting on dirt rather than seasoned oak.

"Come and sit down, Paps."

"All right," he said, standing slightly taller to walk to her and immediately hitting his head again. "Ouch! What's that?"

"The beams supporting the kitchen floor, Paps. They're everywhere." He stooped over and crept to the chair like an old man. How would he do his exercises? He lowered himself gently, to make no sound. The brown velvet upholstery felt like dead moss under his hand, damp and yielding.

Els walked to the other side of a strangely low kitchen table, located behind the sofa. "We cut the legs down," she explained. "People were banging their heads when they got up from meals, and it makes noise upstairs." His satchel sat on the table. Els continued, "Rachel, I want to show you how to close the door from inside. I might be down here and have to run to the front door. People are suspicious of delays." Els led Rachel, their shoulders bent about equally, to the ladder.

"If I don't have time to close up, put your fingers here, and you can seal the hatch right over your head." She demonstrated, and it clicked into place. "Some people with guests lock them in, but I never do. That means"—she met his eyes, then Rachel's and Rose's—"that I am trusting you never, never to come out. They've raided us twice, and they will again. Your job is to stay underground and be quiet. Don't even think of escaping through the kitchen and over the back wall. You're much safer below, like mice." He felt his breath stop for a moment.

"*When* they raid again? That's a certainty?" Rose's voice, which had sounded almost chipper in the kitchen, was hollow.

"Yes. And they can make it just as bad for me and my husband as for you. They ship the hosts right off to the Westerbork Transit Camp along with the Jews and anyone else they're hiding. So we all need to be sure you aren't found while you're here. Is that clear?" They all agreed.

Jacob shifted to the couch to be closer to Rose. His daughter settled in on his other side, making the springs give way. He'd only wanted to protect her and her mother, and hadn't thought beyond that: what it would be like to be prisoners, or where the food would come from, how his shirts would be washed and ironed. He took Rose's chilly hand. Every day, she had kept his life in order, but here she would be helpless.

Els held the keys to their very survival. Who was she, really?

He said, "If you don't mind my asking, who else lives in your house?"

"It's just my husband and me now," Els replied, sitting on the edge of the armchair. "My two daughters are living with my niece in a village in England, away from where the Germans are bombing."

"Oh, good. Can you tell us about the arrangements here before you have to go back upstairs?" Rachel asked.

Els's voice was low. "Of course. I've put some bread and mint tea on the shelves for tomorrow morning's breakfast. More food will come tomorrow, and maybe some coffee substitute. The cistern has water for you to wash with; drinking water is in the jug. Beyond the ladder and behind that curtain, there's a bucket. I'll empty it for you every day. Keep the lid on, of course." No toilet? How could they keep conditions sanitary enough to stay well—especially with no hot running water? The cold from the floor was soaking through his shoes.

Once she'd showed them how to use the electric burner, Els continued, "Jacob and Rose, your bed's beyond the kitchen. I tacked up a curtain to make it separate. Rachel, you're in the opposite corner, near the ladder. It looks like a sleeping mat on the floor, but there are wooden planks under it to keep out the damp."

"Rachel can't sleep on the floor." Jacob blurted out the protest before he could stop himself.

"It's the best I can do." Was that a hint of frost in her voice? Rachel was looking daggers at him, so he bit his tongue.

"Of course, Els," his daughter said. "There's just one little thing, if you could possibly manage it. Could I have a curtain to put up around my bed, too?" Rachel hadn't sounded this timid for years, almost as if she were begging. He had to get them out of here somehow. How could he find another address—especially without offending Els and Wim?

"I'll look in the attic. That's where I got those," Els said, gesturing toward the sofa and chair. "They were my mother's, so I could never bear to re-cover them, even when the velvet was getting worn."

Rose produced a smile that looked forced to him. "It's just what we need. I love my mother's things, too."

"Shhh!" Rachel hissed, and he looked around wildly, but saw nothing different. "Didn't you hear that noise? I heard steps on the floor overhead."

"It's nothing, just Jan," Els said, "but I'm glad you're paying attention. Don't ever make a noise that's loud enough to carry upstairs."

She can't mean that, Jacob thought. *What if I sneeze, or snore?*

Els said, "They can come any time, and some of them know how to be quiet. For now, the basement is all yours. But we may have to hide someone else down here. You know how much worse the raids are lately. People who wouldn't have thought of hiding before are looking for addresses. I'm on my way now, but I'll be back in the morning. I'll make three clear raps on the floor so you'll know it's me." She disappeared upstairs. The hatch closed and the rug swished into place.

Jacob inspected Rachel's bed more closely and saw that it wasn't quite as bad as he'd feared. In the dim light from the kitchen, he made out a thick, low platform that looked quite solid, even if it wasn't a real bed. This time, he remembered not to stand up straight.

"It's all right, Paps. I can manage. We're all tired. Why don't we just unpack a few things, and then we can rest?"

He agreed. Perhaps tomorrow would be better.

Rose was still sitting on the sofa, her expression as vacant as if she were in a poorly lit railway station at midnight. What was she thinking? In a minute, she went behind the curtain, and propped it aside with a chair. He went to help her open the cases on the bed, but she shooed him away.

It seemed to take forever until she'd assembled the basic night things, and Rachel arranged a basin where they could wash their faces in the cold water from the cistern. No one had the energy to heat it up. Jacob saw Rachel bumping into furniture clumsily from sheer exhaustion before she retired. He waited until she and Rose were settled before he extinguished the kitchen light. The blackness was like that of a cave, absolute and damp. Feeling his way along the table, Jacob listened for Rose's movements and breathing, and let them guide him.

At long last, Jacob could get into bed with her. Every day, he looked forward to this moment, and in that one way, tonight was no different. The bedsheets felt clammy and thin, but it was still a relief to climb in and slip toward sleep after the strain of the last few days. As he had for so many nights, he rolled toward Rose, who lay on her back. Her breath was rapid and shallow. She didn't turn to him. Lying on his side, he put his hand lightly on her nearer shoulder. Talking would serve no purpose when she was so withdrawn. Sooner or later, she would soften to his touch. Fatigue sank into his bones, as strong and sure as an opiate, and he felt grateful for it. If only they could do something about that moldy smell.

Just as he began to relax, Jacob jolted to alertness, wondering if the Feldberg baby had croup again. Then he remembered—he couldn't help her anymore. He stretched his cool leg against Rose's warm one.

The day before, when he'd searched for his anatomy text, Jacob had seen his office as if for the first time. He had expected to spend the rest of his life there. For a moment, he had sat still in his chair, creaking but still functional, from his father's medical office in Germany. The sturdy oak seat turned easily, if squeakily, on its wheeled base. His father couldn't have imagined leaving his home to hide in a basement, for any reason. What were conditions like now for Rab and his family? Had the Allied bombing forced them out of their home? It had been months since the last strange coded letter.

At least Jacob hadn't collaborated with the enemy like some doctors. He hadn't even told Rachel and Rose when he decided not to respond to the call for Jewish doctors to certify men's fitness for the work camps in Germany. If he had allowed even one man to go, it would be on his conscience now. Who took care of their medical needs now that they'd been shipped off? Nazis doctors, no doubt, pressing people to hard labor whether they were well or ill. *But I can't help them.* A deep peace stole over his soul. He was ashamed of it. *All I can do is be here with my daughter and my wife, and care for them as well as I can.*

Yet doubts still nagged at the edge of his conscience, like flitting bats: If he had believed Rose's fatalistic predictions, could they have escaped from Holland altogether? Weariness overtook him, and he gathered an unresisting, sleeping Rose into his arms. His thin legs felt the warmth of her full thighs under the duvet. He buried his face in the tangled hair at the back of her neck, and could not help but smile.

Rose

Rose felt Jacob's absence the next morning before she heard him and Rachel a few feet away in the "kitchen." It was so dark that it must still be night. All she wanted to do was sleep until she could finally go home. But the other two were already talking softly, and she could hear every word. The pillow smelled as if it had been moldering here forever. If the basement was this cold and damp in August, what would it be like in November? Surely they'd be out of here long before that.

She stiffened at a slight creak from above.

Rachel whispered to Jacob, just loud enough for Rose to over-hear. "That's Els, I'm almost sure." Muffled voices drifted through the floor, then a faint bang as the door closed, just over Rose's head.

"It's better if Mams sleeps," Rachel said. "There's not much to do. We're going to get so bored." A good point. What could they do down here except wait to be taken away?

"I've always been too busy to be bored. Let's set up a washbasin on the table. I need to shave."

Shave! What for? They were buried in this mausoleum for days, or even weeks. All her energy had fizzled out. Sealing up the house was her last act for a long, long time. Now it was a waiting game.

Jacob and Rachel banged and rattled around. They were making so much noise. Rose, her head under the pillow, finally got back to sleep, by imagining that she was walking along the Amstel River with Rachel discussing new dresses, then with her father on her way to the Diamond Workers' Union Library, or . . . Some hours later, Rose got out of bed. Her feet touched the cold earth. Earth, not a floor. She put on her shoes (no space for slippers in their luggage).

She needed to pee desperately. What would her mother have said about this smelly prison—an expensive one at that? They should have gone to London as soon as they heard about the rampage against the Jewish Germans on Kristallnacht, four years ago. Rose imagined all three of them at Aunt Sophie's country cottage, eating the fresh vegetables her cousin Claire loved to grow. Fresh, crunchy carrots, beets with hearts like a tree's inner rings, lettuces soft as rose petals. Claire probably had a houseful of children sent to the countryside from the bombed cities. Rose ached to see her cousin's face, to taste one of her rich sweet cakes, redolent of rum and raisins.

She emerged into the kitchen area just as a definitive series of three knocks from above announced Els's imminent arrival. That was all Rose needed—a guest before she had used the so-called toilet. She squeezed past Jacob and Rachel and vanished behind the curtain shielding the bucket, but knew her noises would be audible throughout the basement. This was intolerable.

Rose heard the nearby squeak of the ladder as Els descended, all too close to the bucket. The hatch thudded closed, and something clanged nearby.

"Good afternoon," Els said. "Here's some more drinking water and food. Rachel, I found this old piece of blue cotton to use as a curtain. I'll help you rig it up if you like."

She and Rachel were standing just on the other side of the ladder, with only the curtain around the bucket separating them from Rose, who could barely keep her balance. She could smell yesterday's urine. How long could this go on? Her bowels absolutely refused to cooperate. She'd have to wait until later. Replacing the lid without smashing it down hard was a chore.

"Is your mother ill?" Els was asking Rachel.

Rose had no choice but to emerge. Only Jacob normally saw her undressed, before she had brushed her hair. "Good morning," she said, heading directly toward the improvised basin to wash her hands. Inspecting Rachel's so-called curtain, she winced at its flimsiness. Why had the last "guests" really left?

Els stepped in her path and detained her. "Mrs. Klein, it's not morning anymore. You need to get up every day at the usual time, make your bed, and bathe and dress. People who don't do that"—she looked meaningfully at Rose's getup—"lose heart and get careless. And when someone gets careless, we're all in danger."

Although she had almost never wanted to hit someone, Rose would have lunged at Els if their lives weren't dependent on her. How dare this woman speak to her that way? Els was their landlady, and yes, she was taking a risk. But Rose was not a child to be told what to do. She felt herself redden to the roots of her hair. Rose looked at the walls, then at the hatch. She could be up there in an instant. If she was shipped off somewhere, she'd make sure the Nazis got this petty tyrant, too.

Jacob put his arm around Rose, standing as tall as he could manage. She trembled against him. "My wife is exhausted," he said quietly. "She just needs a few days' grace." *A few days!* She'd never change her feelings about this hellhole. Even the tiny, dirty flat where she spent her earliest years had been worlds better than this. On that teeming island near the Waterlooplein, they'd had a proper privy, not a makeshift bucket. And there were windows, light, air— you could go outside and breathe, walk by the river. She had never wanted to go back there, but this was worse, worse than she could ever have imagined. Rose felt as if she had been sent back to the very worst part of her life. Soon, there would be rats.

Els said, "More food will come later today or tomorrow. Here are a few canned things if you need them. And remember, no noise, even if you think I'm alone in the house. That's how they almost caught us once. Let me have that bucket. I already put the clean one by the bottom of the stairs." Els left as abruptly as she had come. Relief at last. After her rage, Rose felt almost drowsy.

"I'll help you get dressed, Mams."

"Why? Leave me in peace. I just want a few minutes to wash myself, that's all. It's freezing down here."

"I could heat some more water." Why was Rachel being so nice all of a sudden? Rose saw pity in her daughter's eyes, and she hated that. Once washed and dressed, she sat at the kitchen table with a broken china cup of mint tea. She held it to her nose to counteract the basement smell. The warm liquid felt good going down, and the taste was intense and fresh.

In their normal life, Jacob had usually been right about her dire predictions. The boiler hadn't blown up just because it hissed; Rachel hadn't been expelled from school for playing cards during her French class. This time was different, with their very lives at stake. Her anger about Jacob's insisting that they not leave Holland rose again, but she had to stifle it. There was no point in excoriating that good man, her husband.

Rose sighed deeply. She looked at his thin, anxious face, and Rachel's fuller, weary one. At least they were together. Their house hadn't been raided before they could hide. Maybe Els wasn't so bad. She went back to the bedroom, propped the curtain between it and the kitchen aside so she'd have more light, and heaved a suitcase onto the bed. As she opened it, a whiff of the lavender her cousin always sent from England almost made her cry.

She mastered herself. Her husband and daughter were sitting where she'd left them. She absolutely must make an effort for them.

"What's on the menu?" she asked aloud. "Is anyone else hungry?"

Rachel and Jacob glanced at each other. The corners of their mouths twitched in just the same way. A few minutes later, under the bare lightbulb, she ate a few bites of tinned herring and stale crackers on the china plates from home. They tasted good.

$$\times \quad \times \quad \times$$

Over the next weeks, as Rose's energy slowly returned, she and Rachel put the kitchen and bedroom areas in some kind of order. Rose hadn't realized that the basement would always be dark except when the electric light was switched on. Even then, there were only pools of light, with twilight around the edges, and darkness in the far reaches. Els added a lamp with an extension cord for their bedroom, but they had to unplug the hot plate to use it. The only part of Rose's life that felt at all normal were her hours in bed with Jacob, although neither of them had touched the other except as two beings wanting each other's warmth. Making love had hardly crossed her mind, which was unusual, but Rachel was not even a wall away.

Rose began to listen to the orchestra of the house, instrument by instrument, determining the nuances of dangerous sounds versus innocuous ones. She watched her loved ones closely. Was it just the dreary lightbulbs, or did Jacob really look a year older every hour? His face was graying to match his beard. She hated to see him and Rachel stooping over to walk. Her daughter's back would straighten up again when this was all over, but Jacob looked as if the stoop had settled permanently.

The house was plagued by almost constant minor groans or ticks or squeaks. She remembered Els's warning: "The first time they raided us, they tiptoed in like gentlemen. The guests didn't hear them until their boots were right overhead. Always be so quiet that no one can hear you. As soon as you hear any visitors heading for the kitchen upstairs, turn the lights out. And cook when I do, in case any smells drift up."

While Rose chafed at living by someone else's hours, it did provide a certain routine. Although she had never been so unwilling to get out of bed, Jacob insisted on their waking early, prompted by an alarm clock tucked deep under his pillow. The first morning he used it, she was shocked. After a whispered argument, they agreed that he would rise within half an hour of the alarm, but they would stay together in bed first. At least he still wrapped his arms around her. When she came close and smelled his body, she could avoid the ever-present musty stench, but he didn't have his old fresh soapy smell.

When those first waking moments had passed, Rose would not allow him to rush her into their empty day. When she was lucky, she slipped back into a semi-dream state, in which she could wander through their old home like a ghost, watering the potted palm (how long until it died?), touching the piano keys, fingering the leather of her favorite chair, smelling the intoxicating mixture of chicken and celery floating up from the kitchen. Rose never tired of this dreaming, painting the canvas of her home back to life every morning.

"How about getting me some tea?" Rose asked as she slipped to the bucket. Seated at the table, Rachel was bedraggled and gaunt under the harsh light, but Jacob looked pinker as he sipped his hot drink carefully. He'd always hated to burn his tongue.

They both looked inquiringly at her, but she headed back to bed after her visit to the stinky bucket. In a moment, the steaming mug sat on the carton that served as a bedside table. Picking it up and cupping her hands around it, Rose felt the heat seep into her fingers. How could it possibly be warm outside, maybe even a sunny day? She inhaled the steam deeply. It was nothing like the teas they would have had in England—china cups redolent of the hillsides of sun-drenched Darjeeling, tempered with the milk of country cows—but at least it smelled of the world outside. She imagined Claire making tea for Aunt Sophie, on a tray with a few freshly picked roses in a little vase.

Jacob was talking about being a boy at camp. Maybe that was his form of escape.

"When did you go?" Rachel was asking her father. Rose realized that none of them could have a private word in the kitchen.

"After we moved to Holland. My parents didn't want me to lose my German, so they sent me back to a camp in the Black Forest."

Rose couldn't help smiling at the thought of her fastidious husband in a tent full of ruffians telling jokes and misbehaving.

"How old were you?"

"Eleven or so the first time, just learning to make a fire and handle a boat. The other campers are probably all Nazis now. I wonder how they'd feel if they knew they'd shared a tent with a Jew. We all exercised every morning at six, and I've kept up the habit over the years."

There's a lot she doesn't know about her father, Rose thought, and picked up her volume of Turgenev.

✕ ✕ ✕

Later that day, Els lingered for a few minutes after delivering water and food.

"Won't you sit?" Rose urged, hearing the plea in her own voice. Any whiff of the world outside was welcome, even Els.

"Just for a moment. The neighbors expect me to be home, unless they see me go out. If I don't answer the door, they could get suspicious." As Els eased her weight down onto the sofa, she winced with pain. "Arthritis," she said in answer to the unspoken query.

"Is something else bothering you?" Rachel asked. She was always a sensitive child.

"Yesterday a man in Looiergracht was sent to Westerbork because his guest couldn't resist coming upstairs for a midnight snack. They caught them both."

"Will they keep them there?" Rose asked. Wasn't Westerbork somewhere near the German border?

"Nobody knows. Most people seem to get sent on somewhere else, but a few find a way to stay right there. It's hard, but better than going on to the work camps. Well, I—"

Rose gestured toward the sack of food. "Thanks for the package. Could we meet the delivery person, just to say hello?" If only she could see someone else, even occasionally, she'd feel less trapped.

Even Jacob livened up at the thought of a new face. "We'd like to say thanks in person."

"I'll ask her." A full smile lit Els's face. "The danger wouldn't bother her. Just the other day she said it was boring to handle packages rather than people."

"People?"

"Getting them safely to hiding places like this. Not everyone is as organized as Rachel was when she came to make the arrangements with me."

Rose remembered that she herself had felt too busy—and too afraid—to visit Els the first time. Rachel had become so independent this last year or more. At first, Rose felt sure that there'd been a boyfriend, but after a while Rachel had looked so sad it must have ended. After that, she seemed busier than ever. *She must have taken me seriously when I told her that I'd have done something against the Nazis if I didn't have Jacob to think of. At least she had sense enough not to tell me what it was. So many people are in jail because somebody knew too much.*

Noticing Els heading for the hatchway, she whispered, "Come when you can."

"I'll do my best." Her foot was already on the bottom rung.

Rachel

Rachel felt a pang when Els's feet disappeared, the rug was moved back into place, and the sturdy table scraped the floor overhead. She settled on the clammy sofa beside her mother. The shadows from the overhead light were unbecoming, to say the least. Her parents looked like prisoners photographed for the warden's record. Just as Els had feared, the doorbell sounded. Her brisk footsteps first passed over their heads, and returned toward the kitchen with someone else's. Rachel got up and shut off the light. Her mother caught her hand and tried to detain her. Shucking her off, Rachel found her way to the hatch in hopes of overhearing a normal conversation. Standing under the ladder, she could decipher words, if not whole sentences.

"Should I—" The other woman began, but then spoke more quietly. Els was bustling between the cupboard and the stove, which made it harder to hear her.

"Why do—have to—?" said the unfamiliar voice, accompanied by the clinking of spoons and china. It was worse than trying to decipher the flickering signal of the BBC.

A grating sound directly overhead made Rachel's heart leap hard until she realized the two women were simply sitting down.

"Of course I knew he was Jewish when I married him! With a name like that, what would you expect? But it didn't matter then. His parents were socialists, and they didn't care about religion."

Rachel held herself still.

Els asked, "More tea? So what happens if you don't register?"

"He says they could—" Her voice dropped again.

"Do you need a place for him to go?"

"Go? But he's safe. He's my husband." Rachel thought immediately of Jan, of his arm around Anna, of the glow at their wedding. Would he still be protected?

"Tell that to the Nazis." Rachel imagined Els's rueful expression. "If I were you, I wouldn't register. If your husband needs a place to hide, I might know someone who could help him."

"Couldn't you help him, Els?"

"No, but I might have friends I could talk to." Rachel was shocked. Els was lying. Why? Then Rachel remembered how much more dangerous it was to help people you knew. She'd already begun to forget.

Els's friend was saying, "I hoped you yourself could . . . well, I'd better go."

The chairs squeaked again, and footsteps shuffled out.

X X X

The most anticipated moment of their day was listening to a radio Els had provided once she came to trust them. Either the clipped tones of the BBC or Radio Oranje from London revealed the latest moves on both sides, played at the lowest audible volume. Rachel and her parents gathered around the radio as if around a hearth, their heads close together. Queen Wilhelmina's scratchy, iron-filled voice exhorted courage, but why didn't she tell the other Dutch citizens directly to help their Jewish comrades? "We might as well keep the radio in plain sight," Rachel had said with a painful laugh. Why conceal it as they had on Lauriergracht? It would be a minor infraction compared to hiding.

SEPTEMBER–NOVEMBER 1942

Rachel

After they turned over the big newsprint calendar page for August, Rachel suggested that they take turns crossing off the dates. They marked the *X* after the evening supper, as if it were dessert to have another day behind them. Leafing through the pages, Rachel wondered who had x-ed out the months before their family arrived. The marks looked wobbly.

Each day, Els brought water and the news of massive raids involving hundreds of addresses. Desperate people struggled to get their identity cards stamped with an exemption. Rachel felt both sorry and glad that she wasn't outside helping people, although the deprivations of the basement wore on her. She craved light. Not a single ray came from anywhere but their few lightbulbs. Even with the additional lamp and cord Els had produced so she could read in bed, it always felt dark around the edges. The tiny windows just under the ceiling at the front of the house were papered over with thick black paper.

Despite the heater Els brought down as the nights got colder, the bedding never dried out. Els took the wash upstairs just a few garments at a time, always things that she or Jan could have worn. "I'm sorry about the sheets, Mrs. Klein," she said. "I can't change them more than once a month. One of our neighbors is already suspicious."

Rachel felt hungry all the time, except when she was actually chewing the potatoes or turnips or carrots, and for half an hour afterward. Her energy sank, and she saw her parents slow down, too. It wasn't long before Jacob had the sniffles, then was so congested that he could scarcely breathe. The snoring that resulted was dangerous. Within a few days, he passed the malady to Rose, whose red nose added color to her lackluster complexion. Rachel hadn't caught the family cold yet, but it was only a matter of time. They had to ask Els for more handkerchiefs.

Rachel took it upon herself to train her parents about safety precautions. Whenever they heard unfamiliar steps, she taught them to put a hand on the light switch. None of their three lamps could be left on without a person nearby. At first, if Els had visitors in the kitchen, they endured an hour or more of darkness. Eventually, Rachel asked Els to signal with two raps (easily concealed) if light was safe, and she agreed—as long as they never spoke above a whisper when anyone else was in the house. It was easier and safer to keep their voices low all the time.

The first time Rose sneezed out loud, Rachel jolted out of the chair where she was taking her second nap since breakfast. She and Jacob rushed over and said, "SHHH!" rebuking Rose as if she were a naughty child. Perhaps because she was sleepy, Rachel was the first to realize the absurdity of the situation and began to chuckle.

"This could be dangerous, and we have to keep it from happening again," Jacob said. "The sneeze is caused—" His learned disquisition started Rachel into peals of stifled laughter, which felt good even if it was silly. Another way to die for a ridiculous reason. After that incident, they reached for pillows rather than handkerchiefs when they sneezed or coughed. When Els witnessed this curious behavior, she relaxed visibly. "I did have a chat with the woman who brings your food. When I asked if she'd like to meet you, she said she was in so deep that it didn't matter if a few more underground 'divers' recognized her. She'll be here this afternoon."

✕ ✕ ✕

Three raps overhead, and Rachel rushed to the foot of the ladder, as if greeting a visiting dignitary. Her parents followed. Overhead, the table squeaked on the floor, the rug swished, and the hatch creaked. A pair of stout brown oxford shoes appeared on the top rung.

"Don't come down, Els," the woman overhead said. "I'll introduce myself." She descended swiftly, and pulled the hatch down over her head.

The woman was in her thirties, wearing a nondescript gray-toned coat. Her mobile face was surprisingly sunny, with a few lines where she had smiled again and again. Her head cocked to one side when she spoke, like a parrot's. She wore a little hat with a jaunty feather, the only distinctive touch in her attire.

"I feel like Alice in Wonderland going down the rabbit hole," she said with a mischievous grin, straightening her head enough to look at each person in turn.

"I loved reading that as a child," Rose said, extending her hand. "I'm—" But Rachel interrupted her. "No names, Mams."

"She's right," the woman said. "Just call me Connie. I'm going to call your husband Doctor Rabbit, and I'll have to decide about you two. Here's the food." Rachel took it and smiled. Connie smelled like the outside air. If only Rachel could walk outdoors, even in the dark, just for a block.

Connie set her bag down on the table. "They offered me a little extra meat at the butcher's for the same ration coupons. I couldn't tell whether they were really sympathetic, or just testing me. Just to be safe, I won't go there again, but meanwhile, here's a little beef for your soup. I bought a few pieces for my brother's kids, too. He has three little mouths to feed."

Rachel gestured toward a chair. "Yes, times are hard for everybody. Do you have a lot of addresses today, or can you stay for tea?" She remembered the pressure of having too much to do. It seemed like a dream now.

"Just for a few minutes." Connie sat suddenly. "If they catch me, better to be having tea with you in comfort than out there in the rain. What a day! This place isn't bad," she added as Rachel boiled the water. "Better than most except for the lack of light, but if you can't see out, they can't see in. So, what shall I call you? Let's start with you, young lady."

Her hands busy with measuring the smallest amount of mint that would produce flavor, Rachel spoke without thinking. "Rebekka," she answered, and remembered Rebekka Feinstein's bulging tummy against hers in that horrible basement wardrobe.

Jacob protested, "This is foolish when Els knows all of us."

"No, doctor, anywhere we can snip the chain, we must do so. And, Mevrouw, your new name?"

Rose said, "Marieken, after a dear friend when I was a little girl, who lived in a beautiful house."

Connie inhaled the steam from the tea. The mint scent swirled around them. "Just like my mother grows at her cottage in Friesland. But it sounds as if you grew up in more exalted surroundings, Marieken."

"Hardly. I grew up in the slums. My parents moved to Diamond Street as soon as they could afford to, to a small house near the factory where my father worked. Marieken had everything, but her parents treated her like a little doll."

"So you learned very young that money isn't everything," Connie said, putting her cup down. Rose nodded. The journey to the past had restored some liveliness to her eyes.

Jacob smiled. "And she acquired a taste for fine things."

"Other people in Amsterdam are as hungry as you are, and I

must go and feed them," Connie said, getting up. "Don't you have something for me to take upstairs?"

"What do you mean?" Rachel asked.

"A bucket?" Connie replied.

Jacob blushed. "Els usually—"

"Let's give her a break. Hand it over, Dr. Rabbit, you can't keep secrets from me." They had to laugh. And when she handed the bucket back down to Rachel a few minutes later, it smelled of disinfectant. Jacob nodded approvingly. Connie said, "I worked in a hospital before the war. See you next week—I hope." Only Rachel shivered.

✕   ✕   ✕

The following evening, Rachel sat engrossed in a game, using cards left behind by their predecessors. "What are you doing?" Jacob asked. She hadn't played since childhood, but it passed the time. The cards felt limp in her hands as she shuffled them. Someone else must have handled them many times.

"Solitaire." Rachel put a black ten on a red jack, and added a tic to her sheet. At least she could keep the fifty-two cards in order.

Her father said, "You need a game that makes you think. I wish I'd brought the chess set."

Rachel looked up immediately, as if she had smelled a roast in the oven, then sighed. "So do I." He'd tried to teach Rachel several times when she was a child, but she hadn't been interested beyond learning how to move each piece. She'd never taken the time to learn strategy or to practice. Then an idea came to her. The next morning, Rachel withdrew behind her curtain with paper, a knife, and a pen. With only filtered light, she worked on an old copy of the *Jewish Weekly*. With effort it became a chess set to present to Jacob, with its pieces folded neatly into a square board. Thoroughly absorbed, Rachel was startled by her father's hand tactfully reaching through the curtain to warn her of quiet footsteps overhead. Her heart hammered hard until she heard the two raps from Els. To calm herself, she returned to her project, sitting right beside the lamp so she could turn it off instantly. She decorated the outside of the board as though it were wrapping paper, with open snowdrops and the neat buds they emerge from. Her hands trembled until the noise stopped, but she kept on drawing.

✕ ✕ ✕

Rachel was awakened by someone shaking her, and the light blasting her eyes. Her breath stopped.

"What's going on? Did you all take a sleeping pill? It's the middle of the day." It was Connie. How had she gotten downstairs without Rachel's hearing a thing?

She sat up shakily. "You scared me half to death. Are my parents asleep, too?"

"I think so." They listened, and heard nothing on the other side of the room.

"Sometimes it's easier for us just to sleep. Tell me the truth." Rachel grasped both of Connie's firm arms and faced her. "What's going on up there?"

Connie whispered more softly than usual. "It looks as if they're trying to force every single Jewish person out of the Netherlands. The Nazis have upped the bounty for turning someone in, so the hiding places aren't as safe as they used to be. My brother says they're rounding people up from all over the city now."

"Your brother?"

"He—he drives a night tram."

"Not one of the trams that take people to the trains?" Rachel's mouth stayed open after she spoke.

Connie's voice was even softer. "He doesn't like the job, of course, but he has three children to feed, and they pay him extra. Two trains run to the Westerbork Transit Camp every night now. He'd lose his job if he refused. And if he didn't drive the tram, someone else would." Connie spoke as if she had rehearsed the arguments in her own mind.

"Does he know what you're doing?"

"Of course not. He doesn't talk much about his work, and I don't talk about mine. He's a nice guy. You'd like him. Maybe after the war, you could meet him and the kids."

"After the war?" Connie and her family might well be together. But Rachel and her parents? Who knew? "What's happening to the people who are sent to Westerbork?"

"The camp is packed, even though they keep shipping people east from there. Nobody knows exactly where they end up, but it's not good." She sighed. "I try not to think about it."

Rachel reminded herself that their survival depended on Connie, and she was a good person—wasn't she? The two were sitting side by side on the low mattress, like confidants. "Tell me. Why are you doing this?"

"Maybe I like excitement," Connie said, turning her face away. "Or maybe I can't let those damned Nazis get away with this." When she looked back, her eyes were glazed with tears. "Or maybe I can keep a few people off my brother's tram. Let's wake your parents up. It's not good for them to sleep the day away. And what if somebody else had tiptoed down instead of me?"

Jacob

The fact that Connie had let herself in without waking any of them disturbed Jacob deeply. He worried about it while a dog barked until dawn. It stopped just long enough for fatigue to start winning over worry, but the jagged noise resumed just as he was dropping off.

The barking was probably due to a neighbor's bitch in heat and not the Nazis, but who could be sure? Because the nights were often disrupted, he knew he was sleeping too much during the day.

The less good food they ate, the sleepier he became. He hated never feeling clean. He'd had a good hot bath every morning for as long as he could remember. Rose's hair was thinning out, and Rachel's nails were splintering. The radio spoke of horrendous roundups throughout the country. Even the Dutch Jewish work camps were being emptied so their inhabitants could be sent to Westerbork and beyond. It was hard to tell how much to believe the BBC's reports about the situation inside Germany. He was torn between wanting his brother to be safe, and wanting the Allies to win so life could get back to normal.

✕   ✕   ✕

One evening, to Jacob's surprise, Rachel handed him a flat, light square package made of decorated newspaper, and insisted that he guess what was inside. Flustered, he made a series of wrong guesses: A poem? A puzzle? A song?

"No," "No," and "No," Rachel responded, with a kind of glee he hadn't seen in her eyes since they arrived here. Rose emerged from the bedroom after still another nap. She yawned and asked, "What's that?"

Jacob unwrapped the flimsy paper package carefully. The last thing he wanted to do was disappoint Rachel by failing to appreciate whatever she'd made. Strange little paper squares revealed themselves; what could they be? When he saw the form of a chess bishop drawn on one, and the crown of the king on another, his chest opened. He said, "Oh, Rachel! Ebony and ivory chessmen, just for me!"

They settled down to play that instant. In his delight, Jacob checkmated his daughter in less than a dozen well-planned moves, which exasperated and hooked her. It wouldn't hurt her a bit to have some real competition for a change. As the days passed, Rachel spent the mornings playing chess with herself, trying out different strategies. She finally won against her father in their thirtieth game, and laughed aloud for the first time in days. He won the next, however, and Rachel fumed, "How did you do that?"

"I planned from the beginning. Let's replay it, and I'll show you."

As Rachel rearranged the pieces to the point where the tide had turned against her, Jacob heard Rose on the sofa, rattling a crumpled newspaper, probably the one the potatoes had been wrapped in. She was breathing faster. "Something in the news, Rose?"

"Nothing new or different." She almost spat. "But don't you see? From the beginning, the Nazis planned what they would do with us. We've only seen a move or two ahead. If we'd recognized it from the beginning—" Her voice rose, and the face she turned to them was blotchy red.

"Stop!" Jacob's whisper had the force of a hammer. "We mustn't think that way. We're together, and we are alive." He couldn't live with her anger in this small space. At home, after an outburst, he'd been able to withdraw to his office, or take a walk if he couldn't soothe her. Here, it was impossible. He was stuck in this basement, in clothes that were barely clean, sleeping on sheets which a beggar might have scorned.

Rose did not stop. She hissed on about the ships they could have taken. "If you had listened to me, we'd be in England right now. You even had connections in the Jewish Council. We didn't have to end up in this stinking basement!"

Jacob's mind was suddenly erased, blank. He felt nothing.

Rachel had gone over to put her arm around her mother. "Mams, please, don't. Please don't."

Jacob couldn't move. He stayed at the table, staring at the chess pieces.

Rose began sobbing deeply. Rachel stood and muffled the noise with her body, stroking her mother's head until she was quiet.

"I'm sorry," Rose whispered, as she reused her wet linen handkerchief. She dried her eyes, and nudged Jacob lightly as she headed for the burner to make tea. Her touch felt like a branding iron.

Rachel broke the silence. "Now, Paps, let's play that game again. Show me how you won, if you can remember." Rachel sat opposite him and looked up expectantly. His blood resumed its flow.

"Of course I remember." Then he showed her, move by move, how he had cornered her queen, then her king, until finally she had nowhere left to go.

X   X   X

Whenever the doorbell rang, everyone held still.

The sound was usually followed by the now familiar tones of the milkman or a neighbor. One day, Jacob heard a different noise: a clumping in the front hall, staccato voices, then an ominous series of steps. It had to be what they all feared most. The boots were tramping only a foot or so above their heads. As he tried to breathe more deeply, the fetid basement smell registered at the back of his throat.

Jacob's eyes were fixed on his daughter's. Though terrified, she looked defiant. Rose did not reach for him, but lowered her head. Her clasped hands trembled. Rachel flipped off the light. Doors opened overhead, and questions were barked out, as if dogs were talking. It seemed to go on for hours. He could do nothing, absolutely nothing, to help the two women he loved, except sit still. His every muscle vibrated with the tension of inaction. The police finally left.

Rachel cried with relief and turned the light back on, but Rose barely reacted. She just went to their bed and refused to get up for dinner—even though she must, like them, be starving. They had stopped talking about food; it was unbearable to think of real meals, and of the sensation they used to have every day, of feeling full of good food their bodies needed and could use. He and Rachel ate their root vegetables alone that night, almost wordlessly.

When Jacob finally joined Rose in bed, she hardly responded to his hand placed gently on her hip. He moved closer, and at last her body slumped toward his.

"My love?" he whispered. But there was no answer. She was asleep, again. Even while she was awake, Rose seemed to be miles away most of the time. She usually stayed in bed and pretended to read, even when he pleaded with her to get up. He often found her face slack and worn an hour later, the book askew in bed beside her.

X   X   X

Three welcome raps from overhead echoed through the basement. The sound could come any time Els was alone in the house to deliver their water, or very occasionally when she came down at night to empty the bucket. Today, she looked more tired than usual.

"Els, this must be awful for you," Rachel said. "If we all get through the war, we'll invite you over to eat cake and anything else you love." He was glad his daughter still remembered their house, even if it might as well have been on the moon.

"For now, we'll have to do without the cake. I brought you some food, though," she said, without explaining why Connie hadn't come. "Not much this week. It's harder to get anything but potatoes and these awful turnips. No meat, but herring is at least some help. I think there's enough for you to have some every day. You look a little sickly to me. How are you feeling?"

Even the thought of food flooded his mouth with saliva. To respond to Els's question, Jacob tried to put his clinical hat on. They were all thinner, he most of all, and a pallor had crept into their cheeks, even Rachel's. Rose rarely left their bed except when he forced her to.

Before he could answer, Rose said, "We're all right. Won't you sit down, Els? Please."

"All right, but briefly," Els replied. "Are you taking the vitamins I brought?" He nodded. Despite the bitter taste, he made sure the pills were taken each day. "And, doctor, I have a case to consult you about. Nervous collapse, I think they call it. It's a girl about twelve years old who won't speak. The people who hid her left her alone in an attic for three months."

"Bring her here," Jacob said. "I can treat her. Rose and Rachel can bring her out of her shell." Then he looked at his wife with her exhausted, shifting eyes, and his pale daughter, and wondered.

"It's too dangerous to move her."

"Then the best treatment is a secure routine, where she knows what to expect."

"Isn't that what we all need, doctor? I have to go upstairs now." Els stood up.

Jacob sighed. For a moment he had thought he would be a doctor again. He imagined his patients' faces, most probably taken away or hidden. After the war, they'd all come back to him, wouldn't they? But first he would go to Germany and find his brother. They would visit twice a year from now on, no matter what.

Trailing after Els, Rose walked over to the ladder. She looked like a little girl as she clung to the other woman's arm. This behavior was as strange as her sleepiness and silences. Only at night while she slept could Jacob feel close to her, even on the clammy sheets. What was happening to them?

Rose said, "Maybe one day we can really visit, Els, you and I."

"Yes," Els said, putting her hand on Rose's briefly but pulling away. "After the war."

DECEMBER 1942–MARCH 1943

Rose

Two people were whispering about a raid. Jacob and Rachel again, alarmed by every tiny sound, sure the Nazis would find them. Rose was barely awake. The night before, she couldn't sleep for Jacob's twitching. With any luck, she could catch another forty winks right now, and the morning would be over by the time she got up. If she decided to.

That must be Rachel rustling to boil water.

Just as Rose was drifting off, Jacob sat on the edge of the bed. She felt it sag, and his hand rested on her shoulder. "Rose, please get up. I don't want to start the day without you."

"Leave me alone." She wanted to be left in peace, especially if they were going to be raided soon. His hand felt heavy, and she shifted away from it.

"Mams," Rachel whispered through the curtain, "I can't find the tea. Do you know where it is?"

How could Rachel be so oblivious? It wasn't as if the cupboards were stuffed with delicacies. Jacob's face looked desolate. All right, Rose would get up for a minute and help. Lifting the musty sheets, she trembled with the chill. Her nightgown felt moist and smelled dank.

Rose found the tea and started to hand it to Rachel. Instead of taking it, she sank onto a chair by the kitchen table and wept, her head on her arms.

Rose put the tea down. She put her hand on her child's thin back. When had the flesh melted away like that? Rose could feel her spine. "Shh," she whispered. "You'll upset your father. What's the matter?"

Rachel blurted, "Can't you at least try? Don't you see how Paps and I feel when you don't get dressed? Have you looked in the mirror lately? Sometimes I think it would be better if they did find us. At least this would be over." Her head slumped back onto her arms.

"Don't say that! What do you mean?" Rose was stunned. Her daughter had everything to live for when the war was over.

"You hardly even talk to us. When we listen to the news, you don't crab about it the way you always used to. You never joke anymore. You're not even reading." She blew her nose.

Retreating to the bedroom, Rose switched on the light and sat on the rumpled bed. Would she ever have clean, pressed linen again? She reached into her useless purse and felt around for her compact. When she opened it, it released a puff of well-perfumed powder. She wiped a thin layer off the mirror, and looked at herself as she had not in weeks. Could that gray-skinned, wrinkled face be hers? She saw herself twenty years hence, resembling Aunt Sophie or her mother. Her cheeks had never been hollow like this. Five hairs had sprouted on her chin.

Rachel was right; she had let herself go. It was this terrible place, and the way it reminded her of life before Diamond Street, in the slum—the fetid smell no matter what you did to clean the dirt that couldn't be scrubbed out, the impossibility of personal hygiene. After the initial shock of being here, Rose had kept up her grooming routines at first, and she must begin again. Now, before she hurt Rachel and Jacob any more.

"Heat some water for me," she told Rachel, and sorted through her clothes until she found something that wouldn't hang as unbecomingly on her depleted body. In a few minutes, Rachel brought a chair with a pot of warm water and a reasonably clean towel. Shivering as she washed—so different from the delights of immersing herself daily in hot bath water—Rose asked herself how she could get through this time except by sleeping. One answer lay in books, just as it had after her infant brother died, and her once adoring parents withdrew from her.

Rose tried to remember how she'd filled her days so happily on Lauriergracht apart from reading. Family life and household management, of course; and the piano. How empty the basement air seemed, with no music soaring through it. How could she maintain her skills? That afternoon, as Jacob and Rachel played chess, Rose retreated to the bedroom and began her own secret project, creating a piano keyboard out of an old *Jewish Weekly*. With a pencil and an improvised ruler, Rose marked out the keys and filled them in.

✕   ✕   ✕

When she began looking in the mirror again every morning, Rose was startled at how much her hair had grown. It really needed to be brushed every night, as did Rachel's, and they restored that ritual from the days when Rachel was a little girl. The rhythm of the strokes gave her peace. One evening, when she had tamed Rachel's curly brown hair and piled it on top of her head, Rose couldn't help exclaiming, "You look so much like your grandmother. What a woman! She would have been right there beside Connie in the underground if she'd lived, probably doing something dangerous."

Rachel smiled, which invited Rose to ask a question she'd been musing about even more lately. "Rachel, I said you should do something against the Nazis if you could. I never pressed you about it before, but can't you tell me now what you were up to?"

"Mams, we could get caught and questioned any time. Forget

it. Just tell me more about Grandma. I know she was against your marrying Paps."

It was time to tell Rachel the whole story. Why not, in these circumstances? And they had the time, as Rachel took her turn brushing. Rose even revealed some of her mother's efforts to dissuade her from marrying Jacob because his family was too religious, and the class divide was too wide. "But I was in love, and I knew your father was right for me, no matter how conservative his family was."

Jacob put one arm around Rose. With his other hand, he turned her face gently to his, and kissed her check.

"Your whiskers are tickling me," she grumbled. Such a sentimentalist.

X   X   X

Later that night, she awoke to find Jacob curled around her, stroking her breasts as he had not in weeks. Nestling back toward him, she felt his ribs against her spine, and realized how thin they had both become—but she felt a surge of joy as her body began opening. What a long drought it had been, she thought, as she turned to face him and hold him. The bed had no springs; Rachel wouldn't hear a thing. Jacob was alive and hard against her. She slipped beneath him and guided him in. She felt a little dry, but it passed quickly. Nothing had changed. They were together again, wave upon wave.

X   X   X

When the family gathered around the radio one December evening, the upper-class accent of Anthony Eden poisoned the air, confirming Rose's very worst fears and the rumors she'd heard. The Nazis were engaged in the mass murder of Jews in Poland, wiping out whole communities. It was as bad as she'd thought. Rose reeled and clutched Jacob's hand. Eden said that other governments were joining Britain in reprimanding Germany. They would do what they could to stop the slaughter, but Eden said there were "immense geographical difficulties" in the way.

Hundreds or even thousands of human beings slaughtered and the rest of the world wouldn't help because of geography? Rose began laughing, a high-pitched sound from the top of her throat. She knew it was too loud, but she couldn't stop. Now she knew what was happening to the thousands of deported Jewish people. She felt a hand pressed against her mouth to muffle her hysterics: Rachel's. No one had done that since Rose was a child. The hand felt smothering, and she wanted to bite it. It did not smell of soap but of a body only superficially washed for weeks. Disgusting. Jacob grabbed his daughter's arm to pull her hand away, but froze and did not. They were all still for a moment. Rachel with her hand clasped over her mother's lips, Jacob's face numb.

Rose was so outraged that she fell silent. How dare her daughter treat her this way? And her husband allowing it, even abetting it? And Hitler—killing Jews as she had said he would, with Jacob telling her she was exaggerating. He had held them back from going to London, forcing them into this absurd situation because he wouldn't listen to her. She grabbed Rachel's hand with both of her own and tried to claw it away, but her daughter was too strong. Rose gave up and dropped her hands, beyond furious.

"Synagogues throughout Britain held a day of mourning," the radio announcer continued. "The House of Commons followed the Prime Minister's speech with a moment of silence." Rachel loosened her hold.

"I'm sorry, Mams," she whispered. "I'm so sorry."

But she could never be sorry enough. Rose felt violated. She pushed her away, rushed to the other side of the room, and flung herself on the bed. In an instant, Jacob tried to put his arms around her, but Rose pushed back. "Don't you dare try to placate me!" she hissed. "And don't defend her, either." Jacob shook his head, and held on. At first she wept, alternately tossed with rage and with sorrow, but finally she relaxed against his beloved, familiar body.

Feeling his arms securely around her, Rose made out the last words of the radio report: "Many first-generation Jews living in England believe they had a lucky escape from the concentration camps." What could that last phrase mean?

✗   ✗   ✗

Rachel

Hearing the end of the report bent Rachel's head down as if a hand had pressed her chin toward her chest. Her breath heaved. Mass murder: Was that in store for the Dutch Jews, too? What about Paula and her family? Were they still at the Westerbork Transit Camp, or had they been sent on somewhere else? Would her own mother ever forgive her? And her father? Rachel felt she would burst if she didn't get out of the basement and away from her parents. Her very bones felt brittle.

When Els appeared to provide water and take the bucket upstairs, Rachel asked her, "Just let me go up to the kitchen, even for fifteen minutes. I'll come down if I hear anything—anything at all." Rachel had not known it was possible to feel so desperate. She didn't even care that her parents were within easy earshot. "I have to stand up and stretch, just once. Please, trust me."

Els turned her head like an owl, taking her time. "I *do* trust you. But they come so fast now. If they run through the alley and over the back wall, you wouldn't have a chance, even if you just stayed in the kitchen."

"Please." Rachel took Els's calloused hand between hers. *If only my parents' lives weren't at stake as well as mine,* Rachel thought, *I would just push past her and pop up through that trapdoor. If I stay down here any longer, I'll go mad.* She did not know how or why she had reached that point, but she had. Her parents appeared from behind the curtain.

Els detached her hand and moved toward the ladder. "I'm sorry," she said over her shoulder.

"Wait," Rose whispered, and walked over. "Rachel doesn't look Jewish, agreed?" Els turned back and nodded cautiously, her face set.

"So why not hide her in plain sight? She has false papers. You could say she's household help. It would give us all some peace."

Rachel looked at her mother with amazement, then at Els with desperate hope. She said, "I've passed so many times! Not just with the Dutch police, but with the Germans. And I speak their language. They like that. Maybe I could keep you out of trouble. Sometimes a few words of German go a long way."

Jacob crept over and put an arm around her. It felt like a vise. "What times we live in! You learned German to read the works of Schiller and Goethe, not to bargain with criminals."

"Don't be a fool, Jacob," Rose snapped. "How do you think she's survived all these months out on the street?" Rachel felt his body recoil at the sharp tone.

Els's voice cut in as she started up the ladder. "I'm sorry, but I can't allow it. If you heard the stories, you'd understand. You'll have to trust my judgment." Her judgment! She had no idea what it was like down here, with a stinking bucket only a few feet and a curtain away from a bed on the dirt.

Shrugging off her father's arm, Rachel spat out, "What else can we do? Shop around for another place?"

"Rachel!" Raised to a normal level, Jacob's voice sounded like a shout. "Excuse her, Els, she doesn't know what she's saying."

"Shhh." Els opened the trapdoor, climbed out, and closed it. They could hear her footsteps muffled when she put the rug back into place.

Rachel stood at the bottom of the ladder, holding it hard, one hand on each side, squeezing it. She wanted to pulverize it. Her father said, "Rachel, you can't—"

"Don't tell me what I can't do! I've probably saved more lives than all your doctoring." She flounced behind her curtain and tore one of the rags she used as a sanitary napkin into little pieces. It felt good. *I'll go up tonight after they're all asleep. They can't stop me. If the Nazis come, I'll run at them so they'll shoot me. No capture, no torture, no secrets told. Then Paps would be sorry.* Here she hesitated even in her fury.

✕ ✕ ✕

Chess games had become more strain than distraction. Her father never met her eyes anymore. For the first time in her life, Rachel had really hurt him, and she didn't know how she could repair it. Part of her wasn't even sorry, which made it harder. After some tense days when she vacillated between utter frustration and wanting to make up, Jacob's birthday was imminent. Rachel brought herself to write him an affectionate verse, and the tension eased. Even her mother slowly got over that awful moment when her daughter had shut her up.

With mixed feelings, Rachel noticed the resumption of her parents' lovemaking at night, with subtle sounds she wished she could not hear. With a smelly pillow over her head, she did deep breathing exercises she'd learned from a friend at school. When her longings for Michiel were unbearable, Rachel waited until her parents' snores were synchronized, then dove into wetness and pleasure. Afterward, though, she wept deeply, and she couldn't fall asleep. It was almost not worth it.

✕   ✕   ✕

"Shhh." Rachel heard the sound overhead first, and Rose held up her right index finger. Nobody moved. Rachel listened above the fast rhythm of her own breathing, her hand poised over the chess game she and her father were playing again.

Yes, a man's low voice was at the door. Had she missed the doorbell? Surely not. Rachel was attuned to every sound. And why would Els open the door to someone who hadn't rung?

They heard friendly farewells: "*Tot ziens!*" Then the door creaked closed overhead.

Rose exhaled. Turning to Rachel, she whispered, "Do you ever wonder if Els might betray us?"

"Of course not," Jacob said.

"It depends on what they do to her," Rachel added. Even Eva had chosen pills rather than put herself to that test.

"Especially if they threaten Jan," Rose added, looking from her husband to Rachel. A silence fell. They exchanged a long look. Mams is really back with us again, Rachel thought, acerbic and logical. She had the look of a woman who would defend her nearest and dearest right to the end. Even if it did no good.

✕   ✕   ✕

Jacob said he began to have trouble concentrating on chess after Connie reported that the Nazis had raided the Jewish psychiatric hospital at Apeldoorn. His conscience was wracked by the thought of all those unstable people being subjected to even more terror. "Just before we came here, I had a man who attempted suicide admitted there. He was a peddler who couldn't support his family anymore because of the Nazis." He shook his head, looking like an old man who doesn't understand the world anymore.

As he retreated into his anatomy book, Rachel and her mother decided to try imaginary tours of their old life, going back to a single ordinary day at different times of year. It was almost inexhaustibly diverting to savor as many details as they could.

"Let's make it spring. Tulip time, or a little before," Rachel said.

"Again? What about a little earlier, maybe the first daffodils?"

"If we're going back that far, let's do a snowdrop day. In fact, let's find the snowdrops for the first time." Their voices were low, as always. "Let's go to the Begijnhof. I missed it last year, but the year before I went by myself for the first time."

"Really? Your father and I didn't go?"

"No. It was February, a cold day, and I went after school. But let's pretend that it was earlier, when I was just a little girl, and you each held one of my hands as we walked." Rachel turned her face away so her mother wouldn't see her tears. When she looked at her parents now, only their eyes looked the same.

Rose

Food deliveries were grand occasions to Rose, especially if Connie came downstairs—even if the amounts were scanty and it was ever more difficult to create something edible with them, much less palatable. A tall, jaunty woman, Connie would have attracted attention on the street if she hadn't dressed down to blend in. Rose was so sick of wearing the same things over and over. If they ever got out of here, she'd cash in some diamonds and buy a whole new wardrobe.

Connie almost always joked. "Potatoes from Queen Wilhelmina's gardens, just for you," she would say. She was grim only occasionally, and they never asked why. Connie made many deliveries, and perhaps one of the other addresses had been raided. Peeling the potatoes, Rose remembered how her mother and Aunt Sophie had taught her to do it with the knife angled precisely against the skin. The chore had seemed penitential at the time, since those hours in the kitchen were stolen from books and playing. But now, in the basement, with her hands busy and efficient, Rose felt nostalgic about sitting at the kitchen table listening to the two sisters visit. Her pangs were as deep as the wooden stakes under the house, driven deep into the muck that Amsterdam was built on.

✕ ✕ ✕

One day, tucked on top of the turnips and an onion, lay a long, narrow paper bag which appeared to have nothing in it.

"What's this?" Rachel asked.

"Don't squeeze it!" Connie cautioned. "There's a surprise in there, to celebrate. Stalingrad has gone our way at last, and Hitler must be wetting his pants! He said the Russians would never hold out this long. Anyway, here's a present for you."

Rose unfolded the top of the bag with gingerly, small movements. As soon as it opened, she caught a scent—sharp, distinctive, and unforgettable—even before she saw the frilly open cup of the single golden daffodil inside.

"Come over here, Jacob." Her soft voice held an ache for the bulb fields, miles of them. Every year, Rose had bought pots of daffodils and put them near the windows in the living room to remind Jacob of the "Jewish flowers" his parents had loved. The light used to fall on them as she practiced the piano, and their fragrance had filled the room.

Rachel reached carefully below the flower and held the naked stem gently. She brought it to her nose and breathed in deeply again and again. As if in a trance, Rachel put the flower in a glass of water on the table. She sat down and looked at it even more closely. While Rose peeled the potatoes, Rachel got up and fetched a pencil and a precious sheet of paper. By then, the fragrance was beginning to impinge on the dampness and the mold. When the potatoes were ready, Rachel's page was full of sketches.

$$\times \quad \times \quad \times$$

"Wake up, dear." Jacob's hand was on Rose's shoulder, and he was already dressed. There was always a split second before she remembered. Try as she might, she could not prolong it. She felt the usual dread, and as quickly snuffed it. He said, "I'll bring you some tea."

As Rose waited, she caught a scent under the stench, and suddenly remembered the daffodil. Around Aunt Sophie's cottage, their yellow heads would be soaked and weighed down with rain and dew, and would be the more beautiful for it.

Knowing that the life of the flower is brief, Rachel drew it every day, even without Rose prompting her. "Oh no!" she exclaimed one morning. "The petals are thinning out." Rose had to agree. The cup had begun its quiet and subtle collapse, and the end of the stem began to split underwater.

After Rose cut off the lower inch in hopes of refreshing the flower, she carefully divided the fresh green into equal thirds.

"Is this the salad course?" Rachel quipped.

Rose felt a little guilty as she ate it, but she would have given anything for the crunch and burst of green filling her mouth.

$$\times \quad \times \quad \times$$

After three knocks, Connie came down late one afternoon. At last! Rose longed to see her. It felt as if they were living inside an egg, and one tap could crack the shell at any time. No matter what the news was from outside, she wanted to hear it from a person she trusted, not a radio with propaganda from both sides.

"Hello," Connie said. "Do you have a few kind words for me

today? Nobody else seems to." She tried to laugh as she cocked her head, but her eyes seemed to hesitate. Her coat's cinched waist was loose. Her expression was tight, as if she were squinting into a cold wind. She forced a smile.

Jacob, ever decorous, offered to help Connie off with her coat, but she declined with a gesture and a shudder. He asked, "What's the matter?"

"Well," she demurred, sitting on the edge of a chair, "everyone seems on edge. They must be planning something big. In fact, I'm sorry but I was told specifically that I couldn't come back here until things cool off. I'm hoping it's just their panic after losing Stalingrad." Connie looked at the floor and fiddled with her coat button.

Rachel coughed and covered her mouth, probably to hide a sob. Even as a faded version of her former self, Connie brought them real cheer. Only she had the temerity to say, "Those Nazis! Back in their villages they wouldn't even be sub-assistant constables."

Rose asked, "Has something happened?" Connie turned away. "Tell us," Rose insisted. She heard the tightness in Connie's voice.

"We don't know why, but they seem to be finding more people. Maybe someone told them where to look. The dogs seem better trained, too." Connie reached inside her worn bag. "I brought you something nice, since I won't see you for a while."

On the table she placed a small oblong package wrapped in brown paper.

Rose fumbled as she undid the fine white string. *Could that be the smell of brandy?* She'd almost forgotten what it was like. As soon as the paper was off, she saw a small, perfect fruitcake, with cherries glistening against dark brown. She could already imagine the cherry's globe in her mouth, then the gush of its flavors.

"Wherever did you get this?" Rose asked, incredulous.

"The back of my mother's pantry in the country," Connie

explained. "I was cleaning the last time I was there. This must have been from the last batch she made."

The last batch, Rose thought, *from a time when sugar and flour and eggs were to be had, and candied cherries, huge and redolent like a child's imagined rubies; nuts fatty and ready for toasting; orange and lemon peels boiled in still more sugar.* Could she even think of accepting this gift? Rachel was already swallowing her saliva, and Jacob was breathing in the scent as if it were cake itself.

I have to give her something in return, Rose thought. She spoke quickly, before she could change her mind. "You've been such a friend to us, Connie, and who knows when we'll meet again? This is for you." She undid the clasp of her silver bracelet, a wide band intricately chased with calligraphic floral and fern fronds. Since she inherited it from her mother, Rose had never taken the bracelet off except to clean it with a worn toothbrush. "You've been so kind to us."

Connie was speechless. Before she could protest, Rose had clasped it around her wrist.

Rachel looked stricken. As a little girl, she had often begged to try the bracelet on, just for a minute. It should have been hers one day. But Connie had risked her life to give them food and cheer, and they might be captured at any time.

"I can't possibly—" Connie began, picking clumsily at the complex clasp.

Then Rose used her hardest voice, that no one could think of opposing. "Take it, Connie. With you, it will be safe."

APRIL 5–6, 1943

Rachel

"We need to talk," Els said, crossing the basement and avoiding Rachel's eyes. They gathered around the table, silently. "The Germans are after a man who killed an informer the other night. The underground can't risk getting him out of Amsterdam. The Nazis have tripled the reward, so everybody's looking for him." The shadows around the basement's edges crept closer. Instead of the fresh spring smell that must be outside by now, rot seeped around them.

So she wants us to take him in, Rachel thought. It would be thrilling to have someone new here, but where could they put him? Besides, if the Nazis want the man that badly and they catch him down here, they'll punish all of us. She shivered.

Rose was saying, "We'll do what we can. Could you lend us another blanket and two bedsheets? He can sleep on the couch."

"He *is* a Gentile," Els said.

"It doesn't matter," Jacob replied.

"I thought you'd say yes, but I wasn't sure." Els's smile was thin. "Frankly, my concern isn't just for you. Jan's starting to get worried." Ah, the mysterious Jan, her unseen husband.

"No wonder. When's the new guy coming?" Rachel asked, hungry to meet any new person, especially someone the Germans were hunting for.

X   X   X

The man tiptoed down the ladder, wrapped in dark clothing so his face and body were barely visible. When he took off his long scarf, Rachel was moved by his bony, utterly exhausted face. He appeared to be twenty-five or so, and he was that rarity, a short Dutchman. After an instant of puzzlement, she remembered him, even though his face was sculpted by hunger: the friend who'd been with Michiel when she went to Leiden to find him, who had given her that searching look. Was there any chance that he'd know what happened to Michiel? Hope began to flutter around her.

"Mevrouw, how do you do?" he said to Rose, as though they were in a parlor. His low, melodious voice didn't sound like a killer's.

When Rachel laughed softly at the incongruity of his fine manners in this rough place, the man looked at her, first dully and then with quickly concealed surprise. Unthinkingly, she reached out her hand and started to speak, but he interrupted her.

"I'm glad to *meet* you," he said, giving her a meaningful look. "I'm Rolf." His hand felt warm and large, almost like Michiel's. Rachel felt an aliveness that hadn't been inside her for months. She already looked forward to talking with him.

Jacob also shook Rolf's hand. They sat down at the table on the hard wooden chairs, which at least didn't smell as the sofa did. A curious comfort pervaded the ensuing hour, as the four of them sipped hot water. It was embarrassing to have absolutely nothing else to offer a guest. The thin soup made from what would once have been compost scraps was all gone. Even the mint tea jar was empty. Rachel's stomach gurgled, and she wondered again whether hot water made her fuller or emptier.

After comfortable preliminaries, Jacob finally said, "We heard a BBC report of a speech by Anthony Eden, talking about mass executions of Jewish people. Is there any evidence of that? Has anyone returned from the work camps in Germany to say what they're like?"

"No. Every now and then, a family gets a postcard in German saying their relative is fine, but that's all. We're beginning to think no one will come back, or very few."

"But that's impossible. They say hundreds of Jewish people have been sent away," Jacob said.

"Yes. And the Germans are drafting every Dutchman they can lay their hands on. They must be getting desperate. So now we're looking for addresses to hide Gentiles, not just Jews—not to mention finding ration coupons to feed them. At least it means more people are willing to help, but it's hard for people in hiding. Some of them get very depressed. You can probably understand that."

Rose nodded. "Yes, but I try to fight it. Believe it or not, I still practice the piano."

"Now? What do you mean?" Rachel couldn't believe she had found a way.

"Just a minute, and I'll show you. I made a paper keyboard." Turning to Rolf, she said, "Jacob gave me the piano when we got engaged. Until Rachel was born, it was my greatest joy in life." After disappearing behind the curtain, she pulled open a roll of old newspaper with the white and black keys drawn in their exact proportions.

Intense as his eyes had been, Rolf's gaze was beginning to droop. He must be exhausted.

"It's been an enjoyable evening, thanks to you," Jacob said. "It's good to have another man around the house. Our toilet facilities are limited, but if you step behind the curtain you will find what we have."

The two women made up the couch. Rose whispered, "Maybe you can even have a little fun with him when he's rested. At least he smells as if he's had a bath lately!"

"Oh, Mams!" Rachel said as she smoothed the blanket. She'd find out what he knew about Michiel, if anything.

When Rolf came back and took off his shoes, they realized he had no other clothing. He dropped onto the sofa and fell fast asleep.

✕ ✕ ✕

"Is he all right, Paps?" Rachel asked, concerned that Rolf had now been sleeping for many hours, only occasionally stirring. When would she get to talk with him? His short body was lying in almost the same position she remembered from hours ago, in his rumpled, worn shirt and pants.

"Yes. It's exhaustion, both physical and nervous. He doesn't seem to me like someone who would go join the underground, much less kill someone. He's not the type."

"Maybe there isn't a type," Rachel replied, "just people who know we have to do something against the Nazis." She saw Jacob's eyes widen at the "we," and looked down. If only Rolf would wake up.

What could she do in the meantime? Her eyes fell on Rolf. He lay on his side, his two hands beneath his cheek. His eyelids, almost transparent, showed tiny blue veins. He breathed almost silently.

"Shhh!" Rachel enjoined her father when he made a slight noise. He smiled.

"Don't worry," he whispered. "That young man could probably sleep for a week. But we should wake him up in time for dinner. He needs to eat."

As the time approached, Rachel felt more restless. The full food delivery hadn't arrived—an inexplicable but not unprecedented disappointment—but Els had passed a big turnip and a few potatoes down the hatch that morning with a whispered "Sorry." Rachel spent half an hour first scrubbing the turnip, then cutting it into centimeter cubes.

She scrambled around the shelf they cynically referred to as the pantry, and unearthed the potatoes. No meat, but at least it was a meal, and she supposed Rolf had gone without many times, by the look of him. If only she could take a walk with him, even for a block. It was hard to believe that she had once roamed the whole city at will, even gone to Oudekerk and the sea on her bicycle. Would she ever see them again? And Sonja, Paula? She wanted to believe that Anna and Jan were still all right, but there was no way to know. *Don't think about it,* she told herself. With luck, at least she'd learn something about Michiel.

Once dinner was in hand, Rachel brought a chair over beside Rolf, and sat near his head, her paper propped against a piece of sturdy cardboard. Soon she was attempting to draw him: the pronounced valley above his upper lip, the cheek flaccid in sleep, the place where his nose narrowed asymmetrically. She hadn't looked at a man so closely since she was with Michiel. The act of close observation itself made her miss him.

Beneath Rolf's translucent eyelids, his eyes flickered. His breathing became shallower, and his mouth twitched as if he were about to say something. Rachel was terrified that he would wake from his dream and speak loudly, or even shout. Who might be upstairs? She first touched him lightly on the arm, then whispered, "Shhh!" her finger to his dry lips.

Rolf

Rolf woke only to use the bucket and drink. Occasionally, he half rose, drank down the glass of water that someone refilled, and fell instantly back to sleep. After unknown hours, he jerked awake in panic, but relaxed when he heard voices, a woman's and a man's, and remembered he was hidden. Drifting again, his mind hovered between alertness and repose, roaming over the events that had brought him to this basement. How strange that the Nazis had put a price on his head as a dangerous terrorist. When he was a boy, his mother had said he was so squeamish he couldn't even pluck a chicken.

If the Nazis hadn't herded his best friend and classmate Jaap onto the truck in the Jonas Daniel Meijerplein and murdered him, Rolf probably wouldn't have gone beyond the protests he originally helped Michiel organize. Jaap, a hearty young man, was the first in his family to go beyond primary school, a football star who still had time for an intellectual like Rolf. Rolf's university-educated parents thought it a little odd that his best friend was the son of a butcher, but they never minded that he was a Jew. Jaap had saved Rolf from complete isolation by teaching him to play ball.

Later, he said, "I felt sorry for you at first, but then I began to like you. And now we're friends until one of us dies."

Or, as it turned out, even after.

×   ×   ×

Feeling a light finger on his lips, Rolf opened his eyes in an instant of coiled alertness, then blankness as he studied Rachel, and finally calm as he remembered where he was. She did look familiar, but he'd met too many people to be sure. Rolf wondered what Rachel had looked like before the war. She was so bony. If he survived, he'd find a round woman whom he could knead like bread. He hadn't thought of a woman that way for months. Rachel was telling him it was close to dinnertime.

Dinner! Had the whole night and day really passed? "How do you know the time?" Rolf asked, as he sat up slowly.

"We still have our watches. Often I'd swear they're wrong. Hours seem to pass in twenty minutes. But our hosts' footsteps upstairs tell time for us, too. It must be creepy for them, knowing we're living under their feet."

Rolf yawned and shook his head, like a dog coming out of the water. He once found the smell of turnips cooking unpleasant, but tonight it made him salivate. He passed his hand over his stubbly chin. "May I shave before dinner? I must look like a criminal."

"You do, but it's all right since you are one," Rachel joked. "I'll ask my father for a razor." Rolf nodded but hardly noticed the humor.

He wondered if she had any idea what kind of criminal he was. Not just a forger or courier. A killer, more than once. He could hardly believe it himself.

By the time Rachel had turned to ask for the razor, it was there, and Rose was heating the water. So, Rolf realized, everything could be overheard in the central space, even whispers.

Sitting down together for dinner gave a sense of occasion, especially with a stubby candle at the center of the table. The good china glowed thin and fine like his own mother's, the pattern of roses broken by the carefully cubed turnips and accompanying potatoes. It was almost convivial, as if Rachel had brought him home for dinner to meet her parents. Rolf was so exhausted that conversation was a chore, but he knew he had to talk. These people had been trapped here for months, and, after all, they'd agreed to take him in, like putting a bomb with a live fuse under their beds. At the least, he had to show them that he was a civilized person. He'd met men who used the underground as a rationale for their bloodthirstiness. For him, it had been so different.

"What were you studying before the war?" Jacob asked.

"I started out in literature, especially poetry, but I ended up in physics, and I'm still interested in both." A second ago, he had had no energy, but the earthy fragrance of hot potatoes and turnip revived him. He speared his food eagerly, and involuntarily smiled at the first bite. The turnip at least had flavor.

Just then, a strange pressure on a floorboard overhead made Rolf catch his breath, but it was followed by normal footfalls. Rachel waved dismissively to indicate all was well. Rolf studied her face closely—the angle of the nose, the graceful cheekbones. She must have been beautiful once, before her skin went sallow and stretched tight over her bones, before her hair lost its sheen and her eyes their glow. He couldn't quite place Rachel, although her signals had been that they had met; she might be one of the dozens of such girls to whom he had passed messages and people.

Dinner passed pleasantly, returning to more neutral topics. Jacob loved physics, and enjoyed hearing Rolf describe his studies. He let himself unwind as he spoke of a world that follows inexorable laws. After the dishes were done, Rachel showed him the chessboard and invited him to play. "I'm not very good," he demurred. He didn't feel like making the effort, though he knew he should. They sat across the table from each other, the handmade "board" and "pieces" between them.

Both took a long time to consider each move, which allowed Rolf to examine her carefully. He was sure now that he had seen her. Then, as Rachel reached for her paper queen, he remembered her hovering near him and Michiel one day. Her presence had made him nervous. Even at that early date, the Nazis had informers on the campus, and he and Michiel had been organizing one of the early protests. Rolf had been unsettled about Rachel even before she approached them, and he had asked Michiel if he knew her. His friend had replied in a tormented voice, "Yes, she's OK. I have to talk with her."

At the time, that incident had made Rolf wonder whether Michiel was a double agent, but the way his life had ended later put any doubts to rest. Michiel had been safe for more than a year, and then someone betrayed him. One of Rolf's contacts knew Michiel was his friend, and told him when and how he died. Rolf felt sick when he thought of it, and resolutely turned his attention to the game and his vulnerable queen.

"The pieces are getting worn," Rachel said. "I could make more, but we have so little paper. As long as we can still tell a pawn from a rook, I guess they'll do."

"At least for now," he agreed. They exchanged a look.

At last Jacob and Rose retired. Rachel motioned to Rolf, and he reluctantly followed her to the other corner of the basement. All he wanted to do was curl up on the couch and sleep. Instead, they sat side by side on her mattress, their backs against the damp wall. He could smell the nearby bucket, even with its cover, under the turnip's thick odor. Whispering even more softly than usual, Rachel began, "So . . . I think I know you."

"I wondered if you did." He had hoped she would have forgotten him, and it was dangerous to be recognized. Even if he never left this basement, the less this girl knew, the better. "But I'm your generic Dutchman, just a little shorter. A lot of people look like me."

"Not all of them were talking with Michiel Drogt on October 11, 1940."

He lowered his face. "You're very precise," he replied. How much did she know?

"I remember because it was so important to me. I have to talk to somebody about Michiel, and it can't be my parents. You knew him, so you can understand why I would love him, first as a friend, then as"—she hesitated, glanced across the basement—"much more than that."

Rolf listened closely, not sure just what was expected of him. She must be the Jewish girlfriend who had jilted Michiel, then reappeared some weeks before he had to hide. Rolf remembered finding what he had thought was a safe address for Michiel, not in Amsterdam but on a Drenthe farm.

"But I love her," Michiel had protested when Rolf pointed out that his staying in touch with Rachel would not only jeopardize her, but also the worker on whom other addresses depended. Rolf half wondered if he had been wrong to cut them off from each other. What difference would it really have made in the end? Then again, Michiel might have been betrayed sooner.

"What's the matter?" Rachel asked Rolf, probably noticing that his attention wandered.

"Nothing. Go on."

She started talking and couldn't stop—their meeting at the café, their common love of books and bike rides, their falling in love, her astonishment at his talking of marriage, her decision to break up and then to return, and finally their all-too-brief love affair.

Listening to Rachel, Rolf felt wistful as well as exhausted. His biggest crush had been on a much older woman who had delighted in teaching him to please her. Flashes of their hours together had often consoled him as he shadowed a potential betrayer, or covered the miles on his bicycle. When she took up with a Dutch Nazi party member, he said he had to leave her, because he wanted to be her only lover. "You silly boy," she said, cuffing him. "Come here."

He had, but for the last time. He sent golden lilies he couldn't afford and a love note that would satisfy her. Afterward, he woke night after night grinding his teeth, his whole body aching. Rolf first thought he could not bear it. Then came the anger, that she would take up with that filthy Nazi.

"Aren't you listening?" Rachel's face was anxious, her forehead rippled.

"Yes," he lied, and amended, "I was just remembering someone." Her face was crumpling and her voice thickened as she described how Michiel had vanished after warning her. "I've hardly heard from him at all—just a postcard."

"I told him not to write," Rolf blurted out before he could stop himself. "It was too dangerous." *Oh no,* he had actually said it. It must be the fatigue. He had almost never slipped up before.

"So you knew him! I was sure of it." Now Rachel's whole body turned to Rolf. He felt her yearning. "How is he? Have you seen him?"

Flinching, Rolf closed his eyes. He was in this basement not just because he was in danger, but also because he couldn't take any more.

"No, I haven't. I have to sleep now." He got up and looked away.

"But you must have heard something—" She pulled on his shirtsleeve.

He brushed her hand away more harshly than he meant to. "Good night" was all he would say before he headed for the couch.

APRIL 7, 1943

Jacob

The next morning, Jacob hushed Rose and Rachel so they wouldn't disturb his patient. How delicious it felt to monitor someone closely again! Rolf looked to him like a man on the brink. If he had really killed someone—which Jacob could not quite believe—it must be haunting his conscience. He looked as if he hadn't had a proper meal for months. When Rolf talked about physics, though, he looked like an ardent teenager rather than a careworn man. Rolf's only in his twenties, Jacob calculated. He returned to re-memorizing the veins in the finger.

$$\times \quad \times \quad \times$$

Rolf slept until noon that day. When he rose, he looked anxiously at Rachel but hardly spoke to her. Jacob had seen them go into Rachel's quarters last night, and heard the soft murmur of voices. The two young people seemed strained with each other today. What had happened?

After another lunch of pale soup, Jacob asked, "How about a game of chess with me this time?" Rolf was only a fair player, but he did think about his moves. Jacob let him drag the game out, postponing the inevitable checkmate. Rachel watched them from the corner of the couch, where she was reknitting a sweater Els had given her into a size she could wear.

That evening, over small portions of herring and potatoes and carrots, Rolf's presence animated Rose. Jacob loved to see her real smile as she reminisced about the Waterlooplein market of her youth.

"The characters you saw there—and the ways they had of depriving fools of their money!" Jacob took his wife's hand under the table when she put down her glass and continued. "My favorite errand was going to the butcher for brisket for the weekend. He was a delight, and had a little boy who was always playing ball in the street outside. After the union was organized, the butcher would say, 'These are good times, my girl, when diamond workers can eat meat every Shabbat and more.'"

"Where was this butcher shop?" Rolf asked, breaking the spell. Something in his tone made Jacob look at him closely. Rolf was as still as a heron.

"On Vlooienburg Island," Rose replied, still carried away by the gaiety of her reminiscences.

"What was the butcher's name?" Rolf's body was motionless.

"The father was Abe Rubens, and the little boy who inherited it was Bernard. He ran it until the Nazis outlawed ritual slaughter. He has a son, too, who didn't go into the business. I can't remember his name."

Rolf whispered lower than usual: "Jaap. His name was Jaap." He pressed his napkin over his mouth and seemed to choke.

"Our butcher's son—you knew him?" Jacob asked, reaching over to pat Rolf's back and help him get his breath. But the young man leaned forward. Retching in his napkin, Rolf staggered up from the table and ran to the bucket.

Against the background of his uncontrollable noise, Rose said, "Remember, Jacob, I read you the death notice in the *Jewish Weekly* when it came out—heart failure, it said. Rachel saw him rounded up on the Jonas Daniel Meijerplein that day. Rolf must have known him."

He didn't want to make Rolf feel ashamed, but Jacob couldn't stand the sounds, which were now sobs. In any case, he had to quiet him down. He found Rolf behind the curtain, on all fours trying futilely to clean up the vomit which had spattered beyond the bucket. Jacob bent over him, extended a hand, and placed it on the boy's quivering shoulder.

"I'm—so—sorry . . ." Rolf's voice trailed off.

Jacob knelt beside him. Rolf's worn clothes were spattered. His breath was foul as he puffed hard, like an exhausted swimmer.

"It's terrible to lose a friend," Jacob offered, "and so many strangers, too." He put an arm around Rolf, who gripped Jacob's other hand with all his strength. Jacob gasped but did not protest. He had seen many women through childbirth.

Comforting Rolf wordlessly, Jacob felt like a doctor again, deep in this encounter with a person who was raw, exposed to the quick.

"Rachel," he whispered across the room, and she came at once. "Bring the brandy from my bag, please. It's beside our bed."

Rolf raised his eyes, saw Rachel's retreating back, and shuddered again. "Michiel's dead, too," he said. "You tell her."

"Who?" Jacob asked. "Someone Rachel knew?" The abrupt change of subject wasn't surprising in a stress victim.

"Boyfriend," Rolf said, and closed his eyes. "Shot. Not right away. Later."

Jacob started. Rachel had a boyfriend he didn't know about? It must have been a schoolgirl flirtation, nothing serious. But she would be sorry to hear he was gone.

"I'll tell her," he replied. It was his duty. He was her father, and this young man was in no condition to give anyone bad news.

Rachel returned as if on cue, bringing a cup and the flask. Jacob poured a small dram and held the cup to Rolf's lips. The young man sipped it between harsh breaths, then leaned his head back and closed his eyes.

At that moment, Rose appeared and admonished, "You two leave so I can get this young man cleaned up." She carried a basin of soapy water, a makeshift pajama top, and a cloth and towel. Rolf nodded slightly. Jacob gave him a quick pat on the shoulder, stood up as straight as the low ceiling allowed, and headed toward the kitchen table. He heard Rose order, "Let's get you out of those clothes. I'll put you in Rachel's bed where you'll be more comfortable. One night on the couch won't hurt that daughter of mine a bit."

As Jacob sat down at the table with Rachel, she said with a tight smile, "Mams doesn't waste any time, does she?"

They heard Rose putting Rolf to bed as if in some faraway land. Jacob knew what he had to do, and took the hand Rachel had rested on the table by her cup.

"I am sorry, my dear, but Rolf asked me to tell you some bad news."

Her eyes were riveted to his. "Michiel?" The name could hardly be heard. Her father nodded, and watched her face collapse first, then her shoulders. She gave no cry or word, but her whole body slumped. This man meant something to her.

"Rachel?" No response. "I'm sorry, dear. He was shot." He forced himself to say it. "Did you love him?"

She retrieved her face and said simply, "Yes. Yes, I do." A pause. "Did." Tears seared her cheeks. Jacob held her hand, cold and flaccid. Why had she kept such a secret from him?

Rose emerged with a bustling air. "Dead to the world," she announced with satisfaction, then looked at her husband and daughter. "What is it now?"

"Did you ever meet a friend of Rachel's named Michiel?"

"No."

"Rolf knew him, and Rachel loved him. He was shot dead."

Rose's eyes widened. Her hand fluttered to her mouth. "Who was he?"

Jacob shook his head to quiet his wife, for Rachel looked as fragile as a lily about to lose every single petal in the next breath of wind. She released her father's hand and turned away from them. "I'm going to bed," she said, heading toward her corner, past the couch.

"But Rolf is—" Jacob began. His wife cupped her hand lightly over his lips, and stopped the words. "Hush," she said. "Let them be."

X X X

As he held Rose in bed, his breath came fast. What if Rolf took advantage of Rachel? Had he abused other women? Whatever had made her go over there?

"Stop, Jacob." Rose spoke as if she had read his mind.

"I'm going to tell Rachel to sleep on the couch where she belongs."

Rose turned so her face was close to his. He couldn't see her but felt her breath on his face—the breath which once was so sweet. Although their poor diet and lack of adequate toothpaste wasn't her fault, it still upset Jacob that his wife did not smell the way she used to.

"Don't," she said. "Do you really think that exhausted man would think of seducing your daughter tonight? Or that she would even consider it if he tried? They're caged here, Jacob, and they don't have love to see them through, as we do. So if they lie down side by side, what's the harm for a night or two?"

"She's our daughter! She had a boyfriend we didn't even know about." Rose tried to put her arms fully around him, but he resisted. He had thought he knew his daughter.

"Shhh, Jacob, most girls have friends they don't tell their parents about. And she would never upset us with a Gentile boyfriend, which he probably was. I'm just guessing. This Rolf seems like a fine young man even if he killed someone—or perhaps because he did. So don't disturb them tonight."

Reluctantly, he agreed, but he couldn't get the image out of his mind of his daughter lying beside that man. At least she'd have to be on the floor; that "mattress" wasn't big enough for one person, much less two. And he'd heard no sounds of her getting undressed. When had she met this Michiel? Was that why Rachel had been out so much in these last months? Had she actually meant to marry him? If he were a Gentile, that would have been unthinkable.

From the moment of Rachel's birth, it had been a miracle to him that she arrived intact and shining into the world, especially because as a doctor he had seen so many births go wrong. When she was small, her adoration coursed through him, buoying his every moment. He'd once loved his parents that way, but it had come to an end when his smallest steps toward independence had terrified his mother. He didn't ever want anything to come between him and Rachel, and now something had.

✕ ✕ ✕

The next morning, when Rolf slept and everyone else read or studied, Jacob heard a creak overhead. It was soft, a note that would have been overlooked in the music of everyday life of Lauriergracht. Perhaps a child's footfall, or a reactive adjustment in a wooden floor to events taking place on the other side of the room. Or an adult foot carefully placed, heel to toe, inadvertently making an unintended sound.

Jacob clenched the anatomy book. His body was instantly tuned to that note, ready to spring and—what? Hide under the table? The only exit from the basement was the hatch. Els had completely blocked off the old loading door that led to the back garden, so they could never be taken by surprise from that direction—but it also meant that they were trapped. Jacob listened for another creak, but only the subtlest sound followed. Someone on tiptoe.

Rose met his eyes across the table where they both sat. Her face was stiff and startled; she must have heard it, too. They waited what seemed like an eternity, but no further sound intruded. Still, neither dared to speak until they decided they must have imagined it, that time.

Rolf

When Rolf woke up, he felt a sleeping body nestled near his. He somehow knew it was a woman's. At first, he didn't remember where he was, or who she was. His bones felt a hard surface through a thin, smelly mattress, her body his only source of warmth. Shifting a little, he remembered Rachel and the basement, but had no memory of her coming there to lie beside him. She lay a few inches lower than he. He felt a folded blanket beneath her on the cold dirt floor. He trembled with cold. Her breath was soft and even. Vaguely, he remembered Rose washing his face, helping him change his shirt, and leading him here.

Just before waking up, he had dreamed of biking with Jaap in the dunes near Bloemendaal, the joy of the smashing salt water first seen, then only heard, as he followed his friend up and down the dunes, first in sight of the sea, then not. So often, in that split second before fully waking up, Rolf could be who he used to be. Then he remembered all that he wanted to forget—not just about Jaap, but about himself—the months it had taken him to go to the Jewish Quarter to offer his condolences to the butcher and his wife. He just couldn't face them before.

By the time he finally went, the shop downstairs was closed, and no one answered the door to the upstairs living quarters. A neighbor he'd met saw him knocking and invited him in. Mrs. Kahn was thin and frayed, single now, wearing an old checked dress. Her generous mouth had sagged, the moles on her face more conspicuous now that her cheeks were no longer pink.

"So you want to know about Abe and Sophie," she said. "Why now? You must have known Jaap was dead." Her gaze drilled into Rolf's eyes across her tiny living room.

"Because . . . because . . ." He faltered, and then found his head in his hands, cradling his skull, sobbing hoarsely. Then he felt Mrs. Kahn shaking his shoulders hard.

"How dare you!" She almost spat. "How dare you! How many others have disappeared just like Abe and Sophie? And why? Because people like you go on working and living as if everything is normal. You want to know what happened? I was standing right there"—she was trembling, her mouth and her whole body, as she pointed— "I cut a slit in that blind, and I saw it all. Three goons banged on the door. In uniform, of course. They smashed it open. Then there was shouting inside, and crashes. They burst back into the street, dragging Abe and Sophie with them. They didn't even have a little suitcase. Now they're gone to those labor camps, God knows where." At this, the storm seemed to have broken; Mrs. Kahn almost fell into her chair, her face grayer than ever.

Rolf was aghast. "But why would they take Abe and Sophie?" he ventured, recoiling. She hardly heard him.

"I don't know. Maybe the people who gassed themselves right after the Nazis invaded were right."

"Isn't there somewhere safer where you could go?"

"No," she replied. "Nobody offered. Not one of my colleagues at the Telephone Exchange. Not one. The day they fired all the Jews, the others could have walked out, or at least asked me if I had a place to go. Or someone could have found me later. They had my address."

"Maybe they didn't know—" Rolf began, but even that phrase filled Mrs. Kahn with rage again.

"Didn't know! How could you live in Amsterdam and not know?"

Rolf drew back, his head and limbs retracting like a turtle's. His vision was blurry and something was caught in his dry mouth. It tasted terrible. "But, Mrs. Kahn, didn't Abe and Sophie know anyone who could help them?"

"Yes," she said. "They knew you. Get out of my house."

After that, Rolf began his serious underground work. Now, in the basement, he saw people as if they were right there—not only Jaap, but the betrayers he had killed. The slump of that first woman's shoulders, her weight in his compressed hands. The people he had sent to addresses which proved to be unsafe: at least one college friend, two neighbors, a whole host family. They all whooshed past him as if he were in a too-fast train and they were standing on the platform—no, as if he stood by the track and they sped past him on the train with no earthly destination. The one that hovered longest was Mrs. Kahn. He'd been so pleased when he went to tell her that he'd found an address where she could hide.

By the time he went back to give her the good news, the neighborhood was almost deserted. When there was no answer to his knock, he broke into her apartment to discover only her body and a terrible smell. It was still in his nose. She had decided not to wait for the Nazis.

Rachel finally stirred, murmuring a little, but still asleep. Automatically, Rolf put his arm around her. She felt so warm, and when she turned toward him and tucked her head under his chin, he felt rest settle into his bones for the first time in months. Then she woke up and jolted away. "Who shot him?" she whispered. His stomach contracted as if punched.

"I don't know," he said. "Let's get up." It would be hard to face her parents after his performance the day before. And what would they think about their daughter sleeping beside him? Better to arise and get it over with.

"Please," she begged, tugging at his sleeve, "just tell me. Was it the Germans, or one of the Dutch police?"

"I don't know. I need to use the toilet." His body somehow knew it was morning, despite the darkness. He detached her hand gently and heard her weeping as he crossed the room. He would never tell her what he had heard. Let her believe that one nice, clean bullet had cut the thread of her lover's life in a single, merciful instant. Exhausted as he was, he had that much compassion left.

After a long day filled with chess, naps, scanty meals, and awkward conversation, Jacob and Rose went to bed. Rachel headed for her corner, and motioned to Rolf to follow. He knew he had to go, and dreaded it. Sitting beside her on her mattress, with pillows behind their backs against the cold wall, he was relieved when she didn't persist in asking him about Michiel. Finally, she stopped talking. He began to drift off, and vaguely noticed when his head drooped onto her shoulder. He woke slightly when she eased him down onto the bed. He'd meant to sleep on the sofa, but he was so tired. Hours later, when he woke up to pee, he felt the kind furnace of her body next to his, and it tinged his sorrows a warmer color, like firelight on old wood.

APRIL 8–9, 1943

Rachel

When Rachel woke up, she was aware both of the cold dirt floor underneath her, and of the living body beside her. The night before, she had thought of sleeping on the couch, but she couldn't make herself leave the comfort of Rolf's body. Michiel was gone, forever. She would never have the chance to marry him now. In sleep, Rolf's face looked like a child's, its etched lines now filled in as if with an artist's pastel. As she watched, he'd squirmed just for an instant to move onto his side, one arm flung out. Her parents wouldn't like her sleeping beside him, but they wouldn't be worried about it—especially given their presence right across the room. Besides, Rolf was Michiel's friend, and neither of them would ever forget that.

The raids were more frequent than ever the next day. They began at six o'clock in the morning, when loud feet pounded the floor right over their heads and woke her. The noise entered her skull and sent a shock through her whole spine and into her ribs. Rachel involuntarily clutched Rolf in the darkness until the rampage was over and boots crashed out the front door. "My parents," she said, turned on the light, and got up to check on them. Rolf didn't move.

Rose and Jacob were already on the couch, sitting close to each other. Her father avoided her gaze. When he opened his mouth to speak, his wife said, "No, Jacob," and asked Rachel, "Are you all right?"

"Yes," she said. She and Rolf were just comforting each other, like two puppies.

Her mother nodded and replied, "What about Els and Jan?" Rolf appeared then, and sat as far away as he could in the small space. For an hour, Rachel tried to convince the others to knock on the hatch, but they ultimately decided not to, and retired to their separate activities: Jacob to his anatomy book and Rose to her piano at the kitchen table. Rachel picked up some sewing on the couch near Rolf, who dozed off in the armchair.

The next raid happened only two hours later. The Nazis must be sure they had missed something—or someone.

When the tramping overhead began, Rachel grabbed Rolf's hand. He woke instantly, and she felt him freeze, but he didn't let go. Jacob and Rose held on to each other. This raid took longer than the morning one, and once they heard boots directly over the hatch. *Wouldn't it be funny if they fell through,* Rachel thought wildly. *Like an American gangster movie.* Eventually, it was over, and the hunger that was always an undercurrent overtook them. It seemed absurd that their bodies still demanded food, but they did. As they ate what there was, they couldn't even talk to each other as they listened between bites.

"Why don't you two play chess?" Rose finally suggested. "Rolf and I will clean up."

The game was welcome but strained. Even Jacob made stupid mistakes and planned only a few moves at a time. Their brief moment of peace was interrupted with a big thump overhead, as if the front door was smashed against the wall of the entryway, and someone— Els?—was thrown to the ground. Rolf again came to full attention immediately, his body rigid. Els's husband, Jan, was shouting, then another thud, and silence. The footsteps were too many to count, and they stomped everywhere, some storming upstairs while others, more threatening, rumbled through the ground floor. Below, Rachel stayed still this time, as if that would help. No one else moved, but Rose hissed, all too loudly, "Let's go! I can't stand it. Through the garden."

"We can't," Rachel reminded her, in a high whisper. "The door's blocked. They'd shoot us." She was afraid even to move toward the light switch.

Rolf looked straight at Rose with more wattage than Rachel would have thought possible. He encircled her upper arms in his hands. "Be quiet," he said. "Or you'll get us killed."

The soldiers spent a full hour going through the house again, and by the time they left, Rachel could see that everyone's nerves were in shreds. Even Rolf looked frayed. She asked again if they shouldn't check on Els or Jan, to see if they were hurt. After a long discussion, they again concluded it was too dangerous for both the upstairs and downstairs residents.

"I wonder what they're looking for," her father asked, and she could hardly contain her impatience. "It can't just be the normal raids. Why would they keep coming back here so often? It doesn't make sense." *Of course it does,* Rachel thought. *They're looking for Rolf.*

Finally, they heard steps in the kitchen, then the knocks, and Els's worn brown shoes came down the ladder. Her face looked puffy, fearful, bruised. "They threw both of us onto the floor," she said, still trembling a little. "Jan just came to, and I've put him to bed with a cold pack. We can't go on this way."

"Oh, Els!" Rachel began. "We talked about checking on you, but we were afraid we'd make things worse if they came back. Let me get you some tea."

"All right," Els agreed, sounding shaky. Rachel busied herself with the hot water, while Rolf steadied Els to the chair.

Jacob examined her face without making her wince. "Just bruising, I'm happy to say. If only we had a beefsteak to put on it."

"Not very likely," Rose said. Rachel handed everyone the fragrant mint tea, but only Els drank.

"They know I'm in the neighborhood, don't they?" Rolf asked quietly, standing by the sofa. Now it was out in the open.

"They must," Els replied. "Next time, they'll find you. One of them said he'd saw through the floorboards to see what was in the basement if he couldn't find the hatch. Then something banged loudly in the street, and the commander ordered them all out to investigate. We were lucky this time, but if they do find you here, they'll send you—and us—to Westerbork, or worse. Jan and I can't go on this way. We're going, as soon as we can pack, to our friends in North Amsterdam." Rachel saw her father wince. Her mother's face was scrunched up with fear.

"What about us?" Rolf asked. Rachel stopped her movements and listened acutely. Rolf's emotions had begun to defrost in these few days of being allowed to be a weary human being. His voice was unsteady. Could he keep himself safe if he had to go back out and charge from one danger to another?

Els replied, "Moving is a huge risk, but it's better than staying here where they're almost sure to find you. Between the raids this morning, I got a new address for the three of you"—she nodded toward Rachel in the kitchen and her parents on the sofa—"but it's not available until the morning, and I don't want you here through the day tomorrow. If the courier gets you out early enough, you should be safe from here to there. Tomorrow is a holiday for the Germans, some Nazi occasion. They told me the new host isn't a pleasant man"—Rachel noticed that they had no choice in the matter—"but the rooms are better. It's an attic."

Els said all this quickly, reluctantly, then handed her empty cup to Rachel. "Someone will come tomorrow morning just after the 6:00 curfew to take you to the new address. She has a key and she'll rap on the kitchen floor the way I would. Take only what you can wear or carry in a satchel or two, do you understand? Nothing like a suitcase that would attract attention."

"Nothing?" Rose asked.

Rachel was ahead of her, as usual. "You can turn that lace table-cloth into a shawl, and we can sew the plates inside Paps's jacket. But what about Rolf?" He couldn't go with them, and she didn't know if she could bear it. He was her only connection to Michiel, to her generation, to the underground worker she had been before she was a prisoner. She walked over and reached for him.

Els turned to Rolf. "Be ready tonight, right before curfew."

He put his light arm around Rachel's shoulders and said, "Isn't the morning soon enough?"

"No." When Rachel let out a little cry, Els added, "I wish it were."

That doesn't count for much, Rachel thought, burying her head into the crook of Rolf's shoulder, not caring what anyone saw or thought.

"At least let us say goodbye to you, Els," Rose said, her voice sounding mechanical and full of effort. "We can never thank—"

"Please," Els interrupted her. "I'm sure you would have done it for us." Tearing herself from Rolf, Rachel came over to kiss Els goodbye, but her face was much too battered to allow for that. Rolf helped Els up the ladder and opened the hatchway. When he returned, he turned to Rachel and gave her the briefest of hugs. She would have to be content with that; she could almost hear his gears shifting. The walls around them seemed closer and danker, the stench heavier and more penetrating than ever.

In a few hours, he'd be entirely gone, but Rolf was already miles from Rachel. She felt him steeling himself to be on the move again, knowing anyone might betray him. As soon as danger closed in, he snapped shut. Before, he'd just wanted food, physical comfort, warmth, and the chance to sleep as much as possible. Els's announcement had jolted him out of that state. *He's already gone,* she thought.

Her mother's hand was on her back, guiding her to the couch.

Rolf was in the kitchen now, getting some water on to boil. "Let's sit down and have some more tea, and talk about how you're going to get safely to the next place," he said, taking charge in a way that he certainly hadn't before. Did his imminent departure give him permission? His jaw was clenched.

Slumping on the corner of the couch, Rachel couldn't stand to look at him. He was as aloof as a general on the battlefield.

"Come on, tea will do you good," he cajoled. Her parents came to the table. Rachel didn't move. He could bring her tea if he wanted her to have it. What would it be like for her and her parents to go outside again? They were hardly safe even here, and the streets must be swarming with Nazis. Wasn't it a form of suicide even to show their faces? Yet she longed for the open air more than anything, more even than a good meal.

Her father's tense face relaxed as he blew on the hot mint tea, making a vapor that dissolved in the chilly air.

Rose spoke slowly. "I hate the thought of going out on the street, even for a few blocks, but it would be worse to be trapped in this awful basement for another raid."

Rolf sounded calm, as if a switch had been flipped, and a different current flowed through his veins. "Your chances of getting to the new place are good. Rachel is as pretty as any girl on the street who isn't being fed by a German. Rose will pass if you put a decent hat on her head and some makeup." Rachel squeezed her hands until they hurt. How could he not look at her?

Rolf was saying, "Doctor, you're the problem. It's not just the nose. That beard has to go."

Jacob was speechless. Rose said, "Jacob has always worn a beard. What if he just covered the lower half of his face?" Rachel couldn't imagine her father without his beard any more than she could envision him without his eyes or his mouth.

"He'd be spotted. It's spring out there. You don't want to be noticed at all. I'm sure the person coming for you has planned a route where the police don't usually go—but some of it is just luck.

Keep your eyes open and evade them before they see you. If you have to stay within their view, look confident. Stand up straight, which Rachel and the doctor haven't done since you came here. Pretend you're free to come and go, just as always. Rachel knows how to do it." He seemed to notice at last that Rachel had no tea, and handed it to her. His eyes were as cold as marbles, but he did ask, "No matter how frightening it is out there, won't you be glad to be outside?"

"Yes. Oh, yes," Rachel said. "I just want to see the light, even for a few minutes." He still didn't really look at her.

Rose spoke up. "What if they do stop us on the way?"

"Then it will be difficult, unless Rachel wins them over." Rolf shook his head. "If there are one or two of them, you might be lucky, Rachel. They may just want a few kisses." Rolf looked down at his hands, which were fidgeting with his sweater. "Remember it's a question of your lives. I'm just being practical. It's ugly, but it may be the only currency they'll accept. Sometimes even diamonds aren't working anymore." Rachel fingered her grandfather's stones around her neck, and Rose clutched involuntarily at the inner seam of her camisole where she had sewn the carats in almost undetectable pouches.

Rolf

"Let's talk about what you can take along to the new place, Mrs. Klein," Rolf said. "They'll be expecting everyone to wear raincoats in this weather. Just be sure yours doesn't look too lumpy." He heard his efficient voice kick in, as if he were a tour guide instructing them about what they'd need on safari. Who knew, they might make it to the new place. Certainly their chances were much better than his.

Rachel asked, "Maybe Els would help us move things? She's been so good to us, and she can go anywhere she wants." Her voice trembled, and she was being totally unrealistic. He'd thought she was braver and smarter than this.

"Not anymore. If they find your things on her, they will certainly arrest her, and maybe torture or kill her. Quickly, if she's lucky."

The next half hour was spent in a parody of a children's dress-up game. Rolf himself could take nothing wherever he was going, but forced himself to consider what they might need. The pile they wanted to take seemed minimal to them, but distributed on three bodies it expanded exponentially. At last, the job was done.

Rose said, "I'm tired, Jacob. Let's take some rest while we can."

Rachel was standing uncertainly by the sofa, her face streaked with tears. Despite himself, Rolf was moved. She had looked like a little girl holding her shell of a bunny, which he had unstuffed for her so she could take it. It wouldn't hurt him to spend a few minutes with her. "Come on," he said, taking her flaccid hand and leading her to her corner. They sat on the bed with their backs against the wall, his knees bent, his heels just on the other side of the mattress. He stared at the curtain. His heart was pounding and racing as it had not since he arrived here, as if fuel were circulating in his body rather than blood. When Rachel surprised him by taking his hand, he had to fight the urge to pull away.

How did the Nazis know to look for him here, in this house? Maybe his number really had come up, after all his escapes. If Els had not been beaten so badly, he would have wondered if she had betrayed them. He probably wouldn't last long on the street, but he had the satisfaction of having avenged Jaap time and again. His hand loosened on Rachel's. He thought of the Jewish children he'd helped tuck away in farms. They would grow up, and they wouldn't forget what had happened to their parents. Now that the Nazis were increasingly after the general population as well as the Jews, more people were helping the underground. If only they had offered those additional addresses earlier, he could have saved more Jewish families. But it was best not to look back. He began calculating strategies, routes, chances.

Rachel let go of his hand and lay down. He heard her head flop onto the pillow, and her body curled up so that only her feet touched him. The expression on her face was bleak and harrowed. Her eyes were closed now. In less than an hour, she would almost surely be lost to him forever.

Across the basement, Rolf heard the soft strains of Rose and Jacob singing a faint lullaby to each other. The music dissolved into the quiet like the honey in a cup of tea, faint but sweetening everything. He suddenly imagined the two of them there, those two older people still finding solace in each other's arms. He would never have that, and suddenly that void was unbearable. He looked down at Rachel, separate, her eyes still closed. Suddenly, he saw her body as never before.

Even under the tired sweater and the barely clean dress, her heart was beating, her whole physical being was buzzing with life. His mind stopped, and he slid in beside her, cupping his body around hers. At first she stiffened. But everything had changed now. She turned to him. It was their last chance, not just with each other but perhaps forever. His hands found her breasts, luscious against her hard ribs. In an instant he was ready to devour every morsel of her that she would give.

Now her breath went ragged, too, and she unbuttoned his shirt, then licked his nipples, which he could hardly bear. He must not cry out, for so many reasons. The curtain was useless as a sound barrier. In the vague distance, he thought he heard Rachel's parents arguing, but it barely registered. His clothes slipped off easily, then hers.

"Do we have time?" she whispered.

For answer, he clasped her close and rolled her on top of him. As their tongues found each other, he could feel that she was already wet and ready everywhere. Her faint smell reached him. She slipped off him onto the bedroll, then pulled his far arm so he was on top of her. When she guided him inside her, it was all he could do not to push hard, once, and have it all be over. But this might be the last time, and he didn't want that, the way it was when he was alone.

As he forced himself to stop, he felt her squeeze and welcome him. Inside, she was moist and shimmering. If she moved much, he would be lost. "Stop," he managed to whisper, then noticed that she was crying.

He asked, "Hurt?"

She shook her head. "No. More."

For all the physical intensity, his body and hers seemed to drift into each other like clouds, more indistinguishable every moment. Then Rachel grabbed Rolf's bottom and pressed him deeper into her, hard. He was finished in seconds, then felt her rippling all around him. They both managed to be quiet. Rachel stroked his hair, which felt sweaty despite the chill, and his hand rested on her cheek.

From a great distance, they heard Rose and Jacob get up. Rose said, "It's almost seven. They'll come for him soon. Not a word to her about this, Jacob. Not a word." Rolf tried to hang on, but Rachel pulled away and took his hands in hers, kissing each finger. She pulled his clothes from the pile at the bottom of the bed, helped him wipe off on the sheet, then dress himself. That brought him back. It was almost time for him to go, and he had to get mentally ready. Reviewing the beauty of her body would not help. In a few moments, she had dressed and left him.

He heard her starting to boil water. How could he face her parents? Rachel and he must reek of sex. Her mother might not be shocked; he was sure he'd caught a knowing glance from her sometimes. But the doctor hadn't met his eyes lately. Maybe he and Rose had been arguing about what was going on behind the curtain. Normally this would have troubled Rolf, but it was the least of his worries as he contemplated his own escape.

He tried to put his clothes back in order. Mechanically, Rolf checked his pockets to be sure he had a knife, and the money they'd given him before he came here. He pushed aside the curtain and took in the tableau of Jacob, pink with what was probably an amalgam of embarrassment and rage, pretending to study his anatomy book but obeying his wife's orders to say nothing; Rose, fidgeting with her piano keyboard; and Rachel, looking absolutely radiant despite the fear that iced over her features. Had it been a terrible mistake to come together, just that once? *I didn't mean to,* he felt like saying. But he couldn't be sorry. He would find the strength to survive outside, or at least give the Nazis a run for their money. If only he didn't have to leave Rachel now, this way . . . but he did.

To his amazement, Rose came over and hugged him. He almost cried. It was her way of saying that it was all right, that nothing had been broken or hurt. Jacob, however, was glowering at him. Rachel's eyes filled when she looked across at her father, and she came over to his armchair. His disapproval would be terrible for her.

"Tea?" Rachel handed her father a cup without making eye contact.

"No," he said in a normal voice. Rachel put it down anyway.

"Shh!" Rolf hissed. Had the man forgotten where they were? Steps sounded upstairs, probably two people.

"Els and Jan must be leaving," Rachel said. Now they would be alone, with no buffers if another raid came. The front door closed overhead.

The four of them drank mint tea and waited for the person who would take Rolf away. If the doctor hadn't been scowling, Rolf would have put his arm around Rachel, but that would only make more of a mess after he left. Stealing a glance, he saw that she looked shaky but resolute.

When a low whistle sounded outside, Rolf's body jerked. "I have to go," he said simply, and turned to Rose and Jacob. "Thank you for everything." He reached for a bag, then remembered that he had none.

"Goodbye" was all Jacob would say, ignoring Rolf's extended hand, but Rose took it and gave him another hug, tighter this time. Her body felt bony like her daughter's.

On the other side of the basement, he saw Rachel reach overhead and begin to push up the hatch, very gradually and listening after each centimeter. Finally, she opened the hatch fully, and came back down, where Rolf stood at the bottom of the few stairs.

"You'd better go," she said quietly. "Be careful." Her face was in blossom like a rose in his mother's garden, every surface soft and fragrant.

He listened closely before taking the next step up.

"Move the rug somewhere credible," she reminded him. "Otherwise it looks suspicious." A real farewell embrace was impossible. Instead, as he went up the ladder, Rachel gave him an imperative, sisterly pat on the bottom as he went up. She lingered on the lower steps of the ladder as he closed the hatch and arranged the rug. He must not look back.

When Rolf opened the front door, he listened, then leaned his head out slightly to glance up and down the street. A man he recognized was waiting to guide him. He stepped out.

Rose

Rose heard the front door close. No shot from the street.

She rushed to the foot of the ladder as Rachel came down in slow motion, then collapsed into her waiting arms. It had been years since she had felt her daughter's full weight. She half-carried her to the couch, and held her in her lap like a child. Jacob stalked off toward their bed. Rose would have to find a way to calm him down. What did he expect, that Rachel would never have a man in her life? She hated to feel the heartbrokenness in her child's body, wracking it.

Rose stroked Rachel's hair until she stopped crying and fell asleep on the couch from shock. Once she had eased her daughter's head onto the cushion, Rose paced as far as she could, then back. At least this basement had been safe until now, unpleasant as it was. Who knew what the next day would bring? Elandsgracht, where their walk would begin, used to be bustling with life and small shops and the city's characters, including the corner bakery with chocolate pastries. When her family emerged, how would they look to the people who had gone on living with a measure of freedom? Their pallor alone might give them away. It wasn't just the unflattering lights that gave them a cadaverous look.

She dreaded going to bed and facing Jacob's anger, and took another turn around the sofa. He would be upset that she had shushed him and hugged Rolf when he came out of Rachel's space rumpled and glowing, but that was just too bad. As long as there was no baby, no harm had been done. If only Jacob could see that they weren't living in the world of his grandparents anymore, with girls saving themselves for marriage. It was wartime now, and even before that, he and she had barely managed to wait themselves. Had he forgotten?

Her legs wearied of pacing. After her simple toilet, she undressed and slipped in beside Jacob. His body was turned away from her, coiled up like a spring, but at least it was warm. She reached for him, and he flipped over.

"How could you—" he began, but Rose just shook her head.

"We don't have time for that, Jacob. Tomorrow they may shoot us in the street. Let's not argue tonight." Rolling toward him, she put her arm across his chest, but he lay on his back and didn't respond. Sleep began to pull the blankets over her mind. She slipped away, then woke terrified hours later from a nightmare as someone pursued her up a long, long staircase. When she clutched Jacob, he patted her shoulder. "There, there," he said, in a voice that showed he had been wide awake all night. She didn't want to be, and fell back to sleep almost immediately.

Jacob woke her at 5:00. She responded first without remembering his anger, throwing her leg over his and squeezing close. When he didn't respond as usual, the evening before came back to her. At least he hadn't recoiled. Maybe the night had brought him some peace. They cleaned up and dressed in silence, as Rose plotted some way to bring the two people she loved together before they had to look confident on the street.

By the time she and Jacob emerged, Rachel had put their last rations onto the table with symmetry and grace. That was a good start, even if her face was swollen from crying. Rose sat between the other two, clasped their hands for a moment, and said, "We have to help each other stay safe. Nothing is more important than that this morning, or any time. We all need to be as calm as we can." Rachel nodded gladly, Jacob more reluctantly, and they finished such breakfast as they had.

As they finished their food, Jacob glanced at his watch. "I'm afraid we need to get ready," he said.

"Let's leave things tidy," Rose said, even though there was no reason to think it would matter to anyone. But Els had been so kind. Once they had finished cleaning up and were dressed in as many layers as they dared, Jacob pulled out his anatomy book and sat in his chair. Was he really studying, or just pretending? In either case, he was composed and ready. If they were captured as soon as they got out on the street, would this be her last real image of him? As awful as this basement had been, it was their home, and safer than most. Connie had told them that the Nazis offered a tidy sum for each Jew someone turned in. Throwing off a shudder, Rose glanced at Rachel, who looked as if she could crumple at any time.

"Get yourself together, young lady," she ordered. "On the street there's no excuse for a face like that. We still have some powder." She produced it and went to work on both herself and Rachel, whose face still showed her youth, and a vestige of her radiance. Anything could happen to them all in the next few hours. All in all she was glad her daughter had known love.

Rachel cocked her head and pointed upward in response to a slight footfall on Els's living room floor. They all stood up and moved toward the hatchway. Leaving the light on wouldn't matter anymore.

Four knocks, then footsteps. Overhead was deliverance, or betrayal. Rachel stood aside. "You first, Mams."

Why should she be the first to face whoever was there? But she went. Rose lifted the hatch and saw a pair of elegantly shod feet in front of her—sleek leather, wet from the outdoors—and above them a shapely and youthful ankle, then a long blue lightweight wool skirt. A hand reached down, and a warm woman's voice said, "Here, let me help you up." When Rose looked into her dark blue eyes, set in the sharp cheekbones of wartime, she took the woman's hand and spoke down to Rachel and Jacob. "It's all right." Stepping into the kitchen, she saw the table set for two, as if Els and Jan were coming back in a moment. The grainy light of early morning graced the china in the cabinet, even the faucets in the sink. The air was delicious.

Rachel, then Jacob, stepped into the kitchen and straightened up with similar grimaces. The woman shook their hands, too. She wasn't yet thirty, but had an air of authority that came from more than her clothes and stature. "We only have a few blocks to go, about ten minutes. You have your papers? Good. Assume we'll be stopped. You've been called to the bedside of an elderly cousin who's very ill. His name is Hermann Neuberger and he lives in the Prinsengracht. I'm a nurse who brought you the news that he got worse during the night and is asking for you. He has no telephone. My name is Mieke. Tell me yours." They gave their false names. "And the address on your papers? Good. Relax as much as you possibly can, but straighten up. They're specifically looking for anybody who might have been hidden."

"Where are we going?" Jacob asked as they headed for the door. Rose met Rachel's eyes and looked heavenward.

"Oh, Paps!" Rachel sighed.

After Mieke opened the door and checked in both directions, they stepped across the threshold. Even the gray early light hurt Rose's eyes. The North Sea wind thrashed the trees. Since the basement had been so cold, the chilly temperature didn't shock her even without a coat, but the gale flung itself at her body like a bludgeon. The fresh air felt harsh on her skin. At least it wasn't raining yet.

Rose took a deep breath and said, "Almost nine months. We've been in there nearly long enough for a baby to be born."

"Forget it." Mieke turned and fixed her with the look of a soldier quelling an errant captive. "Think about your cousin-in-law. He's near death. You're in a hurry. Look the part and come along."

Rose hurried to keep up with Mieke, deliberately leaving Rachel and Jacob together. "I don't know if we can walk that fast," she said, huffing a little herself. "We're out of shape."

"Nonsense," said Mieke. "Cousin Hermann needs you." Almost no one was on the street. At the corner of the Prinsengracht, Mieke turned left, and they followed along the luminous canal. The water rippled toward the Westerkerk, flashing silver along with the brownish green, and just beginning to reflect the first chartreuse leaves breaking on the elms overhead. The Westerkerk carillon played three bars of music to mark the hour—music Rose heard as if for the first time. She turned and smiled at Rachel, who loved the bells as much as she did. They had never been without them for so long. Just seeing the tower reach into the sky made her feel an instant of hope, followed by a deep tug as they approached Lauriergracht. Surely they could go by their house, even if they couldn't go in. She turned to ask Mieke if they could, but Jacob spoke first.

"Don't look," he said, his voice breaking.

If he couldn't stand it, Rose wouldn't even make the request. Her mind immediately returned to getting safely to their new address. She longed to arrive and be secure, but she also wanted to slow this walk down, to feel every step of it, the brick under her feet rather than the basement's cold earthen floor. She wanted to study each house's large windows, fashioned with layers of curved molding like a picture frame. She longed to know each one's facade as intimately as the faces of the people she loved.

Mieke interrupted her thoughts. "Careful. We'd better not look as if we're avoiding those men in uniform." A pair watched them, smoking and talking on the corner of Rosengracht. "Rachel, change places with your mother and smile and chat with me. I love those Italian shoes of yours." She stretched her mouth into a somewhat convincing grin. Rachel stepped forward and smiled back.

"My parents gave them to me for my eighteenth birthday. You'll have to excuse Mams and Paps this morning. They're usually more cheerful, but they're worried about my father's sick cousin." Her voice seemed unnaturally loud, but it was probably the contrast with the basement.

Behind them, Rose took Jacob's arm and shook it. "Think about your patient," she whispered. That would wipe the terror off his face, if he could only imagine it.

Mieke led them down the deserted street, straight toward the uniforms. "If old people have to get that sick, they shouldn't do it at this ungodly hour." She and Rachel kept bantering until they were close to the officers.

If this is the end, Rose thought, let it be here, in the open air, beneath the carillon's tower, with my arm through Jacob's and my daughter just ahead. If our time together must be over, let it end here, not in some faraway camp.

Rachel

The danger went to Rachel's head like champagne. How different from the terror of cowering in the basement, where she could do nothing! This was a game she knew how to play. Up to now she had always won.

The men's eyes traveled lazily up and down her and Mieke's bodies. One Nazi was stout and middle-aged, much older than the other. "Where have you been, out on the town?" he demanded with a wink.

Rachel remembered what Eva taught her about flirtation. "Don't I wish! Unfortunately, it's some old cousin." She looked at the man as if for sympathy from another young person, not someone twenty or more years her senior. His lips twitched a bit.

"You're visiting someone at this hour?" The other soldier sounded German, and looked young and sharp.

"The doctor's cousin." Mieke shrugged. "He got worse overnight and wants to see the old folks before he dies, so I went and got them. It's spooky now, with nobody around. I was scared walking over by myself." Rachel wondered, *Can she make herself blush like that at will? I need to learn that trick myself.*

The young soldier looked closely at Jacob and Rose, and said, "It can be dangerous." If only her father didn't look so pale.

"How about coming along to protect us?" Rachel asked. Pushing it, maybe, but it might work.

The older one sighed. "You'll be all right. Maybe we'll see you later, around the neighborhood." His eyes slid back down to Rachel's breasts. She felt like slapping him.

Instead, she gave a little wave and smile, and Mieke said, "See you!" with a promising look, then "Come on, they're waiting, and he won't last much longer."

As the four of them crossed the bridge, Rachel looked back and waved at the men again. The two seemed to be arguing, which terrified her. They had fooled the older man, but the young one seemed unconvinced.

Mieke counseled in a low voice, "Keep it up. Square your shoulders, doctor." As the carillon's melody for the quarter hour filled the air with joyous notes, Rachel glanced back at her father and implored with her eyes. He had to straighten up. Even her young body hurt when she lengthened her spine, and it must be worse for him.

He met her eyes and rallied, saying "I treated the manager of that office we just passed for a sprained ankle once. A nice fellow from Germany with two daughters. I wonder what happened to them." He sounded more normal than he had all day.

"How much farther?" Rose asked, her voice cracking. "It's been a lot more than ten minutes." No one answered her.

For an instant, intoxicated with real air and the trees overhead, Rachel remembered how the sea pushed the wind in as the clouds tumbled over the gabled rooftops. She wanted to stop and memorize every house so she could draw it.

Returning to reality, Rachel speeded up. Mieke began now to look at the house numbers. The trees were tall, just leafing out over the canal, their branches tangling in the wind. Below them, the water lightened when a space opened between the clouds.

Rachel asked, "What address are you looking for, Mieke? I know all the house numbers."

"199."

"Just a little farther." So these were her last steps outside, at least for now. The houses on the other side of the canal had never looked more alluring, with their pinkish brown brick and ivory-colored molding, and the immense windows to let in the light. *Will all this really be taken from me again?* Rachel thought. *I could probably find that old policeman. He'd surely help me live through the war with good food and silk stockings.* She was horrified at herself, but there it was. That thought.

At 199, Mieke rang the bell. Rachel felt Jacob's arm reach around her as they stood with their backs to the narrow door, gazing out at the canal. The beauty was still there, and he felt it, too. For that moment, her father had returned.

When the door finally opened, they turned. The middle-aged man behind it peered at them with suspicion bordering on hostility. He was tall and fair, with a thin nose and rheumy eyes. His large larynx bobbed as he spoke. "Yes?" he demanded.

"I have the packages you were expecting," Mieke said.

"OK. I'm Han. Come in." He started up the high, steep stairs.

Jacob followed first after Rose gestured to him. The stairway was steep and narrow. Although both parents had gone up now, Rachel hesitated and turned to Mieke. "You have to go?"

"Yes. Good luck. He's not very nice, but it's a good address." She turned and strode off.

Only one step remained for Rachel, across the threshold. A last look at the trees, the sky, the water. At least they were going up the stairs, not down; back into hiding, not into prison. They had made it. She stepped in, closed the door behind her, and followed her parents up three flights of stairs, slowing as their breaths came harder. Her father and Han were talking quietly. When they reached the top, Han lifted a hatch, and some daylight caressed her father's upraised face. Han scrambled up, then reached back to help her parents, then her. His hand was sweaty and held on a little too long.

Toward the canal were two windows in a dormer covered with black paper. A skylight over the stairway was covered only with white—to keep the herons from seeing them?—which meant there was some actual light. Yes, it was better than the basement in every way—but where were the trees she'd just seen again, for those few moments? The wind? The sound of the water and the leaves? Just a thin pane away. Maybe when Han was gone, she could make a tear, just a little one, and peek through. *I'm standing up straight!* she thought, although her shoulders hurt with the unfamiliar position. *And I can breathe.*

Just in front of the windows, practically filling the alcove, was a low bed. The central space adjacent to it was almost square, with plenty of room for a weathered oak table and chairs, and a rounded art deco sofa and armchair with pebbly multicolored upholstery. A coral and burgundy Armenian rug with intricate geometric patterns complemented it perfectly. It almost looked familiar. But Rachel didn't see anywhere where she could sleep. Not the couch?

"What beautiful things!" Rose exclaimed. "Wherever did you get all this, just for an attic?"

Han looked at his shoes. "Someone didn't need it anymore."

"Look, Rose," her father was saying. "A real duvet!"

"The last people left that here. They decided it was too bulky. Better luck for you, I guess. Let's talk about the rent." Han quoted a price that made Jacob blanch, but that he ultimately had to pay.

Han said, "I'm sure you don't expect me to provide meals for that, but if you want something to drink now I'll get my wife to bring up some coffee."

"No meals!" Rose stepped in. "But how can we eat? Of course we expect food to be included. At our last place, I cooked our meals on an electric burner. We could do that here."

Rachel watched this drama as if it were happening on a stage.

"I can't have you cooking up here. The smell would go right to the neighbors. You can boil water, but that's all," Han said. "I can't be too careful, you know." He tried to look like someone who was thinking hard about something that was really against his better judgment. "I'll talk to my wife and see if she'd be willing to do food for three more people. But it will cost more, of course; food is so high these days. And it's dangerous. Let's say double the rent." He darted a quick glance at Jacob to see how he was taking it.

Although he was no mathematician, Rachel saw Jacob wince. Rose again spoke: "As you well know, we have no other way to eat. Ask your wife if she can make us some soup for lunch and a hot dinner, with something light for breakfast. We don't eat pork; it's the one thing my husband asks. She should be able to manage that for 10 percent more than the rent and still make a tidy profit."

"Twenty percent." What could they do but agree? Han kept talking. "Let me just show you a thing or two. If you go through the door back there, you'll find a bucket. It's curtained off from the rest of the storage space. I have some other old stuff stored beyond it. Don't walk back there. You'll be right over our bedrooms and it will creak. You don't want that and neither do I."

Rachel's eyes roamed around the room, taking in the hot plate and basin on a narrow counter behind the table. It looked as if it had been built in on purpose. How long had he been hiding people? And what had happened to the people who had left all this behind?

"*Tot ziens!*" Han turned and disappeared down the stairs, closing the hatch after him. At last, she could let go and ask herself where Rolf was now. Had he even made it out of the city? She sat down. The armchair felt firm, with good springs. The air was so fresh.

"I don't like this," Rose whispered. "He's the type who would turn us in to anybody who offered him enough." She looked around and caught Rachel's eye. "At least it's so much brighter here. And look at that teapot with forget-me-nots and ivy."

Rachel nodded. Who left the china here? She stood up again, and touched the ceiling. Her shoulders felt stabbed with the pain.

Jacob spoke up, "I don't like being so far from the ground. What if they come after us again?" No one tried to answer.

"Where do I sleep? On the couch?" Rachel asked. The large bed was obviously for her parents. She had so hoped that her own space would be better this time. She needed time to herself more than ever. To remember Rolf, their last moments together. She pushed him firmly out of her head for now, but her body still felt stretched and alive from his being inside her.

"No," Jacob said firmly. "As we were coming upstairs, Han promised me two beds with a separate space for you. That's why I agreed to these outrageous prices." Even in her fog, Rachel appreciated the shred of privacy she would have for the first time since they left home.

In the light filtering through the skylight, her father's face looked so odd without his beard. He had ultimately followed Rolf's advice, little as he liked to.

"Your bed must be somewhere," he said firmly.

"What are you going to do, search the storage cupboards?" Rose tried to joke.

Why not, Rachel wondered, and scanned the wall near the floor. She discovered an odd door, a high isosceles triangle on the opposite wall from her parents' alcove. She knelt down and opened the catch. It gave way into a strangely configured dark space, rather like a berth on a yacht. She crawled in and could only just sit up. Her "bed" was again a mattress on the floor, but it was dry. The space was hers alone, and felt enclosed. She liked it, even if it was dark.

After she emerged, Jacob poked his head in. "This will never do," he protested with unusual indignation. "My daughter is not going to sleep in a closet." Rose, who had been moving closer to him, stayed back, and sat in one of the straight chairs by the table.

"Paps?" Rachel was too old to plead with her father, but she had to make him see. She couldn't bear it if he shut her out. "Remember when I made the closet at the top of the stairs my library at home? I like little places."

"Of course I remember. I used to hear you run all the way downstairs whenever I came up for lunch." His shoulders slumped. "I guess this is the best we can do for now," he said. "Maybe the next place will be better."

Rachel put her arm around her father's rounded back. He flinched at first, then eased toward her as she said, "Or maybe we'll stay here until it's over. Maybe we won't need another place."

Rose shook her head. "That's right," she said. "Maybe we won't."

APRIL 10—MAY 1943

Jacob

The journey from basement to attic might have been miles, given how much it had exhausted him. Apart from his fury and confusion about what happened before Rolf left, he couldn't understand how Rachel could have prattled on with that girl—what was her name, Mieke?—when their lives were at stake. She even seemed at ease with the police on the corner, almost friendly. However, when they stood on their new doorstep, he'd seen Rachel's eyes fill with the beauty of the canal and the houses, and even the low sky. For an instant he felt that she was his again, no matter what she had or hadn't done. She'd moved closer to him as they breathed in the open air and trembling water.

The next few nights, he and Rose slept so soundly in their new bed. His anger at her and Rachel was waning; he just didn't have the energy. It was heavenly to smell fresh linen again, and to feel the mattress cradle his tired bones. After they took the black paper off the skylight, the daylight filtering through the white layer was bright. Being able to stand up fully was an immense relief, despite his muscles crying out.

The landlord's capricious visits made Rose and Rachel edgy. Although the food he brought was welcome and much better than what Els had provided, Han seemed to take delight in giving them dire reports almost every day. "More raids last night. They told that Jewish Council of yours to choose seven thousand of their own employees, so they're scrambling. I hear the Schouwburg Theatre is still full, even though they're shipping people off by the hundreds every day." He relished the words.

When Han finally retreated downstairs, Rose said, "That man looks at Rachel and me as if he owns us. What if he betrays us? If they send us to Westerbork to the Transit Camp, there's no way to escape the camps farther on."

"Don't be sure," Rachel replied. "Before we went into hiding, I heard that some people had been there for months, so there must be a way to avoid going east." He couldn't imagine how she picked up information like that. Could she be right?

"Most ways to stay there would be expensive, I imagine," Rose added. Did Rose always have to see the worst in every situation? Jacob's hand went over his eyes.

✕ ✕ ✕

Because their quarters were not above the main floor of the house, quiet movement was possible unless they heard noises directly below. He noticed that Rachel had begun drawing again, both the houses they had passed on their walk, and the attic itself. From early morning until they covered it, the white paper over the skylight gently diffused the sun, or the pearly light that sank through the clouds.

The calm might be an illusion, but he noticed that they all slept better, their bodies readjusting to the normal daylight cycle. When Jacob woke entwined with Rose, she often stirred at about the same time, and Rachel was usually up within an hour. The quality of food available was far beyond Els's supplies—fresher, more varied, and plentiful. He didn't like to think why that might be. After even a few days, they all had more energy.

One morning when he awoke earlier than either Rose or Rachel, he took a flashlight from the kitchen and tiptoed beyond the bucket into the storage area, putting each foot down with great care. The dusty light beam touched on surprisingly lavish furnishings—a ghostly chandelier with hundreds of facets, a gilded armchair, an armoire with marquetry—the sort of thing his parents had, or that Mr. Posner used to sell. What was it doing here?

When Jacob reached the back of the room, he was reassured that the windows were big enough to allow escape onto the rooftops if it was necessary. And it might not be. The moments of panic were fewer than in the basement. While the raids elsewhere were reported as numerous, Han's house was unaffected thus far. Knowing that Rachel was at least one door away gave both him and Rose permission to make love with less restraint. At least their desire for each other had not changed.

X   X   X

Jacob was still troubled by what his daughter had done, but he couldn't help but rejoice in her less anxious manner. Something was different about her now—not only the benefits of better meals, but something else. He couldn't put his finger on it. When they played chess, she was as quick and smart as ever, but at other times she drifted off more and more, often spending hours reading.

Within a few weeks, his calisthenics had begun to be easier, and he'd actually increased the repetitions in some exercises. When he squeezed Rose to him, her ribs were cloaked with a thin layer of flesh, not just skin. Rachel was beginning to show some of the bloom she'd had before, when she was a child with plump cheeks. Occasionally a few fresh spring greens from Han's family in Drenthe appeared on their table. Rose partitioned them carefully so everyone could have a fair share. Only Rachel seemed to be having trouble with their change in diet. He'd heard her throwing up several times, and sometimes she looked queasy during the day.

✕   ✕   ✕

One morning, Han pushed the hatch up almost silently, then proclaimed in a loud voice, "Ta da! Here's your soup—she said it's turnips, beets, an onion, and some beans. I'll bring your water later." Jacob stood up hurriedly from his comfortable chair, still in his bathrobe. Han smirked, seeming to relish the moment of terror he had caused, and put a pot on the table.

Pushing down his anger, Jacob asked, "Han, could you get some antacid for my daughter? She's having stomach problems, and I only have a limited supply. The pharmacist near the Jewish Invalid always has it." Glancing at the other man's face, Jacob added, "We would pay for it separately, of course."

"The Jewish Invalid?" Han said. "They just raided it. Nobody left but a few patients so filthy they couldn't be moved without getting the Green Police dirty. They shipped off more than a hundred patients, and any staff who were stupid enough to stay. Risk your life for your kid, that's one thing—but for some old fool who hardly knows you're there? They're at Westerbork or worse by now, you can be sure of it."

Jacob began to tremble. His eyes blurred, and he squeezed them shut as tightly as he could. Rose's hands were on his shoulders.

"What's the matter?" Han asked sharply. "Did you know somebody there?"

"Yes." Jacob opened his eyes, and everything was blurry through the tears. "I had patients there. The staff whom you"—he almost lost control for a moment—"called stupid were the most dedicated nurses I ever met. They stayed with their patients, as I should have—"

"Jacob!" Rose interrupted. "You couldn't have saved even one of them if you had held on. We're lucky to be here."

Lucky? What about all those who weren't? Why hadn't he been at their side? At least he could have given them some solace at Westerbork or wherever they were going.

Han puffed up. "You were a doctor, were you? That might come in handy. Don't get too upset, will you, miss? You're too pretty for that. You have a lovely daughter there, doctor. Too bad she's wasted up here. See you later. *Tot ziens!*" He disappeared as silently as he had emerged, with a slight thump as the hatch slid back into place.

"Unbearable," Rose hissed. "Just unbearable."

Jacob's head sank into his hands as he calculated who he still knew there, and whether each person would have stayed or gone.

Rose bent over him, her breasts nestling against the back of his neck.

"Come to bed," she ordered. He let her take him there.

Rachel

Watching her parents retreat, Rachel's hands trembled on her coffee cup. She went to her own corner and curled up in bed so she could escape into her imagination. She envisioned the sheen of rain on the paving bricks beside the canals' silvery shimmering. Rolf was out there somewhere, she felt sure, not dead like Michiel. She longed to see him. And even one single tree, its branches quivering in the wind from the North Sea, that seemingly limitless, constantly tossing water, whipped into waves and crashing in.

To stand by the sea now, and feel the wind teasing out the curls in her hair, to lean into that force and know she wouldn't fall, to hear the everlasting roar . . . That's where she would go to ask herself the question that came up every morning from her seething stomach. She'd vomited the last three mornings, and didn't feel right until noon. Her belly, until recently thinner every day, was waxing a sliver at a time, like the moon. Was it the better diet? Or was someone else uncurling inside her belly, hidden for now?

Lying on her back, Rachel could touch the angled ceiling just over her head. The space was just long enough to provide room for her bed, a book or two, a lamp, and her underwear. Even here, she never took off the pouch with her grandfather's diamonds in it. She liked the way they felt between her breasts. Had Rolf noticed them? Probably not, since everything had happened so fast. Even the recollection seemed dreamlike, as if it had happened to someone else.

Rachel smoothed her gown with her hands, starting above her breasts. Pressing a little made her whole inner body come to life, no matter what the news was. Her hands traveled over her ribs, then reached her belly. Would Michiel have understood what happened with Rolf? Reaching the top of her thighs, she realized how wet she was. Michiel was a memory, but Rolf had just left her. She could still feel him stretching her all the way to her spine. *No one will hear me,* she thought, and stroked herself until she laughed quietly, then cried.

✕ ✕ ✕

The next morning, as Rachel crouched over the bucket in the dark, she felt Rose's hand on her back, just as it had been when she was four and ten and even fifteen. Some strange force gripped her and shook her by the spine, and she retched again.

Rose's hand felt cool. "Get it over with," she said. When the bout was finished, Rachel stood up slowly, feeling dizzy, and opened the door. Her mother headed to the water supply. No sign or sound of Jacob. Good. Rachel lowered herself to the couch. She had to face what was happening. She hadn't eaten something that disagreed with her; it would have passed by now. Many women missed periods as they lost weight in hiding, but morning sickness like this was a real sign.

What would pregnancy mean for them? Her mother knew what had happened between her and Rolf, had even encouraged her in a way. But her father? He would never understand anything—what Michiel was to her, how she and Rolf came together only that once. She didn't understand it all herself, but she did feel hope uncurling in her belly like a spring fern's frond. *I'll talk to Mams in another few days,* she thought. *I just need to get used to the idea.* Then they would plan how to tell her father, as they so often had.

Rose was beside her. "Don't swallow this," she instructed, handing Rachel a cup with a little water in it. "Just rinse out your mouth." The young woman obeyed her, as she used to. Rose sat down and hugged her, speaking right into her ear. "Don't worry. It won't be bad for long. You only gave me this kind of trouble for a couple of weeks."

Rachel pulled away to look into her mother's face. Rose nodded. Just then the bedclothes rustled, and Jacob appeared, still in his pajamas. He looked at the two of them, averted his eyes, and went toward the bucket.

"We'll talk later," Rose promised, and went off to heat water. Rachel had still not said a word. Her stomach was boiling again, a volcano gathering its forces to seethe all day. She glanced at the black rectangles of the windows. One breath of sea air, or even standing beside the canal's ripples, would make her feel so much better.

As she and her parents sat down to their meager breakfast, Rachel pondered while attempting to eat a little. Han might throw them out the minute he knew. How had Rebekka Feinstein found an address? Probably only by concealing her condition. Rolf himself had said pregnant women were the hardest to place. It was hard to believe that one encounter could do this—and that she and her parents might even pay for it with their lives. Could she ask that of them? Should she leave? It would break their hearts, but they'd be safer. She had enough diamonds to live elsewhere, at least for a while. Or should she do as Sonja had done? The thought of her father helping her—no. But even if some other doctor could perform the procedure, Rachel couldn't imagine it. Those busy cells inside her were hungry to live, to be born, to become her daughter Rebekka, or a little boy. To stop them would mean to give in completely to fear. Everything else in their lives was ruled by it: where they lived, how they lived, what they ate, even how loudly they could speak. To allow fear also to kill off the possibility of new life felt insupportable.

If they lived through the war, she would have a child and her parents a grandchild, even if an illegitimate one. If they didn't survive, at least they would have had the joy of seeing it learn to smile and perhaps even talk. If that joy brought their deaths, wouldn't it have been worth it? Besides, her father surely could come up with some medicine to keep the child quiet—and so far, the threats in the attic seemed so much less frequent, if Han would let them stay. Or perhaps the child could be sent to the countryside, if she could bear to be parted from it. All day, she dozed on the couch and ruminated, while Rose brought tea at intervals, and Jacob worked out a chess tournament using the pieces she'd made for him. He didn't offer to show her what he was doing.

Jacob

The next evening, Jacob lay next to Rose, who was searching his face. Outside, he imagined the light turning pale and grainy as the evening fell.

"You must have noticed the change in Rachel." Rose was speaking to him in a normal whisper, not right into his ear as she often had in the basement.

He felt rare tears burn his eyes for the second time in a few days.

"Of course I have. I used to be a doctor, remember?" He swallowed, then closed his eyes and put his arms around her. Even after gaining a little weight, how thin she was, as thin as he had always been. He missed her fullness and remembered the voluptuousness of her pregnancy, how they had both delighted in it. Then, in a flash, he remembered and felt the new baby in his arms, her huge milky eyes on his. He swallowed harder.

"Can you blame them?" Rose asked, without any context. But he knew just what she meant. They'd avoided the subject for several weeks, but here it was.

Of course he could blame them: his daughter had been defiled, and right under his nose. Rolf had violated their hospitality, even though they had risked their lives for him. He had taken unconscionable advantage of Rachel's grief for her boyfriend. Why hadn't Jacob rushed over there and stopped them? If Rose hadn't stopped him, he would have. If the worst was true, if Rachel was pregnant, Rolf's impulsive act might even result in their deaths. No one knew when the raiders would come. Absolute silence was essential. Whoever heard of a baby who was quiet on demand?

Jacob held Rose hard as he thought of the criminal carelessness of young love, and how the two young bodies had met as his and Rose's had in their newlywed days. The bed creaked slightly. Jacob realized that he was ready, now, and that Rose knew it. She began pulling his pajama bottoms down; they stuck. She laughed a little for the first time in several days. "Can you blame them? I take it your answer is no," she said.

$$\times \quad \times \quad \times$$

They again woke to the sound of Rachel trying to throw up quietly in the bucket. Jacob groaned, released Rose, and turned toward the side wall of the dormer window. She whispered to him, "Calm down. At least a child would give us something to live for. I'll go help her." She kissed the back of his neck, and he heard her get up.

At dinner, Jacob, morose and silent, moved the bits of turnip and potato and a scrap of meat around, as he once played with tin soldiers as a boy. Rose and Rachel staggered from one innocuous topic to the next: what the mother recalled from reading *Sense and Sensibility*, how the daughter remembered the lilacs which would be blooming about then. So it went until they could clear the table and let Jacob turn his back on them. Even the intricacies of the pelvic muscles couldn't occupy his mind fully.

When Rose finally got into bed with him, she said, "Now look, doctor. You're treating your daughter like a criminal and it won't do."

"She behaved like a slut." How could he think of that word and his own daughter in the same breath? Yet he did. "Who was this Michiel, anyway?" Maybe it started there. Maybe her morals were already corrupted while they were living in their own home. That somehow made it worse.

"I don't know, Jacob. I've told you, he probably was a Gentile, and she knew you wouldn't approve."

"If she cared about what I approve of, would she have been," he faltered, could not supply a word, "a few feet away from us?"

"Remember the night you brought me home, when we were still engaged? My parents were already upstairs for once, and I asked you to come in, supposedly for cocoa? If I hadn't been so afraid, we would have gone further."

"Not that much further. And we were engaged. It's different." Yet he did remember the press of her body against his, that first intimation of how her breasts felt. She was speaking again, her voice soft against his ear as she leaned toward him.

"Rolf will be killed, probably sooner rather than later. He may be dead already. Would we really want our daughter engaged to a marked man? You and I have had each other for years now. Rachel thought this was her last chance to be with a man, even though we hope it wasn't. Just sleep on it, dear." She pulled him closer. "She still loves you, whether you believe that or not."

Jacob let his wife hold him, and her words coursed through him like a harsh antidote, bringing pain and cure at once. He buried his head into Rose's shoulder for the first time in months. And then, at last, he cried and reached the bottom of his grief.

✕　✕　✕

When he heard Rachel at the bucket the next morning, Jacob went to her. She was kneeling on the floor in front of it, throwing up. When the storm had passed, she looked surprised, then happy to see him. But a shadow returned.

"Maybe it's the food," she ventured. He shook his head.

Rachel tried again. "Paps, will you help me?" The words slipped out fast, as if a gush of water carried them.

"I'm a doctor, Rachel. Of course I will," he replied stiffly. Her face suddenly turned soft clay, and he added, "And I'm your father. Don't ever forget that," and reached over to kiss her yearning cheek. When she stood up, he put his arms around her and felt the tender, light flesh barely coating her bones. My grandchild, he thought. My grandchild is coming.

Rose

"Rachel, come lie down in our bed. It's more comfortable," Rose offered as father and daughter appeared. They were smiling at each other in a way they hadn't for days. Although pale, Rachel's face was joyous and relaxed. *Is this how she'll look when she holds the baby the first time?* Rose wondered. She fluffed the pillows and shook out the duvet, then helped Rachel ease herself down. A scratchy noise startled them all, but it was just a bird landing on the roof, probably a heron.

They squeezed in a chair on either side of the bed, Jacob on one side, and Rose on the other. They each took one of her hands as she dozed. Rose remembered so many such times, soothing their three-year-old's nightmares of giant turtles and toads, or nursing her through a bad case of flu a few years later.

It was a kind of idyll, as though the daughter Rachel once was had returned—young and trusting, looking to her mother for counsel and reassurance. In the last years, the war had taken all that away. As Rose held a cold washcloth to Rachel's drowsy forehead, she felt the old tenderness again.

When Rachel finally woke, her father told her, "Don't worry, dear. This nausea is nothing out of line. You may feel this way for another week or two. See if this helps." He gave her a rare spoonful of medicine from his bag, and sat with her while Rose returned to the kitchen.

After she pulled out her mother-in-law's china plates, Rose cut the lumpy boiled potatoes up finer, and began to reheat them, no matter what Han said about smells. She imagined herself and Jacob holding the baby, passing it back and forth, smiling until it smiled, cooing until it cooed. She could heat water for its bath, clean between its tiny toes.

As she laid the silver and plates on the table, she thought of what her common sense mother would say: The space was too small for a baby, apart from the dangers. A baby was uncontrollable, squealing and loud. Why bother to whisper if they were going to take a risk like that? And diapers! Han took the pail of waste down daily, but he'd probably charge a fortune for washing and drying diapers. Or he might well throw the family out on the street.

If he rejected them, how would they find a new address? If it was more expensive than this one, they'd be penniless long before the end of the war. And yet, irrationally, from the depths of her being, Rose wanted to celebrate. Climbing up on a chair to explore the dish cabinet, she discovered real crystal goblets tucked out of sight. Rose washed and polished them until they sparkled like diamonds. The baby would bring hazards, of course, and major ones. But also so much day-by-day joy. She moved everything off the table, spread the lace tablecloth, and set it with her china and the glistening goblets. Anything might happen. Even if a baby brought about their deaths, Rose could not help but welcome it.

Rachel

Rachel drifted in and out of sleep, feeling the anchor of her father's hand. She peeked at his face, so much older than the one she carried in her mind as being his. He looked careworn, but then his eyes caught hers, and joy sprang into them. If they lived, her child would do that for her. When Jacob squeezed Rachel's hand, she went right back to sleep.

Some time later, she felt him shake her shoulder gently. "I have some things to say to you, Rachel." Rose came back and sat on her other side. "Ever since you were born, I looked forward to your marriage and our grandchildren. Now you're pregnant"—he swallowed—"without a husband, and we're hidden up here by a man we can't trust. He'll never tolerate this, and he might use it to his—advantage."

"But Jacob—" her mother said. He interrupted her and continued.

"Still, your baby is the only hopeful thing that's happened since we left home. It might outlive Hitler and his flunkies, or any of us. Pregnancy takes nine months, even under the Nazis. By then, the war may be over."

Rose shook her head. "If not, maybe someone can find us a new address, perhaps where there's already a baby so the noise of crying won't stand out. And even if they catch us, look what we've been through already. We've managed. If we're arrested, we might find a way to stay at Westerbork, rather than being shipped east. We still have our diamonds. Meanwhile, let's keep you out of Han's sight, and feed you extra rations. Are you hungry now?"

"Starving!" Rachel sat up, wiping her eyes. She felt better than she had in days. Before coming to the table, she brushed her hair hard so it shone again, put her light fingers on her belly, and felt the slightest outward curve. Yes, it was real. For that moment, she did not worry.

"Don't spill any of this rich cream soup on my precious table-cloth," Rose joked when they sat down with their watery potato broth.

"Where did you find the crystal?" Rachel breathed in the beauty.

"Hidden on a back shelf. The people before us must have left them. It's a special occasion, so I thought we'd use them." She smiled at her daughter.

They sat together as they had so often. Rose's face shone with excitement, and Jacob's eyes had some of their old sparkle. *Paps looks so happy,* Rachel thought, *now that he gets to be a doctor and a father again.* She felt her parents' love reach deep into her body, to the new creature which was gathering cells, gathering being. She barely registered the cracking noises by the front door, far below.

Jacob picked up his goblet filled with water and stood.

Angry shouts on the stairs swelled upward. Rachel's hands flew to her belly as the noise came closer. Rose's head whipped around toward the hatch, but Jacob ignored the approach of pounding feet, and raised his goblet high.

Rachel had never heard a Hebrew word from him, except on the High Holidays at his parents' home.

"*L'chaim,*" he said. "To life."

AFTERWORD

I never expected to write about the Holocaust, much less spend thirteen years researching it. The subject was much too disturbing, and it felt distant to a Gentile born in 1948. Although I had friends who lost family in the camps, I didn't take the Holocaust personally. Until.

Until I ate lunch with resistance worker René Raindorf, who told me, "The Holocaust is not only about the Jews. It is about the rest of humanity," and showed me the misshapen numbers tattooed on his arm.

Until our Belgian hostess, my mentor and close friend Eliane Vogel Polsky, revealed that she had been hidden in plain sight in a convent school. After twenty years together, I had not even known that she was born Jewish. Her stories trickled out over the next decade, and color every page of this book.

Until I fell in love with the city of Amsterdam.

On February 1, 2001, my lifelong dream of living in Europe finally came true. I'd have three whole months to explore Amsterdam and write. To me, it was a city of canals and great museums and architecture, the tolerant city that probably sheltered my Huguenot ancestors when they were driven out of France, the liberal city where my female partner and I could feel equal to any other committed couple.

As I wandered along the curved canals through the chilly

February fog and rain, I loved the miles of austere but exquisitely crafted houses, candlelit cafés, gently arched bridges, and endlessly varied carillon music. The last thing on my mind was the mass murder of the Jewish people who had found refuge there for the four hundred years prior to 1940.

After a few weeks of revisiting the museums I'd rushed through as a tourist, the Jewish History Museum rose to the top of my "new" list. One rainy morning, I mistakenly braced myself for rooms of lurid photographs of deportation and worse. Instead, almost all the exhibits showcased Dutch Jewish citizens' innumerable contributions to the city since the 1500s: in the diamond industry and banking, health and child care, cabaret and classical music, and essential merchandise like textiles and fish and vegetables.

Only one exhibit was devoted to 1940-45. A photograph of a beaming girl and boy depicted them wearing their Nazi-required Stars of David like costume decorations. Their smiles showed that there was much more to their story than misery and victimhood, and that the period I had assumed was only horrible was far more complicated than I'd thought. For the first time, I wanted to know more, and headed for the nearby Verzetsmuseum, the Museum of Dutch Resistance.

I stepped into the dark exhibit hall and heard the recorded footsteps of advancing German soldiers pounding against a background of turgid Nazi propaganda music. Before me was a credible, step-by-step explanation of how any "civilized" people can participate in mass murder, and why the Dutch experience holds particular lessons for everyone from the Americas to Zimbabwe. The inescapable fact is more than 100,000 of the Netherlands' 140,000 Jewish citizens and others were murdered, partly because of their fellow countrymen's collaboration and passive collusion. Some did find ways to resist— Jews and Gentiles, women and men. Their efforts are sometimes dismissed because so many died anyway, but that does not change my respect for the courage of anyone who stood in the way of the Nazis, even for a moment.

When I later saw a photograph of a roundup that took place right in front of our beloved apartment in Geldersekade, I finally understood that the Holocaust was about me and my own neighbors. The Nazis had rounded up Jewish citizens on my doorstep. But for an accident of time and place, I would have had to face tormenting questions about whether to collaborate, collude, or resist. Nor am I exempt now. I must face them in my own time if I am to learn anything from the suffering of the past.

In winter 2002, we lived a stone's throw from the Anne Frank House. Our landlords were Willem de Vries Lentsch, a vigorous man in his eighties, and his wife, Connie. She in particular had lost many friends in the Holocaust because of her profession as a cabaret artist. Her husband's shipbuilding firm had manufactured less than a fourth as many boats as usual when they were forced to work for the Nazis. On a sunny afternoon, Willem took us upstairs to the attic which had been his office. I commented on how light it was.

"I replaced the windows up here," he said, "but some people thought I shouldn't."

I asked why not.

"The old ones had bullet holes. The Nazis fired at the Jewish people who were hidden here when they tried to escape over the roofs."

"Who were they? What happened to them?"

"I don't know. It was before I owned this house." He shook his head.

Within a few days, I began to imagine them.

During long stays in Amsterdam, I learned about their world, exploring sites, exhibits, archives, books, papers, memorabilia, and photos, as well as visiting libraries and museums in the United States and Canada. I felt and feel the void left by Amsterdam's missing

Jewish people, as well as those who tried to help them and were caught—partly because I love the city where they lived, which they helped to create. I can't begin to explain all the threads that tie me to Amsterdam and the war years, but I know they go back to my childhood in North Carolina, when the first black child entered my all-white school. I had to decide whether to collude, collaborate, or resist. Those choices are still before all of us, every day, as we read about the latest environmental outrage, or the unmet needs of desperate people. I think of Rachel, of how she did the right thing again and again, in peril of her life, even when she was tired and scared. She's my heroine.

Mary Dingee Fillmore, 2016

ACKNOWLEDGMENTS

I have done everything I could to make the public events in this book accurate, but I am sure errors have seeped in and would appreciate corrections.

Many people deserve thanks for helping me create this book and the conversations I hope it will provoke, and I'm sure over the thirteen years of this project I have forgotten some significant contributions. My apologies in advance to anyone not mentioned specifically here.

I would never have gone to Amsterdam, nor found the courage and means to be a writer, without my partner and spouse, Joanna Rankin. My best friend, Eliane Vogel Polsky, cracked open the subject of the Holocaust for me when she revealed that she had been hidden in plain sight as a Jewish teenager in Liège. Eliane spent many years reviewing drafts and dredging up painful memories to make this work as realistic as possible before her death on November 13, 2015. She asked about this book in our last conversation.

More than thirty years ago, my indefatigable mentor Mae Morris encouraged me to write fiction, and I dismissed the idea. I am glad she can see this book published at last. Her constant and abundant support has been instrumental in this and many other growing edges of my life.

The muse was watching over me when she brought Professor

Laureen Nussbaum to Vermont to give a talk about the Netherlands in 1940–45, based both on her personal experience and her scholarship. With consummate generosity, Laureen (and her husband Rudi while he lived) answered my innumerable questions, reviewed my poems and ultimately my whole novel manuscript. Laureen's knowledge of the historical context reassured me that the bones of the story were sound. While the novel is not about an historic individual, it reassured me that someone who lived in that place and time felt that it could have happened.

Diane Lefer, an extraordinary editor and author in her own right, worked with me on several early drafts of the book and pushed it consistently in the right direction. Others who helped shape the manuscript by reading it (in some cases twice!) were the inimitable and insightful Jane Baluss, Roz Feldberg, Jan Green, Barbara Haber, Katherine Bradley Johnson, Mae Morris, Jane Pincus, and Stephanie Young. Each brought insight, a pen, and a sharp pair of scissors. Amy Belding Brown coached me through the final versions with sensitivity and professional aplomb, and Marian Sandmaier offered her seasoned wisdom to get the book out into the world.

The Champlain Writers Group has chewed on countless drafts of countless pieces of this novel. All hail to Mary Harwood, Joan Zipko, and Laurie di Cesare for their skill and endurance, and thanks to KK Wilder and Michele Patenaude for starting the group. The support of the Sunapee Writers and Artists was also crucial (Paula Doress-Worters, Jane Pincus, Hilary Salk, Wendy Sanford, and Norma Swenson). The significant Vermont College of Fine Arts faculty and fellow students are literally too numerous to mention, but my first advisor, Betsy Sholl, convinced me I was a poet. My neighbors and friends at Burlington Co-housing East Village have helped see me through the whole process. She Writes Press has been a wonderful home for my book, and the counsel of my sister writers along the way has been essential.

The opportunity to study with David Barnouw, editor of *The Diary of Anne Frank: The Critical Edition* and an authority on this period, was invaluable. Our other Dutch friends have also done a great deal to make the 1940–45 period comprehensible to me, particularly Els de Vries and Mieke Visscher. I appreciate the support and counsel of Erika Prins of the Anne Frank House. Thanks also to the staffs at the Verzetsmuseum, the Simon Wiesenthal Center, the US Holocaust Memorial Museum, the Jewish History Museum Library and Photo Service, the Montreal Holocaust Museum Center, the Amsterdam Museum, and the Netherlands Institute for War, Holocaust and Genocide Studies. Despite all their assistance, my errors are my own.

On a broader level, the visionary and healer Deena Metzger has been my teacher and guide for decades. She forced me into the light as a writer and has sustained me there, as has my dear friend Andy Lewis, who shares my preoccupations and handwringing.

Neither of my parents lived to read *An Address in Amsterdam*, but they would both see themselves in it, their wisdom and grace as well as their follies. I can never be too grateful to them, nor to Judy Norsigian and her husband, Irv Zola, for giving me a home, and to Geneva Cooper. Kyra Zola Norsigian, Elizabeth Sonia Cooper, Samantha Tilton, and their husbands reassure me that generations to come will still be haunted and compelled by these stories to act, and to resist.

RESOURCES

In the course of learning about the Holocaust and resistance to the Nazi occupation of the Netherlands, I've visited countless exhibits in many locations. None inspires and challenges me more than the Verzetsmuseum in Amsterdam, even after many visits, so I encourage anyone with a real interest in this subject to go there first, then to the Jewish History Museum and other sites in the Jewish Cultural Quarter. As a guide to help you appreciate a multitude of other places, *Jewish Amsterdam* (J. Stoutenbeek and others) will be your best friend.

If you want to learn somewhat more without traveling or delving into this whole list (which could be much more extensive), I recommend first Bob Moore's *Victims and Survivors: The Nazi Persecution of the Jews in the Netherlands, 1940–1945,* and then the classic *Ashes in the Wind* by Jacob Presser which Moore and others update but never supersede.

While most websites are too quickly out of date to list here, I would be remiss not to mention The Digital Monument to the Jewish Community in the Netherlands, http://www.joodsmonument.nl. Especially for those who are traveling to Amsterdam, look for the Jewish Cultural Quarter's website at http://www.jhm.nl/visit/jewish-cultural-quarter. I hope my own website at http://seehiddenamsterdam.com/ will also prove useful.

Film is not my specialty, but I strongly recommend Michèle Ohayon's *Steal a Pencil for Me,* a moving 2007 documentary about the enduringness of even unconventional love, and its ability to sustain people in horrifying circumstances. For the story of Hannelore Cahn, whose picture is on the cover of this book, see *Westerbork Girl* by Steffie van den Oord, a compelling film with enough English for most English speakers to catch the complex story. Paul Verhoeven's feature *Black Book* gives a feel for the agonizing dilemmas of the period, and was once voted the best Dutch film of all time.

Here is a selection of the books I consulted along the way:

Asscher-Pinkhof, C. (1986). *Star Children.* Detroit: Wayne State University Press.

Blom, J. C. (2002). "Dutch Jews, Jewish Dutchmen and Jews in the Netherlands 1870–1940" (In: *Dutch Jewry: Its History and Secular Culture,* pp. 215–224.) J. Israel.

Boas, J. (1985). *Boulevard des Misères: The Story of Transit Camp Westerbork.* Hamden, CT: Archon Books.

Brasz, Chaya, and Kaplan, Yosef, Symposium on the History of the Jews in the Netherlands, B., and Kaplan, Y. (2001). *Dutch Jews as Perceived by Themselves and by Others: Proceedings of the Eighth International Symposium on the History of the Jews in the Netherlands.* Leiden: Brill.

Bregstein, P., Bloemgarten, S., and Barends, J. K. (2004). *Remembering Jewish Amsterdam.* New York: Holmes & Meier.

Coster, T. (2011). *We All Wore Stars: Memories of Anne Frank by Her Classmates.* New York: Macmillan.

Dogar, S. (2010). *Annexed.* Boston: Houghton Mifflin Harcourt.

Eman, D. and Schaap, J. C. (1994). *Things We Couldn't Say*. Grand Rapids, MI: W.B. Eerdmans.

Englishman, M. (2007). *163256: A Memoir of Resistance*. Waterloo, ON: Wilfrid Laurier University Press.

Evans, M. (1991). *Lest We Forget*. Berrien Springs, MI: Andrews University Press.

Feldman, E. (2014). *The Boy Who Loved Anne Frank*. New York: W.W. Norton.

Frank, A., Barnouw, D., van der Stroom, G., Pomerans, A., Mooyaart-Doubleday, B. M., and Massotty, S. (2003). *The Diary of Anne Frank: The Revised Critical Edition*. New York: Random House.

Frishman, J. and Berg, H. (2007). *Dutch Jewry in a Cultural Maelstrom, 1880–1940*. Amsterdam: Aksant.

Garcia, M. R. and Garcia, P. A. (1979). *As Long as I Remain Alive*. Tuscaloosa, AL: Portals.

Gies, M. and Gold, A. (2009). *Anne Frank Remembered*. London: Simon & Schuster UK.

Glaser, P. (2013). *Dancing with the Enemy*. New York: Random House.

Hekking, V. and Bool, F. (1995). *De Illegale Camera 1940–45*. Naarden: V & K Publishing.

Hermans, W.F. (2009). *The Darkroom of Damocles*. New York: Overlook Press.

Hilberg, R. (1985). *The Destruction of the European Jews*. New York: Holmes & Meier.

Hillesum, E., and Gaarlandt, J. G. (1996). *An Interrupted Life: The Diaries, 1941–1943 and Letters from Westerbork*. New York: Henry Holt.

Israel, J. I. and Salverda, R. (2002). *Dutch Jewry: Its History and Secular Culture (1500–2000)*. Leiden: Brill.

Janssen, P. (1970). *A Moment of Silence*. Forge Village, MA: McClelland and Stewart.

de Jong, L. (1990). *The Netherlands and Nazi Germany*. Cambridge, MA: Harvard.

Kasaboski, T. and Den, H. K. (2008). *The Occupied Garden: Recovering the Story of a Family in the War-Torn Netherlands*. Toronto, ON: McClelland & Stewart.

Keilson, H. and Searls, D. (2010). *Comedy in a Minor Key*. New York: Farrar, Straus and Giroux.

Kohner, H., Kohner, W., and Kohner, F. (1984). *Hanna and Walter: A Love Story*. New York: Random House.

Kugt, B. (1995). *Our Story*. New York: Vantage.

Lee, C. A. (2003). *The Hidden Life of Otto Frank*. New York: Morrow.

Lee, C.A. (2000). *Roses from the Earth: The Biography of Anne Frank*. New York: Penguin.

Leydesdorff, S. (1994). *We Lived with Dignity: The Jewish Proletariat of Amsterdam, 1900–1940*. Detroit: Wayne State University.

de Loo, T. (2001). *The Twins*. London: Arcadia.

Lourie, R. (2007). *A Hatred for Tulips*. New York: Thomas Dunne Books.

Maas, W. (1970). *The Netherlands at War 1940–45*. London: Abelard-Schuman.

Mason, H. L. (1984). *Testing Human Bonds Within Nations: Jews in the Occupied Netherlands*. New York: Academy of Political Science.

Mathews, A. (2015). *The Apothecary's House*. London: Endeavour Press.

Mechanicus, P. (1968). *Waiting for Death: A Diary*. London: Calder & Boyars.

Moore, B. (1997). *Victims and Survivors: The Nazi Persecution of the Jews in the Netherlands, 1940–1945*. London: Arnold.

Mulisch, H. (1985). *The Assault*. New York: Pantheon Books.

Muller, M. (1999). *Anne Frank: The Biography*. New York: Macmillan.

Nooijen, T. S. (1995). *Freedom's Clothesline: Dutch Citizens during World War II*. New Orleans, LA: Good Reading Books.

Obstfeld, J. (2004). *My Early Years*. Miami: Biblio Books.

Oliner, S. P. and Oliner, P. M. (1988). *The Altruistic Personality: Rescuers of Jews in Nazi Europe*. New York: Free Press.

Polak, J. and Soep, I. (2000). *Steal a Pencil for Me: Love Letters from Camp Bergen-Belsen and Westerbork*. Scarsdale, NY: Lion Books.

Presser, J. (1988). *Ashes in the Wind: The Destruction of Dutch Jewry*. Detroit: Wayne State University Press.

Pressler, M. and Elias, G. (2011). *Treasures from the Attic: The Extraordinary Story of Anne Frank's Family*. New York: Doubleday.

Romijn, P. and Nederlands Instituut voor Oorlogsdocumentatie (2012). *The Persecution of the Jews in the Netherlands, 1940–1945: New Perspectives.* Amsterdam: Vossiuspers UvA.

Rose, L. (1978). *The Tulips Are Red.* Jerusalem: Yad Vashem, the Holocaust Martyrs' and Heroes' Remembrance Authority.

Schloss, E. and Kent, E. J. (1988). *Eva's Story: A Survivor's Tale.* New York: St. Martin's Press.

Schogt, H. (2003). *The Curtain: Witness and Memory in Wartime Holland.* Waterloo, ON: Wilfrid Laurier University Press.

Scott, A. and Scott, G. (2016). *Behind the Fireplace: Memoirs of a Girl Working in the Dutch Resistance.* Amazon Digital Services.

Slier, F. (2008). *Hidden Letters.* Cambridge: Star Bright Books.

Sluyser, M. (2005). *Mr. Monday and Other Tales of Jewish Amsterdam.* Chandler, AZ: Five Star Publications.

Stein, A. (1988). *Quiet Heroes: True Stories of the Rescue of Jews by Christians in Nazi-Occupied Holland.* New York: New York University Press.

Stoutenbeek, J., Vigeveno, P., and Henselmans, S. (2003). *Jewish Amsterdam.* Amsterdam: Ludion.

Ten Boom, C., Sherrill, J. L., and Sherrill, E. (1971). *The Hiding Place.* Washington Depot, CT: Chosen Books.

Thompson, P. R. and Burchardt, N. (1982). *Our Common History: The Transformation of Europe.* Atlantic Highlands, NJ: Humanities Press.

Trap, E. (2015). *A World War II Memoir: My Impressions and Experiences of Being in Hiding.* Amazon Digital Services.

Van Den Brink, H.M. (2001). *On the Water.* New York: Grove Press.

Van Beek,. F. (2008). *Flory: A Miraculous Story of Survival.* New York: HarperOne.

Velmans, E. (1999). *Edith's Story.* New York: Soho.

Voolen, E., Belinfante, J. C., and Joods Historisch Museum (Amsterdam, Netherlands) (1989). *1940–1945: From Isolation to Murder: The Persecution of the Jews in the Netherlands.* Toronto, ON: Holocaust Remembrance Committee, Toronto Jewish Congress.

Wasserstein, B. (2014). *The Ambiguity of Virtue: Gertrude Van Tijn and the Fate of the Dutch Jews.* Cambridge: Harvard University Press.

Wolf, D. (2007). *Beyond Anne Frank: Hidden Children and Postwar Families in Holland.* Berkeley: University of California Press.

Zilversmit, K. (1995). *Yours Always: A Holocaust Love Story.* Bethesda, MD: CDL Press.

A BRIEF CHRONOLOGY OF
SELECTED EVENTS FROM 1940–43
IN AMSTERDAM

1940

May   Germany invades the neutral Netherlands

The Dutch royal family flees to England

Rotterdam is bombed, destroying the city and killing more than 1,000 people

The Dutch surrender after threats to bomb other cities

Anti-Nazi leaflets appear almost immediately, which eventually develop into hundreds of underground newspapers

July   Jewish Dutch citizens are prohibited from volunteering for the civil air guard, even though this means there are not enough volunteers

September   Jews are excluded from the civil service

Jews are banned from most markets in Amsterdam

Nazis define a Jew as someone with one Jewish grandparent who had been a community member

October	Civil servants must sign an "Aryan attestation" about their backgrounds
	Many Dutch Reformed Churches protest it
	Jewish businesses must register with Nazi authorities
November	Jews are banned from public office
	Dutch Supreme Court votes 12–5 in favor of dismissing Lodewijk Visser, their Jewish president, who speaks out fearlessly until his death in 1942
	Jewish professors are fired, and some colleagues protest loudly
	Students strike and begin to organize
	Some are arrested or go underground by the end of the year
December	Restrictions imposed on Jewish students
Overall	Violence instigated by Dutch Nazis is permitted by German authorities

1941

January	Jews living in the Netherlands (mostly citizens) must register as Jewish
	Jews are banned from cinemas
February	Jewish self-defense groups respond to violence
	A Nazi dies of his wounds, and a huge state funeral is held
	Germans define and seal off the "Jewish Quarter," and establish a Jewish Council to carry out their policies
	Nazis raid Koco's Ice Cream Parlor, and it is defended

In retaliation, 425 young Jewish men are rounded up and sent away

Feb 25   The only general strike in Europe to protest the first roundup is organized

The city comes to a halt and some other Dutch cities follow suit

Reprisals are swift and Amsterdam is back to work a few days later

Scattered efforts to resist the occupation spread

March   Small Jewish businesses must dissolve; large or essential ones must register and have a Gentile overseer

April   *The Jewish Weekly* is published as a Nazi organ, and all other Jewish publications are banned

Jews may not have radios

New identity cards are issued for everyone, with photos and other features that are difficult to forge

May   Jewish doctors and other professionals may not work for non-Jews

June   Jews may not move freely around the country

First roundups in neighborhoods begin, supposedly in retaliation for resistance attacks on the airport and a Nazi officers' club

More bans are instituted, e.g., swimming pools, having shops open on Sundays

More Jewish people begin asking friends for help in going underground

August   Jews must register their assets with the Lippmann-Rosenthal bank

September	Jewish children are segregated into separate schools
	"Forbidden for Jews" signs go up in parks, zoos, restaurants, hotels, concerts, libraries, theatres, cabarets, and more
October	A card index of Jews in the Netherlands is created by the Jewish Council
November	Jews are forced to resign from associations with non-Jewish members
	All Jews living in the Netherlands but not native there are forced to register for "voluntary emigration"

1942

January	Jews may not employ non-Jewish domestic help
	Jews are not permitted in public education
	The first Jewish people from Amsterdam are sent to work camps
	Jewish people from all over the country are to be concentrated in Amsterdam
	Identity cards of Jewish people must be stamped with a *J*, so more forged documents are produced underground
February	Some church representatives protest how Jews are treated
March	Prohibitions on Jews expand, such as no selling furniture or household goods, and bans on marriage with non-Jews
April	Most Jewish butchers must close
	Police organize special units to track down Jews in hiding

May	Jewish people must wear the Star of David
	Jews must hand in all assets and possessions of significant value
June	Jews must hand in their bicycles, and may not travel without prior permission
	Jews may not buy fruit and vegetables in non-Jewish shops
	No more sports are permitted
	Deportation to the Westerbork Transit Camp in the eastern Netherlands begins
July	Jews prevented from using telephones or visiting non-Jews
	Churches protest the deportation plans
	More raids are carried out in Amsterdam, and the first trainload leaves the city
	First trains go from Westerbork Transit Camp to Auschwitz
	Ministers read protests against the persecution
	Margot Frank (Anne's older sister) receives her notice to report for deportation, and the Franks go into hiding
	Many independent resistance efforts are happening by now, not only forging documents and distributing newspapers but helping people hide
	Several major networks are organizing to rescue Jewish children
August	The National Theatre (renamed The Jewish Theatre) becomes an assembly point for deportation for adults, with children held across the street at Miss Henriette Pimental's child care center

Some escape from both places, but most are deported

Extensive raids are carried out

Several groups of Zionist Palestine Pioneers are smuggled out

September   Many Jewish people are hiding in the city and countryside by this time, particularly in Drenthe, Friesland, and Groningen, aided by rescue networks

Babies and children who don't "look Jewish" are easiest to place in the countryside

December   The largest network to hide adults, Landelijke Organisatie voor Hulp aan Onderduikers (LO), is created to assist Dutch men who are subject to the general labor draft. It is too late to help most Jews.

1943

January   Circulation of underground newspapers is estimated at 500,000

March   Amsterdam Population Registry is set afire by the resistance

Someone betrays the organizers who are found and executed

April   The Dutch countryside is declared "free of Jews"

The bounty for any Jew found in hiding increases steadily, up to 40 guilders in summer of 1944, a very significant sum

May   Jews in mixed marriages must choose deportation or sterilization

The Jewish Council is forced to select 7,000 of its employees for deportation

May–June   Intensive and widespread raids take place in Amsterdam

September   The last major raid happens in Amsterdam, and the Jewish Council is terminated

Transports from Westerbork to Auschwitz-Birkenau and other camps continue

December   By the end of the year, those who hunted Jews for pay had turned in something like 6,000 hidden people in all

The year after this novel's ending, the Allies lost the crucial "bridge too far" at Arnhem in September 1944, partly because they ignored local resistance intelligence. Amsterdam then suffered through the frigid Hunger Winter of 1944–45, in which more than 20,000 Dutch people died of starvation and cold. Homes of deported Jewish people were looted for food and anything that would burn. Canadian forces liberated the Netherlands on May 6, 1945.

Of approximately 140,000 Jewish people in the Netherlands before the war, more than 100,000 were murdered in the Holocaust, as well as non-Jewish resistance workers, Roma and Sinti people (so-called gypsies), homosexuals, people with disabilities, and others. Those who hid stood the best chance of survival. About 74 percent of Jews living in the Netherlands were ultimately murdered, the highest percentage in Western Europe.

DISCUSSION QUESTIONS

1. When the Nazis invade, Rachel's parents perceive the situation very differently: Jacob is relatively calm, and Rose is alarmed. Since we know what happened later, we are more sympathetic to her. At the time, however, many people felt as Jacob did, and only slowly came to believe that the situation was dangerous, especially to Jewish people. Why do you think they minimized the risks?

2. In the early part of the book, Rachel is absorbed with Michiel and falling in love, then rejects him because she feels he's too serious about her and she can never marry him. What makes her change her mind and seek him out again? How does she justify a sexual relationship outside of marriage?

3. When Rachel suspects that Michiel is working against the Nazis, she tries to get more information from him, but he tells her very little. Later, when she has her own secrets to keep as an underground worker, she understands why he was so cautious and regrets pressuring him. How would it have increased the danger for each of them had he revealed more?

4. Rachel almost decides not to go and meet Eva that first time, when she is being recruited into the underground. What detains her? What makes her go anyway?

5. As they discuss assignments and much more, Eva becomes a mentor to Rachel, providing guidance about how to survive on the streets and to guard her secrets. What does Eva teach by example? What does she tell Rachel directly? After Eva dies, how do these lessons play out? Is there a time when Rachel doesn't do what Eva might have wished her to?

6. What are the different kinds of underground work depicted in the novel? What seems to be most effective? Which are most dangerous? Which might you have done? What would you have weighed as you considered whether to do it?

7. Did you find Rachel's character as an underground worker realistic? Why or why not?

8. What are the different kinds of heroism which are depicted in the book – for example, the newsagent, Eva, Mr. de Vries, Connie, Els, and Rachel herself? How do we know they are human as well as heroic?

9. Rose implies at times that she is somewhat aware of Rachel's underground activities and hidden personal life. How does she encourage her daughter to be her own person in both senses?

10. When the family moves to the basement, Part II is written in multiple points of view, so that for the first time the reader sees directly into the minds of Jacob and Rose as well as Rachel. What difference does that make in how you see those characters? What did the author gain by giving you that additional insight?

11. Living in the basement strips the characters of almost everything they usually enjoy and desire, as well as the remnants of their freedom. What sustains each of them after they must move to the basement? How does each person adapt?

12. In their normal life, Rachel and her parents had some privacy from each other, but they can't keep it up in the changed circumstances. What hidden aspects of the three main characters emerge in the basement? What do they learn about each other and how?

13. Throughout Part I and the beginning of Part II, Rose often blames Jacob for their predicament overall, particularly the move to the basement. Why? How do we know that she has stopped holding him personally responsible? What helps her overcome her feelings?

14. Before the war, Rolf was a gentle soul, a lover of science and literature. What are the experiences that made him join the underground at all, ultimately doing the ethically difficult work of an assassin? Is it believable that a person could change so much under those conditions?

15. Before they move to the basement, how does Jacob see his daughter? How does his view change as a result of living so closely together under extreme conditions?

16. The move to the attic is another huge upheaval for Rachel and her parents. Once they navigate the perilous journey there, the overall conditions are better than in the basement – except for the host. What are the positive changes? How do their host's character flaws endanger them? Do you think he was betraying them, or planning to betray them?

17. Did the "Brief Chronology of Selected Events" clarify anything for you? Was it in keeping with what you thought you knew about the Holocaust and resistance in the Netherlands? What affected you most?

18. The backdrop of the Nazi occupation of the Netherlands is the same as in Anne Frank's *Diary*, and the families are hidden only a few blocks from each other. Apart from the fact that Anne Frank is an historic figure and Rachel Klein is fictional, Anne was about to be 11 when the Nazis invaded, and Rachel was 18. How would you contrast them and their perspectives?

19. What are the possibilities for what happens to the characters after the end of the book? Why do you think the author refrained from supplying details of what happens next?

20. What will haunt you after reading this book?

ABOUT THE AUTHOR

© Karen Pike

Mary Dingee Fillmore fell in love with Amsterdam in 2001 and has been returning there and researching its complex history ever since. A longtime professional facilitator for nonprofits and government, she gives talks for the Vermont Humanities Council and others, titled "Anne Frank's Neighbors: What Did They Do?" Mary earned an MFA at Vermont College of Fine Arts in 2005, and writes at www.maryfillmore.com and www.seehiddenamsterdam.com.

SELECTED TITLES FROM SHE WRITES PRESS

She Writes Press is an independent publishing company
founded to serve women writers everywhere.
Visit us at www.shewritespress.com.

Even in Darkness by Barbara Stark-Nemon
$16.95, 978-1-63152-956-6
From privileged young German-Jewish woman to concentration camp refugee, Kläre Kohler navigates the horrors of war and—through unlikely sources—finds the strength, hope, and love she needs to survive.

All the Light There Was by Nancy Kricorian
$16.95, 978-1-63152-905-4
A lyrical, finely wrought tale of loyalty, love, and the many faces of resistance, told from the perspective of an Armenian girl living in Paris during the Nazi occupation of the 1940s.

The Sweetness by Sande Boritz Berger
$16.95, 978-1-63152-907-8
A compelling and powerful story of two girls—cousins living on separate continents—whose strikingly different lives are forever changed when the Nazis invade Vilna, Lithuania.

Faint Promise of Rain by Anjali Mitter Duva
$16.95, 978-1-938314-97-1
Adhira, a young girl born to a family of Hindu temple dancers, is raised to be dutiful—but ultimately, as the world around her changes, it is her own bold choice that will determine the fate of her family and of their tradition.

Portrait of a Woman in White by Susan Winkler
$16.95, 978-1-938314-83-4
When the Nazis steal a Matisse portrait from the eccentric, art-loving Rosenswigs, the Parisian family is thrust into the tumult of war and separation, their fates intertwined with that of their beloved portrait.

Tasa's Song by Linda Kass
$16.95, 978-1-63152-064-8
From a peaceful village in eastern Poland to a partitioned post-war Vienna, from a promising childhood to a year living underground, Tasa's Song celebrates the bonds of love, the power of memory, the solace of music, and the enduring strength of the human spirit.